A large, green sport utility drove up as Angie reached the rear chain link gate of the school, a vehicle she didn't recognize. A woman—perhaps in her mid thirties—got out, dressed in jeans and a chambray shirt. Her square-jawed smile was tentative. "Are you Angela Donalson?"

"Yes," Angie acknowledged, puzzled. "Do I know you?"

A back door opened and a dark-haired man got out. Also in his thirties, he was dressed in denim. He stepped backward, a grin on his face. Angie felt a tremendous shoving force square in the middle of her backpack, and she was pushed into the arms of the smiling man, who reached up to steady her, or so she thought. Instead of helping her stand, he seemed to fall backwards, pulling her into the backseat, literally on top of him. The door slammed behind them, the woman got back into the front seat, and the vehicle pulled away. With his arms wrapped around her, Angie's face was mashed into the chambray-clad chest of her captor. A needle jabbed into her upper right arm.

"What's that? Why are you doing this?" Angie's yell was stifled as she struggled to move her face away from his chest.

"It's a drug to make you sleep. You have about thirty seconds." The woman's voice was calm and matter-of-fact.

"You don't understand. You have the wrong girl." Angie's voice trailed off, and she had trouble keeping her eyes open. The chambray shirt melted into a swirl of colors, then into blackness.

The Gift Horse

Pamela J. Dodd

March 2004

Booklocker.com, Inc.
2004

For my mother, Irene Dodd, who taught me everything from which authors wrote the best "mysteries" to how to fry okra just right. She would have been proud of me for getting the job done.

For my husband, David, who encouraged me in every possible way.

And for my friend, Sarah Trippe, my first reader, who told me to get it published.

Chapter 1

"Aw, Coach, I haven't got a prayer. Everybody knows how much I want to get a good scholarship, but I'll bet that every incoming freshman will fill out this one."

"Come on, Angie. Someone will win. You've filled out more of these things than anyone in the county—that experience ought to count for something." Coach Chuck Doyle grinned as he fell into stride with Angela Donalson. "This one is kinda different. The company is sending a representative to conduct area interviews, which just happen to be good old Adamsville High, so you won't have to go anywhere. It'll cost you a stamp and a class period."

"Well, okay. Since you put it that way, I guess I should. Hey, maybe I'll get out of Mrs. Harris's class." Angie paused on her way to American Literature.

"Angie, this is important. Someone is gonna win, and that someone might be you. Your future is at stake." Doyle's voice was sincere and caring. Too caring.

"Don't tell me, you need a sitter for tonight?" Angie voiced her suspicion.

"Yep, we could use you. Got a game over in Americus, and Suzanne is gonna take some pictures for the yearbook." Doyle turned toward the gym. "The twins say they'd rather have you than anyone in town. We'll need you from the time school is out until about 10:00. How about it?"

"Okay, I'll call my aunt." Angie sighed as she turned onto the English hall. Coach Doyle's eight-year-old twins were mischief personified, but she needed the money even more than she needed his goodwill. Realistically, she needed both.

"Thanks, Angie. Meet me at the gym after school."

"I'll be there."

As Mrs. Harris droned on about some dude named Emerson, Angie perused the form. Avery Electronics might be sponsoring it, but it was just another scholarship; the questions seemed typical.

Halfway listening to a poem about a snowstorm, Angie began to sketch out answers to each item. Being Adamsville High's queen of scholarships, she had begun early, in her junior year, looking for anything that might cause her college years to be spent studying, rather than at a part-time job. What Angie wanted, more than love, more than clothes... and she loved clothes... was to have people see her as she walked down the street and say, "There goes Angela Donalson—she's...." But with the capriciousness that is common in high school, she kept changing what went into the blank. Angie applied for everything—nursing scholarships, information technology scholarships, journalism scholarships and education scholarships. She wrote each essay as if whatever was being offered had been her greatest goal since she emerged from diapers. So, today she brainstormed a list, working up a keen desire to be an electronics engineer.

According to everyone who could remember, Angie's mother had loved her redheaded daughter with all her heart, but that same heart, never strong, had given out when Angie was just a toddler, so Angie's dad had been doubly important to her. After her mother's death, Angie and Bill Donalson had moved in with his older, spinster sister, Claire Donalson. Angie supposed that Aunt Claire was loving in her way, but she suspected that Claire had never married because it was hard to get through the rather distant facade which she directed toward most of the world. The family lived modestly on Bill's salary, earned by driving an eighteen-wheeler, until he died in an accident. Afterward, Angie and Claire, who had never worked outside her home, faced harder times.

Although her parents were gone, their desire to have their daughter "be somebody" was alive and well within Angie. Each week she studied the board outside the counselor's office, looking for yet another avenue to make her goal a reality.

A few weeks later, Angie was summoned to Ms. Greeson's office, next in line for the interview.

Wearing the closest thing she had to preppy clothes—khaki pants and a pullover sweater, Angie rose to greet the interviewer.

Mrs. Greeson introduced them. "Mr. Arnold, this is Angie Donalson. A junior."

"Hello, Angie." Mr. Arnold was wearing a glen plaid suit, traditional white shirt, and a dark silk tie.

"Hi."

"I've read your application and your essay. A most impressive essay."

"Thank you, sir." Mrs. Greeson waved Angie into a chair.

"You're only a junior. Most of the students I've talked to are seniors."

"Some scholarships are open to both, and I want to do everything I can to obtain the best one possible."

"Why do you want to study engineering?"

"Well, sir, to be honest, I'd be willing to study any number of things, if I could get the proper financial support. My parents are dead, and my aunt and I will have a difficult time when I go to college. But with or without a scholarship, I intend to go to college. Please understand, it's not that I mind hard work. I just want to devote myself to my studies as much as I can. Your scholarship could make that possible." Angie chose to focus on his tie, because looking at his face was making her nervous.

"Do you have any hobbies, Angie?"

"I like to read. The library is my favorite place in town. Fiction, some classics, even the newspaper. Especially the paper. I like to know what's going on. Here, and everywhere."

Mr. Arnold smiled and thumbed through the papers on his lap. Angie tried to ignore the video camera, which was sitting on a tripod, running.

"Some students don't want to study; they just enjoy getting away from home and having a good time." Mr. Arnold observed.

"Yes, sir, I guess that does happen. My mom and dad would want me to finish school. If I win, the money will be used, uh, in the way you would want. Some folks do just want a good time, but I need that degree. It's been my goal for a long time."

Mr. Arnold nodded, a gesture of dismissal.

"Thank you, Angie. It was nice meeting you."

Mrs. Greeson motioned her out the door. Angie glanced at her watch. She hadn't spent more than ten minutes in the interview. So much for getting out of class!

Pamela J. Dodd

*   *   *

Marcus Avery, Jr. was in his father's private lounge, holding a watered down drink and discussing his latest project. "The estate is shaping up—twelve thousand square foot house, five hundred acres, in the foothills. Stables, tennis courts, pool. I've hired Matt Chapman's sister as the estate manager."

"Billie? She's career Navy, isn't she?" The elder Avery searched his mind for Miss Chapman.

"Marines. She retired three months ago. She's hired a small staff, and renovations will be finished soon. I plan to spend the weekends there as much as possible."

"Won't that ruin your social life?"

"Right now, I just want to have an outlet for stress. Tennessee is a restful place, and Billie Chapman is most efficient. It's going to be great."

*   *   *

At that moment, Billie Chapman was supervising the addition of steel bars to the windows in the two adjoining upstairs bedrooms on the north wing of Avery's country estate. She had already had steel doors installed from each room to the hallway, and a steel door in between the rooms. A pair of pocket doors, made of chain link fencing within a heavy steel frame, had been added to close off the hallway from the rest of the house. The girl's room was furnished with good quality furniture, in light feminine colors. With enough square feet to make two rooms, it had a study/sitting area at one end and the bedroom furniture close to the bathroom. Through the connecting door was Avery's room; although somewhat smaller, its furnishings were even more elegant.

Danny Watson, one of the permanent staff, looked at Billie through the open window as he screwed on the heavy metal grill. "You expecting burglars, Billie?" he asked, grinning.

"No questions, Danny. You agreed before you took the job."

"Yes, ma'am. No questions."

"And you'll get no answers from me."

"Yes, ma'am."

Janice Rule came upstairs with shopping bags in her hands. "I have the purchases you asked me to make, Billie."

Chapman glanced in the bags. "These look fine. Cut off the tags and hang them in the closet. Underwear in the chest. Put the reading material on the desk and tables." Janice put the items away, making neat rows in the drawer and an attractive display on the table, then she left. Chapman looked around the room again, nodded, and moved on to the next job.

*   *   *

Angie was excited when Mrs. Greeson informed her that she was a finalist for the scholarship. The second interview was a bit longer, and Mr. Arnold was accompanied by Marc Avery, Jr., who was introduced as the son of the CEO of Avery Electronics. Winning a scholarship generous enough to pay her every expense was an awesome thought. Although she was nervous, she dressed in her best outfit and tried to impress the committee with her maturity, as well as her desire to learn and succeed.

As she left the counselor's office, she felt that she had indeed swayed them, especially the handsome Marc Avery. He was, she supposed, any girl's dream man—six feet, two inches, blonde, with an athletic spring in his step and penetrating blue eyes. Despite the difference in age and social class, he'd seemed to show real interest in her, which surprised her. The connection, however fleeting, made her feel that her chances at winning had just gotten a whole lot better.

*   *   *

Marc Avery practically leaped from the helicopter when it landed on its pad at his country house near Apple Valley, Tennessee. The estate wasn't huge, but the five hundred acres of rolling hills provided ample privacy. The grounds surrounding the house were verdant in the early spring, and he could see some obvious improvements since his last visit. New beds of azaleas were in bloom, and some more formal flowerbeds had been added, ready for planting once any danger of frost was past. The lawn had been cut, and a privacy fence had been added around the pool. The stable had a new coat of white and green paint, and four horses grazed in the paddock beside it.

The drive, graveled with creek pebbles, led from the main gate. A new chain link fence surrounded the exterior perimeter of the grounds, eight feet high and electrified. The five car garage held a BMW, a Ford Explorer, and a flatbed Dodge truck for hauling materials around the estate. A latticework breezeway, covered by a green metal roof, connected the garage with the main house. This was a knock-off colonial design in the traditional white, with huge columns and two wings branching out from the main hall.

Billie Chapman, dressed in neat khaki pants and a navy polo shirt, strode up. Her military uniforms might have been left behind; her aura of authority had remained. "Good evening, Mr. Avery. I believe that we are ready."

Avery nodded. "The grounds look great. How about the inside?"

"Ready there, too."

"Then we're ready to go get the girl?"

"Right," said Chapman. "Of course, that is subject to specific information. I can't plan the mission without the details."

"Got it right here," Avery said, waving his soft leather briefcase. "I think that you'll have everything you need—we have the initial application, the video tape interview, and the P.I. report."

"After I have reviewed the materials, what's the timeline for this operation?"

"As soon as possible," Avery replied, starting for the house. "I'm going to be out of town for a while, more than two weeks, but I would want her to have a few days to settle in before I see her, anyway."

"You'll want to inspect the rooms where we'll be keeping her, right, sir?"

"Yes."

Chapman opened the door for Avery.

As they entered the wide entry hall, Avery dropped his briefcase on a bench at the right. Chapman followed him as he bounded up the stairs.

"I have your keys, sir. Do you want them now?"

"No, no need as yet." He stopped before the wire gate. Chapman used her keys to unlock the gate, then she slid it away into the partition walls on either side of the hall. Hinged moldings covered the openings, making the gate invisible for the moment. The first room was Avery's; Chapman used her key to open the steel paneled door. They entered it and proceeded to the door between the rooms, which she also had to unlock. As he entered the girl's room, Avery glanced at the furnishings.

"As a security measure, the gate will be locked before any door to her room is unlocked. There are bars on the windows in both rooms. There is no possibility of escape, as long as we follow standard operating procedures." Chapman assured him.

"And the detention cell?" Avery hoped that it wouldn't be used, but he figured that his little redhead would put up a fight. She seemed to know her own mind, despite her youth. Chapman led him to a room across the hall from the girl's room. Another steel panel door was there, but this one had a gap under it of about four inches.

Chapman opened the door. Dark gray painted walls, an iron framed cot, a basic sink, and a seatless toilet made up the furnishings. There was a security camera mounted high in one corner. Chapman gestured to the camera. "The green room, next door, has the security monitors for the entire estate, so a single staff member can monitor the girl's suite and the rest of the grounds, if necessary. There is an additional monitor station in my office, which can be switched to monitor any camera, or it can be set to rotate among the cameras at a fixed interval."

They went into the room beside the cell. The longest wall had a huge desk set against it, with a hutch filled with small monitor screens. Chapman turned on the system, and views of the front gate, two views from the exterior of the house, the interior of the front hall, the detention cell, and four views of the girl's suite—two in the bedroom and two of the bathroom—came up in rapid succession. Another wall of the room had a pegboard with hooks that held several different types of restraints including handcuffs and leg cuffs, as well as an electronic stun gun, and even a riding crop.

Chapman gestured toward the pegboard. "Mr. Avery, I am concerned about how much punishment I can use on her, without doing any permanent damage—either physical or psychological."

"You have several options. Use the detention cell if necessary. I hope you won't need it, but it's there. You'll no doubt need to use the handcuffs and the whip at least at first. Let her know who is boss, right from the start. If she's unreasonable, then use more force."

"Yes, sir." Chapman agreed that in order to break the girl, a certain amount of force would be necessary. "But how do you want her treated?"

"With utmost courtesy, whenever possible. I know it'll be a balancing act—but be very polite, even formal. Still, she does need to be broken in a bit. You do that yourself. Train her to respond to your commands. Search her every time she goes off this floor and every time she comes back. You have two reasons for that—for security and to get her used to your touch. Monitor her in the bathroom. That is your first, biggest risk. Search her again before bed. I hope that suicide never crosses her mind, but at first, any sort of reaction is possible." Avery paused, thinking aloud. "Billie, she'll need to lose some of her modesty, her shyness. You can see her naked, or without much in the way of clothing. But *you* conduct all searches and any punishment which must occur. Only you. Limit her contact with the staff as much as possible."

"I can't do everything, Mr. Avery."

"No, of course not. Janice and Danny are trustworthy—but you must do most of the oversight."

"How do I address her?"

"As *Miss* Donalson. We want her to behave like a lady, so we'll treat her as one. Make some attempt to help her realize that as soon as she learns how to act, she'll have the run of the place."

"Yes, sir."

"Don't answer questions, if you can help it. It will be up to me to tell her why she's here. Go ahead and start breaking her to her role, but any mention of sex will come from me. Don't allow her clothes, just a nightgown, at first. That should make her less likely to try to get away from you. After I've spoken with her, I'll make the decision as to when she can dress and be allowed out of the suite upstairs. We'll give her more freedom as she becomes more trustworthy."

"Okay, we can do that," Chapman acknowledged.

*   *   *

Along with Danny Watson and Janice Rule, Chapman was cruising around a small Georgia town, looking for a tall girl, with sparkling green eyes and copper-red hair. Today she drove a Lincoln SUV that she had rented in Macon, an hour to the east. Each day she had rented a different vehicle, because she didn't want anyone becoming suspicious of a certain car. If they could find her alone, all they would need was two minutes without a witness—just two minutes.

*   *   *

Angie stood at the back of the gym, waiting for Sheila, her best friend, to give her a ride home. Ever since Sheila had gotten her new car, Robert had come over to talk to her in the afternoons after school. Angie couldn't fault Sheila, because she had plotted long enough to get both the car and Robert. Certainly, Sheila didn't want her friend hanging around. That was the reason for the planned gym door pick-up. Angie hated being left out here alone, plagued by all the guys who had nothing to do but drive around and around the school, yelling stupid stuff. Today, even the cruds had gone home—or wherever they went. The gym parking lot was deserted, so Angie decided to hike the two miles home.

A large, green sport utility drove up as Angie reached the rear chain link gate of the school, a vehicle she didn't recognize. A woman—perhaps in her mid thirties—got out, dressed in jeans and a chambray shirt. Her square-jawed smile was tentative. "Are you Angela Donalson?"

"Yes," Angie acknowledged, puzzled. "Do I know you?"

A back door opened and a dark-haired man got out. Also in his thirties, he was dressed in denim. He stepped backward, a grin on his face. Angie felt a tremendous shoving force square in the middle of her backpack, and she was pushed into the arms of the smiling man, who reached up to steady her, or so she thought. Instead of helping her stand, he seemed to fall backwards, pulling her into the backseat, literally on top of him. The door slammed behind them, the woman got back into the front seat, and the vehicle pulled away. With his arms wrapped around her, Angie's face was mashed into the chambray-clad chest of her captor. A needle jabbed into her upper right arm.

"What's that? Why are you doing this?" Angie's yell was stifled as she struggled to move her face away from his chest.

"It's a drug to make you sleep. You have about thirty seconds." The woman's voice was calm and matter-of-fact.

"You don't understand. You have the wrong girl." Angie's voice trailed off, and she had trouble keeping her eyes open. The chambray shirt melted into a swirl of colors, then into blackness.

Chapter 2

At first, Angie was only aware that she was in a strange place, and that caused her to rouse with a jerk. Morning light streamed in through long, barred windows. The bed in which she lay was king sized, with sturdy posts of cast iron at the four corners and vertical bars with scrollwork in between. The finish was an unusual creamy vanilla color which looked almost like stone. The corners rose high, and a silky canopy of cream-colored cloth looped over her head; an upholstered bench sat against the foot of the bed. A chest of drawers and an oval mirror of washed wood, which complimented the bed, stood against one wall. Near the windows was a low table with two armchairs and a chaise lounge. A desk with a hutch was against the wall next to the windows. Angie had never seen the room, or anything like it, except in magazines.

Where was she? Why was she there? As she sat up, her memory returned, full force.

She threw back the covers to leap out of the bed, eyes focused on the door, intending to run. She had no specific destination in mind; she just wanted out of the room. However, her flight was stopped before it began. Something held her back. Looking down, she realized that a shiny circle of steel was fastened around her right ankle, with a chain attached that ran to the foot of the bed. Following it, she realized that it was welded to the bed frame. For a moment she sat, dumbfounded by this discovery. As panic set in, Angie thrashed about, throwing the pillows and tugging with all her might on the ankle chain. The cuff bruised her leg, but didn't give.

Angie didn't notice as the door to the hall opened. The woman who had given her the shot was now in the room, launching herself onto the bed, crushing her. Angie was turned face down, her abductor on her back, wrapping her upper body in an embrace that was none too gentle. In her ear, a voice commanded, "Miss Donalson, be still." After a few seconds, Angie accepted the fact that she couldn't buck her captor off, so she obeyed. Angie lay motionless, her face mashed against the mattress.

After a moment, Angie found enough air to ask, "Who the hell are you?"

Her captor let go, sliding off the bed to stand beside her. Angie turned to a sitting position, still held in the bed by the chain connected to her ankle.

"My name is Ms. Chapman. I haven't had time to introduce myself until now." Angie's captor seemed taller now, with short brown hair, dressed in khaki trousers and a navy blue polo shirt. A wide belt held gadgets, including a key chain and a radio. A certain aura surrounded her—this woman meant business.

"Well, Ms. Chapman," Angie asked, putting some iron into her voice, "just why am I here, instead of where I'm supposed to be?"

"As far as I'm concerned, Miss Donalson, you are right where you're supposed to be," Chapman replied in a level voice. "First things first. How do you feel?"

During all that threshing about Angie hadn't stopped to consider her physical state. She perused her body, noticing some bruising on the inside of her right arm. There was a Band-Aid on the inside of the elbow joint. The gown she wore was rucked up above her thighs. Automatically, she smoothed it down. After a quick mental inventory, she realized that apart from a slight headache, a sore right arm, and a need to use the bathroom, she felt fine. Angie told her about the headache and the stiff right arm.

Chapman nodded. "All that seems normal. Good."

There was a knock on the door, and Chapman opened it. An attractive young woman in her late twenties stood in the doorway, dressed in the same khaki pants and polo shirt as Ms. Chapman, a tray in her hands.

"Would you like breakfast?" Chapman turned back to Angie in the bed.

"No. I want you to unlock this chain, gimme back my clothes, and let me go."

"We can't do that, Miss Donalson."

"Then I wanna see whoever is in charge here."

Chapman grinned and exchanged glances with the other woman, who still held the tray.

"I am in charge," Chapman said. "At least until the master comes, and that will be several days."

"The master?" Angie asked. Then she muttered more to herself than to her captors. "This is getting weirder and weirder. Who is this 'master'?"

"You'll simply have to wait. We have instructions to allow you to get up, although you'll be confined to this room after we have seen to your basic needs."

"How about going to the bathroom?" Angie inquired, a bit of sarcasm creeping into her voice.

"Yes, I suppose that qualifies as a basic need." Chapman swept back the covers, pulled the huge key ring from her belt and unlocked the cuff. Without a thought for her state of dress... or undress, since she was wearing only a short cotton knit nightgown and underpants... or any plan of escape, Angie jumped off the bed. Her long legs unfolded like a coiled spring that had been released, and she bolted past the attendant—who still held the tray—and out the door. Noting a window at one end of the corridor, Angie turned and went the other way. Hearing Chapman yell, "Stop!" she turned her head toward the sound, and at that moment ran headlong into a gate made of chain link fencing which she had failed to see. The gate didn't give much. Suddenly dizzy, she sank to the carpeted floor.

Chapman grabbed her, one hand wrapped around the girl's waist, the other around her right wrist. With surprising strength, Chapman dragged her charge back to the bedroom, throwing her across the bench at the foot of the bed. She produced a pair of handcuffs from the wide belt and, while Angie was still disoriented, snapped them on her wrists. Angie was sprawled across the bench on her stomach, hands stretched out in front. Chapman took a riding crop from her belt and swatted Angie's bottom three times—hard. Involuntary tears sprang into Angie's eyes, but she managed to choke off any outcry.

"No more of that, Miss Donalson. You will remain in this room until I say you may go. Janice, leave the tray. Our young lady will have to manage as best she can." Chapman ushered the woman named Janice out, followed her, and locked the door behind them. Angie was alone.

*   *   *

Standing up and ruefully looking at the shiny steel bonds on her wrists, Angie noted that each cuff had a small ring attached to two links of chain. Chapman had placed them in front rather than behind, so she could indeed manage, but certain maneuvers were going to be awkward. Angie sauntered into the bathroom, which was quite a bit larger than her bedroom at Aunt Claire's house. Wow, this was the darnedest thing! The luxury of the huge whirlpool tub and two large vanity areas, each with its own sink was enthralling. A shower stall had jets built into the sides, and a toilet was in its own separate little room. Shelves held plants, towels, and even little soap bars that were color coordinated with the furnishings. Angie admired it, used it, and went back out to see what breakfast was like for captives of Ms. Chapman. Realizing that she hadn't eaten anything after consuming the horrors offered in the lunchroom the previous day, she heard her stomach rumble with hunger.

The tray held a bowl of cereal, a small pitcher of milk, a banana, some buttered toast and jelly, a goblet of juice, and a carafe of coffee. There was also a copy of a newspaper from Knoxville, Tennessee. "Toto, I don't think we're in Georgia anymore," Angie muttered, almost absently. She ate, her movements clumsy due to the restraints on her wrists. Afterward, she searched the paper for anything about her disappearance, but found nothing. Later, she explored the room, having nothing else to do.

The sitting area had chairs upholstered in off-white brocade, with a matching chaise lounge. Feeling a bit like Goldilocks, Angie tried each piece of furniture, but settled in no one spot. The desk had a hutch designed for books; several recent bestsellers resided there. Copies of teen and fashion magazines were arranged on the low table near the chairs. A small CD/tape player was set up on another of the bookshelves, with an assortment of CD's stacked beside it. Angie sat on the chaise lounge, looking at a couple of magazines, balancing each one on her knees so she could turn the pages. The furniture was comfortable, but the situation was just too weird. Angie looked down at her cuffed wrists and shook her head in disbelief.

Restless, she resumed her exploration. A pair of mirrored doors opened to reveal a huge walk-in closet, bigger than the kitchen at Aunt Claire's. Stop making comparisons, Angie chided herself. The three walls of white wire shelves were empty, and only one of the many racks had any hangers, all holding only nightgowns. The drawers of the chest held some underpants—her size. The bathroom held the usual items, including a lot of sample size shampoos, other hair products, and cosmetic samples, occupying a big basket. She wondered if she wouldn't be there long, or perhaps they were trying them out to see what she might like. Angie hoped that it was the former rather than the latter.

When she returned to the bedroom sitting area, she stood looking out the long windows at the grounds surrounding the house. Clipped lawns and flowerbeds with blooming azaleas surrounded the foundation area around the house. Farther away were more flowerbeds, a park bench facing a fountain in a little pond, and some white board fencing in the distance. Everywhere, luxury encircled her. What kidnap victim is surrounded by such beauty? Admittedly, her prior experience with being abducted was from the movies, of course, but this didn't seem to fit. Kidnapped people were tied up in shacks, waiting for someone to pay the ransom. But Angie was not being held in a shack, and no one in her whole town—much less Aunt Claire—could pay a ransom that these folks would even notice. However, she was tied up, and she eyed the handcuffs with loathing. She had never realized how annoying it was to have one wrist held within three inches of the other. The simplest tasks became challenging.

Baffled, Angie spent the day reading and listening to music, or simply pacing beside the windows, interrupted only by Janice bringing in meals. Janice was always accompanied by Chapman, who made sure that Angie had no opportunity to make another exit. The clock radio on the nightstand read 9:30 when Chapman returned, alone, with the riding crop in her hand. Angie cowered against the chaise lounge, fearing another whipping, but Chapman went to the closet and picked out a gown. Moving to the chest, she produced underwear.

"Come here," Chapman commanded, and Angie obeyed, her movements reluctant. After unlocking the cuffs, Chapman handed the girl the clothing and instructed her to go take a bath. As she turned toward the bathroom, Angie saw her captor sit down in a chair to wait.

Angie took her time in the bathroom, figuring that she'd be chained to the bed when she emerged. Her intuition proved correct. As she returned, dressed in the new nightgown, she noticed that the bed was turned down and the chain had been pulled out, ready.

Chapman met her halfway to the bed and barked commands, as if she were a drill sergeant. "About face, at rest."

"Huh?" Confused, Angie stood motionless.

"About face, at rest."

"Look, lady, you're gonna have to tell me what you mean."

Chapman explained in a voice one would use with an imbecile, "Turn away from me, toward the wall, crossing your hands behind your back. Eyes down, looking at the floor. Spread your legs 18 inches apart and hold the position."

Angie hesitated for a moment, wondering just how much of this crap she was going to have to take.

Chapman touched her right thigh with the riding crop, just a touch, but enough to get her attention. "Miss Donalson, you must follow my orders, or you will receive punishment. That is not a threat; it's a promise."

Sighing, Angie turned and followed the instructions. Chapman's hands were gentle but thorough—very thorough—as she searched. She then ran the riding crop in between Angie's legs, spreading them farther apart, a most humiliating procedure. Angie's face became hot and flushed, her redhead's complexion hiding none of her embarrassment. Chapman checked every possible hiding place. Apparently she was satisfied that all the razors were still in the bathroom, because she ordered Angie to sit on the bed while she inspected the ring of bruises around her right ankle. She locked the chain around the left.

"You have a remote control for the ceiling fan on the nightstand at your left, which you can reach. There is a bedpan under the left side of the bed, near the foot. I will awaken you at 7:00, but if you can't make it for some reason, it's there."

Angie pulled up the sheet, hiding her body from further scrutiny.

"Good night, Miss Donalson," Chapman said, turning out the light and locking the door. Angie turned to the pillows and cried. Tears ran onto the soft surface, soaking it. For the first time in a while, Angie recalled the pain which followed her father's death. Bill Donalson had died in his semi, halfway across the country. An image like a snapshot flashed into her mind. Her Dad was in an unaccustomed suit, pale and waxy in his coffin. She was thirteen, already 5' 10", with a figure like a sapling. The loss had left her and Aunt Claire bankrupt—emotionally and literally. Now she was alone, kidnapped and held by strangers. Angie wallowed in her grief, crying herself to sleep for the first time since her daddy had died.

The second day was a frustrating repetition of the first. She saw no one but Janice, who brought her meals, and Chapman, who snapped the handcuffs on her wrists before she unlocked the ankle chain and removed them at 9:30, when she told Angie to go bathe. Angie endured another search after the bath, and once again she was chained to the bed. All questions yielded curt replies which told her nothing. The following morning, Chapman informed her charge that because she had behaved well, there would be no handcuffs.

Puzzled and exasperated with the wooden faces of her captors, Angie decided to provoke some action, be it good or bad. The moment Chapman's key turned in the door lock, she picked up a china vase from the nightstand and hurled it at the door, where it shattered. A crystal clock from the desk went crashing through the window, where it hit one of metal bars and bounced back into the room, lying in the splintered glass. By that time, Chapman had her cornered.

"Get over there in front of the bed!" she yelled, brandishing the riding crop in Angie's face.

Angie stood her ground, determined to test the limits. "No!"

"Move it, " Chapman said in a quieter voice, but with plenty of authority.

"No, I won't."

Chapman's strong hands were on Angie, one hand on her right wrist, one encircling her neck, pressing on the nerves. She propelled her out of the room, straight across the hall, and into a small room with dark walls. Chapman forced her onto her knees and handcuffed her to the end rail of the small cot. Her nightgown was ripped off, and her underwear yanked away. Angie was naked, still kneeling on the floor. Chapman put a foot on Angie's back and pressed her down toward the floor. She smacked the girl's bottom with the whip, then told her to count to ten. Angie shook her head.

"I'm going whip you until you start counting, then we're going to ten anyway, so you had better get started." She rapped her again on the bottom—which stung with a pain that caused Angie to gasp.

Angie began to count. Chapman hit her once per count, each one progressively harder. When they reached ten, Angie was sobbing. Chapman transferred the cuffs from around the bed rail to behind the girl's back and left her, still naked, still crying, kneeling in the little room. Angie got up and parked her sore backside on the cot. Looking around the room, she saw the red light of a security camera, pointed at the cot where she sat. Shaking, she tried to get herself under control. Despite the pain in her bottom, she had no wish to entertain her captors with a show of tears.

*   *   *

Angie thought she had been miserable locked in the beautiful bedroom with no answers to her questions, but she revised that notion as she gingerly lowered herself to her bare knees on the rough plywood floor of her new prison. The bare light bulb in the ceiling must have been very low wattage, because everything was gloomy. The walls were sealed with the same rough plywood, and everything was painted a flat, dark gray, just like the In School Suspension room at Adamsville High. Angie had spent one day in there for skipping class with Heather Goshen. She remembered how depressing the dark cubicle had been. Looking around at a whole room of darkness, she decided that this was worse, much worse.

As she knelt over a double dog dish with milk on one side and slices of bread on the other, the sort one would use to feed a small dog, she tried to figure out how to eat lunch without eating her long auburn hair. Her hands were still held behind her by the loathsome handcuffs. "Next time, throw your fit after breakfast, Angie," she told herself aloud. Because she was so humiliated, part of her wanted to ignore the food, but it had been hours since dinner. Considering that she had no way of knowing when she would be released, the practical side won out.

Tossing her head to get her hair all over one shoulder, she bent down to the dish, pulling a bread slice free with her teeth. She sat up on her sore haunches and consumed the bread. Angie repeated the procedure for the other five slices, then drank the milk from the other side of the dish. When she finished, she shoved it away from the wide space below the door with her foot. Perhaps one of her captors would come in to retrieve the dish. Then, maybe, she would get out of the dark cell.

*   *   *

Chapman was waiting in her office for Marc Avery's call. When the phone rang, she picked it up after the first ring. "Yes."

"Billie, Marc Avery here. How's Angie doing?"

"Locked up right now in the detention cell. She started throwing things yesterday. I stripped her, gave her a good whipping, handcuffed her hands behind her, and gave her nothing but bread and milk in a doggie dish. She's still wearing handcuffs, but we've allowed her to have her hands in front of her today—and she's had regular meals from the kitchen. I plan to let her back in her room tomorrow if she continues to behave."

"Okay. Sounds like she's put up a bit of a fight. But how has it been, Billie? Give me a blow by blow account."

"The actual operation was smooth. No witnesses. We have an investigator monitoring the police down in Georgia. They're looking, but she's listed as missing, possibly endangered. Anyway, she was out approximately 16 hours. When she first came to, she was kind of wild, throwing pillows and such. But she settled down soon enough. When we let her loose from the chain, she ran right out the door. Our security measures were adequate, though; she didn't get past the gate in the hall," Chapman informed him.

"Good."

"We've kept a close watch on her, via the monitors in the green room. Someone has been on duty there whenever she's not chained in bed. The first night, she cried herself to sleep. She was shaking and crying when I finished the whipping yesterday. Apart from that, she's been well composed. There have been a number of questions, but we haven't told her anything. Naturally, the situation is stressful, Mr. Avery, but I think she's doing pretty well for a seventeen-year old kid."

"Glad to hear it, Billie. I'll see you either Friday or Saturday, depending on the weather and my golf game. Call me in Charleston if you need anything."

* * *

Janice joined Chapman in the green room. The camera in the cell was rigged for low light, so it sent an acceptable, if not crystal clear, picture. Angie sat on the bunk, handcuffed hands around her long legs, which were drawn up against her nude body. The chain was taut—as it had been for hours and looked as if she thought that enough pressure exerted for enough time would somehow free her from the bonds.

"How long has she been like that?" Janice asked.

"Quite a while. I don't know if she's hiding herself from the camera or testing the handcuffs. They're double locked, so they won't tighten—otherwise she couldn't stand it."

"Billie," Janice questioned, "Is this going as badly as I think it is?"

"I don't know what you're thinking, but it's going okay. She was bound to put up some fight. I expected it. She hasn't acted crazy or tried to hurt herself; I count those as positives. The girl has to test our strength. We need to show her that she can't win. That's all this is— we're testing each other. Sooner or later she'll give up."

"What about her throwing stuff?"

"That was frustration. Think about it from her point of view. She wants to learn more about her situation, and we aren't cooperating.

What would you do, if you were in her shoes?" Chapman leaned back in the chair, continuing to observe her charge. Janice shrugged, and they watched in silence for a few moments.

"When will you let her out?" Janice asked.

"Has she at least been civil when you took in her meals?" Chapman inquired, turning to face Janice.

"She hasn't said a thing." Janice's tone was bitter.

"Is she eating?"

"Yes, most everything."

"Good enough. She gets out tomorrow morning, if we have no further trouble."

*   *   *

Chapman strode into the little cell and told Angie to hold out her wrists. She took out her key ring and unlocked the handcuffs, placing them in a black nylon case on her wide belt.

"You may go back to your room if you wish, Miss Donalson."

"I wish," Angie replied, rubbing her sore wrists. Chapman opened the door and gestured for her charge to enter the room across the hall. Angie crossed the hall in three quick strides. Once in the room, she stood there, still quite naked, and looked around.

"You will behave as a young lady, Miss Donalson, or you will go back to the detention cell. Do you understand that?" Chapman's voice was low, in her ear.

"Yes, ma'am." Angie's voice was also soft.

The window that Angie had broken had been replaced, and new china vase sat on the nightstand. Chapman went to the closet, brought out a nightgown, and suggested a bath.

"Ms. Chapman, when did you say this 'master' would be here to answer my questions?" Angie asked in a formal tone.

"The master said he would be home either Friday or Saturday."

"What day is it?" she asked, feeling foolish. Angie had lost track of time, locked up in the dark room where the light never changed.

Chapman grinned. "Today is Tuesday, Miss," she said and handed the clean clothing to her charge.

"Thank you."

Chapman gestured toward the bathroom, and Angie took her nightie and underwear into the room, draping it across a bench in front of the vanity. While she stood there, she surveyed her body in the huge mirror. Fading red marks marred her hips and buttocks, the telltale signs of Chapman's punishment. Angie stared at them and sighed, wondering if her tantrum had been worth it. Not really, she decided.

When she came out of the bathroom, a breakfast tray sat on the desk. She ate and looked at the newspaper that accompanied it. Again, there was nothing concerning her disappearance. As before, she had the entire day to herself. Although she was most delighted to be out of the little room across the hall, glad to be free of any chains, and pleased that her bottom wasn't too sore to sit upon, nevertheless, she was exceedingly bored. Angie paced the room most of the day.

That night, Angie posed a question as Chapman was searching her, the whip in hand, and Angie was in the "at rest" position with her face toward the floor, her hands behind her back.

"Ms. Chapman, why do you chain me to the bed? You keep the door locked."

Chapman answered while continuing the search. "If you thought you could get away, you might be tempted to try something stupid. In a way, by searching you and chaining you to the bed, I'm giving you an opportunity to sleep soundly. I'm making sure that you have nothing else to do."

"I see," Angie said. Chapman touched her bottom, just a touch, and gestured toward the bed. Angie climbed in and extended her leg at Chapman's order.

"I'd sleep better," Angie told Chapman as she snapped the cuff on the right ankle, "if I could get some exercise."

"I agree. We'll see what we can do about that," Chapman promised. "Good night, Miss Donalson."

The light went out, and Angie heard the key in the lock. With a sigh, she settled in for another long night.

Ms. Chapman was as good as her word. The next day she took her prisoner outside after lunch, searching her first. While Angie was in position, Chapman placed the handcuffs on Angie's wrists, locking them behind her. Angie felt most peculiar, for she was still wearing just a nightgown.

"Ms. Chapman, aren't you going to give me some clothes? Don't you have what I was wearing—when you grabbed me?"

Chapman ignored this reference to the abduction and simply addressed the issue of clothing. "We're just going to tour a section of the grounds today, Miss Donalson. You won't see anyone, except me and Janice—therefore, no one will see you. The gown will do." Chapman's voice was firm, but not unkind.

Janice had conjured up a pair of leather and fabric sandals which more or less fit, and Angie was grateful, because she toured quite a bit of territory. The estate seemed quite large, with beautifully landscaped grounds. Graveled paths led in several directions, and Chapman led her along a number of them.

Taking no chances, Chapman stayed right beside her prisoner, a hand at her elbow, guiding her along each path. She escorted Angie inside the stable, pausing to show her a smallish bay mare. "This one is half Arabian, half Quarter horse and very gentle. She is to be yours. You'll have to think of a name for her."

Angie didn't respond. From the stables, they went to the swimming pool; Chapman explained the cover had just been removed. The pool was large and had a white painted fence six feet high around it. Chairs and two umbrella tables flanked the pool.

"You'll get some of your exercise here when it is a bit warmer," Chapman said. "Are you a good swimmer?"

"No, not really. I never had much opportunity," Angie replied. Part of her had no wish to converse with Chapman. But she needed to know more about her situation, so she listened closely and answered Chapman's questions.

Chapman touched her arm to turn her toward the gate. "We'll have to fix that," she said. "The Master will want you to be comfortable in the water." Next on the tour was the helipad, near the southern portion of the house. This was a round circle of creek gravel, circled by green lawn, to make it look like a target from the air.

"The Master usually comes via helicopter. It's much faster than coming by car. This estate is fairly remote," Chapman told her. Next they went to the two tennis courts, both with artificial surfaces and lights for night play. From there they headed back toward the house. The flower garden, which could be seen from Angie's room on the second floor, was next on the tour. Chapman seemed to be in no hurry; she went out of her way to show Angie that there were all sorts of things to do.

"You'll have the run of the property, in due time. All you have to do is learn your place," Chapman promised.

"Place? What exactly is my place?" Angie wanted to gesture toward the grounds, but she found it hard to express herself with her arms bound behind her back. Her long auburn hair waving in the slight breeze, Angie stood still and glared at her captor.

"For that, Miss Donalson, you must wait and ask the Master." Chapman's voice was inscrutable.

Chapter 3

The next few days were uneventful. Chapman took Angie for a walk each afternoon, always in a gown, always with her hands fastened behind her with the horrid handcuffs. Of course, that left many other hours to fill. Since Angie was reading everything at a voracious pace, Chapman allowed her to visit the library on the first floor to replenish her supply of reading material. "The Master" didn't come Friday, and by Saturday afternoon Angie had decided that he didn't exist. About 4:30 she heard a helicopter. Angie rushed to the windows, forgetting that the helipad was on the other side of the house.

Angie sat on the bench at the foot of the bed and waited, every nerve and sinew imbued with tension. Fifteen minutes later Marc Avery came striding through the connecting door, which up to then had always been locked. Angie was ecstatic—thrilled at just laying eyes on someone she knew.

"Mr. Avery, thank God it's you. Did you pay my ransom? It has been horrible! This crazy bunch of people kidnapped me, and I've been whipped and they won't give me any clothes and—" She broke off, sobbing, then stood up and went over to hug her rescuer. Only then did it register that he carried the riding crop in his hand, the same one that Chapman had used on her. Although she was no longer sore, and the marks were fading when she'd inspected her backside in the mirror, she remembered the pain all too well. Instead of embracing him, she stepped back, putting a hand to her mouth. Angie bit her lip to keep from crying out.

"Oh no," she said under her breath. "Oh, God, this can't be."

"Yes, Angie. I'm the one they call the Master. This is my house. My employees have looked after you. That's because I am your Master now."

She looked up at him, absolutely dumbfounded, silent as his words sank in, and he let her think it over.

"Why… why are you doing this to me?" Angie found her voice, and she needed answers.

"It's simple, really. I decided some time ago that I wanted a mistress. Not a hired whore, not some society girl like I usually have chasing me, but an old fashioned mistress. I knew that I needed a young girl—someone who had not been spoiled by another man, or a series of men, someone who could be trained to suit me. We went through the scholarship applications and interviewed girls, and you won. The house was ready; the staff was ready. All I needed was the right girl to teach. You qualify. Congratulations."

"You… are… absolutely… crazy."

"Oh, no. I've been very cautious. The police have no leads and are making no further efforts to find you. You're just another teenage runaway to them. So you belong to me. Your body and your soul are mine. Once you've accepted the situation, we'll both be quite happy. You'll have the things you always wanted, and I'll have the perfect paramour." Avery smiled at her, which was even more frightening.

"I will never accept this—never!" Angie declared it, as if saying it would give her more courage.

"Don't be so sure. You've already started." Avery didn't gloat, but his voice held confidence. "When Billie gives an order, you obey. You obey because you have to."

"Who the hell is Billie?"

"Billie Chapman. I know you've met."

"Oh, yes. She's the one who hit me with that damned whip!"

"Only when you defy her. If you behave and do as I say, there will be no more of that."

"I'm not going to do whatever you say. I don't care who you are!"

"Yes, you will. You have resisted, some, and you've been punished, some. Every time you fight us—every time you fail to meet our expectations—you will suffer. You may resist some more, but in a short time, you'll come to accept all this. I'm sure of it. Angie, I studied your profile. You came out of nothing. Think, girl—you just left food stamps and free lunches at the school cafeteria behind. Here, you'll be pampered, like you've never been pampered before. You'll have more than you ever dreamed possible. And all you have to do is cooperate."

Angie shook her head. "I can't believe this."

"You'd better start. Billie's orders are to be followed, and so are mine. I am the Master and I will be obeyed." Avery punctuated this statement by taking her by the shoulders and shaking her. "Remember this, Angie. I'd be better off with you dead, than with you *ever* getting away. The staff here knows that. There will be no escape. We'll use you to fertilize a flowerbed before we let you go."

He released her, and she collapsed onto the bench, like a leaking helium balloon. Avery's anger had escalated and he paced the room, as if to work it off. Angie sat, brooding, embroiled in her own tumultuous thoughts. In mid stride, Avery paused in front of her.

"Take off that gown."

Angie looked up at him, her mind blank. She was still so stunned that the order didn't really filter into her brain. Pain arced through her legs as he brought the riding crop down across her bare thighs.

"Take it off, Angie. I spent a lot of money finding you, bringing you here. I want to look at the merchandise." He gestured for the girl to rise, so as she stared at the whip she rose, reluctantly. She stood before him and slipped the straps off her shoulders, allowing the gown to slide down and puddle at her feet. Avery used the end of the crop as a prod and motioned for her to remove her underpants. Angie hooked her thumbs into the sides and pushed downward. The wisp of satin joined the puddle of cloth on the floor.

"Walk to the desk and back." Avery's voice seemed tight. She did so, instinct making her cross her arms in front of her breasts. Avery touched her right arm with the riding crop, shaking his head, and she lowered her arms to her sides. He did not approach her; he just stared.

"Turn around, please."

Angie obeyed, never taking her eyes from the whip. She knew that her bottom still bore marks from that same whip, and she found that she feared pain more than embarrassment. Angie stood, her face as red as her hair, waiting.

Avery smiled his approval. "Excellent. Your body is as beautiful as your lovely face. You move with grace and poise. Your physique is mature—for a teenager." At this, he gestured toward rounded breasts. Angie shuddered involuntarily. "I know that I'll enjoy you when the time comes." He paused. "As you become more trustworthy, we'll let you out a bit—have your hair done by a real professional, shop and get a wardrobe. Angie, you'll have everything you need."

"What you're saying is that I won't be a prisoner here, forever?" There was a tremor of hope in Angie's voice. Her arms crossed in front again, and Avery made no move to stop her.

"Eventually you'll have the run of the estate. Later, you'll travel with me. But only when you are obedient. You belong to me. Get that through your head, then I'll give you the world." He held his arms wide, as if to illustrate what she could, one day, receive.

"I want to be somebody, Mr. Avery. I told you that in my interview. But I want to do it myself."

"You'll be more than you ever imagined. But you will do so on my arm."

"No!" She struggled to control her voice.

"Your goals will be met. You'll finish your high school work. I already have a tutor lined up. Then college is a possibility, if you're ready."

"Great. I'm glad you're thinking only about my education. Could I put my gown on now?"

"Sure." Avery turned to go. "Just remember, Angie. Obey and you will have everything you ever dreamed of having. Resist and you'll face increasing levels of punishment." He disappeared through the connecting door. Angie heard the bolt slide home.

She looked at the closed door with some relief, but her dreams were evaporating like a small puddle in the path of a strong wind. Angie realized that she was trapped, with no way out. Hope had kept her going for the past week, and now the whole situation seemed impossible. Worse, Avery had begun hinting at the most psychologically disturbing of crimes—rape.

For a moment, she glared at the connecting door, hating the man who had just gone through it. Reaching over and picking up the gown, she slid it over her head. Angie crossed to the hall door and hammered on it until her fists were aching. She stood there, the tears flowing hot and fast, rolling down her face, making little runnels to her chin, and blurring her vision. Angie was sobbing out her misery, and certainly not expecting company. Chapman surprised her by opening the door. She stumbled back, expecting more punishment.

34

"Are you all right, Miss Donalson?"

"No." She shook her head, flinging tears.

Chapman guided her away from the door, over to the chaise lounge in the sitting area, offering tissues to dry the tears that streaked down her face. Angie was shocked when Chapman clasped her around the shoulders and gave her a quick embrace. Just as abruptly, she released Angie's shoulders, but stood beside her, offering support.

"Just rest for a while," Chapman comforted her. "Try not to think about anything for a bit. Okay?" Her hand patted Angie's shoulder once more, then dropped to her side, but she remained close to her charge.

Angie wanted to yell at Chapman, to tell her that she had destroyed her life. But her kindness was so unexpected that Angie didn't want to alienate the only possible friend she had in this place. So she sat and tried to think of pleasant things—memories of her dad, and of playing in the tiny yard behind Aunt Claire's cottage in Adamsville. She paged through memories of her friends at Adamsville High, as if looking at a friend's yearbook. Angie realized that these were things that she might never again experience. Her body shook with fierce emotions. Chapman patted her again, but didn't speak. Angie closed her mind to her surroundings and wept for all she had lost.

After a few moments, Chapman left. Angie had never felt so alone. She was in a daze, unaware of the passage of time, until Janice entered the room with a tray.

"Miss Donalson, would you like this in the sitting area, or at the desk?"

Angie shrugged, so Janice placed the tray on the coffee table in front of her.

Absently, Angie picked at the food, then went back to wallowing in her memories. Chapman interrupted this reverie with the usual bath and bed ritual, but her voice was gentle and her search perfunctory. She also offered Angie a pill to help her sleep, and Angie took it.

"Good night, Miss D. Get a good rest. I'll see you in the morning."

Angie closed her eyes, not sure that she'd ever sleep. Angie pulled on the chain, a tangible reminder of her prisoner status. She had to get away; she had to get out of this room, out of this house. How could she sleep, knowing what she knew? Maybe it was the pill; maybe her brain had to shut down for a while, but she did sleep.

The next morning, Avery joined her for breakfast. Janice brought two trays, and Angie's was placed over her while she was still in bed. Avery ate at the nightstand. He seemed just a bit more reserved than the night before. Perhaps seeing her chained up put him off. When he finished, he kissed her on the forehead and caressed her face. He vanished through the connecting door, and within seconds Chapman came to let her up.

"Well, Miss, are you feeling better today?"

"Yeah, I guess so." Angie's hint of a smile was rueful. "I'll put it this way—once again, boredom seems to be my biggest problem."

"Mr. Avery hasn't said if he has any plans for you. He did, however, bring a few things for you to wear. I'll bring them up a little later."

"Okay." Angie went into the bathroom. Chapman was gone when she came out. She checked the door, a habit that she'd gotten into. Of course, it was locked. She took up her favorite post by the window and perused the grounds. No one was around, but she remembered that today was Sunday. Angie had the morning to herself, so she read. Around mid-day she was surprised to see Janice wheeling in a rack of clothing. Janice smiled and suggested that Angie take a look and find something to wear to lunch downstairs.

The rack was filled with a variety of clothes, all in Angie's size— an entire wardrobe of T-shirts, shorts, dresses, pants, shirts, suits, even shoes—all much nicer than anything she had ever owned. After spending more than a week in nothing but nightgowns, any clothing would have been a relief. Although not every piece was to her exact taste, it seemed that the clothes had been chosen with her in mind. Angie selected a pants outfit in emerald green with gold trim; it was cut like a sexy uniform. There were even matching shoes of a metallic gold.

When Angie finished dressing, Chapman entered the room. She smiled as Angie pirouetted, showing off her new outfit. "Ready for lunch, Miss Donalson?"

"I guess so." She faltered, thinking of Avery and his glib plans.

"About face, at rest." Chapman's voice was commanding. Without hesitation, Angie turned and placed her hands behind her, spreading her legs for Chapman to do her search. Angie had learned that her captor was serious about these searches. This time Chapman was quick about it, but when she finished Angie felt her click a cuff on her right wrist.

"What's this?" Angie inquired, annoyed.

"Another pair of pretty bracelets for you to play with. These go in front. About face." Angie turned and Chapman fastened the other cuff to the girl's left wrist. There were about 12 inches of chain from one cuff to the other, giving Angie more freedom than the handcuffs, but her movements were somewhat restricted. "Mr. Avery wants you to join him in the dining room, but right now I require some sort of restraint if you leave this hall."

"Don't you trust me?"

"Not at all, Miss Donalson, not at all."

*   *   *

Avery, clad in a golf shirt and lightweight pants, stood at the foot of the stairs in the foyer of the country house. Angie was coming down to the dining room for the first time. Chapman had insisted on the restraint, but allowing her out of the secure area still represented progress, a great deal of progress. Marc looked forward to the time when a well-trained and well-groomed auburn-haired beauty was his companion whenever and wherever he wanted her. His gaze moved upward as he heard the clanking noise of Chapman storing the chain link gate in its home, in the upstairs hallway. Angie emerged onto the landing, her captive beauty fulfilling his longtime fantasy. Only the shiny cuffs and swinging chain reminded him that this was a work in progress.

Chapman was two steps behind on the stairs, a riding crop in one hand, ready to stop any undesirable behavior on the part of her charge. Angie came down without haste, looking around, ignoring her keeper. As she reached the bottom, Marc joined her, kissing her on the cheek, chastely. With one hand at her elbow, he guided her to the dining room.

"This way, Angie. I hope you like Italian food. The cook has made some fabulous manicotti—it's one of my favorites." Marc's voice was warm and welcoming. "I like the suit; it really sets off your hair. Beautiful color." Marc reached up to brush the long locks behind her shoulder. Angie stopped and allowed him to touch her, but her manner indicated that she was enduring rather than appreciating his caress.

The dining table was set for two, at one corner. Marc guided her to the end of the table and helped her get seated. Angie placed her manacled hands in her lap and sat straight and tall in her seat. Janice served, while Chapman took a seat in the hall outside, ready to step in if Angie misbehaved. Janice, clad in her ubiquitous khaki pants, served Caesar salad, offering to grate fresh Parmesan cheese. Angie spoke only when it seemed that she must, but she ate as if she enjoyed the meal, if not the company. A good part of her time was spent gazing at her surroundings, which included the dining room itself. She counted twenty-two seats. A pair of huge crystal chandeliers were suspended over the table, and a sideboard, set with gleaming silver and crystal candlesticks, flanked the table. A wine cooler, half-filled, resided in an enclosure near the swinging door to the kitchen. Janice brought the main course—creamy, cheese-stuffed pasta in marinara sauce. Angie turned to the view outside the tall windows. These faced the front of the house, a different view than the one from her room. Now she could see the circular drive, softened with blooming shrubs, which curved into some woods.

"What sorts of activities do you think you'll want to do here?" Marc asked her, again trying to engage her in conversation. "Billie gave you the grand tour one day, I believe. Surely something looked like fun."

"I just want you to let me go. Mr. Avery, please let me go home. I won't tell anyone where I've been. I promise to keep it all a secret. My aunt has no one but me, and she's old. She needs me!"

"I'm sure she'll be fine. And I'll keep you here for as long as I need to, until you are trustworthy." Marc Avery touched her hand, the one resting on the table. She put it in her lap, clasping the other hand, the chain forming a puddle in her lap.

"I think you'll be surprised, Mr. Avery. You may find that you are spending too much keeping me here and getting too little out of it. I know you're rich, but surely you can find something better to do with your money."

"Oh, it'll be money well spent. I can see that right now." His gaze was appreciative. "The way you fill that suit is a perfect example."

"A suit bought with your money, right?"

"Right. And it is perfect. Just like you. Get used to it, Angie. I'm your master."

Angie glared at him.

"Ah, if looks could kill, I'd be a dead man."

Angie held her gaze steady.

Marc shrugged and smiled anyway. "Finished? Would you like coffee?"

"Nothing else—no."

"Let's tour the house, then." He rose and pulled out her chair, helping her up. They left the dining room and returned to the foyer.

Chapman joined them for the tour. Avery showed Angie the library, the great room, the breakfast room and kitchen, the sunroom, the exercise room, and his private study. Down another hall were the guestrooms, eight of them. Then they went outdoors for a walk in the flower gardens, even though she'd already seen those. Marc kept an arm around her waist, and she stood erect and stiff, as if relaxation meant enjoyment. Obviously, she wanted him to understand that her cooperation was nothing more than an avoidance of punishment.

"I'm heading back to the city tonight, Angie. You will begin an exercise program next week, and you can start riding and tennis lessons. The staff here can handle all that. Later, you will have some schoolwork to complete. I'm sending you back upstairs for a while; then we will have an early dinner before I go. See you later."

Chapman took her arm and guided her back up the stairs. She paused to lock the gate at the top of the stairs, then she took the girl into her room. Once inside, she unlocked the cuffs and barked her usual order, "About face."

"This is so stupid," Angie muttered, but she turned around.

"At rest," Chapman continued, and the girl placed her hands behind her and spread her legs with some renitence. Chapman, noting

Angie's reluctant manner, tapped her inner thigh with the crop to make her adjust her legs and searched her thoroughly, moving her hands over the girl's lithe body. When the search was finished, instead of the usual gentle pat on her bottom, Chapman swatted her, and Angie jumped.

"What was that for?" Angie complained.

"Look sharp, Miss Donalson," Chapman said with an edge in her voice. "I will return for you at dinner time."

Angie glared at the door that Chapman had just closed behind her. Ms. Chapman was being unnecessarily harsh. She flopped down on the chaise lounge, noting that the bed had been made and the room cleaned in her absence. The clothes rack was gone, but its contents now hung in the huge closet. Angie kicked off the gold pumps, picked up the remote control for the CD player and grabbed the book she'd been reading. Which was, of all things, a romance between a kidnapper and his victim.

Janice knocked and entered at 5:45. Angie looked up with a questioning glance.

"Miss Donalson, I'm here to help you dress for dinner," Janice said.

"I'm dressed," Angie said with a slight edge of sarcasm in her voice.

"The Master wants you in something a bit more formal, Miss. You will please take a quick shower while I get things in order."

"No, I'm happy with what I have on."

Janice left the room, and Chapman was with her when she returned. Chapman looked displeased, and she had the riding crop in her hand. "I understand that you're not being cooperative."

"Ms. Chapman, I like what I have on. I'm happy to have the clothes, but I see no need to change."

"Mr. Avery was reared in a household which dressed formally for dinner. He will no doubt want to do that here, at least some of the time. It is his house; he is the Master here. You will dress for dinner," Chapman said with quiet determination. "Go take a shower, and Janice will help you with your dress, hair, and make-up. *Now*."

Angie stood her ground for a moment, and Chapman sensed that she wasn't sure if this was worth a battle. The whip slashed

40

downward, a sharp blow that stung through the cloth of the pants Angie wore.

"Move it, Miss Donalson." Chapman's other hand shoved her toward the bathroom. Angie went without further prompting.

Janice picked out a dress of midnight blue with slits halfway up the thigh, blue pumps and dark hose. When Angie emerged from the bath in her terry cloth robe, Janice handed her appropriate underwear. After Angie had donned them, Janice showed her to the dressing table in the bathroom. A manicure was first, shaping and coloring Angie's nails a dark wine-color. Janice applied a base coat of foundation and plaited Angie's striking auburn hair into a French braid. Then she completed the make-up, achieving a level of sophistication that Angie would never have thought possible. The dress, hose, and shoes came next. Janice checked everything and picked up a small radio. "Billie, she's ready."

Chapman came up to secure her charge. She paused, regarding Angela Donalson. "Wow, you sure do clean up nice."

Angie scowled and made for the door.

"Just a moment. Let's get this over with. About face." Chapman's voice was commanding—but Angie stopped and turned to complain.

"Billie, you searched me when I came up here, just a few hours ago. This is getting pretty dumb, don't you think?"

"Turn around, Miss Donalson. I'd hate to mess up Janice's handiwork." Chapman's contralto was firm. Angie turned. "Hands on the wall." Angie complied.

Chapman's hands moved up and down her legs, torso and arms, snapping the cuff around her right wrist.

"In front, again," Chapman said, and as the girl swiveled back, she snapped the left cuff into place. Chapman grasped her elbow and they moved toward the door together.

*   *   *

Once again, Avery was waiting for her. Chapman was close to her elbow, no doubt expecting her little rebellion to surface again, but Angie did her best to ignore the compact woman. Marc took Angie's hand as she came to the last step and brushed it with his lips. The chain between her wrists kept this from being as elegant as he no doubt intended.

Marc placed his hand at the small of her back to guide her to the dining room. They were seated as before, at a corner with Angie at the end of the table. Janice poured glasses of a blush colored wine for each of them. The first course she served was Oysters Florentine, followed by pasta in a tomato sauce. After that, she brought an Italian salad with cheese and olives. A smooth and creamy cheesecake with raspberries completed the meal. Avery did most of the talking, seemingly able to carry on without much help from Angie.

Angie relaxed just a bit after imbibing a couple of glasses of the unaccustomed wine, in spite of her reluctance to be with her 'Master.' Avery looked very handsome in his dinner jacket and formal striped trousers. He spoke of his business and travels. Angie wasn't able to respond to much of this, and any talk of her past seemed to be unbearable for either of them. Any talk of Angie's future, as Avery saw it anyway, was too disturbing for her. Often, the room fell silent.

At the close of the meal, Chapman escorted Angie to the library, offering to give her an opportunity to pick out some more books for her room. Chapman stayed with her charge, watching as Angie perused the shelves. Avery was upstairs, changing for his trip back to the city. As he came back down, Angie heard the helicopter landing on the helipad on the south side.

Chapman carried Avery's briefcase and a riding crop. Marc put his arm around Angie and escorted her to the helipad. Just before he boarded the craft, he ordered the girl to kiss him goodbye. Angie shook her head. Without speaking, he held out his hand and Chapman put the riding crop into it. Immediately, Angie felt the sting as it connected with her buttocks. Rather than wait for another blow, she stretched up to peck his cheek.

Avery tossed the whip to Chapman, took his briefcase and climbed up into the chopper, which headed off, then Chapman escorted Angie back to the house and into her room. At Chapman's order, she took off the fancy blue dress, cleaned off the makeup, and unwound her long auburn hair. When she had dressed for bed, Chapman searched her again and locked the cuff around her right ankle. As she turned to go, Angie grasped the chain and tugged, but it didn't give.

"Why bother doing that? It's welded to the bed frame, and it's not coming loose," Chapman told her, an amused half smile on her lips.

"I hate this thing."

"Good night, Miss Donalson." Chapman ignored the complaint.

"Good night," Angie echoed.

*   *   *

Chapman woke her charge at 7:00. Angie was still groggy when Chapman unlocked the ankle chain and ordered her to the bathroom. She emerged, expecting to see Janice with a tray, but Chapman tossed her a pair of thick mesh shorts and a T-shirt.

"Get those on, and these shoes," she said, pulling a pair of Nikes from the closet.

"Why?"

"The Master told you yesterday—your exercise program begins today. You'll be out of shape and .fat if you keep eating stuff like you did this weekend without working it off. Besides, you told me last week that you wanted some exercise."

As Angie finished dressing, Chapman motioned for her to turn away.

"Aw, Billie, you just watched me dress, for God's sake."

"About face, Miss Donalson."

Angie turned. Chapman looped a chain around her waist and fastened it.

"What's this?"

As Angie turned back around, Chapman snapped cuffs around each wrist. A short chain fastened each handcuff to the one at her waist. Angie found that she could move her hands, but not far from her side. Nose scratching was definitely out. Chapman fastened a leather collar around her neck, running her finger under it to see that its fit was loose.

"What is all this?" Angie asked again. Glancing in the mirror, Angie saw an image she didn't like. She looked like a dog on the way to the pound, but she decided to keep the thought to herself, noting the determined expression on her keeper's face.

"You'll be going on a walk around the estate. And you're going to cooperate." Chapman motioned for her prisoner to precede her. "We'll begin with two and a half miles today. By next week, we'll be up to four a day."

They went out the door near the kitchen, across a wide patio, and down the graveled path. Chapman guided her to the stable. There, Chapman fastened a long rope to the collar and mounted a horse. Angie stood motionless for a moment. The rope tightened, and she realized that she had no choice but to follow the plodding horse. Although the rope was just clipped onto the collar, the wrist restraints would not allow Angie to reach it. If Angie stopped, she'd be dragged by the neck, unable to free herself. Waves of anger washed over Angie. This was so damned humiliating.

Angie walked behind the horse for what seemed an eternity. Chapman followed a path which wound through woods and meadows. The ground had been cleared and the path was graveled, but it was hilly and provided a good workout, especially since Angie had been confined, for the most part, to one room for almost two weeks.

Being early morning, it was cool, but as she kept walking, Angie became quite warm. Sweat broke out, but she couldn't wipe anything or even push the hair away from her face because the manacles kept her hands near her sides. She felt weary and decided that she probably looked worse, when they arrived back at the stable. Chapman got off the horse and a man Angie had seen working in the yard came out to take it. As she looked at him through the curtain of hair across her face, Angie decided that this man had been Chapman's accomplice during her abduction.

"Thanks, Danny," said Chapman. She disconnected the rope from the neck collar, coiled it, and gave it to him. Chapman guided her charge back to the house and to her room. This time, there was no search, and the restraints were quickly removed. At Chapman's suggestion Angie went to take a shower. When she emerged, wearing her terry cloth robe, with damp auburn hair streaming down her back, she saw that Janice was bringing in a breakfast tray. Janice raised the domed lid with a bit of a flourish. Biscuits and sausage patties occupied the single plate.

"Janice, is there an agenda for the rest of today?" Glad to see some southern food, Angie was already munching.

"I don't know about the whole day. I heard Billie mention that tennis is later this morning."

"Who does that?"

"Not me." Janice snorted. "Danny is good with a racket. Probably he'll be the one to teach you."

"So more shorts?"

"Yes, I suppose so. Enjoy your breakfast, Miss." Janice smiled as she withdrew, locking the door behind her.

Angie picked up the plate and sat on the chaise lounge, gazing out the low windows. Once again a newspaper had been in the side pocket of the tray, so she perused another Knoxville paper. Angie noticed the date. She'd been gone from home eleven days! She wondered what Aunt Claire thought—and her friends. Angie wondered what Coach Doyle was saying about her. If he hadn't given her that application, she wouldn't be a prisoner here. "I can't believe I am still here." Angie flamed with anger, remembering the humiliation of her early morning "exercise."

"And I'm being friendly with them." Angie found herself questioning her lack of resolve. She needed to get away from this place. Avery's efficient staff made it all too easy to just do as she was told and concentrate on their plans, rather than formulate one of her own. Why wasn't she fighting back? Angie glanced at the furniture, at the sheer number of square feet in the room. She wondered if her reason for staying was the elaborate appointments which adorned her suite, or the fancy dinners served on fine china. Angry, she sprawled on the bed, tears rolling down her cheeks as she thought of never seeing her aunt again... of not having her senior year at Adamsville High. She had never even had a decent date! This situation was so unfair.

Life ain't fair. Angie could still hear her Dad's voice; she guessed she'd repeated the expression a few times herself, if the truth be known. But this was beyond unfair. Yet, it was hard to put up resistance. Chapman had thwarted the few moves she'd made. Rebellion had simply led to a beating and a visit to the dark room across the hall. Angie had not stopped looking for a chance, but

Chapman had been most effective. As she reviewed the time of her captivity, she remembered Chapman's attention to detail. There had been no opportunities. If she waited long enough, Chapman would no doubt relax her vigilance. But how long would it be? And what would Avery do to her while she was waiting for Chapman to trust her? However, with trust would come opportunity.

Angie pondered all this as she rested from the walk through the woods. Based on Janice's prediction, Angie dressed in shorts, a T-shirt and tennis shoes. Around 10:00, Chapman returned with a pair of conventional handcuffs in her hand. Angie anticipated her order and turned away with her hands crossed at the small of her back, ready for the search and the snap of the handcuffs.

"I'm waiting, Billie," Angie said, tapping her foot. Angie turned to glance at her captor, noting a surprised look on her face. Chapman grinned a lopsided grin. Then, Angie felt the cuffs snap as her hands were restrained behind her.

"How are you at tennis, Miss Donalson?" Chapman inquired as she guided Angie down the hall.

"I've never played much, except for during Lifetime Sports last semester." Angie shrugged. "I never went out for the team or anything like that. But it was fun."

"I never played much myself. But Danny is pretty good, so I asked him to teach you and be your partner." She paused as they went out the back door. "He's a member of the permanent staff, so he knows about you and what you're allowed to do and what you're not. Don't try anything stupid, okay?"

"Okay, I'll save that for you." Angie's tone was playful. Prancing down the steps, she took the lead and headed for the tennis courts. She had decided to foster the impression that she was going along with it all—every little thing—hoping that Chapman would relax her vigilance—before Avery took away something that she would never get back.

*   *   *

Chapman watched as Angie chased the yellow tennis ball. Danny was easy on her at the beginning of the lesson, but as she proved herself able, he stepped up the pressure. Lounging on a bench in the shade, Chapman enjoyed the sight of her charge being tired out by continuous changes of direction across the green court. Bit by bit, Angie's seventeen-year-old energy was worn down by the thirty-something Danny's skill.

"I give up!" she shouted and flung her arms into the air in defeat. She collapsed onto the bench beside Chapman and lay with her chest heaving. Chapman stood up, concerned, watching her charge for signs of being overheated, but the girl looked fine, just tired.

Angie grinned at her and sat up. "Don't worry, Billie. I'm not gonna die on you."

"You'd better not! I'd be dog meat for sure if I let anything happen to you."

"Me, too," Danny said as he joined her on the bench. "You were pretty good, for someone who says she hasn't played much."

"I really haven't. Believe me, my aunt and I don't have a tennis court in the backyard. We barely have a backyard. Our whole house isn't much bigger than the great room in this house." Angie spoke without envy. "But it's okay. Aunt Claire is always there for me." Her voice cracked. A knowing glance passed over her head as Danny caught Chapman's eye.

"Let's get you back, Miss Donalson." Chapman ended Angie's reverie with a hand up. "About face, if you would be so kind." She kept her tone light. Angie obeyed, albeit very slowly, and Chapman wondered if her lack of speed was due to the turn in the conversation or if she was just fatigued. After snapping the handcuffs in place, Chapman nodded to Danny, who was putting the rackets and balls into the locker outside the fence.

"Thanks again, Danny." Chapman touched Angie's elbow to guide her back toward the house. "Miss Donalson, it's almost warm enough to swim. I have a couple of catalogs; you need to pick out some swimwear. I can order some for you. We want to get you in the pool soon, also."

"Who's the swimming instructor?"

"I am. Do you need instruction?"

"Well, in all likelihood, I wouldn't drown, but I don't know any fancy strokes or anything like that." Angie continued playing along, feigning interest.

"I know a few. Let's let the water warm up a bit more. How about horseback riding?"

"Never tried. I don't know much about it—never had a chance to try it. I've heard it makes you sore. If you ride for very long, I mean," Angie said.

"We can begin that after lunch. Have you thought of a name for the mare?"

"Yeah, she looks like a Bessie to me."

"Bessie it is, then. Danny will have Bessie ready for you at 1:30."

They entered through the back door, and Chapman followed her captive up the stairs, locking the chain gate behind her. As they entered the room, Angie stopped, legs spread enough for the search, with her head bowed. Chapman slid her hands over the girl in a perfunctory manner and unlocked the handcuffs.

Janice brought lunch and, at Angie's request, braided her hair into a long rope down her back. After fighting the hair all morning, Angie was grateful to have it out of her face. She ate the garden salad and baked potato that Janice had brought, then read until Chapman returned for her. Once again, Angie made Chapman's job easier by assuming positions before the order came, and Chapman rewarded her by making each procedure quick and more or less painless.

Once on the horse, Angie concentrated on staying on. She didn't want to fall off and embarrass herself in front of her captors, so she abandoned her search for opportunities to escape and focused on the lesson. By mid afternoon, Angie was getting the hang of it, and Chapman mounted another horse, taking her for a ride along the same path she had walked earlier.

When Angie returned to her room, she was worn out. The day had been full, and after her days with little to do, it was quite a contrast. She ate dinner and read for a while. At 9:30, Chapman came to put her to bed, so Angie did a quick turn around in the shower, because she found that she was ready for sleep. There was no sign of protest when Chapman fastened the chain about her left ankle and told her good night.

*   *   *

Angie had a long walk again on Tuesday morning. This one was worse in one way—she was sore from all the exercise of the day before. Despite her exemplary behavior, she was once again wearing chains at her waist and the collar at her neck. She had kept the braid in, and that was some help. At least she wasn't peering through hair half of the time. Angie found it hard to get a rhythm going with her arm movements restricted, but Chapman refused to consider letting her walk without restraint. The walking did work out some of the soreness in her legs, however, and by the time she finished, Angie felt better.

After breakfast, she went horseback riding again. Because her muscles ached quite a bit, Chapman didn't have her stay on quite as long, so she managed. Chapman seemed determined to keep her charge busy, while avoiding total exhaustion. Angie was back in the second floor room by 11:30, and once again, she read until lunch. Afterwards, Chapman escorted her to the exercise room and showed her how to use some of the machines. Chapman devised a regimen of upper and lower body exercises for Angie to do each week. Also, she had Angie stand on a scale, and she took her measurements.

"Okay, Miss D. You're five feet, ten inches tall. Weight is 136 pounds." This information Chapman recorded at the bottom of the chart. "We'll check this every month."

Angie's jaw dropped open. She was surprised that even the ever-efficient Ms. Chapman would go to such lengths.

"I want to keep tabs on your physical condition. Your weight is appropriate for your height—you might even be a bit underweight. You do need to develop some more muscle," Chapman explained as she finished her work on the chart. "The weights will help build your muscles, while the walking and other aerobics will help your general fitness. The cook has been instructed to keep in mind the calorie and mineral requirements of a growing, teenage body."

"I just wish you'd give me ordinary food instead of all the fancy crap. I would rather have hamburgers and fries. If it has to be healthy, how about pizza? Or macaroni and cheese?"

"We'll stay with the fruits, veggies, and a few lean meats—you'll adjust."

"At least you folks have plenty of food."

Chapman considered her, puzzled. Angie guessed that Chapman had never run short of food. Aunt Claire and Angie hadn't always been so fortunate since Bill Donalson died, leaving them with so little income. After a moment, the concept seemed to dawn on Chapman.

"Yes, Miss Donalson. You may not always like it, but you will have enough to eat. Always."

Chapman walked her back to the second floor bedroom, and for once, gave no orders for her to move into position to be restrained. They just strolled along, talking. Once they arrived, Chapman asked her to pick out some items from catalogs—mostly swimwear and exercise clothes. As a reward for her good behavior, Angie was allowed to eat dinner in the dining room. Of course, she didn't get dressed up as she had for Marc, but she did don a simple skirt and blouse... and the manacles, at Chapman's insistence... instead of shorts and T-shirt. Angie felt odd, being served four courses in the elaborate room, all by herself. Janice served, sometimes pointing out which piece of silverware to use. Angie smiled at the thought of having an etiquette lesson with dinner, but Janice acted as if it was the most natural thing in the world.

Chapman took her for a walk in the flower garden after dinner. In the twilight, they sat on a bench beside a little pond with goldfish in it and talked. Angie decided that the best thing about her decision to play along with Chapman was that the conversation level had quadrupled. Certainly the past two weeks had been the loneliest time of her entire life. Angie regarded her captor—tousled, short, brown hair, square-jawed face, and realized that she wanted to talk to her, needed to talk to her, and have her talk back.

"Ms. Chapman, you may not answer this, either by Mr. Avery's orders or by choice, but I have wondered about something. How on earth did you get the job of being my... keeper?"

Chapman leaned back and chuckled to herself. She ran a hand through her hair, adjusted the wide belt, and seemed to think about what she might or might not say. "I was in the military for a while, Miss Donalson. I can't say just what I did there. But while I was in service, my brother, who works for Mr. Avery, needed a kidney transplant. My family couldn't afford it, so Mr. Avery took care of everything. Everything. I have only my brother, and he is very important to me. When Mr. Avery needed someone to oversee this operation, he called upon me."

"I knew you were exceedingly loyal to him, of course." Angie faltered, searching for the right words. "But most people wouldn't risk what you did. Kidnapping is, well, it's a serious crime. I mean, you can get into a lot of trouble if something goes wrong, can't you?" Angie was struggling to keep any resentment out of her voice. She wanted information.

"Sure." Chapman grinned at her innocence. "Angie, we were careful. I knew the location of every police officer in Adamsville the day we took you. And for three days before that. We waited until conditions were perfect before we made any attempt."

"Do you mean that y'all were out there for days, just waiting?"

"And the others—Janice? And Danny?" Angie wanted to gesture, but the chain between her wrists made her self-conscious. She put her hands back in her lap.

"I think it would be up to them to share their stories, if they so desire. But they are as loyal to Mr. Avery as I am. I guess you're fishing for some weaknesses. I would, if I were sitting where you are. I don't think you'll find one. We are totally loyal, totally dedicated, and we will follow Mr. Avery's instructions to the letter. Regardless." Chapman's voice took on the commanding edge again. "Miss Donalson, I have told you over and over, but I believe it to be true. Follow instructions, behave, and you will have a good life here. We've been told to keep you safe and sound, and that's because Mr. Avery has great plans for you. Look around you, young lady. This life is going to be much better than your former one."

"Hey, I've been good today, haven't I?" Angie kept her voice bright, one of her best drama performances ever. She felt desperation coming on. Any mention of the future here exacerbated her sense of foreboding.

"Yes, yes, you have." Chapman stood up. "Ready to go in? It's getting close to bedtime."

Angie rose to her feet, the chain between her wrists clinking as she did so. "Sure. I'm ready."

They strolled back to the house, and in half an hour she was chained into the big bed in the upstairs suite with new things to ponder.

Chapter 4

When Angie woke, Chapman sent her to the bathroom. The sheets were stained. Angie knew where the appropriate accoutrements were, so she took care of the situation. As soon as she came out, Chapman stopped her.

"Hands on the wall," she ordered. Angie was still wearing only a nightgown and underpants. Chapman searched her, pulling her underpants down and swabbing the upper portion of her hip with a cold wipe. "Don't move." Without warning, she rammed a needle into Angie's upper hip.

"Ouch," Angie protested, twisting away. Chapman bade her be still and pushed the plunger in, then withdrew the needle. "What are you doing? What was that?" Chapman placed a Band-Aid on the injection site.

"Depo provera, Miss Donalson. It's good for three months of birth control. It must be administered during the first five days of menstruation," she said briskly, and signaled for her charge to release the position.

"Oh, God," Angie said, slumping against the wall.

"You can get dressed now," Chapman said. "We're going three and a half miles this morning."

"I'm not going anywhere." Angie's resolve to cooperate had just evaporated.

"Oh, yes, you will," Chapman promised, her voice firm. She picked out some shorts and a cropped tank top and tossed them at Angie's feet. "You have ten minutes, Miss Donalson." Chapman left, turning the key in the lock.

After a moment of hesitation, Angie bent down, retrieved the clothing, and dressed, putting her hair in a ponytail, since she lacked Janice's skill with braiding. Finished, she sat on the bench at the end of the bed and waited. Chapman came back, her hands filled with chains and the riding crop, which Angie hadn't seen for days.

"About face, at rest," Chapman ordered.

Angie sat still, trying to decide what to do. Birth control. They must believe that she was ready to go along with anything. Anything.

Chapman used the crop to get Angie's attention, slamming it into the bedclothes beside her charge, then poking the girl in the midriff with the tip. "Move. Into position. Now."

Without haste, Angie rose and turned, placing her hands at the small of her back. Chapman followed the ritual, first fastening the waist chain, then cuffing her hands. Last, she fixed the leather collar around Angie's neck, not too tight, but close enough that it wouldn't come over her head.

After three miles, some of her anger had worked itself off, but Angie was still very unhappy. This must have shown, for Chapman made no effort at conversation. Back in the second floor room, Chapman freed her of the chains and collar, and Janice served a light breakfast of muffins and coffee.

Angie had the morning to herself—no tennis or horseback riding. Chapman told her, as she brought lunch, that Danny was scheduled to play tennis at 1:30.

"Ms. Chapman, I'm in no mood to chase that dumb yellow ball all over the court." Angie's reply was succinct.

Chapman sighed. "Okay, I won't force you. However, you need to work out today, to stay on schedule. We'll do your lower body instead." Chapman's tone was firm, but kind. "I know you're upset. That's understandable. I gave you the injection when you weren't expecting it, thinking it would be less painful. In retrospect, I guess I should have discussed it with you. Our orders were to give it, though, and if you had protested, we would've had to do it anyway." She paused. "Let's go do the workout. You have to do something besides sit around and brood about it."

"I'm going to do the workout. It'll keep me from being so sore. But I need some time to sort things out." Angie's tone was bitter.

"Would you like to talk about, uh, the things that are on your mind?" Chapman asked.

"Talk to *you*—isn't there something wrong with this picture? You do remember that in the two weeks I've known you, you've kidnapped me, beaten me with that damn whip, used every sort of chain imaginable to confine me—and now you are preparing me for rape." Angie scoffed at her suggestion.

"Well, there's Janice, or Danny. They're the only other options. Would you like to talk to either of them?"

"What I would like," Angie said, with less acrimony than she felt, "is to get the hell out of here before something happen... something that I can't handle. I have to get away. I don't know how, but I have to."

Angie sighed. She had just done what she didn't want to do; she had allowed Chapman to see past her ruse of the past couple of days, no doubt ruining any immediate opportunity. Worse, she had let Chapman see how scared she was.

"Do you have any questions?" Chapman seemed to want to help.

"You don't answer questions. I've found that out the hard way." Angie's tone was harsh.

"Angie, I was under orders to refuse to provide answers—at least until Mr. Avery had talked with you. Today that's not the case. Perhaps I can help settle your mind."

"Okay. When will that shot start working?"

"By the time you're fertile, the depo will have prevented ovulation. It will also probably cause irregular bleeding. Eventually you'll cease to menstruate. Don't be alarmed when these changes occur."

"When does Mr. Avery intend to try it out?"

"I can't answer that. I really don't know. My job is to keep you secure and get you accustomed to your life here." Chapman reached down and clasped Angie's right hand. "Let's go do lower body. Maybe you'll feel better if you exercise."

Chapman escorted her to the exercise room without any bonds, which surprised Angie. She did leg presses and curls and extensions and rode a stationary bike. Chapman urged her to do extra reps or try higher weight—whatever, just to make her think about muscles instead of other, more painful topics.

When they finished, Chapman picked up her radio. "Danny, saddle Bessie and Thor. We're going on a ride." She turned to Angie. "Let's go for a ride through the woods. I think it would do you good."

"You're just trying to distract me." Angie protested, but she turned around at Chapman's signal, hands at the small of her back. Chapman took handcuffs from her belt pouch and secured Angie's wrists.

Angie went riding in the same clothes that she had used for the workout, a stretch pair of shorts and a sports bra under an oversized sleeveless shirt. The sun felt good against Angie's bare skin. The pair went through the woods and fields, not fast, just ambling along. Chapman stayed close to her charge. As her stiff muscles stretched out, Angie began to feel much better. She wouldn't have acknowledged it, but the black mood of the morning was gone.

*   *   *

Angie's schedule varied somewhat from day to day, but each one was filled with exercise, usually with Chapman or Danny supervising. She also spent time learning how to be Avery's companion. Angie had to acquire some sophistication, and Janice was her teacher. During occasional solo meals in the dining room, she learned about place settings and wine selection; her lessons even covered how to eat escargot! Angie decided that it wasn't too bad if she forgot that she used to sprinkle salt on the back door step to discourage the little buggers from sliming everything. At first, Janice's lessons in etiquette, hair care, wardrobe, and make-up seemed impromptu, but Angie came to understand that all this was just part of the plan to make her the perfect mistress for Marcus Avery, Jr.

All of Angie's activities outside the house were supervised. A few times, Chapman took her to the flower garden and chained her to a park bench, which was set in a brick platform near the fishpond. There she could read or watch the fish, but since she had only a six-foot chain, she couldn't get any exercise. These rare occasions were simply a chance to get out of her room for a while—and although she hated having another date with an ankle chain, she was glad to have the additional time outside.

During those first weeks, Chapman continued to bend her captive to her will. Angie had to submit to random searches, and she wore handcuffs or manacles when she left her room. As time went on, Chapman became more casual about it. Often the last order Angie obeyed was to chain herself to the bed. Every so often Angie tried to push the envelope, but such efforts inevitably met with some punishment. In Angie's eyes, Chapman seemed to be everywhere and know everything. She was the first person Angie saw in the morning, when she tossed her the keys so she could let herself up. Of course, Chapman was the last one Angie saw at night, when she conducted the search before bed.

*   *   *

Chapman was dog-tired. She'd been on for four weeks straight. Sure, there had been plenty of rest periods early on, when they had left Angie alone for hours at a time, but now that the girl was more active, the staff had been stretched to the limit to provide security for her. Janice had taken some afternoons off, and Danny had taken the weekends, but Chapman had been at the point for weeks, and it was telling on her.

When Avery did his check-in Wednesday night, Chapman was frank with him.

"Miss Donalson is secure, and we've made significant progress toward making her submit to us. But we can't keep going without relief. I can't keep going. She needs the exercise and the attention, but I need some time off. Janice and Danny need more time, too. I've not allowed contact with anyone else. I need additional staff who can be trusted with this duty. What might be better is for you to take some time off and get better acquainted with your mistress."

"You want me to be in charge of her, without you. Is she ready for that?" Avery seemed worried.

"You need to be cautious—I am. But you could handle her, I think. Janice knows the rules for the house, and Danny has handled the outside enough to know what works there. With them on, you should be able to do it for a long weekend. That's what I'm asking for, a long weekend." She sighed, thinking of all the hard work devoted to making Angie obey. She hoped that Avery wouldn't destroy it all in a few days' time.

"Okay, Billie. I'll be there Friday night and stay until Tuesday evening. That would give you almost four days."

"Thank you, sir. I look forward to seeing you."

Chapter 5

Angie learned that the Master would be returning Friday, and she was certain that her virginity was on the line. While she'd been able to push the idea of the birth control injection to the back of her mind, it was still lurking there. Avery had told her from the outset that he wanted her for his mistress, and the injection had to mean that he intended to claim her sooner rather than later.

Chapman remained cautious, requiring restraints when Angie left the upstairs. Of course, this was more of a psychological necessity than a physical one. Chapman realized that as long as Angie thought escape impossible, it was. She simply would never try it. Angie wanted very much to flee and return to her home, but as long as she waited for a better chance, she would remain a captive.

On Friday evening, Chapman placed manacles with a foot-long connecting chain on Angie's wrists. The girl was dressed in an amber and navy outfit with long, flowing pants and a graceful tunic top. Once again, Janice had done her hair and make-up. They met Avery at the helipad, and he beamed at the sight of his mistress. As before, he was surprised at the girl's mature, yet innocent, appearance.

Angie didn't look pleased to see him; however, she didn't draw away when he reached out to her. She possessed a natural dignity that made her able to keep her distance emotionally without a physical withdrawal. She held herself straight and didn't relax in Avery's presence. But Chapman could see the stiffness—a barrier that, for whatever reason, Angie did not erect with her. Perhaps some time together would make them closer. Chapman hoped, for both their sakes, that this was the case. She had observed Angie, before the abduction, and had concluded that the girl would be better off with Avery. The grinding poverty, the hopelessness of her existence, had caused Chapman to agree that Angie would be perfect for the role. Angie had everything to gain and so little to lose. As she watched the awkwardness between them, Chapman wondered again if this business would ever work out.

Chapman gave Avery some last minute advice and jumped into the Ford Explorer, heading for her brother's house in Chattanooga. As she drove, she could feel the tension, which had been building up bit by bit, easing. She couldn't wait to see Matthew again. And it would be good to see her nieces and nephews, although there was a certain irony in that—Matthew's oldest was a seventeen-year-old girl.

*   *   *

Avery had brought some movies with him; accordingly, for the evening's entertainment, he suggested that Angie choose something for them to watch. Angie was in her room with the pile of videos on her desk. She finally chose an action adventure, hoping it would be suspenseful enough to keep Avery from thinking too much about her.

Danny was in the green room, watching her via the hidden cameras. Right now, as she stood near the desk, he got a close-up view, although the picture quality was slightly distorted. He turned, looking at the various tools for restraining their captive, and settled on a pair of leg irons. To him it seemed that they would be best for the meal and television. Angie would have to walk downstairs with them—awkward, but possible. Then she would only have to go across the hall to the family room, with its large screen television. Best of all, the restraint would be out of sight during the meal.

A light flashed in the com center; Danny answered.

"Dinner will be ready in five minutes."

Mrs. Bowen probably wondered just what was going on, but like the others, she'd been told to avoid questions about their guest. Danny phoned Avery in his room and took the leg irons off the hook.

Angie was surprised to see Danny and even more surprised to see the leg chain. She stood stock-still, looking at him, wondering what he might do. Danny had watched Chapman often enough to know the routine, so he did his best to emulate her.

"About face, Miss Donalson," he said, motioning for her to turn around. Angie stared at him and didn't comply. "You are familiar with this procedure. Turn around."

Without haste, Angie turned around. Danny fastened the cuffs around each of her ankles, omitting the body search. Angie watched his awkward movements, offering no resistance. When he finished, he gestured for her to precede him out the door. Angie picked up her chosen video and shuffled toward the door, her strides limited to fourteen inches by the chain.

"Where's Billie? Did she get the night off?" Angie asked Danny as he followed her slow progress down the stairs.

"Something like that." Danny hoped Billie was correct, and that the right combination of supervision and restraint would keep Angie from trying anything. As they reached the landing, Avery caught up with them. He had changed into casual slacks and a striped knit shirt. He motioned Danny aside and joined Angie.

"Hello, again. What did you pick?"

Angie handed him the movie; as they crept toward the dining room, they discussed the actors and what they had heard regarding the film. Avery seated her at the end of the table again. Once she was seated, with the chain out of sight, it was easy for him to pretend that she was there of her own free will, and not as his prisoner. Although Angie didn't initiate any topics, she conversed a bit more freely than during his last visit, so Avery believed that she was beginning to soften.

Janice, clad in her khakis and navy polo, served them a pasta salad, followed by grilled chicken and stir-fried vegetables. Afterward they went across the hall and sat on the big sectional sofa, with a bowl of popcorn and some sodas. Avery popped the movie in the player and put his arm around Angie's shoulders. The video was indeed suspenseful, and because Angie hadn't seen television since she'd been abducted, she enjoyed it more than she would ever have admitted.

When it was over, Avery leaned over Angie and kissed her, tenderly, while caressing her breasts and her neck. Angie stiffened, although she sensed that a rebellion would bring Avery's anger. To avoid punishment, she allowed his touch, but she gave no sign that she enjoyed his efforts.

Avery pulled back and looked at her in the soft light of the track units in the back of the room. Her makeup was sheer tonight, and the soft freckles which ran together on her nose were visible. She looked young and vulnerable. Angie returned his gaze, and he wondered what was going on behind those dark green eyes. Did she hate him? Would she ever stop hating him?

"Angie, I enjoyed the movie. Good choice." He chose to converse about trivialities, for the real issues were too dangerous.

"Thanks. Good popcorn." Angie's voice was unreadable. She might have been sarcastic; she might have been content with the down home evening—he was unsure.

"I have the responsibility of tucking you in," Avery said, standing and extending a hand to help her up.

"Danny is off duty, huh?"

"Yes. He's scheduled to do the morning workout. And you need to get rested up for it." Avery pulled her to her feet and guided her toward the stairs. After locking the gate at the top of the stairs, he took Angie into her room and locked that door as well. Once inside, he asked her to slide up onto the bed. Sitting beside her, he used his keys to unlock the leg irons.

"I understand that it's time for your bath." Avery grinned. "Do you need any help with that?"

Angie jumped off the bed. "I can manage by myself," she replied.

With some haste, Angie went to the closet and chose a nightgown—the thickest, longest one she could find. She went to the chest for underwear and then into the bathroom, closing the door. Avery took the chain back to the green room and glanced at the monitor. A wireless camera hidden in a potted plant on a shelf in the bathroom gave him a tantalizing glimpse of Angie's naked backside as she leaned over to check the water in the Jacuzzi. He stood watching until she got into the bathtub, then he returned to his post in her room.

When Angie emerged, she was wearing both the nightgown and a terry cloth robe. Chapman wouldn't have allowed the robe, but Avery wasn't Chapman. He approached her as she waited beside the bed. Angie seemed uncertain. Chapman always performed a search, and she always had the chain pulled out, ready.

Avery seemed to have something else in mind. He pushed her down onto the bed and lay beside her, on top of the covers. He kissed her, on the forehead, on the cheeks, and just a touch on the lips. His hands slid along her long arms and longer legs. With the softness of a bird alighting on a branch, he touched her breasts, moving the robe aside to continue his tender fondling. Part of Angie's mind was wrestling with thoughts of escape, but she knew the door was locked, and the gate in the hallway was locked as well. Since she was stuck, she lay still, willing her body to show no reaction.

"Angie, you are so incredibly beautiful. You have a body made for love. It's your destiny. Please don't deny me. Don't deny yourself!"

Angie made no reply; instead, she turned away from his body and fixed her gaze on the darkened windows. "Angie, I will have you. You can make it easy on yourself, or you can make it painful. It really is up to you." His voice came over her shoulder; his hand rested on the highest point of her hip. "I can have my people chain your arms and legs, and you'll be helpless. Or you can have it nice and gentle. I'll wait a little while longer, but I won't wait forever."

His hand was gone, then his weight was no longer on the bed. He jerked the covers aside, found the chain and snapped it on her ankle. Angie didn't look at him; she didn't move. Marc disappeared through the connecting door. Angie rearranged the bedclothes and turned her face to the pillows. However, it was a long time before she found sleep, a very long time.

*   *   *

Angie was awake when Janice came. Not only did she have trouble going to sleep, but she woke ahead of the usual time as well. Angie went to the bathroom and dressed in shorts, T-shirt, and Nikes without being told. Janice braided Angie's hair and put the manacles on her wrists. Danny was at the back door, dressed in a T-shirt and knit shorts.

"Miss Donalson, I thought we'd walk together. I need the exercise myself. Billie left instructions that we do three and a half miles. I've got a route worked out which gives us that. Billie wants you to jog it someday soon, so we may run part of the way. If you promise that you'll stay with me, I'll take the chain off."

"I promise," Angie said automatically, holding out her wrists. Angie didn't really mean it, for if she saw an opportunity, she intended to take it. But, she hated being fettered—in any way. By far, she had found this to be the most distasteful aspect of her captivity.

He unlocked the cuffs and tucked them into the cargo pocket of his shorts. They started off at an easy trot, and Angie stayed with him for a while, but because she was unused to even a short jog, she began to lag behind. Danny slowed to a walk and they finished at that pace. During the trek, they never went near a gate, and Angie saw no opportunities to leave her unwanted companion. Danny escorted her to the house and upstairs, locking both doors behind her. Angie had the rest of the morning to herself. Avery had Janice and Danny bring her down for lunch, but Janice put the leg irons on her before she left the bedroom. The afternoon was spent on the tennis court and in the exercise room. Avery played tennis part of the time with her and part of the time with Danny, while Angie watched. Avery and Danny helped her do the upper body routine that Chapman had planned. Afterward, Avery said that they'd have another homebody evening. "Pick out another movie, Angie," he instructed.

Apart from Angie's choice of a comedy, the evening was a repeat of the previous one. Avery did try to seduce her earlier in the film. Once again, she used passive resistance. Marc was patient at first, then he seemed to grow angry as his efforts yielded no results.

"All right, let's get you to bed, little miss virgin," he said, his voice harsh, and he pulled her to her feet. Angie followed him up the stairs, her pace slowed by the chain between her legs. His touch was rough as he removed it.

"I want you wearing only your birthday suit when you come out of that door," he said and sat down to wait. He sounded cross.

Angie took quite a bit of time in the bathroom. She knew that going back through that door to the bedroom would be the beginning of the end. After dawdling around for a while, she realized that she just couldn't do it. Instead of returning to the bedroom, she sat, wrapped in a towel, on the edge of the tub. Avery came in after her.

"I thought I told you to come out, without any clothing." His voice was ruthless.

"I'm not out yet," she said, wondering what he would do.

"Drop the towel and go into the bedroom—right now."

"Mr. Avery, please. Just let me go. This is crazy." Angie rose to her feet, keeping the towel around her. He reached out, grabbed the towel and jerked it off. Angie almost reached for it, then stopped.

Trying to cover herself would just cause an even greater loss of dignity. Instead, she drew herself up to her full height and held her head high. Poise, she told herself. Not panic—poise.

With as much composure as she could muster, she stepped around him and moved into the bedroom. "Are you going to just stand there, or are you going to let me go to bed?" A slight tremor in her voice betrayed only some of her nervousness.

Avery looked at her—really looked, as if he'd never seen her before.

"Angie, you are so beautiful. I just have to have you." He grasped her arms, throwing her onto the bed, but she kept on rolling, right off the other side. Angie eluded him for a few moments by using the furniture as obstacles, then his right hand caught her wrist. Avery bent her arm behind her and forced her back to the bed. Operating in panic mode, Angie clawed him with her nails, causing him to twist her arm brutally. He gripped her throat, cutting off her breath. She continued to struggle, despite the chokehold, but he managed to get the chain on her ankle.

"How dare you do this to me, you son of a bitch!" Angie's voice was pitched high and loud.

Avery left her on the bed, gasping for air, while he went to get more restraints. In spite of her efforts to resist, he attached each of her hands to a bar on the headboard. As she fought him the handcuffs tightened. Angie felt his touch, no longer gentle, on her body. She stopped resisting because she couldn't think of anything but the pain in her wrists.

Angie begged, "Please, Mr. Avery, please—" He silenced her with his tongue, which he thrust into her mouth. She focused on the pain—living through the pain. She was aware of his exploration of her nude body, but her mind focused on her wrists and ankle. Tears ran down her cheeks, and she arched upward, trying to relieve the pain. Angie no longer feared rape; she feared being left in agony all night long.

"Please," she sobbed as he came up for air. "Please let me go. I won't fight anymore. I can't stand the pain."

Avery seemed to listen then. "Pain?"

"My wrists," she said and began sobbing again.

Avery looked at her wrists. They were chafed red and already swelling against the tight cuffs. His weight shifted off the bed as he got his keys from the nightstand. He unlocked each wrist, and she sat up rubbing them. For the moment, Angie was oblivious to her nakedness. Nothing mattered but getting those tight cuffs off.

"Thanks." Her voice was soft and husky.

"Is your leg okay?" He looked at the ankle chain, which wasn't as tight as the ones that had confined her wrists, but the struggle had made her ankle raw. He moved the chain from the right to the undamaged left.

"Angie, I told you. Don't resist. You're going to get hurt if you do. I could have finished it tonight, but I'll wait for some other night, because I don't want to hurt you. If you'll simply cooperate, then this will never happen again." He gestured to her raw and swollen wrists.

Avery flipped the light off and went through the connecting door. A nightlight shown from one of the electrical outlets, and moonlight streamed in the windows. Angie sat in the dim light, looking at her wrists for a few moments. She raised her eyes, and only then did she notice that his keys were still on the nightstand. Her ankle was chained to the foot of the bed, as always, but there was enough slack in the chain for her to reach the keys, if she stretched as far as she could.

Angie lay on the bed, heart pounding. She was elated, yet scared. This was what she had sought for so long—opportunity.

Would he realize it and come back? She reached out, pulling against the chain, and snatched the keys, hiding them in the covers beside her. Angie rubbed her wrists, which still hurt, but the jumble of keys beside her was doing a lot to kill the pain. Now her mind focused on planning. What she needed was a course of action.

Clothes were first. Angie couldn't go through the house without some covering for her body. But the closet was filled with clothes. She thought over what she had seen on the hangers and decided on a pair of dressy shorts and their coordinating top. Quiet shoes, of course—the tennis shoes would do. She had to get out of the door and through the chain link fence in the hall. Perhaps the outer doors of the house would be locked. Angie decided that she must get to the garage. If any of those keys fit any vehicle down there, she would make it!

Admittedly, her driving skills weren't the best. Aunt Claire had begun teaching her after her dad had died. Angie had never taken the test for a real license, but she felt sure she could cope until she could get someplace safe. She knew a chase would be an utter disaster, but she could manage well enough if she could sneak away without immediate pursuit.

Chapman had allowed Angie to use the keys to free herself on several occasions, so she had no problem locating the right key and unlocking the cuff. She slipped into the closet to search for some clothes.

Chapter 6

Danny was supposed to be off duty, but insomnia had struck again, so he decided to go to the second floor green room to check on the estate. He grinned to himself, thinking about Avery and that sexy redhead. If he was lucky, he might get a glimpse of the pair of them on her room monitors. Danny glanced at the monitors, seeing no one. He propped up in the big comfortable office chair, his feet on the desk, and his eyes caught an unusual strip of light. Danny leaned toward the monitor, peering at the dusky image, and realized it was the closet door, slightly ajar, with the light on. Next he observed Angie, dressed in shorts and tennis shoes, move across the room and out of his line of sight.

He sat, paralyzed, for a moment. Had she overpowered Avery? That seemed impossible. There was no camera in Avery's room, but it was conceivable that she had simply stolen his keys, or... Danny ran out of possibilities. The hall monitor showed her coming out of her door. She glanced at the camera, moving with stealth, something dangling from her hand.

Danny called Janice on the intercom. She was still awake and responded without delay. The monitor showed Angie fumbling with something, probably the keys. He turned his eyes to the pegboard and selected a stun gun. He had to stop her, and stop her now.

Angie had found the right key and had the gate open when Danny came racing down the hall. He lunged against her, jamming the gun against her back and hitting the trigger, holding it down. Angie yelped and shook violently, falling in a heap on the floor. Janice came bounding up the stairs and stopped short at the sight of the helpless girl.

"What now?" she asked, upset at seeing the crumpled figure.

"Don't worry, it's just a stun. She should recover soon. Let's get her into the detention cell and make her secure. Then we'd better check and see if Mr. Avery is all right."

Together they lugged the girl into the dark room and put her on the bunk. Danny put a pair of handcuffs on her wrists and locked the door. Janice went to the green room to watch the display that monitored the cell, while Danny knocked on Avery's door.

"What is it?" Avery said, irritation in his voice.

Danny held up the key ring.

Avery's eyes widened, and he turned on the light in his room. He glanced around, then checked the pocket of his discarded pants. Avery shook his head, his disbelief obvious. "Yes, they're mine. Where did you find them?"

"Miss Donalson was using them to unlock the gate, sir."

"Angie? I chained her in bed. She should be there."

"She's in the detention cell, sir. I used a stun gun. She hasn't recovered yet."

"How did you—?" Avery seemed to have trouble framing the question.

"I had trouble sleeping, so I decided to check the monitors. I saw her leave her closet, dressed, and then she came out of her room. With some luck, I got her before she left this floor."

"Thanks, Danny." The warmth in Avery's voice was real. "She might just have made it with that much head start."

"Did she lift the keys from you, sir?" Danny didn't want to anger his employer, but the details just might include facts he needed to know.

Avery shook his head. "I guess I got careless. They must've been on the table in her room." Avery paused. "I was angry when I left her."

"Any orders regarding her, sir?" Danny asked, a serious expression on his face. "I think she must face some punishment for trying to escape. If Billie's plan is to be followed, Miss Donalson will have to be made to regret this. Otherwise—" Danny spread his hands, allowing Avery to draw his own conclusions.

Once again, Avery shook his head. "I ought to be the one punished. I screwed up." Avery paused, thinking. "But Billie's right—we have to come up with some punitive action, or she might be just as bold if there is another slip-up. Any suggestions?"

"Leave her in there for a while. It's not a torture chamber, but it isn't any fun either. If you want, we can keep her from eating, or at least make that less pleasant. Billie fed her bread and milk in a dog dish when she had trouble with her."

"Okay, I guess that'll do." Avery seemed to be at a loss as to what punishment to inflict. "It should be enough. I'll bet the stun gun was painful."

"No doubt," Danny said. "If she's not cooperative, we could just stun her again."

"You mean just walk up and hit her with it? I don't think so. I just don't want to have this happen again." Avery was no longer angry, just concerned.

"Yes, sir. We got lucky on this one," Danny repeated.

"Did you use any restraint?" Avery inquired.

"Handcuffs, in front."

"Take them off. I tried cuffing her to the bed, and she struggled until her wrists were pretty raw. One ankle is in good shape. Use that and chain her to the bed, like Billie does. You can take her clothes. I gather that she has the usual aversion to nakedness."

"Okay. Billie stripped her, too. I'm not going in there without Janice, though." Danny got the leg chain from the green room and motioned for her to join him.

Avery slipped into the green room to watch as his employees stripped the girl and chained her up. Part of him enjoyed it, since she had angered him, but another part of him found it very hard to watch. Angie seemed quite aware and was beginning to move around as they left.

"She's locked up and chained to the bunk. Do you want one of us on duty, sir?" Danny asked, returning to the green room.

"No, Danny, you've done well. I'll just watch here until I'm sure she has recovered from the stun. Then I'll go on to bed. You might as well cancel all the activities scheduled tomorrow. We'll do some monitoring from here, but I think we should keep her in there one day, at least."

*   *   *

Angie lay still, unable to move much more than her eyes. She didn't know for sure what had happened—but she had collapsed, still holding the keys. Whatever Danny had done hurt. A lot. Almost as painful had been the helplessness. They had picked her up and hauled her onto the cot as if she was a large sack of potatoes. Her body was tingling, but it was beginning to work again.

Angie rotated her head to gaze down at her body. The clothes she had selected from the closet were gone. The cuff of one end of the leg iron was around her left ankle, and the other was fastened to the bed's bottom rail, thus tethering her to the bed. The dim light was on, but it wouldn't prevent sleep—if she could relax that much. Angie was hurt, angry, and disappointed. Somehow, Danny had caught her and prevented what would surely have been her escape.

She couldn't believe her bad luck. Was she destined to remain a prisoner forever? The chain rattled, reminding her of the futility of her situation. Once more, she cried—for her aching wrists, for her naked body, and out of sheer frustration. Turning onto her side, back to the camera, she sobbed. For what seemed to be hours, she wept, but sleep did eventually come.

Early on Sunday morning, Janice entered the cell, waking her. Janice transferred the cuff from the bed rail to her other ankle, freeing her from bed, but limiting her stride. Later, she was given a double dog dish with milk and bread, the same menu as during her last visit to the dark cell. Humiliating as it was, she ate, because she needed her strength. The only thing she saw all day was a glimpse of Janice's shoes when she brought the dish and slid it through the opening under the door. Angie had a small collection of the dishes when Avery came to see her Monday afternoon.

The door opened as Avery strode into the little cell. Angie heard the lock turn behind him. Avery appeared rather uncomfortable. After a moment, she moved so that he could sit beside her on the bunk.

"You decide to visit the jail?" Angie asked him, sarcastically.

"I left my keys outside," he said with a rueful smile. "Angie, I feel responsible for what happened. I tempted you."

"I found it very tempting, yes. What happens now? Is this my new home, Master?" Her voice held a challenge. With Chapman—who made her life hell—at least Angie admired and respected her. Avery, despite all his money, power, and sophistication, struck her as a bit of a nincompoop. He might be rich, but he had inherited his wealth and position. As she regarded him, she observed no strength of character.

"I'll discuss a course of action with Billie. We can keep you in here from now to eternity, but that's not what anyone wants. We want to be able to trust you. Angie, you can finish high school, go to college, and have some social life. There'll be a few restrictions, of course, but you can have a life. But only when we can let you go out the door and be assured that you'll come back. Until then, you will remain a captive."

"I'll never come back here willingly," Angie declared. She sighed and tried a different tack. "Just let me go. Then I'll cease to be a problem."

"I've told you no. I meant it." Avery was firm. "If you'll promise to behave, I'll instruct Billie not to punish you any further."

"I'm not going to promise you a damn thing."

"Okay. Enjoy your stay." Avery knocked and the door opened. As he left, Janice came in, retrieved the stack of doggie dishes, and locked the door behind her.

*   *   *

Avery phoned Chapman before she left her brother's house. In a terse conversation, he related his mistake and Angie's attempt to capitalize on it. He also reported her stubborn attitude since her failed escape attempt. Avery was out of his depth, and he needed Chapman's reassurance that things would work out. Chapman had halfway expected some sort of rebellion in her absence. The incident with the keys might have made it worse, but it wasn't unexpected.

As she drove out of Chattanooga, she eyed a military surplus store, and she had an idea. Chapman turned around and made a few purchases, thinking about the new recruits that she had helped train. Now was the time to take the reins and do what should've been done in the first place, regardless of Avery's wishes.

When Chapman took over from Avery, she lugged a wooden, olive green footlocker to the detention cell and deposited it in a corner. While Angie looked on, she stocked it with gray-green camouflage shorts, sleeveless olive drab T-shirts, olive drab socks, plain black T-back bras, and black cotton underpants. On top of the locker, she placed the girl's running shoes. Finally, she placed an olive drab cloth bag filled with toiletries beside the shoes. Chapman refused to answer any questions until she had finished her task. Once the locker was stuffed, she turned to her seventeen-year-old charge.

"We are going to start over, Angie. You evidently needed a firmer hand than what you got when you first came. Now you will get it. This—" Chapman gestured to the dark cell, "will be your quarters for the next few weeks. Your new wardrobe is right here. You won't have any clothing decisions to make. Same shorts, same shirt, every day—your uniform. You will wake up at 0545 and we will *run* four miles. After that, you'll have breakfast downstairs—patio or kitchen, whatever is convenient for the staff. Janice won't be lugging trays up and down the stairs. I will give you a supervised morning work detail. I'm sure Danny has plenty for you to do, like cutting the grass, weeding, and so forth. Lunch will be downstairs; again, at whatever location is convenient. Afternoons will be spent in workout and additional work details. You'll get some supper at 1730, and lights out will be at 2030. No more Oysters Florentine. I just gave the cook two weeks off. As of right now, you are leaving fancy dinners, tennis, and riding lessons behind. No books, no CD's, no Jacuzzi. You can shower down at the pool house."

"Billie, why're you doing this?" The girl sat on the bunk, her long legs drawn up against her naked body, covering the most sensitive areas from Chapman's scrutiny. Chapman glanced down at her, noting the light shining off the chrome plated leg irons. Despite being locked up, without a chance to groom herself, the girl was quite attractive.

"That's Ms. Chapman. Angie, you haven't learned anything because you've been so damned spoiled. We've waited on you hand and foot, and gotten nothing for our trouble. Those days are over. You're going to earn your keep, and you're going learn to do what you're told at the same time. You dress when I say so, you work and rest when I say so, and you even use the bathroom when I say so. Oh, and I want all that hair out of the way, or I will cut it myself. And I have never been to cosmetology school! You have a comb and some hair bands in the bag. Use them."

"And if I refuse to obey your orders?" Angie's voice held a challenge.

"You've only had a taste of the discipline we can use with you." Chapman's voice was matter of fact. "Have you ever heard of a flying carpet ride?"

"Sure. I watched *1,001 Nights* with Coach Doyle's kids."

"This wasn't in the movie. That stun gun brought you down quick enough. A flying carpet ride involves using it in a location right between those long legs of yours. That is just one sample. I can make your life a living hell and never leave a scratch on that gorgeous body."

There was a moment of silence while Angie considered Chapman's threats. "Okay, okay. I get the picture. You said a few weeks—just how long do you intend to keep me in here?"

"That depends on you. Four weeks at a minimum. Disciplinary infractions will yield demerits. Any refusal to obey a direct order will yield a demerit; every time I give you a demerit, you get one more day over here. I'll keep a chart on the wall beside the door. We will mark off each week, and we'll keep up with infractions which bring a demerit. It may take us a while, but you will learn obedience and respect."

"I think you have some interesting delusions." Angie was pushing Chapman, looking for the limits.

"Miss Donalson, from here on out there are only three phrases I want to hear from you—'Yes, ma'am,' 'No, ma'am,' and 'No excuse, ma'am,' You got that?"

Angie stared at the determined face of her captor, which brooked no rebellion.

"You got that?" Chapman's voice wasn't loud, but it demanded her attention.

"Yes, ma'am," Angie replied.

Chapman pulled her keys from her pocket and unlocked the cuffs from the girl's ankles. "You won't be needing these. Get some sleep. It'll be 5:45 before you know it."

Chapman coiled the cuffs into her pocket and locked the door behind her.

*　　*　　*

The next morning was a rude awakening for Angie.

Chapman, dressed in combat fatigues, leaned over the bunk and yelled into her ear, "You have five minutes to fall out that door, ready to run. Five minutes—I mean five. You got that?" Chapman left the door open and timed her. Angie managed to be dressed and out in ten.

"You're going to move your lazy ass faster. You will move your ass, and I mean move it, whenever I say so." Angie braced to attention as she endured the tirade. Mentally, she reviewed her phrase book—'Yes, ma'am', 'No, ma'am', and 'No excuse, ma'am'—but Chapman gave her no opportunity for speech. Chapman's diatribe ended after she explained just what a worthless piece of crap Angie had been all the days of her miserable life.

They covered the predicted four miles. Chapman started them out, jogging at a brisk pace. After watching Chapman on horseback, leading the walk, Angie was amazed to see her captor not just keeping pace, but setting it. Angie was panting and about done in when they marched up the back steps to the patio. Janice set a plate with buttered toast, a bowl of corn flakes, and a banana on an outside table. For a few moments, Angie sat, holding her head in her hands. Then she ate there with Janice's watchful eyes upon her. When Angie finished eating, Janice told her that she had ten minutes in the hall bathroom.

Waiting in the hall, Angie saw Chapman marching toward her. Five minutes later, she was listening to Danny, who indicated two areas of grass which needed mowing. He showed her how to start the gasoline-powered lawn mower. Angie pushed it for about two hours before completing the assigned areas. Danny inspected her work, then handed her a metal trowel and told her to weed and mulch a large flowerbed. This task was finished at lunchtime, so Danny escorted her back to the patio. Chapman set a paper plate with two peanut butter and jelly sandwiches, a glass of milk, and a container of applesauce in front of her. Compared to the elaborate meals she had been eating, it was indeed plain fare, but Angie wolfed it down.

Chapman took her to the gym to do weights for an hour. Later on she set the girl to scrubbing down the tiled kitchen floor—with a bucket and a scrub brush. By the time Angie finished that chore, she could hardly move. She made no protest as Chapman escorted her to the pool house for a shower —only cold water!—and back to the detention cell. Angie collapsed on the bunk, her muscles aching, and Janice had to awaken her to eat the bologna sandwich and carrot sticks that were dinner.

Reflecting on the events of the day, Angie realized that she had not seen any restraints at all—only hard work and constant supervision. However, she was too tired to worry about not having opportunities to escape. The next day was almost identical. Danny gave her a pair of leather gloves and a tool basket and had her weed and fertilize another flowerbed. Then, she helped him cut brush in the woods for the rest of the morning. Because it was hot, he offered Angie a sports drink from the cooler he kept on the back of the truck. They drank thirstily and returned to cutting and stacking brush. After lunch, she did her lower body workout with Chapman supervising, then Janice had her vacuum the carpet and dust the furniture in the guest wing of the house—eight bedrooms, hallway, and rec room. At last, she went upstairs for fresh clothing, down to the pool house for a shower, and back to the kitchen for a light supper before returning to the detention cell. Once again, she was so exhausted that her muscles were trembling by the time she sagged onto the bunk.

Each day, except Sunday, was a continuation of those first days. Angie dressed in the splotchy gray/green camo shorts, olive green shirt, and running shoes that Chapman referred to as her uniform. Each day began with the four mile run. After that Angie *worked*—she cleaned the pool and scrubbed down the concrete which surrounded it. She cut grass, pushed a little cart with fertilizer in it all over the lawn, and did weeding and mulching. Also, she planted flowers and helped install an irrigation system for some of the shrubs. Some days she cleaned out the stable or cut brush and piled it up for burning. Inside, she polished silver, cleaned floors and cabinets; she even shampooed the carpet.

*   *   *

Janice Rule stepped through the door of Chapman's office with Angie's olive drab laundry bag in her hand. Chapman, in her fatigues, was going through some accounts. She looked up, eyes not yet focused on Janice.

"Billie, I have something for you to see."

Chapman seemed confused. "What?"

Janice dumped the contents right into Chapman's lap.

"What is the meaning of this?" Chapman gathered up the dirty clothing and placed it on an empty corner of the desk.

"Everything in this bag is soaking wet."

"Is Angie taking showers with her clothes on?"

"Billie—that's sweat. You're going to work the girl to death. It's hot! She's not used to so much physical work. It's like this every day. She's going to have a heat stroke or something. Mr. Avery wants us to care for this girl, not kill her."

Chapman sighed and stuffed the clothing back into the bag.

"Jan, you're being insubordinate. But I suppose you feel justified. I know this isn't what we planned. However, it *is* working. The girl has stopped spending her spare time trying to figure out how to get away. Look, she's too exhausted to escape, therefore she is secure— mission goal accomplished. If you'll recall, another of our mission goals was to acquaint her with the estate and how it is run. Angie knows more about it than Mr. Avery does, already. Because I have rotated her tasks, she is building knowledge of what it takes to keep this place going—second mission goal accomplished. Still another aspect of the mission was to get her used to the staff. By alternating jobs and supervisors, she's gotten to know all of us better. Goal three—accomplished."

Janice slid into the single chair in front of Chapman's desk. Her black hair swung in a line along her cheekbone. She grimaced as she gestured toward the bag. "But what is she really learning? To hate us even more?"

"We were already her captors. I doubt her feelings for us could get worse. But as she sees us work, doing real jobs, not just fastening her restraints, we'll earn some of her respect. Think, Jan, hasn't her attitude toward you changed in the past couple of weeks?"

Janice paused, considering Chapman's words. Angie had been more responsive of late. Before, Angie had treated her as if she was part of the furniture. Janice picked up the bag as she rose to her feet.

"Okay, but I still think you might lighten up a bit. She looked awful at lunch today."

"I'll speak to Danny about keeping her hydrated and giving her more breaks. But this won't work if she gets time to brood about being a captive."

"Yes, ma'am." Janice lugged the bag down the corridor, and Chapman returned to her accounts.

*　　*　　*

By degrees, Chapman instilled her military style discipline on Angie. Chapman taught her to brace to attention when a superior entered the room and ordered her to drop for pushups when she failed at some task. Any reluctance to obey bought her extra work details, extra pushups, and a few demerits. The combination of brisk command and swift punishment yielded fast results. Angie soon came to rely on "Yes, ma'am," "No, ma'am," and "No excuse, ma'am" as her entire verbal repertoire. Within two weeks, thoughts of escape had faded from Angie's mind. Instead, she was just trying to get through each day with a minimum of pain, humiliation, and exhaustion.

Angie's only relief came on Sundays, when she had a half-day off. She got a breakfast tray in her quarters accompanied by a Sunday paper and a couple of magazines. This meant that she got to sleep late and read a while. But after lunch, there was always another work detail.

"Billie's Basic," as Danny referred to it, lasted four weeks. On a Sunday afternoon, Angie had been working in the study, taking all the books off the shelves and dusting them, when she encountered Avery. She hadn't seen him for a month. He stared at her "uniform" —her now well broken-in camouflage shorts and T-shirt—and her hair, which was tightly plaited and hanging down her back. She nodded at him, then went back to her work. Any slowness on her part would result in a dressing down and a demerit on the board. Angie needed to finish before Chapman came to check on her workmanship, for the former Marine was an exacting taskmaster.

"Angie, it's been a while. How are you?"

"I'm okay. I just have to finish these shelves." She was pulling books out, dusting and putting them back, straightened.

"And what happens then?"

"I hope I get a shower and some rest. But I have to finish by 1700. I don't want any more demerits." Angie glanced at her watch, a basic military design on a black nylon band.

"What happens if you get those?"

"I spend even more days working. Don't you and Billie ever talk anymore?"

"Not lately." Avery watched for a few more minutes as Angie worked through the higher shelves, bracing herself on the ladder. "I'll be seeing you around."

"Sure," she said and kept on with the job. Although she was at the end of the four weeks, she had earned another week in demerits already. But Angie was so busy that she had little time to think about it. She just tried to keep ahead of the tasks of the day. Janice came in as she finished and told her to go back to her quarters.

"Billie is coming by here to check your work; then she'll see you there. I think she wants to talk to you about something, because she told me to be sure you were waiting."

"Okay, Janice."

Angie took the stairs two at a time, realizing that her stamina had increased three-fold with the hard work that Chapman had required. She swung into the dark room, ignoring the rough plywood walls and rude furnishings. Per instructions, Angie sat down to wait.

She didn't wait long. Chapman, dressed in her fatigues, came through the door. Angie stood, braced to attention and waited, being certain that the only thing that moved was her diaphragm. That was the sort of month it had been.

"About face, at rest."

Angie placed her right toe behind her left heel and pivoted 180 degrees, precisely as Chapman had taught her, and assumed the position for a body search. By now, Angie was accustomed to having Chapman's hands run lightly over her body.

"About face. Parade rest."

Angie turned again and stood before her, hands clasped behind, legs spread a foot and a half apart. The girl fixed her gaze straight in front, as she had been taught. Chapman stepped back and looked up at her. Angie found it disconcerting, because Chapman was five inches shorter than she was, but they had to be standing next to each other for the girl to realize it. In Angie's mind, Chapman seemed huge. Must be her character, Angie mused. She remained motionless, but she was wondering what was on Chapman's mind.

The former Marine eyed her up and down, and there was, for the first time in weeks, a hint of a smile. "You will be going back across the hall in a few minutes. Your demerits will be worked off on Wednesdays. That means that every Tuesday night at 2000 you'll dress in your uniform and return to this room. Wednesday, you will get up at 0545 and do your run and your work details—just as you have done for the past four weeks. Then you can go back across the hall at 2000 in the evening. This happens every Wednesday until the demerits are cleared, so right now you have a month and a half of Wednesdays to work off. If you get more demerits, then you will lose even more Wednesdays. If your behavior, or the lack of it, warrants it, you'll go through this whole training session again."

She paused. Angie still stood, silent, waiting for her next orders. Ironically, she had found "Billie's Basic" preferable to the uncertainty of Avery's whims. Angie was hoping that Chapman would keep her away from him longer, but his appearance in the library and Chapman's words seemed to make that scenario doubtful.

"Angie, you've learned a lot in these past four weeks. I have been pleased at your progress. I know that we're going to have better conduct from you from now on. But, I warn you, do not violate my trust. Before you say or do anything, I want you to ask yourself, 'What will Ms. Chapman do if I—? ' Fill in the blank with whatever you might be contemplating. If you know you'll get into trouble, then don't even think about doing it." She paused again. "I've come to realize just how much you despise having to wear restraints. The only reason we used them was to insure proper conduct. If you want to leave them behind, then you must meet my expectations for your behavior. The demerit system is still in place. If the count goes beyond what you can serve in two months time, you go back to daily training. And you are close, very close. Understood?"

"Yes, ma'am."

"You can shower and change in your room across the hall. Mr. Avery wishes to have dinner with you, and formal dress is required. I'll send Janice to help you in a little while. Dinner is at 7:30."

"Ms. Chapman," Angie stopped her. "Uh, I'm used to eating at 5:30; could I go to the kitchen for a snack? I worked hard this afternoon, and I'm hungry. Please?"

"I'll have Janice bring you something. We won't make you eat in the kitchen anymore."

"I'd rather go down myself," she told her, meaning it.

"Perhaps, but I'll order a tray."

"Yes, ma'am."

"Dismissed."

Angie went across the hall and found the door to her room unlocked. The room was as she had left it, except a new computer desk had been installed right beside the writing desk and bookshelf combination. This was a handsome desk that matched the other wooden furnishings; it held a computer, a printer and a rack of software. Angie stood looking at it, reading the program titles, when Janice came in with a tray. A small crystal bowl of mixed fruit with shredded cheese surrounded by a collection of assorted crackers sat upon it. An elegant "snack" indeed, but Angie decided that she'd rather have had another of Chapman's peanut butter sandwiches.

Angie sat at the desk and ate. As she did so, she caught a glimpse of herself in the mirrored closet doors. There was a dirty smudge across her freckled nose and the worn olive green tee and camo shorts looked out of place in the elegant room. However, she found herself somewhat reluctant to shower and change. She leaned back and shook her head, wondering at this clinging to "Billie's Basic." Across the hall in the spare, barracks-like room, the situation had seemed almost normal. Over here, it was ridiculous.

Returning to the tray, Angie finished the snack and went to take a shower. Hot water! This was worth a celebration. She reveled in it for a while, then came out wearing a terry cloth robe. Tossing the camo clothes into the laundry basket in the closet, Angie turned to the task of finding something formal. The blue dress was there, the one she had worn when Avery first wanted to dine with her. And there was another, a white dress with sequins and braid, which would no doubt do. With all the sun she'd gotten while working outside, it might even be a more flattering choice.

Janice returned. She joined Angie in her perusal of the closet. "We need to work on this wardrobe. It's just not adequate. Maybe we can do that next week—I'll have to talk to Billie. For tonight, I think the white is best. Let's see what we have to go with it."

Once again, Janice worked her magic. Angie would never have taken the time that Janice did getting her ready. They began with a manicure... a tough job for Janice since the girl had been working her fingers off, literally... and a pedicure. After that she put Angie's long, auburn hair up and did another splendid job with make-up. The freckles, which had multiplied under the hot Tennessee sun, faded with each layer. Finally, Janice disguised her tan line with a fancy necklace with sparkling stones which glittered like diamonds.

"Miss Donalson," Janice said as she finished, "that should do it. You are expected downstairs."

"What, no handcuffs?" Angie's tone was teasing, but there was a real question in it. She'd never had dinner with Mr. Avery without a search and some sort of restraint.

"No, miss. Just go to the dining room, please." Janice shook her head, grinning. "Do me a favor and walk slowly. I have to serve."

"Sure," Angie said, chuckling as Janice sped out the door.

At 7:25, Angie came down the stairs, making something of an entrance. Chapman and Avery were waiting in the foyer, and they looked up, their faces showing disbelief. The transition from the camouflage-clad servant to Miss Donalson in evening attire was quite remarkable. Although she didn't laugh, Angie couldn't quite keep the grin off her face, either. Avery returned the gesture, and Angie found herself smiling even more broadly. She had never felt so feminine, so alluring.

"You look great, Angie." Avery's admiration was apparent in his face and his voice.

"Thanks, but Janice is the wizard. I just sat still for her," Angie told him with complete honesty.

"Janice may be an artist, but you are a beautiful canvas."

Not knowing what to say to his compliment, Angie grinned. Avery touched her cheek, a simple caress, and stood back to admire her flawless face.

"Come into the dining room; Mrs. B. has been whipping up something delicious."

"And probably dirtying up every pot in the kitchen," Angie responded dryly. In the past four weeks, she'd been kitchen patrol enough to know that the woman could dirty five pots and pans to make one cute little plate of appetizers. She had talent all right.

"If you can act sociable, I'll make sure you don't have to do the dishes," Avery said, his tone light.

She'd probably prefer washing dishes, but Angie left the remark unsaid. Instead, she favored him with a wry half-smile. He held out his arm in a formal gesture, and Angie played along, slipping her arm through his, like being escorted at a wedding. She felt that way, anyway, with the fancy white dress and all.

*   *   *

After dinner, they listened to a new CD Avery had brought and talked music. The eight years between them were readily apparent, and the conversation soon sputtered and died like her aunt's car on a cold morning. Angie yawned, then apologized for it. "Ms. Chapman usually gets me up before six, and I'm used to an early bedtime," she explained to Marc.

"I'll bet it was rough, wasn't it?" Avery grinned. "Billie strikes me as a tough lady, very tough."

"She is," Angie agreed. "But despite the fact that she has jabbed me with needles, used all sorts of chains on me, made me work like a slave, and even whipped me a couple of times—I kind of like her." Angie's voice was hesitant, almost reluctant. "I don't know. It's hard to explain, but she is a real together person. She commands respect. You get the feeling that she's lived life and knows the score. I'd trust her in a crisis."

"You're right. I couldn't agree more. I trust her when I would trust no one else. That is why she's here, in charge of you." Avery's tone was sincere. "Angie, you are important to me. I want this to work out.

You are beautiful and intelligent. Billie tells me you have strong moral character—and a good work ethic. Those attributes make you the companion I need. You don't realize it just yet, but we'll both enjoy the relationship. Billie has made quite an impression on you. That's great, because she's here to help us get a good start."

"Mr. Avery, I don't want any more demerits. I don't really want to sleep on a tiny cot and work eleven and twelve hours a day, so I have to be careful of what I say. But again, I am respectfully asking you to just let me go home. My aunt has no one but me. She *needs* me. I *need* her." Angie looked at him with equal sincerity and entreated him assiduously. "I want to finish my schooling, ordinary stuff... senior pictures... the SAT. I want a normal life." She gestured, holding out her hand as if it held the entire estate. "This junk means nothing to me. I don't need material things. I never had them. I need my life back. Please. And please note that I've been very polite and diplomatic. You be sure and tell Billie that when you tell her about my negative attitude."

Angie plopped down on the sofa, her pose anything but elegant, despite the dress. The country girl was out of her depth—way out. She'd been more comfortable in the kitchen eating peanut butter and jelly sandwiches. His life was not her life. Angie needed to get away from this—from him. Somehow Avery had to see it. He just had to.

Angie looked up at him, hoping for some sympathy, for some understanding.

Avery sat beside her and took her hand in his. His tone seemed heartfelt.

"You're young yet. Sure, you feel out of place right now. But as you live here, as you're exposed to more and more new things, you'll grow into it. But the foundation, the moral character, will still be there. We can graft on some sophistication, but I couldn't take a shallow person and give her your inner strength. That's why I need *you*." He shook his head, then continued, his voice low.

"Enough of this. Billie is waiting to take you upstairs. Then she is off duty for a couple of days. Angie, we had trouble the last time she was gone. I'll be the first person to admit that I was part of the problem. But I need your cooperation. Promise me you'll behave. For her sake. She needs the time off."

"I promise. Not because I want to be here, and *not* because I feel sorry for Ms. Chapman, either. It's just that I got into enough trouble last time." Angie rose from the sofa and stepped into the hall, Avery following. Chapman was there, ready to accompany them. At the top of the stairs, for once, Chapman didn't pause to lock the gate. Avery went into his room and Chapman followed Angie into the big bedroom.

"About face, at rest." Chapman sounded tired.

"Yes, ma'am." Angie's response was crisp. She braced to attention before turning, a bit awkward on her high heels. The search was accomplished in record time. Angie straightened up and looked down at her keeper. "You look exhausted. I'll get myself ready for bed—go on."

"No, I'm on duty until you're tucked in."

"I'll hurry." And she did. Angie had changed out of the fancy dress and into the nightgown Chapman had chosen, was free of make-up, and had her hair down in less than fifteen minutes. Chapman had the bed turned down and the chain out.

Angie stared at it, her face growing red beneath the freckles. "I thought you said that if I behaved, I would be free of restraints." Angie didn't take her eyes from the chain. "I've been perfect—absolutely perfect!"

"This is the only one, Miss Donalson. And only when Mr. Avery is here." She sounded defensive.

"What's he afraid of? That I'll kill him in his sleep? The door is locked on his side. Or if he's real worried, he could sleep downstairs. God knows, there are enough rooms."

Chapman sighed at her innocence. "It's not my place to tell you this. But Mr. Avery might feel the need for some advantage in bed. You are a strong girl." Chapman watched as comprehension dawned on her. "Make it easy on yourself. Don't put up a fight."

"What would you do, if it were you?"

"I don't know." Her voice, normally so self-assured, sounded doubtful.

"I think I do. You are hardly a weakling," Angie looked straight into her eyes.

Chapman shrugged and gestured for the girl to climb into the bed. "He's a nice man, for the most part. He's rich and handsome. He has made elaborate plans for you—most of this estate was designed with you in mind. He'll pay your every expense. Many young ladies would jump at the chance. Angie, you've been handed a gift horse. This man has taken you from the poverty you were in and shared his wealth. By now, you must realize that he can give you everything a woman could want. You just don't look a gift horse in the mouth, girl." She snapped the cuff around Angie's ankle. "Good night. I'll see you Tuesday evening—in your uniform." She turned out the light and closed the door. Angie heard the lock turn and the door rattle as Chapman checked it. She lay thinking about Chapman's last remarks. A gift horse. She wondered if it was just that—a way to get what she had always wanted. "To be somebody—" Maybe this was fate's way of fulfilling her desires, her expectations. Sometimes the bad came with the good. A tear trickled down her face. She swiped at it and wiped her hand on the satiny sheet.

Lying in bed, wearing an emerald green negligee, with the cuff around her ankle, Angie gazed out the windows. A pale, three-quarter moon illuminated the grounds. A portion of the flower garden and tennis court filled the bottom half of her view. She glanced about the moonlit room. The exquisite furnishings weren't a part of her dream; hell, they were *better* than any dream she'd ever had. And Avery, himself—tall, athletic, handsome, cultured—just what a woman would want in a man. He obviously thought she was something special. Even the estate had been named for her—*Angelhurst*.

The moonlight revealed the connecting door as it opened. The master of Angelhurst slipped quietly into the room. Angie could see that he was naked, and she knew fear... revulsion... and an emotion she hadn't bargained for—anticipation. 'Cut it out, you fool, it'll be more like rape', she chided herself.

Avery came over to the bed without speaking and raised the sheet. Angie lay in the soft moonlight, cowering back as far as the slender chain would allow. Her leg was drawn tight, and Avery moved his hand over its smooth surface, from the top of her thigh to her ankle, feeling the muscle tense underneath.

Angie grasped his wrist, her grip very strong. "No." Her voice was a desperate whisper. "I don't want you. I've never wanted you. Leave me the hell alone."

"Angie, take it easy. I'm not going to hurt you. I didn't bring you here to torture you," he said, sitting on the bed beside her.

"Didn't you?"

"I've explained it all before. The time for talk is over."

Angie was sitting up now; Avery wrapped his arms around her in an attempt to soften her stiff body.

"You haven't given me a decent explanation because there isn't one—unless it's that you've lost your friggin' mind." Angie twisted in his arms, trying to free herself from his embrace. She knew that getting away was impossible; she was stalling.

"For as long as the earth has been populated by men and women, the women have traded their feminine wiles for what men could give them." Avery's voice was lighter than his subject matter. He pulled her down onto the pillows.

"They chose the trade—I didn't!" Angie pushed against the growing weight of his body.

"Some did, some didn't, at least not at first. You *will* come to value the exchange." Avery's voice was low in her ear as he pressed her down into the bedclothes. "It's time we did more than talk," he said, and his mouth was on hers. He caressed her, kissed her, and insisted on her cooperation.

"Spread your legs," he told her, pushing them apart with his knee. Chapman's advice not to fight was still in her mind, yet the temptation was to use those hard-earned muscles to repel her unwanted lover. She held his wrist still, and her other hand held his chest away from her. Mentally she weighed the balance, and she knew that chained to the bed, as she was, she couldn't hold him off forever. Angie decided that she couldn't win, and that Avery could summon help. After a few moments of intense mental debate, she chose passive resistance. When he moved her body, he had to work for it; she held herself very still, not reacting to his lovemaking. Avery took his time, stroking her body, looking for sites which might arouse her, but Angie managed to show neither distaste nor passion.

When it was over, Avery slept and Angie extracted herself from his arms, being careful not to awaken him. She crawled as far away as her tether would allow and, after a very long time, slept herself.

Avery wanted her again, just before dawn. He woke her with a kiss, and immediately she stiffened. He crossed her wrists and held them above her head, forcing her legs apart with his knee. Angie knew that she could make trouble. As Chapman had pointed out, she was plenty strong enough to fight him. But then he would use the restraints and do it anyway. She kept her resistance minimal, just enough so that he would know that she didn't welcome his advances. He held her with a solid grasp until he was satisfied, then rolled off her, dozing. Angie turned to the pillows and wept silent tears.

* * *

Danny knew that Billie had worried about leaving just as Angie was coming off the month of training. Angie had been easy to handle when they'd kept her exhausted and under close supervision. But what would she do when faced with fulfilling Avery's expectations *and* having more time on her hands?

In the green room, Danny used the monitors to check on her. He was scheduled to take her for a four mile run, but when he saw Avery in her bed with an arm wrapped possessively around her middle, he decided that they'd have to cancel... or at least postpone... it for this day. He watched for a few moments, but he saw no movement, so he went downstairs. If Angie needed to get up, Avery had a key.

* * *

Angie needed the bathroom. Badly. She looked at the clock radio, which read 7:30. Her usual schedule would have her finished with the morning run and having breakfast by this time. Her body's internal clock said she was overdue for her morning ablutions. Angie looked at Avery, who was still on his stomach, snoring. Pulling on the chain was a useless gesture. She wasn't going anywhere without a key.

"Um, I, um." She was having trouble articulating for some reason. Embarrassment, she supposed. With some hesitation, she touched him on his shoulder. "Mr. Avery, I need for you to wake up."

He turned over and mumbled something.

"I need for you to wake up. Please."

"Oh, hi, Angie. You look great. You were great."

"Do you have the keys?" She gestured to the chain holding her in bed.

"In my room."

"I need the bathroom. Please."

He was still groggy, but the message was getting through. "Oh, sure. Just a minute." He got off the bed, stumbled a bit and went through the connecting door. Moments later, he came back with the keys and unlocked the cuff. Angie leapt from the bed and sprinted though the door to the big bathroom.

While there, she went ahead to the shower. Angie decided that she needed a good, hot shower. More than anything, she needed to scrub Avery off of her. She was lathering her head when the shower door opened, and Avery's naked body slipped in beside hers.

He took the soap from the holder and washed her back, her breasts, and finally the part that needed it the worst. Angie stood quite still, tolerating his ministrations. He handed the soap to her and turned his back. For a moment, Angie just stood, water dripping over her slender form.

"My turn," he said. "I always have trouble reaching that part." She began washing his back. In a moment, he turned and grinned. "The front needs some of your kind attention, my lady." Angie washed his chest, but avoided other areas. He moved her hand, still grasping the soap, down to the nether regions, so she washed him, but in as cursory a fashion as she thought would get by. They exited the shower together and wrapped towels around their naked bodies.

"I'll get some breakfast up here," Avery said and passed through to his room to use the intercom. He came back wearing a toweling robe. Angie entered the walk-in closet and found a pair of shorts and a thick mesh polo shirt. She emerged already dressed, damp hair streaming down over one shoulder. Her hair had been long before her abduction; now it was very long.

"No fair," Avery said. "I wanted to see you dress."

"I'm supposed to go jogging before breakfast," Angie said, intending to change the subject.

"I imagine they thought better of it. Come here."

Angie approached him, and he pulled her down on the chaise lounge beside him. His arm was around her shoulders, and he explored her slender face and neck with his free hand. "You'll come to appreciate me," Avery was saying in her ear. "Angie, just let go and enjoy yourself. You can have a good time, if you'll just let go of your inhibitions."

There was a knock at the door. Avery went to answer. Janice had a tray laden with fruit, cinnamon rolls, coffee, and a couple of newspapers. She set it on the table in front of the chaise lounge, nodded to Mr. Avery, and left.

The pair shared breakfast and the papers. Avery talked of the business and of the way economic growth was affecting sales. Angie listened, having no experience in such matters. For a while, she perused the newspapers, but found little to interest her.

"Am I boring you, Angie?"

Angie found herself searching for a diplomatic answer. "Not exactly. But I don't know much about your business. I had a course in economics—but that was in tenth grade, and it was sort of general."

"So what do you want to talk about?"

"I... I'm not sure. We really have very little in common. Other than the fact that you had me kidnapped and brought here. No one asked *me* if I was interested in your little trade." Angie shrugged and poured another cup of coffee.

"Let's talk about that, then. At least indirectly." The bantering tone was gone from his voice. "I know that you've worried about your aunt. She's fine. By the way, she won a contest, held by a subsidiary of Avery Electronics, for $10,000. That should help her adjust to the loss of your Social Security checks. You're officially a missing person, but the local police think you're a runaway. Billie was careful. And it's no secret that you wanted to get the hell out of Adamsville. Angie, there was no evidence of foul play in your disappearance. The investigators realized pretty quickly that your home was something that one might want to escape. No one is looking too hard for you."

Avery set his coffee cup back on the tray. "Billie has instructions to take you to a hairdresser as soon as she deems you trustworthy enough to be taken beyond the gates. We'll take care of your other needs as well, as soon as you prove yourself. My staff here is able to look after your immediate needs, but you'll need to see a dentist and a doctor eventually. There is nothing much wrong with you; Billie drew a blood sample and had it tested while you were still unconscious." Avery looked at her, his gaze appreciating her legs, which were revealed by the rather short shorts. "I have arranged tutoring by a private learning center that assists home schooled students. You'll complete your senior year studies via that method."

"What happens if I fail to cooperate?" she asked with muted defiance.

"You are already cooperating quite nicely," Avery said with a smile, as he glanced at the bed. Angie felt her face color. "But if you give me or anyone else trouble, I feel sure that Billie will deal with you. I understand that you're going to be rather busy on Wednesdays this summer."

Angie had almost forgotten "Billie's Basic." She didn't answer Marc; instead she was lost in thought, trying to adjust to the life that Marc was predicting.

"It's in your own best interest to work with the tutor, Angie. It will be her job to get you ready for college. I'll send you to college if you are accepted. *If* we can trust you. Of course, you'll have other opportunities for learning as well." Avery smiled his knowing smile. "If you learn at the rate I think you will, there'll be some travelling. You'll learn more than trig and British lit this year." Once again, Avery looked rather smug. Angie scowled at him.

"Let's go play some tennis, okay?" He changed the subject again.

Angie started to protest that she just wanted to be left alone, then she remembered her promise to Chapman. "Sure. I'll lose, though. It's been a month since Danny's last lesson."

"All the more reason to play you today, then. You'll no doubt start back on your lessons, now that we're more or less back to normal. And with Danny teaching you, I soon won't have a chance."

The Gift Horse

*   *   *

Somehow, Angie got through the day. Avery left for Charleston
via helicopter after an early dinner. Angie sighed with relief when the
chopper lifted off the helipad, and Danny escorted her back to her
room, informing her that she was on her own until her morning run.
Alone at last, she sat on the chaise lounge and let the tears flow
unchecked. With time on her hands, she analyzed her situation and
found little to cheer her. When she went to bed, she doubted that
sleep would come, but she slept better than she would have thought.

Janice woke her and Danny took her for her morning run; then she
had a riding lesson, a tennis lesson, and a session in the weight room.
Even in Chapman's absence, her staff was true to her word...
although the doors were locked, she had not seen any sort of restraint.
Mrs. Bowen sent her usual elegantly served, healthful meals. Angie
spent a little time exploring the new computer, thankful for the
computer tech class she'd been taking her junior year. At 7:15, Janice
came in with her camouflage outfit and a reminder to be across the
hall by 8:00. Ms. Chapman was back, and she came in at lights out to
inspect her and to remind her that she would be up at 5:45.

Angie's work details included cutting grass, washing the truck,
and cleaning out the pantry in the kitchen. She finished each task on
time, and Chapman seemed quite pleased that no problems had
occurred in her absence.

Chapter 7

Ms. Chapman and Danny took Angie to a shopping mall for a haircut and some additional clothes on Thursday. Before they even left her bedroom, Chapman sat on an armchair opposite Angie, a pair of hinged... translate "highly restrictive"... handcuffs, in hand.

"Miss Donalson, Mr. Avery has encouraged me to let you off the grounds. But security is my responsibility. You will promise cooperation—or you will not set foot off the estate."

"What do you mean, cooperation?"

"First, you won't be allowed to see the route we take away from Angelhurst. Second, you will speak only about matters at hand, and only to us. Third, you stay with your escort at all times. Oh, and you will wear these restraints in the car."

"Do you really think that I'm gonna jump out of the car?"

"I would hope not, but I refuse to take any chances."

"Please, put those things away. I'll cooperate."

In the garage, Chapman handed her a pair of wrap-around sunglasses. They looked ordinary enough, but when Angie put them on, she found that they'd been painted black on the inside. With a faint smile of admiration, Angie realized that it wouldn't be obvious to passing motorists that she was blindfolded. Chapman pushed her into place in the car, fastened her seat belt and seated herself beside her. Angie wasn't allowed to take off the glasses until they had stopped in the parking lot of the mall. Once there, Chapman went everywhere with her, including dressing rooms, so she had no opportunities to escape.

The hairdresser was skilled; Angie walked out with about six inches less hair than before. Angie's auburn locks now curled just above her shoulders, but there was still enough hair to do a braid or a ponytail, if she wanted the hair out of the way. Sherry, the hairdresser, told her that this cut—much shorter than she had ever worn—was much more sophisticated, just what a young lady who was outgrowing her teen years needed.

So were the clothes. Angie had gravitated toward sportswear, and Chapman did let her choose one outfit there. After that, Chapman steered her toward the eveningwear.

"Ms. Chapman, this stuff is expensive," Angie whispered in amazement, looking at the price tag while they were closeted in the dressing room.

"Mr. Avery has assured me that this is what he wants." Ms. Chapman's tone was confident.

They emerged from the store with five dresses that Chapman called dinner dresses. Angie called them "fancy dresses." More attire for evenings with Avery, of course. Angie could not recall a time in her life when she hadn't owned a single pair of jeans, but for the moment she did not.

Angie also got some swimwear and some new running shoes. Angie tried to keep a mental total of what Chapman was spending on her, but she lost track. She couldn't comprehend expending so much money. Several months of Social Security checks would cover only the items in one department. However, Chapman seemed to think nothing of it.

As a reward for her good behavior, Angie got to pick lunch at the food court. She had pepperoni pizza with a greasy crust and stringy cheese, for the first time in months. Heaven! After a late lunch, they returned to the car, where Chapman handed her the dark glasses once again. She could see just a few odd fragments above and below the glasses; as usual, Chapman's method was quite effective. As Chapman removed the glasses in the garage at Angelhurst, Angie realized that she didn't even know the name of the city they had visited, much less how to get back there.

*   *   *

Later that day, Chapman wore a plain navy blue tank suit and sat with her legs dangling in the pool. Angie was doing laps, demonstrating the two new strokes she had learned—the breaststroke and the backstroke. There was a strong contrast between the royal blue racing style suit that the girl wore and her pink skin. Chapman wasn't sure how much of that was sun and how much was exertion.

93

She'd been working Angie hard. The more she supervised her, the more she realized that meaningful activity was the key to keeping Angie in line. When Angie was occupied or fatigued, she was no trouble.

Making her feel comfortable in the water was the current goal, and Chapman was determined to teach Angie every stroke she knew herself. Also, Chapman wanted her able to swim long distances without stopping, as a safety measure. Chapman had lifeguard certification, and she intended that Angie be able to do everything necessary to be eligible for it herself.

"I'm exhausted," Angie announced, standing up in the shallow end of the pool with the water lapping around her thighs.

"You need to be able to do twice that number of laps, Miss Donalson." Chapman's voice held a slight reprimand.

"On the first day?" Angie's protest was almost a whine.

"By next week, anyway."

"Maybe you ought to go back and kidnap an athlete."

"We'll just have to make one of you," Chapman said with a grin. "Rest for ten minutes, then try the backstroke again."

Angie pulled herself up on the side and stretched out on the warm concrete, still panting.

*   *   *

On Friday, Chapman took her charge to the exercise room for a weight and measurement check. She grumbled that they were two weeks behind, but Angie reminded her that the whole staff had been busy recreating boot camp at the four-week interval. While Angie was standing on the scale, Chapman noted that her weight had dropped three pounds, to 133, and Chapman pronounced her a perfect size ten. Angie was able to bench press fifteen pounds more than she had done six weeks earlier, and her leg extensions and curls were up ten pounds each.

"Not bad, but we need to get these weights up higher. You could still trade in some fat for muscle."

"I am not fat. I know I'm not skinny, but I'm not fat."

"Miss Donalson, I never said you were. But if you don't set goals, you don't improve yourself. A twenty-percent increase in strength is not unreasonable. That's where I want you in three months."

"Yes, ma'am."

*　　*　　*

The weekend was like the previous one, in many ways. Avery flew in on Friday evening, and Angie had dinner with him in the dining room, dressed in one of the new dresses. After the meal, they moved over to the den and spent the rest of the evening watching a movie. Chapman chained her up at bedtime, and Avery came in later. Angie didn't enjoy his visit, but she didn't show overt resistance, either. She had a tangible reminder, the one surrounding her left ankle, that she could not fight and win that battle, so she didn't try. Avery seemed satisfied with what he was getting, and Angie found herself surviving it. On Saturday and Sunday, they spent much of their time together during the day, playing tennis or riding, and they ate together. The evenings were probably meant to be seductive, but Angie just set herself to endure. After he'd done what he wanted, Avery put an arm around her and dozed. Angie fought back tears, but saw little point in making any physical resistance.

This became a typical pattern for their weekends. Avery flew in on Friday afternoon or evening and stayed until Sunday evening. Occasionally, he came earlier or remained longer. As the weeks came and went, Janice taught Angie more about doing her hair and makeup—and how to dress for elegant dinners, as well as for less formal occasions. Layer by layer, the staff of Angelhurst grafted on the veneer of sophistication that Avery desired.

*　　*　　*

"About face, at rest," Chapman said, and Angie swiveled, her movements as crisp as a Marine recruit, and assumed the position for the search. The girl was wearing a very brief, seductive negligee in soft purple silk, so the examination was quickly performed. Chapman

95

touched her and signaled for her to get into the bed, which had been turned down in readiness.

"I would like you to forget the chain." Angie's voice was soft and pleading.

"You know that I can't do that just yet," Chapman informed her and fastened the cuff around her ankle.

"This whole scene is bad enough without the humiliation of being chained like an animal," Angie informed her.

"Miss Donalson, you are not an animal, and we don't treat you as one." Chapman sounded annoyed. "I'm simply insuring cooperation for Mr. Avery. If you want up, and he's satisfied with your behavior, then he has a key."

"Billie—please."

"No. You will comply with all our rules—including this one. It may not be pleasant, but you're not in any pain. Good night."

* * *

Angie tried to get away when Chapman and Janice took her to see a gynecologist. That was, perhaps, their closest call. The doctor's office was in a building down the street from—of all the most wonderful things—a police station. Chapman always had her wear the black-painted glasses until the car stopped at any destination. As she pulled the glasses off her face, Angie noticed the police station. They let her get out of the car and escorted her, a woman on either side, into the doctor's office. Chapman took care of the paperwork, only asking her one or two questions. The nurse seemed to think that it was unusual for anyone to accompany a patient in the exam room, but Chapman never left her side. She helped Angie undress, and stood by her head while the doctor did the physical exam. The whole time Angie was there, she kept looking for some way to capitalize on her discovery. At last, as Chapman went to the desk to take care of the bill, Angie slipped past Janice and ran across the road to the police station.

Angie was running as fast as her heels would permit. Entering the double glass paneled door, she skidded to a stop at a counter with a glass window, which had an opening for sliding papers back and forth.

"Can I help you?" asked a woman in uniform.

"Please, I need your help. I've been kidnapped!" Angie was breathless with the effort of escaping from Chapman.

In retrospect, she supposed that she had hardly looked kidnapped. She was wearing a stunning black dress, and the hairdresser had done wonders. Of course, Janice had done her makeup with her usual skill—so Angie looked like a society girl instead of a victim.

Before Angie could give much of an explanation, Chapman entered, wearing a white coat and a nametag with a medical insignia on it. She caught the attention of an officer who was coming down the hall, and Angie heard her begin, "Please pardon the intrusion. We have had Miss Donalson over at the therapist's…" Angie didn't hear all of what she said, but two more police officers from the station actually helped them get her, kicking and screaming, into the car. Angie did hear Chapman telling the officers "… how distraught she is after one of the sessions…."

The older officer agreed, "It's pitiful to see such delusions in someone so young."

Back in the car, Chapman produced a pair of handcuffs and snapped the cuffs so that her hands were held together, in front. The sunglasses were replaced, and Angie rode in stiff silence all the way back to the estate. For that little escapade, Angie was taken to the detention room, where she spent the rest of the day in handcuffs, her clothing confiscated, eating bread and milk; after that, she got six consecutive days back in "Billie's Basic."

All in all, Angie spent quite a bit of the summer dressed in her camouflage uniform doing work details. But, in time, Chapman taught her that being obedient was ever so much easier than trying to rebel against her captors.

*   *   *

Once Avery had taken her to bed, Angie gradually accepted her role. There were protests now and then, but overall Avery and his staff had a much easier job of it. She was reserved, seldom asking for anything. Each Tuesday evening she reported to the little room across the hall, ready to work off her demerits. When she was given work details, she tackled the tasks assigned to her without question. Her riding lessons and tennis lessons continued, and swimming was added to her list of scheduled activities. Because she'd shown some aptitude in the culinary arts, she was assigned to help Mrs. Bowen two evenings each week. Chapman kept a schedule of activities for her, and she was kept busy most of the time.

Chapman continued to use the ankle chain at night whenever Avery was there, giving Angie a tremendous disadvantage if she attempted to fight her bedtime duties. So Angie submitted to him, seemingly without emotion.

Toward the end of summer, the tutor, Mrs. Carter, began working with Angie in the library for two hours a day, three times a week. The tutor left assignments that she completed on her own. Avery had shown the tutor Angie's high school transcript... obtained from her scholarship packet... and a course of study was planned for her "senior year"—two semesters, with a holiday at Christmas time. She studied British literature, SAT prep, and world history for five months, then trig, Spanish, and ecology.

Angie was amused when it came time to take the SAT. In order to monitor her, Janice and Chapman also took the test, which was given at a high school about thirty miles from the estate. Angie was elated when the scores came back, and she had beaten her captors by some 200 points—each.

*   *   *

When she allowed herself to think about it, and that wasn't often, Angie didn't remember giving up. She just became used to being Avery's mistress. Her initial struggles had met with so much punishment that she'd found it easier to go along with everything. Certainly, she had set her mind to look for opportunities, but they never came. Angie had to work hard to keep up the schedule which Chapman set for her, and after a while she just sort of forgot to challenge things. There were a few incidents early on, sure. She got two demerits for pitching a fit when Janice did her first bikini wax, which was quite embarrassing and hurt like hell. But Chapman, with no hesitation, chained her hands to the headboard, tethered her feet to the footboard, and Janice continued with the procedure. Angie called them names and threatened both of them as Janice continued working. When Janice had finished, Chapman told her that she had two more Wednesdays to work off, one for resisting and one for having such a foul mouth. So, the next time, Angie just let her do it. Angie got used to it, though it took a few sessions.

* * *

As the weather cooled down into autumn, Angie found that she had served all the demerit days, and she was allowed a little more freedom. During the first eight months, she wore the improvised blindfold whenever they left the estate. For much longer, Chapman never allowed Angie to go anywhere without her and Janice. As time went by, Chapman reached a point where Angie was allowed to go to get a haircut, or to buy clothes, with just Janice as her driver/escort. Before any such foray, Chapman sat her charge down and elicited a promise that Angie would behave during the trip and return without protest. Either she promised, or she didn't get through the gates.

Christmas was a milestone of sorts. Avery had decreed that the staff of Angelhurst should be able to spend Christmas with their relatives. Ultimately, Avery and Chapman persuaded Angie to give her word that she would cause no problems during a weeklong trip away from the estate. Angie went with Avery to visit his father for a few days, which was her first overnight trip with him and was also the first time she'd left the estate with her vision unobstructed. After months of wondering, Angie got a good look at the area surrounding Angelhurst. With great interest she sat beside Marc in his BMW as they drove past the gatekeeper's cottage, through tall wrought iron gates, and into the mountainous country surrounding the estate. The trip was a daylong drive, and she was glad that Avery had suggested that she take a book. Despite the novelty of traveling without her blindfold, she eventually tired of trying to figure out escape routes and relaxed a bit.

Angie wondered about Aunt Claire. They had done little to celebrate Christmas since her childhood. No tree, no wreath—as neighbors and friends often did. However, there were some small gifts, and perhaps a special dinner. What would Claire do this year, without her? Did Aunt Claire worry, wondering what had happened? Angie longed for a way to get in touch with her, even if she couldn't leave Avery. She though of voicing a request, but she already knew the answer. During the first few months of her captivity, Angie had asked over and over, and she never got any sympathy. Knowing that, and remembering her promise to Chapman, she kept silent, but the resentment she felt was like a barrier between them, even as they sat within inches of each other.

At first, the elder Mr. Avery didn't seem to know what to make of her. Nor did Angie know how much *he* knew. But Marc acted as if she belonged there; after a short time, Mr. Avery did as well. Marc and Angie slept in the same room, and she helped with everything from last minute gift wrapping to preparing the food.

On the way back from Charleston, Marc surprised her by pulling into a country grocery with wooden floors and crowded shelves, which reminded her of a little store outside Adamsville where her father had taken her when she was small. Inside, Marc chatted with the proprietor, telling Angie to stock up on food for a few days. They drove up a winding road, turning onto a graveled drive so steep that the BMW groaned in protest. Marc laughed at Angie clutching the parcels as he skidded around tight curves. On the ridge of the mountain was a rustic cabin, with a view of the Blue Ridge Mountains. Marc and Angie spent another three days there, and she did most of the cooking.

* * *

The interior of the cabin was finished in grooved wood, the insides of the logs, Angie guessed. Above her head, early morning light filtered in the window, illuminating the room. Her breath was visible, because the temperature in the cabin had dropped as the flames in the fireplace diminished into a smoldering heap. Marc lay beside her, his body radiating heat like a furnace. His breathing was regular, his face relaxed. Any opportunity to sleep late was a joy, but she was never able to fully relish it, for Chapman's pattern of early exercise had become ingrained in her.

For some time, Angie had mentally swung between hating Marc, for his arrogance, for his egotism, for his lust and appreciating his attention to detail and the way he relished her as a woman. What she felt for him couldn't be called love, but she no longer loathed his presence. Sighing, she turned away from him and willed herself to avoid thinking of him at either end of her mental balance; she didn't want to be in bed with either a rapist or Santa Claus. Whatever else he was, Marc was a rich kid, a person who'd always been given anything he wanted, and thus had never achieved maturity. That he desired her was an arbitrary twist of fate, nothing more.

As the room brightened, he stirred. His hand came around her middle, pulling her toward him. He cupped one breast in his hand and caressed her face, running his fingers from the tip of her jawbone to the point of her chin. Turning toward him, Angie almost kissed him. Shocked by her own reaction, she pulled back and lay still.

"Something wrong, doll?" Marc's voice was husky with sleep.

"No. I was thinking it's time to get up."

"There's no Billie here," he chuckled. "Enjoy it. Let's exercise in a different way." Once again, he pulled her close and caressed her naked form. "We'll probably use more muscles doing this than you use in the weight room. And it's bound to be more fun."

Acquiescing, she reached out and stroked his chest, tracing the pectoral muscles.

"That's my girl," he praised her, and it was a while before they got out of bed.

* * *

Each day, they put on hiking boots and jeans, loaded a daypack and headed across the ridge. The trails were steep and marked only with blue paint arrows on an occasional tree. Without Marc's help, Angie would've been lost within minutes. Angie was delighted when they saw snow flurries on their last trek in the woods surrounding the cabin. Although she tried to remain aloof from him, Angie was drawn to her companion, whether it was finding their way back to the cabin, preparing simple meals in the small kitchen, or just roasting marshmallows by the fireplace in the evenings. How could this man, who had been behind her abduction, be so charming?

*   *   *

In early February, a stone faced Angie sat at the dining room table, having just finished another of Mrs. Bowen's culinary masterpieces. Once again, Angie was unhappy with Avery. An airline ticket folder was beside her used plate.

"Do you want to go or not?" Avery was exasperated.

"Do I have a choice?" Her tone was ugly, clashing with her elegant appearance. Tonight she wore a deep green dress with sequins on the bodice; her hair was fluffed out so that it softened the lines of her face, and her make-up was flawless.

"If you didn't, I wouldn't have bothered *asking* you." Avery was exasperated with her lack of gratitude.

Angie looked up at him. "If you think," she said in a controlled voice, "that I want to go off with you, pretending to be your lover to anyone and everyone, you're nuts."

"Okay, then you can just rot here! If you wish your sole function to be that of my whore, then so be it."

"How dare you call me a whore!" Angie got to her feet and raised her hand to slap him. He caught it before she connected and spun her around on her high-heeled sandals. Angie was heading out of the room and up the stairs before Avery could collect himself.

Chapman heard the end of the exchange as she came down the stairs. She met Angie and took her upper arms in a powerful grip, holding her in place on the stairs. Angie met Chapman's gaze and stopped dead in her tracks.

"Have you finished your conversation with Miss Donalson, sir?" Chapman asked in a dispassionate tone.

"Yes." Avery's voice echoed through the open hallway.

She released her grip without hesitation, allowing Angie to continue up the stairs. Chapman joined Avery in the foyer, a questioning look on her face.

"Billie, talk to her about this trip next week. Then call me if she changes her mind."

Chapman picked up the folder containing first class tickets to the Virgin Islands.

"What is it that she might change her mind about?"

"I was hoping to combine business with pleasure. I have a sales meeting in Miami, and I planned to have Angie join me at the end. I thought a trip to the beach would be a nice change for her. Sort of an early birthday present."

"And she looks better in a swimsuit than anyone on your R & D team, right?"

Avery grinned.

"Sure, I'll talk to her," Chapman said.

"Billie, she thinks a lot more of you than she does of me." Avery was frustrated. "Christmas went so well. What happened?"

"I'm not sure. Sometimes Angie seems content with her situation, sometimes she resents being here," Chapman explained. "Women are often said to be fickle. Especially pretty ones."

Chapman smiled at the cliché. Avery scowled.

"You knew it would take time, Mr. Avery," Chapman reminded him. "I've spent a great deal of time with your young lady. I know her better than you do. She's really a good kid, but in many ways, she's still a kid."

*   *   *

The last day of the trip, Angie stayed too long on the beach and got sunburned. After Avery and Angie spent two and a half hours on a commercial flight back to Charleston, she had three and a half hours in a helicopter; so she was tired and sore and in a horrible mood when she got back to Angelhurst. Chapman stood beside the helipad, ready to help with the bags. Angie got her purse and her small suitcase leaving Chapman to handle her large garment bag. As she hefted the big bag, she noted the burned skin and grinned at her infuriatingly.

Angie climbed the stairs, grateful for the solitude of her room. The worst part of the trip had been playing the role, pretending to be in love with Avery. Everyone who saw them together assumed that they were lovers, and that wasn't accurate. While they *made* love, they were not *in* love, Angie told herself for the fifty-seventh time.

Angie was in the bathroom, toweling off after a quick shower, when Chapman came in without knocking. The girl turned to stare at her. "What the hell are you doing here?"

"Miss Donalson, I am responsible for your welfare. Redheads don't have the best complexions for forays in sunny climates. " Chapman held up a tube of aloe vera gel. "I'm here to help you with… with the places you can't reach. About face."

Angie dropped the towel and turned. After all, Chapman had seen her naked on several occasions. Chapman anointed the places that needed it, soothing Angie's burning skin.

"Did you have a good time?"

Angie had not stopped to think about this before. She remembered the first-class hotel, the restaurants, and snorkeling in the clear, blue water. To her surprise, the whole experience, sunburn included, had been fun. "Yes, I did."

"You sound surprised." Chapman finished and handed her the tube of gel.

Angie turned to face her. "Frankly, I am, a bit."

Chapman nodded and looked at her, perceptively. "Good night, Angie."

"Good night."

Chapter 8

Above all else, Chapman and her staff seemed resolved to control Angie by keeping her busy. She had a schedule that Chapman kept in a notebook—it included several athletic activities and Angie's sessions with Mrs. Carter, her tutor. On a Wednesday evening in early April, Angie sat at the computer, working on her term paper for ecology. Bleary eyed, she shook her head and forced her exhaustion away from her consciousness. Chapman brought her dinner tray herself and sat down on a chair across from the chaise lounge. Angie kept on laboring at the computer; the tray could wait.

"What are you working on?" Chapman sounded insulted that her charge had ignored the dinner she'd brought.

Angie sat back in the big high-backed swivel chair and rubbed her burning eyes. "My term paper—Mrs. Carter wants it done by Friday. I'm not even close to finished."

"Don't you think you ought to take a break? For dinner, at least."

"Okay, okay." Angie got up and went to the tray, which held tuna salad on fresh spinach leaves, whole wheat crackers, herbed tomatoes, and a dish of baked apples in a caramel sauce, served on china and crystal. Mrs. B. always prepared elegant meals—even when Angie was oblivious to them.

"This is very tough."

"Really? We had that—and I though it was quite good."

"Not the food." Angie chuckled. "I was talking about my schedule. I'm taking three academic classes, plus running four or five miles a day, plus weight training five days a week, plus tennis three days a week, plus riding five days a week. And that doesn't include being Marc's entertainment two or three nights almost every week."

"Miss Donalson, are you saying that you're overstressed?" She sounded more amused than sympathetic.

"Yes, Ms. Chapman, that is exactly what I'm saying. And please don't give me any demerits for being ungrateful, 'cause I don't think I could possibly give up any Wednesdays." Angie ate more tuna salad.

"Are you asking me to alter your schedule?"

"Couldn't we? I'm dog-tired. I'll have to stay up late for the next two nights to finish this paper for Mrs. Carter. And you know what you'll say if she tells you I failed to do an assignment."

Chapman grinned. "I'll cut tennis back to twice a week—the same for riding lessons. We can do the weights in four days, if we do upper body twice and lower body twice. You'll continue the morning run. No reduction there—you have to maintain a certain level of fitness. Angie, the exercise is necessary to balance the time you spend sitting on your behind, and to keep your weight down. You know that you have to have both strength training and aerobic activity. Still, those changes should give you an additional five or six hours a week."

"Thanks. Really!" Angie was afraid that she sounded sarcastic. "This term paper is killing me. And I've let other stuff slide to get it done." Angie finished her meal and pushed back onto the chaise lounge.

"If you think this is bad, just wait until next year. College is bound to be worse."

"Gee, thanks for all your kind words, Billie."

"Anything else I can do?" Chapman stood to take the tray back to the kitchen.

"No, ma'am. I'll just keep on keeping on." Angie marched back to the computer.

*   *   *

Angie went to bed at midnight; Chapman had her running at 7:00. Mrs. Carter came at 9:30, and Angie skipped down the stairs to the study, dressed in white jeans and a striped tank top. Chapman had instructed her to dress like a typical teenager when Mrs. Carter came, and Janice had allowed her to roam shops which catered to teens long enough to procure appropriate clothing. Mrs. Carter was a fortyish lady who had tired of fighting the battle in the public schools, and an excellent tutor. As a matter of fact, she was perhaps the best teacher Angie had ever had—absolutely no nonsense, and quite well versed in a variety of subject matters. During the year, Angie had learned that she had degrees in modern languages and science, as well as advanced course work in math and history. As she bent over Marc

Avery's desk in the study, Mrs. Carter frowned in concentration while she looked over Angie's Spanish vocabulary exercises and her trig problems, which were kept in notebooks. Afterward, they discussed the two chapters she had read in the ecology book and went over the questions at the end of each chapter. At the end of the session, Mrs. Carter read the fairy tale that Angie had translated into Spanish. She made new assignments and checked on Angie's progress on the term paper. The session ended at 11:45. Angie realized that she'd gotten more out of it than a whole day at Adamsville High.

"When is your next appointment?" Angie asked her, making conversation as Mrs. Carter packed up her things.

"You're it for today. I usually work Monday, Wednesday, and Friday. But your guardian said you were usually tied up on Wednesday, so we moved that session to Thursday for you."

"Yes, sometimes Wednesday is my busiest day. Would you like some lunch before you go?" Angie asked her on impulse.

"Oh, I wouldn't want to impose." Mrs. Carter smiled.

Angie was sure that the offer was unusual. Somehow the world didn't view teachers as real people. "There's no place close, and I know it won't be a problem. Mrs. Bowen cooks for the staff anyway. Let me tell her we'll need an extra plate."

"Well, if you're sure."

Angie left Mrs. Carter in the study and popped into the kitchen. Mrs. B. was, sure enough, fixing up soup and salad. Angie leaned over the cook's wide shoulders and asked if she could invite her tutor to lunch. Since Angie had been assigned to help her from time to time, Mrs. B. had become quite maternal. Angie smiled, sure that she wouldn't refuse.

"Of course you can, honey. You two go to the dining room in about fifteen minutes, and I'll have Janice bring it in."

"Thanks, Mrs. B." Angie squeezed her shoulders with a playful hug and went back to Mrs. Carter. She managed to kill off fifteen minutes by giving her tutor a quick tour of the downstairs of the house. Angie didn't dare take her upstairs to see the steel doors with the big locks, of course. When they finished the tour, Angie took her to the dining room. Janice had already set out crystal goblets of water, along with rolls and butter.

Angie soon realized that the poor lady was just a bit intimidated by the whole scenario—Janice served them only three courses—soup, salad, and dessert. But, Angie was aware that Marc's dining room was an elegant place—even if the lunch menu was light. At the end of the meal, Angie escorted Mrs. Carter to the door and assured her that the term paper would be ready when she came on Friday.

As soon as Mrs. Carter left, Angie made a beeline for the computer. Grinning to herself, she hoped that lunch was good for a few extra points.

*   *   *

Angie was awake, putting the finishing touches on the term paper, when Chapman came to get her for their morning run. She unlocked the door and came in, dressed in her usual knit shorts and tee shirt, the one with *Marines* emblazoned across the chest. Chapman seemed surprised when she saw Angie at the computer.

"I'm glad you're up, Miss Donalson. But I told you, you will run every day but Sunday."

"I know, I know," Angie said, swiveling in her chair. "I'm finished, I think. I'm going to set this to print while we are gone, then I'll be ready in five minutes."

In a couple of minutes, she left the computer and picked up her jogging clothes—just a sports bra, oversized lightweight tee and shorts, as warm as it was—and took them into the bathroom. In five minutes she emerged, tall and slender, with well-rounded breasts and just enough hips to give her slim figure a feminine silhouette. Angie slipped on her running shoes, which were parked near the bench at the foot of the bed, stood, and told Chapman she was ready.

The course, which took them just over four miles, began outside the patio door, went through the flower gardens, beside the stables, and down a path through the woods which they also used for horseback riding. As they jogged, they covered rolling hills and went single file along a bridge that crossed a small creek. The path was lovely, and over time, Angie had discovered that this was indeed a good way to start the day. Her problems vanished as her body struggled to keep up with Chapman. The former Marine set a quick pace, and although she'd been doing this for months, Angie still had trouble keeping up.

Dawn was just breaking when the pair set out; a radiant sun was showing through the morning mist as they climbed the steps back to the patio. Janice had set breakfast on one of the glass-topped tables, and Chapman and Angie ate together.

"So you finished the paper?" Chapman asked as she poured milk over her granola.

"Um, yes. I need to do a final proofreading. But it's finished."

"Are you catching up on your other studies?"

"I am a bit behind in the vocabulary and math study books. But since I've already taken the SAT, that isn't a top priority. I still have to watch a video in Spanish and write a movie review. I'm going to try to find time for that this weekend."

"I heard you invited Mrs. Carter to lunch yesterday."

Angie grinned. "Yep. Think it's worth a few points?"

"Can't hurt." Chapman smiled back. "You'll be finished with your classes in just a few weeks. Are you looking forward to that?"

"Sure. I guess. I really will miss Mrs. Carter, though. She's a very good teacher."

"She seems to be. Has Mr. Avery discussed any summer plans with you?"

"Not much. He mentioned that we might go to the beach, but he didn't say when. Has he said anything to you?"

"Nothing specific. He just indicated that we might get some time off."

"That will be good for all of you." Angie pushed back her plate and got another cup of coffee. "I guess it's been a long year."

"Yes. It has. You certainly made it an interesting one." Chapman regarded her over the coffee cup. "I wasn't sure that you remembered."

"One year, as of tomorrow, isn't it?"

"Yes, I think that's right." Chapman looked at her charge, as if Angie should say something profound. "You've learned quite a lot in the past year."

"Yes, ma'am. Including how to be cooperative. You have nothing to worry about." Angie finished the coffee and stood. "I need to go shower and change. Mrs. Carter will be here pretty soon."

"See you at lunch," Chapman said. She rose to get another cup of coffee.

Angie had the feeling that she was still watching her as she went up the stairs to her room.

*   *   *

The session with Mrs. Carter covered many topics in rapid succession, as usual. She left her pupil with only a couple of additional assignments and told her to enjoy the weekend. After lunch, Angie went riding and worked on the assignments. When she finished, Chapman joined her, and they went down to meet Marc at the helipad.

He jumped from the helicopter as if he was glad to leave the burdens of his workweek behind. He asked Angie about her schoolwork and her other activities. They went upstairs together, and he joined her in her room after he had changed into casual pants and a sports shirt. This was a typical start to a weekend together.

Over time, they had learned more about each other. Marc was driven to make just as big a mark on the electronics business as his father had done. So he often worked long hours and tried to keep up with many aspects of research and development. His travel made his job seem even more demanding. He often related stories about his work, so Angie was becoming more familiar with the issues he dealt with there.

In turn, he had made a real effort to make friends with Angie. At first, she'd only been a bedmate, Angie realized. However, he always made time to talk to her about schoolwork and her activities. Sometimes he suggested movies or books, just to have something in common to talk about. As for Angie, she had mixed emotions regarding him. Despite the passage of time, she could never forget that he'd been behind the kidnapping and those first dark days when she'd been restrained with chains and beaten. He also continued to use her body, not asking, but assuming that she wanted him as much as he seemed to want her. Despite his egotism, he was also the person who provided her extensive wardrobe, saw that she had the best medical care, made sure the staff looked after her every need; he even hired the tutor. Though it was easy to hate him, it was impossible to not be somewhat grateful for all that he'd given her.

As for the bedroom, Marc still visited her most nights when they were together. On the occasions when they traveled, she slept in his room. Chapman had stopped using the ankle chain on her after "Billie's Basic," except the times Marc came for a visit, but since the visit to the Virgin Islands, Chapman had ceased using the restraint. As the months rolled by, Angie had also become more responsive in bed. Although she never initiated lovemaking, she was also not quite the wooden doll that she'd been ten months ago.

Marc often brought her presents, and this weekend was no exception. At dinner, he presented her with a new watch, replacing the simple sport watch that Chapman had provided when she was trying to finish work details by a specific time.

"It's an anniversary of sorts, Angie." His grin was sheepish. "I know that you probably won't view it as something to celebrate, but aren't you better off now than you were a year ago?"

Angie made no comment regarding that, but she did thank him for the watch.

*   *   *

Marc had another present for Angie; waiting in his briefcase was an acceptance letter from a small college, just 40 miles away. A college where his father sat on the board of directors, and one where Angie should be safe and well educated.

Marc used the intercom phone in his room to speak with Danny.

"We're going out to dinner, and I expect we'll need a driver. Bring the BMW to the front. Angie and I'll be down in fifteen minutes."

After a courtesy knock on the connecting door, Marc entered Angie's room. Janice had already left, but her handiwork was in evidence—Angie's black dress was cut low in front, with slits up the sides, a simple, yet sophisticated look. Her upswept hair added height

111

and grace to her carriage, and her flawless makeup enabled her to pass for several years older than she had looked only that morning.

"Ready?" Marc said, his eyes focused appreciatively on his paramour.

"Um, yes, I think so." Angie picked up a beaded black evening bag. She glanced at her left wrist, and he noted that she wore the new watch.

"Our chariot awaits. I've asked Danny to be charioteer." With a gallant gesture, he ushered her out into the hallway.

"Oh. Don't you feel like driving?" Angie's tone was serious.

"I won't, by the time we return." He chuckled, and they descended the stairs together.

Danny exhibited the same skill while driving the BMW that he had with all mechanical devices. As the powerful sedan covered the miles, Marc made an effort to cheer Angie, who seemed to be in a dark mood.

"Do you think Mrs. Carter has done a good job, Angie?"

"The best. I've never had a tutor before, but she's a great teacher. I've learned a lot."

"Good. I've decided to give her a bonus when you finish. What do you think about that?"

"Sounds great. I'm sure she can use the money."

"Angie, when you first came to us," Marc leaned over to caress her cheek, "I told you that if you cooperated that you would have the opportunity to accomplish your goals. Mrs. Carter is part of that, but only the first part."

Marc pulled an envelope from his jacket pocket and handed it to her. Puzzled, she pulled it open and read the single page acceptance letter. "Is this… do you mean it? You'll send me to college?"

"Sure. Billie will give you some rules to follow, just as she does at Angelhurst. But if you adhere to the rules, then your education will continue. I'll pay your every expense. This is a better scholarship than the one you applied for last year, I do assure you."

"I can't believe it. College. Wow! This will be so cool."

Although she wasn't bubbling with enthusiasm, her expression was much more pleasant, he thought. Marc stroked her shoulder, feeling the firm flesh beneath smooth skin.

"You'll be a commuter student, so you can continue your duties at Angelhurst."

Some of her elation evaporated. "So nothing there will change?"

"Is it so onerous?"

Unwilling to anger him and yet unwilling to acquiesce, Angie fell silent.

After a while, Danny broke the silence. "Did you decide where I'm to take you, Mr. Avery?"

"Yes. We'll dine at the Equestrian Estates. Then we'll head over to the Classic Theatre on Broad Street for a play. While we're at the theatre, I want you to pick up a few items."

Marc handed him a list, and gave directions to the restaurant, which did indeed have an equine theme, from a few old carriages on the grounds to horse pictures scattered on the walls. Even the wallpaper in the restroom had a horsy border, Angie noted.

Blessing Billie's exercise program, Angie was able to dine without regard for the calorie count. When the check was paid, Marc escorted her to the car, and Danny piloted them to the playhouse. Emerging from the theatre two hours later, they made themselves comfortable in the back seat of the BMW.

"Here you are, Mr. Avery," Danny said, handing back a chilled bottle of champagne and two glasses.

"It's a night to celebrate," Marc reminded Angie and handed her a glass filled with the sparkling wine. By the time they climbed the stairs, she was too inebriated to spend any time brooding about the day she had lost her old life. Marc made love to her, and she responded with more passion than usual. Indeed, Angie seemed to be enjoying her gift horse.

*   *   *

Angie didn't have to run on Sunday. Chapman had started taking off most weekends, which meant that Angie didn't have a partner anyway, since Danny was also off on Sunday. Marc often joined her in other activities, but the early morning run was one that didn't appeal to him. Usually, Janice brought them a breakfast tray, and the pair had a leisurely breakfast while they read the Sunday paper.

The morning after her "anniversary," Angie awakened later than usual. She supposed the lack of sleep early in the week was catching up with her. Marc was already out of the bed, and she smelled coffee. When Marc noticed that she was awake, he came back to lie beside her. He caressed her body—legs, stomach, and breasts. Angie lay still, enjoying his gentle touch. Sighing, she curled up, drawing her legs up against her stomach.

"Something wrong, Angie?" Marc's voice was filled with concern.

"I don't think so. I'm just tired. I had a paper due to Mrs. Carter on Friday, and I spent too many hours on it. I have to catch up on some more school—and sleep."

"Billie told me she'd cut back your activities so you could have more time on your school work."

"Yes, she did. But I'm still exhausted. It should be better from this point on, but I had a rough week." Angie stretched out and yawned.

"You might have a hang-over." Marc grinned. "You aren't used to alcohol."

"Perhaps that's a part of it," she admitted.

"Are you excited about college? It's a good school. You should learn a great deal—and have fun doing it."

"Yes, sure. Going to college was what I always wanted. It's what got me into this—" Angie sat up and gestured to the room, "in the first place. I'll bet Coach Doyle would never have given me that scholarship application if he'd known something like this could happen."

"I guess not." Marc changed the subject. "It's raining. We'll have an inside day, looks like."

Angie got up and went into the bathroom. She took a shower and was dressed only in a robe when she came out again. After a while, she had grown accustomed to being undressed in front of Marc. Angie got coffee and a Danish and started accumulating a group of department store sales flyers from the paper.

The two of them spent most of the day together, just reading and talking in the morning; then they went to the exercise room for the afternoon—there was a treadmill wide enough for two there, so they ran together. After that, Angie did her upper body workout, with

Marc spotting for her. Later, they watched a movie and dined together before his helicopter came and took him back to the city.

*　　*　　*

Marc took Chapman with him when he went to the learning center for his "parent conference" with Mrs. Carter. They met in a small conference room. Mrs. Carter produced a grade report and printouts of Angie's scores on the SAT.

"I hope you're as pleased as I am, Mr. Avery. Angie is a wonderful student. I taught AP classes for a number of years, and Angie ranks among the best I ever taught. Her term paper in ecology was especially impressive."

"She worked very hard on that," Chapman pointed out.

"It showed. I know she had exceptional resources; your library is good, and she had access to the Internet, but the writing was her own."

"What about college?" Marc asked. "She's been accepted."

"Mr. Avery, I should think any college would be happy to have her. I understand that she was being home schooled due to emotional problems resulting from her father's death, but I saw none. I've found her to be even tempered and hard working. I think you and Ms. Chapman have been most supportive of Angie and her education."

"Thank you for your efforts as well. Billie and Angie have told me how dedicated you are to your work." Marc concluded the conference with a smile.

*　　*　　*

Angie finished her lessons with Mrs. Carter, who seemed quite happy with the bonus check from Marc. Angie was, as she had speculated, sorry to end the relationship, for the teacher had been her steady companion for almost a year. Also, because Mrs. Carter had no knowledge of Angie's peculiar circumstances, she could pretend, for a few hours a week, to be a normal teenager again. But doing all that Mrs. Carter required and all that Chapman insisted she do had been a strain, so Angie was ready to enjoy a lighter schedule. However,

Chapman increased her sessions in tennis and swimming, and she added another session with Mrs. Bowen each week. Chapman had decided that Angie needed to learn more about cooking, especially more sophisticated dishes. Angie had known how to do some cooking prior to her abduction, but as Chapman pointed out, Mr. Avery's expectations had always been a bit beyond macaroni and cheese! Angie also volunteered to help Danny a couple of days a week with the yard work. Despite the activity load, she had found that she really did enjoy gardening, and she wanted to learn more. Once again, Angie was busy to the point of exhaustion.

Chapter 9

Angie began her first college courses in August. This situation created a whole new set of security headaches for Chapman to solve. She couldn't turn Angie loose just yet, so she compromised by having Janice drive to the school and audit the classes that Angie took. The plan resulted in the loss of Janice's work for several hours a week, but having Angie unsupervised seemed much too risky, so Chapman sacrificed her service for the time that Angie was gone from the estate.

Many aspects of college pleased Angie, but being around people her own age was what she relished most. She hadn't realized how much she missed even casual conversation with peers. Angie's social life was somewhat constrained by Janice's tendency to stick too close to her, but it seemed a small price for being allowed to attend classes at the college, instead of at home.

Since the day of her abduction, Angie had been somewhat reserved with her captors, and they had treated her in a formal manner, starting with calling her "Miss Donalson." Indeed, Janice had found it difficult to switch to "Angie" at school; she had slipped up and spoken formally more than once. Since the professors at this school tended to call students Mr. So and So and Miss So and So, the others took her slip-ups as a joke of sorts.

As Janice drove Angie to class each day, they had more time for conversation. One day, Angie asked Janice the inevitable question, "So, how did you wind up helping Billie with this kidnapping thing?"

Janice blanched, but kept her eyes on the road and her hands on the wheel. "Miss Donalson, I don't think we're supposed to talk about that."

"Of course, it's up to you. But Billie did tell me a little bit. I know about the Averys helping her brother. And Billie told me that you were just as loyal to Mr. Avery. Danny, too. But she didn't say why."

"When did she tell you?"

"I don't remember. Before "Billie's Basic." Early on, in fact. I asked, and she said there were things she couldn't tell me—but that she could tell me some. At the time, I was just curious. I think that

Billie had a different reason. She wanted me to think that no one would help me escape."

"Ah." Janice nodded, slowing down for a turn. "That makes sense, I guess."

"Look, Janice. It's been almost two years. You can trust me. Enough to explain why someone like you is wasting time watching me go to college."

Janice grinned. "Okay, I'll try. I grew up not too far from one of the Avery manufacturing facilities. My dad worked for it at one time, although he's with another company now. We weren't rich, like the Averys, but we were comfortable. Mom didn't work—she did volunteer stuff and went to the country club. As a matter of fact, I worked one summer at the club. That's where I learned how to serve a meal." She laughed, a bit rueful.

"I ran around with some kids who had money and lots of free time. Some of them were into drinking and drugs, and after a while I did those things, too. Just to fit in, at first. What they call peer pressure, I guess. And I got hooked." Janice swallowed. She seemed to have trouble with the story.

"Go on."

"My folks figured it out. They say the parents are the last to know, but mine must have been smarter or something. Anyway, they got mad; then they got me some treatment. I got out of rehab and did okay for a while, but later, I went back to my friends and back to the drugs. I was more careful, so I hid it longer, but my folks found out. They were even madder, yet they still loved me. So it was back to rehab."

"But, you're clean now. I can't see Billie putting up with anything like that," Angie observed.

"Yes, you're right about that. During the second rehab—I was in my junior year of college when that happened—I realized that I couldn't stay clean and be near my friends. I told my dad that, flat out. He helped me look for a job which would get me out of that lifestyle. Mr. Avery had just bought the estate, and they were looking for a live-in staff. After I met Billie, I knew that one, she would never let me get involved with drugs again, and two, that she really needed me. Can you imagine Billie in charge of decor for the house? Camouflage curtains or something!"

Both of them laughed.

"Did you know about me when you took the job?"

"No, I don't think I would've taken it. We worked for several months, just getting the place up and running. After we were about finished with that, Billie told Danny and me what the real job was going to be. We were both, well, shocked. But she let us see the tape at the scholarship interview. Then we went to see your home, and we even saw you walking home from school one day."

Janice glanced away from the road, to Angie's face.

"Please don't take this the wrong way, but you looked like you would benefit from what we could provide. Billie made a good case for it, anyway. I knew, from that moment, that I had been hired to help you fit in. You saw me as the maid, but I was and am a teacher—of sorts. I'm paid quite well for a domestic, and I can keep most of the money, because I have only a few expenses."

Angie chuckled. "When y'all first took me, I remember trying to figure you out. I mean, you obviously had too much education to be serving food on trays and doing the housecleaning. It seemed such a waste."

"If I can stay out of trouble, I'll dress like Billie and vacuum the carpet. I don't care." Janice spoke with determination. "Besides, your classes are a good refresher. Maybe I'll finish my degree when we get you through. But I'll work for Mr. Avery and Billie as long as they'll have me."

*　　*　　*

Janice learned quite a lot during this time as well, and not just in the classes. Angie was a good student and quickly stood out as one of the brightest and most articulate. She also learned that Angie could attract a crowd of boys without effort. Of course, Angie had been nice looking when they had first taken her, but in the eighteen months she'd been with them, she had become much more elegant and poised. Mrs. Carter had polished her grammar, and Janice had taught her how to look and act, so the unaffected country girl had become a bit of a sophisticate. This mature self-confidence sometimes caused the crowd to close in around her.

Had it been allowed, Angie could have had any number of dates, but as instructed, she told any and all that she was seeing someone. So Angie attended the day classes, then she returned home to Angelhurst to study and do assignments. Since she was only auditing, Janice did none of the work and the professors didn't call upon her to answer questions. But Janice enjoyed Angie's freshman required courses, all the same.

*   *   *

In late February, Marc asked Chapman what he should get Angie for her birthday. Chapman frowned and shook her head. "I can't think of a thing. Angie has most anything she needs. And she has never been one to beg. I don't know."

Marc asked Janice, who also seemed at a loss.

"Why don't you ask Angie?" Janice suggested.

"What if she says she wants to go home?"

"I don't think she wants that. Not anymore," Janice assured him.

Marc knocked on the connecting door and entered Angie's room. She was dressed casually, in dark trousers and a white fisherman knit sweater, sitting at her computer, obviously working on an assignment. She looked up, eyebrows arched to ask an unspoken question. Marc stood behind her and swiveled her chair to face him. "This is the end of your teen years," Marc said, his tone mockingly serious. "What would you like to do to celebrate?"

Angie scowled at him, also mocking. "Do you think I'll be old next year?"

"Well, I don't know. We might have to get you a rocking chair when you turn twenty."

"If I'm such a kid, take me to Disney World!"

"You're kidding, right?"

"No, I'm not. We had to give a speech entitled 'my most embarrassing moment' at school, and one girl told about losing her lunch on a ride at Disney. We didn't get to do things like that, when I was growing up. So, take your nineteen-year-old to Disney."

Marc peered at her upturned face. Although she was amused, she also seemed sincere. "Okay, you got it. I'll have Janice make the arrangements. But you'll have to make up any schoolwork you miss."

Marc's staff was as efficient as ever. Janice made reservations for a long weekend at a resort on the grounds. Chapman drove Angie to a community airport on Thursday afternoon, where Marc met her, in a small hired jet. They flew to Florida, and the pair visited theme parks on Friday and Saturday. Angie found the parks fascinating, never having seen so much packed into one place.

After a more leisurely Sunday morning, the same jet took them to Charleston, Marc's weekday home, and Angie boarded a helicopter for the flight back to Tennessee. It had been a fun weekend, and Angie returned to Angelhurst exhausted, but happy.

On Sunday evening, Chapman met Angie at the helipad and helped her with her luggage. "Did you have good time, Miss D.?" she inquired as they went up the stairs.

"Yes, I did. We did some fun things. I'm tired, but it was great."

"Glad to hear it. Janice wanted me to remind you that you have to read the third act of *Hamlet* for your lit course."

"Oh, God. I forgot." Angie sighed. "I guess I'll be up late."

"I'll see you at 6:30 for your morning run." Chapman turned to go. "Good night."

"Good night."

*　　　*　　　*

Angie made the dean's list her second semester. Despite having Janice as a chaperone, she enjoyed college. As time went on, she thought less and less about what it would be like to leave Angelhurst and go home to Aunt Claire. The estate became home; her captors became her family. She enjoyed having the material wealth—the state-of-the-art computer, the beautiful wardrobe, the tennis courts, the horses, the pool. Mrs. Bowen prepared her excellent meals, and Janice did her laundry and general cleaning. Chapman kept her busy, but she also allowed the girl some growing room, giving her opportunities to make more decisions on her own.

Pamela J. Dodd

Marc continued seeing her most weekends and took her on trips from time to time. He treated her with great courtesy as long as she didn't refuse him her sexual favors, and she had given in on that long before. Her attitude was just what he had predicted so long ago— living with Marc was a trade for material wealth. Angie came to view the situation as a fair trade. Compared to her life before Marc, she was wealthy and happy. When the second anniversary of her kidnapping came around, Marc once again treated her to a gift and an evening out; this time Angie didn't consider it a bittersweet occasion—it was merely the celebration of her entry into a better way of life.

*   *   *

Angie started her sophomore year without Janice auditing her classes. Instead, one of the staff, usually Danny, drove her to her campus and picked her up after her last class. For the first time, Angie could have gone to campus security, told them her story and been returned to her home. But Angie had been gone for more than two years, and she had no real desire to return to Adamsville to live in the tired little mill village cottage that had been her home. So she leapt from the car to attend her classes and returned to Angelhurst in the evenings.

Chapman still ran with her when the weather was cooperative. When it was too cold or wet, Angie tried to make it up on the treadmill. She still went riding several days a week, sometimes with Chapman or Danny, sometimes alone.

On a cool October Friday afternoon, Angie went to the stable for her ride; Bessie had thrown a shoe, so Danny asked if she wanted one of the other horses. Angie chose Thor, the spirited gelding that Chapman often rode.

"Are you certain that you can handle him?" Danny's tone was doubtful.

"Sure. I've been riding quite a while now. I'll be okay, really."

"Just be careful, Miss. He's a lot more horse than you're used to."

"Will do," she promised. Mounting him, she rode down the forest path. Danny watched her manage him with ease then went back to his work.

Angie found Thor an exhilarating ride. He was faster and more powerful than the mare she usually rode. They had covered quite a bit of ground at a fast clip, then slowed to a prancing walk as they went into the thickest part of the woods, near the back fence. Somewhere, a gun went off—probably a hunter on the property next to Marc's. Bessie would have taken the sound in stride, so Angie didn't anticipate Thor's violent reaction. He leaped, bucking for a couple of strides, nearly unseating her. Then he took off through the trees at a breakneck pace. Angie pulled on the reins, trying to slow him, speaking soothingly to him, but he continued his headlong rush. Instead of taking the next curve, he veered right through the forest, and her left ankle was crushed between his flank and a huge oak tree. Angie yelped and lost her grip on the saddle. Branches clawed at her, and she lost consciousness as she hit the ground.

When she woke, the sun had set and there was no moon, so the only light she saw was generated by the stars. Her left ankle was throbbing; her extremities were cold. Angie looked at her left wrist, but she was wearing the dress watch Marc had given her, rather than the one from Chapman, which had a light. All she saw was darkness. Angie tried to rise, but she heard the bones grind when she put weight on her left foot. She grunted and settled back against a tree.

Later, much later, she heard someone in the brush outside the fence. She called out, "Hello! Who's there?"

"Miss Donalson?"

"Yes. Danny, is that you?"

"Yes. We were checking the perimeter. When Thor came back without a rider, we rode through the paths, calling for you. We didn't find you, so Billie split us up, looking for a break in the fence."

Angie grinned, thinking that escape had been the last thing on her mind.

"I guess I hit my head. I came to a while ago, but I can't get up—my ankle hurts."

"I have a radio. I'll get Billie to drive the Explorer as close as she can to your position." His voice sounded troubled. "It may be a while. You're pretty far off the path."

"I understand." There was a rueful tone in her chuckle. "I won't say take your time, it hurts too bad. But I'm not going anywhere. That's for sure."

Their arrival did indeed take a while. Angie first saw lights, then she heard her rescuers coming through the trees, each bearing a flashlight. Angie called out; Chapman found her first, then Marc was there. They had rigged up a makeshift stretcher, but before they moved her, Chapman checked her over.

"How are you injured, Angie?" she asked, checking over her body with skillful, thorough hands.

"Left ankle. I can't put any weight on it. And I must have hit my head on the way down; I don't know how long I was out. I think that's okay now."

"Anything else?"

"No."

Chapman got to the left ankle, and the girl screeched with pain. Chapman focused her flashlight on that leg. "Mr. Avery, she has swelled against that boot. It needs to come off. I have a knife, but this is going to hurt her."

"Billie, no!"

"Angie, it's a long way to a hospital from here. We need to restore your circulation. I'm cutting it off." Chapman straddled her legs. "Mr. Avery, hold her hands."

"No, please, no." Angie remembered saying that. Then Chapman started cutting; Angie screamed, then she slumped over, still.

*   *   *

Angie was in the back of the Explorer when she woke again. Marc was holding her; the seat was folded down, and she lay at an angle. Every bump was agony. Angie cried and held onto him for comfort. He stroked her hair and whispered encouragement. Finally, Chapman got them there—then there was a long wait for an orthopedic surgeon to come perform surgery on the girl's crushed ankle. Angie saw Marc and Chapman standing in the hallway as they took her into the operating room.

Chapman was at her side when she woke up. The hospital was small, and the nurses let her come back into the recovery area as soon as Angie was remotely alert. Chapman held her hand and told her that Marc had stayed into the night, but that she'd gotten Danny to come take him back to Angelhurst. In the few minutes she had, Chapman assured Angie that the school situation would be handled, and that someone would be with her each evening until she could return home.

*   *   *

Angie had a cast from the thigh down to start with, which made many activities rather difficult. She spent three days in the hospital, and it was a week before she made any attempt to go to class. Janice had gone to school and made arrangements to have the lectures tape recorded, and she picked up Angie's assignments. Marc sent a basket of mixed flowers, but didn't return until the following weekend. Chapman and Danny split up visiting and helping her learn to maneuver on crutches. They also rented a wheelchair for her to use until she got a shorter cast. Janice moved her personal items to a downstairs guestroom for the duration of her confinement. The cast was cut down after three weeks so that she could bend at the knee. After eight weeks, Angie graduated to a brace—which made a nice Christmas present.

During the recovery period, most of her athletic activities ceased. Chapman took her to the weight room, and she did upper body exercises and a few strength exercises with her good leg. Marc suggested that she spend some of her free time in the kitchen with Mrs. Bowen, who could keep her busy while she remained seated. He also hired an art instructor who came twice a week to help her learn something about drawing and painting. Art was pretty much a bust—Angie admitted to Marc that she had no talent. However, Mrs. Bowen continued to find her an apt pupil as they progressed through the finer aspects of culinary artistry.

In January, Angie began physical therapy. Before long, she started back on the treadmill. By spring she was able to jog again, although she had a great deal of trouble keeping up with Chapman. Tennis was also difficult; the quick changes of direction stressed her weak ankle. As soon as it was warm enough, swimming became her chief exercise, and Chapman insisted that she swim every day unless the weather was totally uncooperative. Angie didn't resume riding until summer, and she stopped going alone. As her sophomore year ended, once again Angie made excellent grades and had settled on a degree in instructional technology.

Also, earlier that spring, Marc asked her if she would like to start driving again.

"Actually, I still had only a learner's permit when... when you had me brought here," she confessed. "And that was a long time ago. I'd have to learn again."

"Billie could teach you, or Danny. Would you like to learn to drive?"

Angie was surprised that he trusted her that much. "Yes, I would."

So in addition to her other duties, Chapman took her to the garage, allowing her to practice driving for a few evenings. After a few weeks, they took short trips outside the gates. By her twentieth birthday, Angie was ready to take her driver's test. So, four years behind most folks, she got a driver's license. On that same day, Marc gave her a birthday present—a Mazda Miata convertible. Red, of course.

"I think it clashes with her hair, Mr. Avery," Danny kidded the young woman as he put it into the garage.

"We could change it," Chapman suggested.

"No, I love it," Angie protested. "Don't you dare change anything about that car."

"I meant your hair," Chapman said, clapping her on the shoulder. "I saw a gal with green hair the last time we went to the mall."

"I don't think so!" Marc chimed in.

Angie had requested to celebrate her birthday at home this year, a sort of family picnic with the whole staff eating barbecue together on the wide patio at the back of the house. As they finished the meal, Janice began picking up, and Angie rose to help her.

"No, Angie." Janice stopped her. "It's your birthday, and Mr. Avery is here. You need to go on in and enjoy yourselves. Besides, he gave us the weekend off."

"Everyone?" Angie whispered. She couldn't recall a time when Chapman didn't have someone on the property to serve as her keeper.

"Uh huh. We'll take care of this, because in the morning, you are on your own. I doubt that Mr. Avery knows much about housekeeping."

Nodding, Angie turned toward the stairs, grasping Marc's hand.

"Ready to pay me back for your birthday present?" he asked, surprised at her gesture of affection.

"I'll try to think of something," she replied and tugged him up the steps.

*   *   *

Just the two of them sharing the huge house seemed strange. They ate at the small table in the kitchen, and they rode the horses and cared for them. Angie found that, in many ways, she was the leader in this endeavor. She was surprised that Marc didn't know much about running his own estate. During her days in "Billie's Basic," Angie had learned about most of the real work of running Angelhurst.

They also took several drives in Angie's new car though it was simple and basic compared to the BMW that Marc drove, she was thrilled, nevertheless. Marc promised her that she would be allowed to drive herself to school after a few weeks. "We'll let Jan ride with you for a while to see if you're doing okay," Marc told her.

Marc had a car phone installed, and he assured Angie that this would add to her freedom. He promised that she'd be given chances to drive herself to town to shop. "I can even call and have you drive down to meet me in Charleston." Marc grinned.

"That's a long way," Angie commented. "I doubt that Billie would allow that."

Marc let her drive the Miata to class on Monday; then he took the wheel and drove back to town while she attended her Monday classes. Marc picked her up, letting her drive home as well. Angie cooked lasagna for dinner, while Marc looked after the horses. Chapman and the staff returned late that evening, and Marc left for Charleston. Angie found that she had enjoyed this birthday more than any in recent memory—not just the fabulous gift, but also leaving her teen years behind.

*   *   *

Chapman watched Angie drive off in the little red convertible, alone. She was astonished at how much the girl had matured in the three years that she'd been supervising her. Shaking her head, she found it almost impossible to remember the frightened seventeen-year-old that she'd brought up from Georgia. This Angela Donalson was finishing her sophomore year in college, an honor student. No longer a back country teenager, she was a woman, poised, polished, with a cultured voice, fashionable clothes and hair, and manners that could make her comfortable most anywhere.

The innocent girl who had been awed by the dining room at Angelhurst and astonished by a shopping spree had now been to fine restaurants, the theatre, and the symphony. She had a wardrobe which included attire for any occasion, a new car, even a Coach handbag and a platinum credit card in her wallet. The young lady who had ordered that her car be brought to the door and who drove down the pebbled drive toward the gate was, at least in part, what Chapman had made her. Chapman was proud of Angie —very proud.

While she had gained a veneer of sophistication, she still possessed the core values which had been instilled by her working class father and aunt. Angie worked hard at school, making top grades, even though she had no need for a scholarship. She exercised and did occasional chores around the house without complaint. Chapman admired the way she dealt with her sexual obligations as well. Without any protest, Angie took care of Marc's needs, although she didn't appear to be in love with him. Chapman was quite pleased with the way everything had worked out. There had been some rough spots, and many doubts, but it looked as if the project had become successful.

Chapter 10

Driving her own car to school—it seemed too good to be true. Of course, Angie had to call Angelhurst when she reached campus. Each day she was to call when she got in the car to return home. Everyone knew that it took fifty minutes to make the trip, so she was monitored on either end. It was not unusual for the phone to ring while she was en route, and Chapman would ask for the nearest landmark. In a way she was free, in a way not—Marc's staff watched her closely.

Still, it was quite an improvement. Angie had to inform Chapman if she had extra time obligations—and with the photography class she was taking, she seemed to be spending inordinate amounts of time beyond what was normal. Angie had to fight for darkroom time, and she had to travel looking for something new to photograph. Old Dr. Osborne had been teaching the course for years, insisting that everything be done "the way it used to be." It took some creativity to find a subject that he hadn't seen before.

Her lab partner was a junior named Justin. He was very tall, about six feet four, and had black hair that curled around his head. With his classic good looks, he could have been mistaken for a Greek god in another millennia. Although he was shy at first, the hours in the darkroom and in the mat cutting and mounting lab led to friendship. Angie supposed that it was a bit like the camaraderie common in the military. Toward the end of the semester, it seemed that they were going through photography hell together.

Angie had a beautiful Canon camera that Marc had bought for her when she signed up for the course. Justin had an old Minolta, and he was having a difficult time with it. The light meter seemed to be out of adjustment. After a grueling class one day, they decided to take some pictures together at a state park that Justin had visited, about a half-hour drive from campus. They decided that they would both use the Canon, every button, and every built-in program, hoping for something that would impress Dr. Osborne. Angie called Chapman, telling her that she would be working late, and they took off in the convertible for the park.

There were some children playing on a playground, a waterfall, and a few rustic buildings. The park seemed to be a good place for pictures, so each of them shot a roll of film with the Canon. After they finished the second roll, they got back into the car. Justin asked if he could drive, so Angie took the passenger's seat. Justin drove to an overlook and pulled off the road.

They sat and talked about school, and Angie enjoyed his company. As the sun became lower in the sky, she realized that she had lost track of the time. Angie knew that she should report in. Chapman, was going to be worried, or mad, or both. As he took her face in his hands, Justin was telling her beautiful she was, and she knew that he was going to kiss her. Angie was no longer thinking about Ms. Chapman.

In a haze that seemed like a dream sequence in a movie, Angie saw Chapman out of the corner of her eye. She was dressed in denim, just like the day she had abducted Angie. Justin grunted and slumped over the steering wheel as Chapman hit him in the back of the neck with the stun gun. A cloth sack came down over his head, and she pulled him out of the car and pushed him to the ground. Angie was sure that Justin never saw his attacker.

Angie, too, cried out, but in protest, "What the hell do you think you're doing?"

Danny was beside her, clicking a handcuff on her right wrist. Twisting her arm behind her, he grabbed her left arm, and she was restrained. He dragged her to the Explorer and threw her into the backseat, slamming the door. Chapman was already climbing into the front—she drove the Explorer and Danny drove the Mazda. Angie looked for Justin, but he must have been left behind. The whole incident had taken less than two minutes, and there were no witnesses.

"Listen. You have this all wrong. I didn't do anything with him. He didn't do anything with me. You shouldn't have hurt him, and you can't just leave him."

"Lover boy will be fine in a few minutes. Danny will call the park rangers from a pay phone just outside the park gates, to tell them where he is. It was a lover's triangle, and your new boyfriend got decked."

"It was assault, and you're going to be arrested." Angie was struggling to keep from sliding all over the leather seat. Her hands were behind her, keeping her from sitting back in the seat properly, and the road though the park was curvy and steep.

"Lover boy didn't see anything but his red-headed girlfriend—and she just disappeared. There were no witnesses and no real evidence. Just his word that *someone* did *something* to him. He isn't too sure what it was."

"Billie—why did you do that? We just came to take pictures."

"I didn't see any camera. For the past month, you've needed more and more time. This evening, your car was off the scope. It took us a while, but we tracked you here. Danny and I had been watching you for the last few minutes, from another overlook. And you are right, nothing happened. But if we hadn't come, something would've happened."

"We were just talking." Angie spoke the truth. She also knew that Chapman was right about where the evening was headed. Part of her did feel guilty. Not about having a romantic interlude, but about Justin's being assaulted. Angie just never thought that she was being monitored that closely.

"You knew the rules. No dating. No socializing with the opposite sex. Your instructions were quite clear."

"It wasn't a date. We came to take pictures. We did take them, two rolls. Okay, we did talk quite a bit afterward. I admit, I lost track of the time. But, I swear, Ms. Chapman, we did nothing wrong." Angie was becoming angrier with each passing minute.

"You broke the rules. It's as simple as that."

Angie sat as rigidly as she could. She wondered what would happen when they got home, but she didn't want to grovel. Angie had explained enough. Anything more would seem defensive, and she didn't want that. So she sat, silent, as Chapman covered the miles back to Angelhurst. The ride was a long one. Angie hadn't known how tired she was until Chapman dragged her out of the truck and into the house.

Janice opened the door and raised her eyebrows as she took in the scowl on Chapman's face, and the handcuffs. Angie was escorted to the detention cell, which she hadn't entered in at least two years.

Hearing the door slam behind her, she sat down on the bunk and hoped that someone would have enough sense, or compassion, to come back and unlock the handcuffs. Her wrists were already chafed and beginning to swell.

Although it was a bit of a wait, eventually Janice brought a sandwich and an apple, and she unlocked the cuffs so that Angie could eat. Janice returned a little later with clean bedding and told her to undress. Angie took off the lightweight pants and embroidered knit shirt that she had put on that morning, an eternity ago. She stood in bra and underpants, looking puzzled.

"Everything off, Miss Donalson. Billie said to take everything." Janice seemed to find her task difficult.

Angie complied, removing her underwear. She had enough experience with Chapman to know that she might as well cooperate. They no doubt had that riding crop stored somewhere close by.

"Janice, I need to go to class tomorrow. The end of the semester is near. I cannot bear to think that I have spent all these months for nothing. Please. Talk some sense into Billie."

"I'll mention it, Miss. But I'm sure Billie is attempting to contact Mr. Avery. It'll be his decision, I would think."

"You know, better than anyone else here, how important this is to me. And how difficult it would be to make up the time. Talk to them."

"I'll try." Janice folded her clothes into a neat bundle, not really looking at the girl, no doubt trying to avoid embarrassing her. "I guess it won't be easy, but do your best to get some sleep."

"Yes, I have a lot to think about." Angie's voice was bitter.

"Good night, Miss Donalson."

There was no response.

*   *   *

Chapman was still angry when she talked to Marc. Despite her indignation, she had not lost all of her objectivity. She relayed what she and Danny observed, and Angie's explanation, to her boss. Since Janice had stressed the problems associated with holding Angie out of school, she brought that up for discussion, also.

While Marc wasn't happy about the incident, he wasn't as angry as Chapman was. He pointed out that Angie was an attractive girl, and there was probably some truth in her story. Chuckling, he told Chapman that when he was a college student, he might have tried to capitalize on being in a park with a beautiful girl, whether or not they were there to take pictures. For once, Marc's instructions were tempered with sympathy.

"Billie, we've handled an extended absence from school before. Angie had to miss a week's worth of classes when she broke her ankle. Have Janice go over and set up something similar. Tell them that Angie had another riding accident and that we're dealing with a head injury. Explain that she has to be kept under observation. We'll let her return in a few days to finish up and take the exams, but with an escort—for health reasons, of course. It's not too unusual to have seizures after a head injury. That will explain the need for an escort. She can finish the semester, then it will be summer break, and we can keep Angie at home for a while."

"I should be able to arrange all that," Chapman agreed. "What do you want me to do right now?"

"You didn't see her *doing* anything. I'm not happy that she got herself into a compromising situation, but she's a good-looking girl who's inexperienced in some respects. It's important to keep her away from this classmate. But I'm not going to have you inflict some disproportionate punishment. Put that out of your mind. She can remain in the detention cell through this weekend, and she can wear the army clothes, if that suits you. You can have her do some work details, just to keep her busy, *but no real punishment.*"

"She's not seventeen anymore. I seriously doubt that the training will work the way it did before," Chapman observed.

"I'm not talking about training. Just keep her busy until I have time to talk to her. I can't be there until Sunday. You can let her go back to class early next week. By then she'll have so much to do finishing up the semester that you should have no problems. Ride herd on her, and we'll get through this. She is to be escorted at all times. I know it's a strain on you and your personnel, but it is only two and a half weeks." Marc sounded reassuring.

"Right, sir. I'll have it arranged." Chapman terse voice did little to hide her unhappiness.

"Billie, are you sure that we won't have any, uh, legal problems?"

"I think the operation was clean. Especially considering the lack of preparation." Chapman sounded confident.

"Okay. Go see about our young lady—when you've calmed down."

"I'll wait until morning. She's secure."

*   *   *

Chapman didn't knock when she opened the door to the detention room—she strode in with Angie's uniform, neatly folded, and handed it to her.

"It's 5:45. I want you out the door at 5:55."

Angie yawned and stretched, but didn't look surprised. She got out from under the blanket, used the facilities and dressed on the double. Her hair was short enough to need no restraint, so a quick few passes with a comb, and she was ready.

Four miles later, but without conversation, Angie and Chapman climbed the steps to the patio. Breakfast was waiting—just cereal, toast, and coffee. They helped themselves and sat opposite each other at one of the glass-topped tables.

Angie regarded her keeper, reluctant to begin. "All right, Ms. Chapman. What's on my agenda? I take it from your choice of attire that I'm not going to class."

"That's right. You had another riding accident. Hit your head falling off, so you won't be able to return to class for a few days."

"What *will* I be doing—while I'm 'incapacitated'?"

"Morning detail, cut the grass on the upper side of the stable, then down the drive. Weed the flowerbed next to the stable and the one next to the garage. Danny will supervise." Chapman's voice was ambivalent, not reflecting her real emotions. "This afternoon, Mrs. Bowen is preparing for a party on Sunday and needs your help with some sort of appetizers. I can't remember what she called them, but it's something to prepare today and cook Sunday. You will assist her.

You also need to do upper body today; we'll take care of that when you finish in the kitchen."

"Why'd you have Janice take my clothes last night?"

"Because you don't like it, and I was pissed at you. Fortunately for you, Mr. Avery isn't as upset as I am."

"So 'Billie's Basic' is just temporary." Angie tried to keep from sounding too hopeful.

"Depends. Mr. Avery says you can finish this semester, with some restrictions, of course. If you're cooperative, then this may end it. If not, we have all summer."

"If we go all summer, I hope you'll get me some bigger shorts. These are too tight." Angie ran her finger around her waistband.

"Getting fat in your old age?" Chapman almost sounded like her old self.

"Could be. I've left my teens behind." For once, Angie sounded wistful.

"Wait until you hit your forties... it'll get worse."

Angie was shocked by the revelation. Chapman would pass for mid thirties, easy. "You're not forty. No way."

"No, I'm forty-two." Chapman was matter of fact.

Angie, having finished her breakfast, stood. "Ten minutes in the hall bathroom, right?"

"Right. I'll walk you down to Danny."

"Just don't chain me up, and I'll cooperate," Angie promised, hoping to avoid any more bouts with handcuffs.

"You'll cooperate anyway," Chapman said with iron in her voice.

*　　*　　*

Angie hadn't realized how out of shape she had become. She was pouring sweat after she cut the grass, and the situation didn't get much better when she weeded the flowers. Angie went to the patio for lunch, and Chapman grinned when she saw her charge's dripping face and sweat-stained clothing. Chapman didn't comment until Angie had finished eating, then she suggested that Angie shower and change before she reported to Mrs. Bowen. Janice met her with another uniform in her room, so she was a bit more presentable when she went to work on the party stuff.

By 5:30, Angie was exhausted. She sat with a sandwich and some pretzels in the detention cell. Angie ate sitting on the bunk. Afterward, she slid the tray through the gap in the door and lay down. For a while she slept, then she got up and paced the floor, knowing that she might be observed. For once, she didn't care. She knew the staff well, and they knew her.

Angie grew tired of pacing and returned to the bunk, sure that she'd be up early.

Saturday was much the same. Different work details, but much the same otherwise. Sunday, she got a regular breakfast tray and some reading material, but she was still held in the cell. Angie was sitting on the bunk, still dressed in camo, reading the Sunday magazine of the paper when Marc opened the door.

"Hi, Angie."

"Hello, Marc. Did you come for visitor's day?"

"Yes. Had to leave the saw and file at the desk, though."

"Darn."

Marc sat down on the bunk, his navy blue trousers creased sharply, his cream colored polo shirt clinging to his muscular arms in a way that made Angie long to have those arms around her. His dark blonde hair seemed almost brown in the dim light, but it was well groomed, and he smelled musky and masculine. Angie felt awful, dressed as she was. Her clothes were old and worn, and a little tight—she really had gained weight. Moving away as far away from him as she could, she realized that she hadn't had a shower since Saturday afternoon.

"Did you want to talk about what happened?"

"Nope. I imagine that Billie told you. At least from her perspective. I didn't even kiss that guy. Yes, I let him use my camera and drive my car. We spent a great deal of time together. I do feel guilty for getting Justin into that situation—I feel terrible about it. I don't feel bad about anything else, though."

"The young man is fine. A park ranger picked him up. They believe that your jealous boyfriend assaulted him. No charges were levied against him. No charges are pending against the unknown assailant, either. It seems the unfortunate young man cannot identify his attacker and didn't want to reveal the identity of the young lady. Nothing to worry about."

"What do I say to him when I go back to school? Sorry about nearly getting you electrocuted?" Angie made no effort to keep the sarcasm out of her voice.

"I don't think it will be an issue. Your professors have been told that you've had a couple of seizures following a head injury which you got falling off a horse. Janice has arranged for you to do your labs independently—with someone to look after you in case you have more seizures. Janice will also be with you during class. I doubt that this young man will want to have a heart to heart with her standing there. Just smile and go about your business."

"When will I have recovered enough to go back to class?"

"Tuesday. If Billie has nothing negative to report."

"Okay. I'll toe the line. At least until I get back to school."

"Angie, you need to toe the line, as you put it, until the end of the semester. I told Billie that if I had a chance to make-out with a good-looking girl like you, I would have tried it. So I can't blame the young man too much. But you're not without some culpability. I won't let you have a relationship with anyone else. You are mine, and mine alone. That's hardly news. Billie has told you the rules. Don't violate them again. I'd hate to revoke any more of your privileges."

He put out a hand to caress her face. When Angie failed to respond to his touch, he removed his hand, sitting back and looking at her, which she found disconcerting. She stared at the floor. After a few minutes, he turned to go.

"I'll see you next weekend. There's a research team party in a few minutes that I'll be hosting. I had hoped to have you on my arm, but that's impossible. I guess you can spend the next few hours remembering what you missed because you didn't know when to say no."

He left, and Angie rose to check the door, which was locked, of course. She plopped down on the bunk, knowing that with the staff busy with the party, she'd be locked up until the last guest left.

*   *   *

137

Angie's afternoon work detail became an evening one—she and Janice had to clean up the mess after the party. And it was quite a mess. Angie picked up linens and dishes from the patio and surrounding grounds. After that, she swept the patio and cleaned the tables. She and Danny stored the extra tables and chairs. She reported to the kitchen, where she washed dishes for over an hour. By then it was late, and they were all quite tired when the kitchen was in reasonable shape. At last Chapman called it quits and escorted her to the cell upstairs.

At 5:45, Angie was up, dressing for her morning jog. She had run a comb through her hair and slipped on the camouflage outfit—ready in less than ten minutes. After three years, the four-mile run wasn't too difficult, so she still had some spring in her step when she climbed the stairs to the patio. Janice had set breakfast there—as was their custom in warm weather.

Chapman seemed in a better mood. They had a civil conversation as they discussed the tasks of the day and the details of Angie's return to school on Tuesday. Janice had reminded Chapman that Angie was largely unused to physical work, so Danny gave her an easy task, and he had her take breaks twice during the morning. After lunch, she did some mopping and vacuuming in the lower floor of the house, since the staff was still cleaning up from the party. Finally, Angie was allowed to return to her room and Janice brought the tapes of her professor's lectures and the reading assignments.

At first, Angie was overwhelmed by it all. Thinking it over, she divided and prioritized the tasks, then tackled them in order. She remembered that there would be quite a bit of time in the car, since she wouldn't be allowed to drive. After an intense evening, Angie went to bed at 11:30, her alarm set for 6:00, knowing that Chapman would make her run regardless of what else she had to do.

Just as Marc had predicted, Justin did nothing more than greet her, because Janice was sitting close by. At the beginning of class, Angie fielded a couple of inquiries regarding her health, and the class progressed as usual. Afterward, Angie gathered up her books and laptop and stuffed them into her backpack. Janice stuck right with her as Angie went to the professor's office to discuss her make-up work.

A week later, Angie was back on track, having spent almost all day Saturday in the darkroom... with special dispensation from the professor, and an escort into the building by campus security. As Janice drove home, Angie went to sleep in the car.

"Wake up, sleeping beauty, we're home." Janice nudged her charge as she steered the Explorer up to the front door.

"Um... sorry, Janice. I'm tired." Angie stirred and sat up, still groggy.

"Go upstairs and finish your nap. I'll talk to Billie. All that you have left are the exams, so you need to be well rested—and you need time to study."

Angie shouldered the backpack, trudging up the steps to her room. Once there, she reclined on the chaise lounge and drifted off to sleep.

In the green room, Chapman glanced at the monitor that showed most of the girl's room. Sitting in the swivel chair, she could see Angie slumped on the white chaise—she checked the other monitors and saw her staff on the stairway, climbing up. Danny and Janice joined her for a strategy session.

"Mr. Avery wants Miss Donalson to join him for a week long trip to St. Simons Island in mid June, and a two week trip to the west coast is still being finalized, but probably in late July. He also wants to spend some weekends at the cabin. Most of those dates will be vacation time for us. But Miss D. needs to be kept occupied the rest of the time. Any suggestions?"

"We could invite that young man over. The one y'all stunned a couple of weeks ago—" Janice's voice was light, but Chapman's eyes were shooting daggers at her. "Bad joke, huh?" Janice concluded.

"I can always use extra help with grounds maintenance," Danny said, hopeful. "I know that Mr. Avery doesn't want her overworked, but she's almost always helped me some in the summer, and I don't think I can do it without her."

"We may have to hire someone, maybe a teenager looking for a summer job." Chapman said. "I have no objection to using Miss Donalson, but I don't want it to be routine. Otherwise, it's useless for discipline. If she volunteers, you'll have her help."

"Is there to be any further punishment for her little indiscretion in the park?" Danny asked.

"You'd like that, wouldn't you?" Chapman grinned. "Unfortunately, Mr. Avery said to keep her away from the young man, and to keep her too busy to think much about it. He said no punishment."

"Billie, she broke the no fraternization rule." Danny was pressing for an assistant.

"Yes, and that has been dealt with—remember, she missed some classes and had to do make-up work… and there were four days of work details. That's a sufficient disciplinary procedure."

"Do I have to accompany her to her exams?" Janice looked as if that would be the most boring job in the world.

"Yes—for security and to keep up the head wound fiction. Take a good book to read." Chapman didn't look sympathetic.

"Will she be allowed to drive alone again?" Danny wondered aloud.

"Not for a good while. She can drive with one of us along— shopping and so forth." Chapman sighed. "Back to the original question. Can we keep her busy?"

"Not without working her in some way. Otherwise, she's so much work that we can't keep our own areas in shape," Danny was frank.

"So we need her to do work details, regardless of infractions, just to keep her out of our hair?"

"I agree," Janice stated. "I don't really think it's right. She needs to know when she's done something wrong; we've used work as a punishment, so working her when she's behaved well sends the wrong message. The problem is, we treat her like a queen when she's good, and there are not enough people in the royal entourage. I'm behind now, just because I've had to drive her to school and play nursemaid."

"Maybe that's it. She has to contribute to the running of the household," Chapman mused. "I think we can compromise, but I'll use the incident with the unfortunate Justin. That will, I hope, address the reason for her having to work."

"Mr. Avery won't like it. Not based on what you just said," Janice observed.

"Mr. Avery probably won't notice. We'll work around him."

Chapman dismissed her staff, and after glancing at the monitor, she decided to let Angie nap a little longer. She had some planning to do.

Chapter 11

Chapman and Angie had finished their usual four miles for the morning and were breakfasting on muffins and Danish. Chapman buttered a muffin and looked at Angie in an appraising manner, like someone who was about to buy a horse.

"What's on your mind, Billie?" Angie asked.

"We need to discuss the summer. I'm going to have you to do some work around here, more than in the past. You'll be doing work details three days a week—Monday, Wednesday, and Friday, both morning and afternoon. This isn't to be viewed as punishment; there will be no restrictions on your living quarters or wardrobe. But it's a strain for us to look after the estate and you, too. Janice is behind with her house duties, primarily because she's been providing security for you at school. You're the problem, so you might as well be part of the solution."

"You could just let me drive myself."

"Miss Donalson, we'll talk about that in August when the new semester starts. Until then, you'll have an escort whenever you leave the estate. More work for us, hence the need for your assistance." Chapman's voice had taken on what Angie considered her "drill sergeant voice," one that was meant to be obeyed, without question. Because Angie didn't object to doing some jobs—it beat staying in her room alone—she offered no protest regarding summer work.

"I have exams the rest of this week."

"So Janice said. You'll jog every morning as always. You need to stay up on your upper and lower body exercises in the weight room. Apart from that, you may study as much as you deem necessary. Janice will drive you whenever you need to go—just let her know the day before what your schedule is to be."

"And after exams?"

"Have your work clothes ready—Monday, Wednesday, and Friday. I'll make the assignments at breakfast."

*   *   *

142

Sweat rolled off Angie's head and upper body as she finished the patch of grass near the garage. She bunched her shirt together and wiped her face, making a huge dark spot in the area just below her breasts. Dragging the lawn mower, she went to the area around the helipad, her next task. Her watch was in her pocket; she pulled it out and looked—only 10:45. She had to go until 12:00 or until she ran out of grass. The summer was hot, and she was tired, but Friday had finally arrived!

*   *   *

Angie had lost five pounds by the time the new semester rolled around. She thought that if she hadn't been off with Marc so much she might have lost more. When they went on trips, Marc took her to some great restaurants. The Chinese food in San Francisco was so fine, she thought as she recalled the trip.

She also tried her hand at more cooking than ever before, because Marc had her go with him to the cabin on several weekends. In the years that Mrs. Bowen had been instructing Angie, her culinary skills had gone from heating up frozen chicken nuggets to Eggs Benedict... with real hollandaise sauce, no less. Of course, that was another factor in her weight never again dropping near the 135 pounds of her seventeenth year.

Angie's summer work was typical—she had cut grass, weeded the flowers, groomed and fed the horses. Whatever needed doing. She found time on the off days for tennis, swimming, and horseback riding—the usual entertainment of Angelhurst. Marc kept her busy on the weekends. Sometimes he came to her, sometimes Chapman dropped her off at the cabin, and a few times she rode the chopper to his home in Charleston. For the infrequent occasions that she drove her car, a member of the staff sat in the passenger seat.

Angie realized that it had been quite a while since she'd asked to leave Marc. After three years, she really couldn't imagine living anywhere else. With some surprise, she realized that she was in love with Marc Avery. From the first time he'd entered her room carrying that ridiculous whip, she had vowed that she'd never, ever submit to him willingly. And for years she had managed to remain emotionally

143

detached. She had bartered her sensuality for the material gain that his wealth could provide. Marc was still the spoiled egotist, yes. But his attraction to her seemed real. Their relationship had evolved, she decided, but it took her that whole summer to acknowledge the truth. Angie no longer dreaded Friday nights; instead, she counted the hours until he came. What she dreaded was the sound of the helicopter on Sunday evening. Angie longed for the day when they would live together all the time—not just weekends.

From time to time, she thought of Aunt Claire. Angie hoped that she was well, that she had gotten over any trauma caused by Angie's disappearance. But she had stopped asking to return to Adamsville. Angie would've been horrified to return to her life there—the poverty, the routine nature of life. With Marc, there was a comfortable routine, certainly, but there were college classes, occasional parties and vacation trips, and weekends in the mountains. Angie had little to complain about, so she didn't.

Angie did worry that she might see Justin in the fall. When the new semester commenced, she did see him once or twice. But she didn't have a class with him, and what had happened seemed to be in the far distant past. Angie had fewer guys express any interest in her, so she figured the jealous boyfriend story had gotten around campus. Because this made it easier to be faithful to Marc, whom she loved, she welcomed their distance.

*   *   *

Angie's junior and senior years passed more or less uneventfully. She was allowed to drive herself once again, but she learned to limit any social contacts. If some social event was necessary, she called in on the car phone—with a destination and an ETA back at Angelhurst. Knowing that Chapman had a homing device in the car made it imperative that she be straightforward with her keeper regarding her whereabouts.

Angie's love for Marc deepened, but the relationship stayed pretty much the same. For Angie, at least, the sex was better. However, the frequency of his visits remained consistent until the end of Angie's senior year. Then it seemed that he was busy more and more of the time, and Angie had trouble meeting him because of her own schedule. She had taken a part-time job for the summer supervising a computer lab at a summer academic camp at a local school—she had been offered the position through the IT department at the college. Angie was a bit surprised when both Marc and Chapman had agreed to allow her to accept the job. Thus, Angie had her first regular paying job, and she had started her first checking account.

Each day she arrived at 8:45 to have the machines up and running by 9:00. The campers/students came in for three different sessions of 90 minutes, then she did whatever maintenance was needed and went home. Angie had weekdays from mid-afternoon and weekends free, so it seemed to be an ideal position.

The kids were interesting, and they all seemed to like working with the machines, so it was a good entry into the working world. Angie's experience with baby sitting... especially Coach Doyle's little monsters... helped her to get along with her charges, and she believed that Mr. Adams, the principal, was pleased with the way everything was going.

As for her relationship with Marc, Angie wondered if he was no longer enamored with her. She glanced in the mirror as she sat at the gate at Angelhurst, waiting for Mr. Simpson, their new gatekeeper, to open the gate. Angie noted a smattering of freckles over clear ivory skin, green eyes, and a sleek bob of coppery red hair. Nope, same old Angie Donalson.

Her body was as trim as ever. Chapman had her running and lifting weights and doing aerobics as always. Chapman saw herself as the guardian of Angie's fitness, and Chapman took that the way she took all responsibilities, seriously. Angie's weight hovered about 145 pounds, and she wore a size twelve—not bad for a seventy-inch long frame. Chapman still kept a chart of her weight and measurements month by month. As she charted Angie's performance on several weight machines, Chapman had often reminded Angie that long term use of depo provera was a good reason for emphasizing fitness activities.

"Keep yourself active and fit, Miss Donalson. Average weight gain on this drug is sixteen pounds in four years. You don't want to gain four pounds a year, do you?"

Angie had gained ten, but she had also grown from a teenager into a woman.

At Chapman's request, Mrs. Bowen made sure that Angie's meals were balanced for her weight and activity level. Thus, she had a personal trainer and a nutritionist attending to her every day.

Janice served as fashion coordinator. She managed to keep Mr. Avery's lady looking like she shopped in the big city. For the most part, they bought from local stores, but Janice was very selective. Janice also taught her how to do things herself—make-up, hair, nails. Angie had learned that many times beauty was in the details. When she first came to Angelhurst, Angie thought that Janice was crazy— taking hours sometimes to get ready for dinner. Over time, Angie came to realize that getting ready for a date involved more than a shower and a few quick swipes with a comb. When Angie was told to be ready, she knew how to make herself beautiful.

Marc had taught her the ways of love. She'd been quite innocent when he started his trips into her room. Five years later, she was an experienced lover. Angie acknowledged that she'd learned to enjoy his caresses and to return affection to him. More than anything, she wanted him to love her the way she loved him. Right now, she missed him and wondered why he was leaving her to vegetate in the country—alone.

The gate swung open as Mr. Simpson hit the switch, and Angie put the car into gear and proceeded up the drive at a pace just beyond crawling. Chapman had hired a gatekeeper, because everyone was tired of the electronic one giving trouble, especially when it rained. The area's ever increasing tourist population often needed more than a strong hint that they were on private property, so Simpson had that duty as well. Once through the wrought iron gates, Angie piloted the Mazda up to the front door and left it for Danny to garage.

Some evenings and weekends when Marc wasn't coming, she worked in the yards with Danny. Marc also had given her a new computer system, so she spent some time tweaking it. After spending several hours at the computers every morning, however, she found that she liked the gardening better. Because this was another Marc-less weekend, Angie decided to do her stint at weeding on Saturday morning. The afternoon would be spent shopping in town—after seeing Sherry for her usual appointment.

Angie got her gloves, tool basket, and a wheelbarrow of mulch. She went to work near the helipad. After spending about an hour and a half digging in the dirt, getting grubby, she used a lawn mower to cut the area around the gravel pad. Now she was sweaty, too—so she showered and changed into a simple camp shirt, shorts, and sandals for her trip into town.

Angie told Janice that she'd be lunching at the mall and back before supper. "I'll get dinner tonight," she promised, looking over the pantry. Mrs. Bowen had the weekend off, and Angie was sure that Janice was weary of wearing two hats. Janice looked grateful and told her to drive with care.

"Always!" Angie assured her as she grabbed her purse and strode off to the garage.

She slowed the Mazda convertible as she approached the gate. Ellis Simpson wasn't at his post—again. The top was down, and Angie glanced at the small cottage where he and his son lived, wondering why he wasn't on duty. She started to sound the horn, but thought, 'That's the way rich people are—sit in the car and wait to be waited on.' Determined to be more self-reliant, Angie got out, went to the little guard shack, and reached inside to hit the button that opened the gate. As she straightened a sharp blow struck her on the side of her head.

Angie crumpled, unconscious, and Joel Simpson, the gatekeeper's ne'er do well son, scooped her up and took her to the shed next to the gatekeeper's cottage. He laid out her limp body on the sleeping bag that he had placed there, in readiness, and pulled out a length of chain which was bolted to a four-by-four post. The free end of this he wrapped around one ankle and fastened with a small padlock. He tugged on it, and she seemed secure. Not to take any chances, he found the other chain, bolted to a four-by-four on the opposite side of the shed. The free end of the chain he fastened around her neck with another small padlock. Now she was going nowhere.

When she awakened, she might make noise, so he had a gag ready. A curious triangle shaped ceramic blob, it had a small chain sprouting from either side. He had made it himself, after experimenting with designs that would keep the tongue depressed and the mouth filled. This he would place in her mouth and secure with another padlock, but he decided to wait until she was coming around. He didn't want to interfere with her breathing as long as she wasn't conscious.

He decided to hide the car, but he'd have to be able to get back to Little Redhead soon, so he could gag her. Joel checked her pulse and respiration, which indicated that she was alive, and her pupils, which were dilated, indicating that she would be out for a bit longer.

Joel sprinted to the little Mazda, which was still idling beside the now open gate. Sliding into the driver's seat, he put it into gear and drove out of the gate and onto the highway. There was a steep embankment around the first curve. After pulling off the road, he put the car into neutral and gave it a shove with all his might. Once he got the car rolling, the embankment was so steep that the convertible rolled out of sight and into the trees. He heard a crunch and the engine went dead.

Joel hiked back through the trees at the edge of the woods, but he was obliged to follow the drive on the estate, due to the electrified fence. He closed the gate and went by the cottage to tell his dad that he had done the morning shift for him, so it was now his turn to be on duty. Joel was doubly blessed—the morning had given him Little Red, and Dad being out of the way gave him the afternoon with her.

*   *   *

Angie woke up with a tremendous headache. She didn't remember the gatehouse, not at first. Angie knew that she was supposed to go to town. Now she was stuck in a far worse situation than she'd ever been. Although she'd been awake only moments, she was already cognizant of how bad this predicament was. She had dealt with an ankle chain many times, of course, but Chapman's chain ended in a cuff that fit snugly, but without causing any pain. Now she had a tight chain wrapped around her ankle, cutting and chaffing her flesh. Her neck was in similar shape, just not quite as tight. Worse than either of those was the thing in her mouth—it filled it and kept her from saying anything intelligible. When she made noises in her throat, all she could do, her captor hit her—hard with his billy club.

Angie lay still, trying not to make any noise. She could sit up, and her hands were free, but she couldn't rise to her feet because there wasn't enough slack in the chains. Angie used her hands to check on the security of her bonds. She soon confirmed that she was held fast and would be there until the man released her. Looking at her captor, Angie saw a tall, husky man not far from her own age dressed in a worn tiger camo jumpsuit. His stringy blond hair hung out from an orange hunter's cap, and his eyes focused on her, just as hers were upon him. After a few moments of staring, she tried to communicate. Angie pointed to the gag and sent him a questioning look. She needed it out, because it was keeping her from closing her mouth, which was drying out her tongue and the insides of her lips. The chain on it cut into the tender flesh at the back of her neck.

He ignored her signals. Angie lay back down, trying to find a comfortable way to remove the pressure on the chains on her ankle and the back of her neck. She wondered how long he would try to hold her in such circumstances. Angie couldn't see any facilities for relieving herself, and she already needed to go. She doubted that she could drink with the gag in place—certainly eating would be out of the question.

The man came over to her, giving her hope for some respite. He took a pair of shears and cut the clothes off of her body. Her shorts, underpants, shirt, bra—even her sandals were reduced to ruins. He threw the clothing in a corner of the shed, stood over her, and looked at her naked body.

Angie couldn't cover herself without trying to get under the sleeping bag, so she sat up and tried to get the zipper undone. The young man pushed her back down and threatened her again with the billy club. Angie lay back, hoping that she wouldn't receive another blow. Her head still throbbed, and her left thigh was already bruised and turning dark where he had hit her, just to keep her quiet.

The club was tossed aside when she became still. Ready to enjoy his conquest, he knelt beside her and began fondling her breasts. He didn't stop there. His hands probed her body, spots tender and not so tender. Angie tried to be as still as a marble statue, offering him no excuse to hit her again. She was choking on the gag, and she was desperate to urinate.

There was a sound from outside, and he stood up. He stopped in the corner and picked up a plastic wrapped package. Working in some haste, he fastened a diaper of sorts around her and left without a backward glance. Angie looked at the diaper, seeing how it worked— a sort of hook and loop system held it in place. Angie used the diaper, then took it off, thinking it better to be naked and dry than almost naked and wet.

Alone, she looked at the ankle chain; it was tight and the links were fine enough to keep her from being able to slip it over her foot. Even if she could do that, there was the chain around her neck. Angie tried to find a way to slip the chain on the gag over her head. She was unsuccessful in that, as well. The blob in her mouth was hard and shaped like her mouth, wider in front and narrowing at the throat, thicker at the front and thinner at the back. She could move it very little, and her teeth were held apart by the links of the chain as they passed through at the corners.

Angie was hungry and very thirsty, and she had a long time to wait. A very long time. Her captor apparently had better things to do than wait on her. All afternoon and evening she lay naked, sweating, and fearful.

*   *   *

"Billie, I think we have a problem." Janice's voice sounded tinny over the intercom. The weekend was unusual in that everyone was on duty except Mrs. Bowen. So Janice had answered the main phone when Sherry, Angie's hairdresser, had called to ask if Angie had forgotten her appointment.

Janice, who had seen Angie leave, told Sherry that Angie had gone into town. Perhaps she had forgotten, Janice told her and rescheduled the appointment. Janice got off the phone as fast as possible, so she could alert Billie. Angie might have run, but she could've had car trouble; she could've had an accident. Any number of things *could* have happened.

"Yes," Chapman replied from the stable, where she and Danny were going over a list of supplies.

Janice ran down the situation. Danny's eyes widened as he looked at his watch and heard the 2:00 appointment time.

"We'll take the Explorer and try to locate the vehicle," Chapman said. "Have you tried to call her on the cell phone?"

"Yes, ma'am. I got call forwarding. It isn't working."

"Stay by the phone, Janice. We'll be in touch."

Chapman thought about taking some tools or weapons, but not knowing what she might face, she had Danny pick up a pair of handcuffs and the stun gun. She put portable radios and a first aid kit in the toolbox. They turned on the scope... and were astonished to see a blip within a mile.

Chapter 12

He was back—with a water bottle! Angie sat up and gestured toward the gag.

"Little Red, I'll bet you're ready for something to drink. But no noise. None. If you say one thing—if you make one sound, the gag goes back and the water can wait until tomorrow."

He unlocked the gag, and she spat it out. An oddly shaped piece of white ceramic with a chrome-plated chain coming out of either side fell into her lap. Angie reached for the bottle, which he handed to her with a great flourish. Slugging down the tepid water, Angie glanced at him. Her captor was watching her, and she figured rape was on his mind.

After a few minutes, he started talking to her... dirty talk. He used words like "fuck" and "cunt"—words she had read, but seldom heard. For whatever reason, this seemed to be necessary for his arousal. Her naked body—she sensed it wasn't enough. He had to have something more. The talk became more and more vulgar, more and more threatening as he spoke of his plans for her—what he'd make her do and what he'd do to her. After a few moments of this, he lowered himself on her and without any preparation—with no foreplay at all—he used her. Angie had made love many times, but this was different. He raped her. The experience was painful and degrading. Without a caress or a compliment, he got up and put on his pants, still watching her, as silent tears rolled down her cheeks.

He seemed to have more time, so he took a rope and tethered her hands to the chain which ran from the four by four post to her neck, turning her on her stomach as he did so. He replaced the gag and sat on her back, crushing her diaphragm. Angie felt enormous pain as he grabbed her by the hair and pulled her head up. With his other hand, he took a sharp pointed tool—like a screwdriver which had been sharpened—and pushed it through the flesh of her nose, right between the nostrils. After he pulled the oversized needle out, he inserted a large metal ring, which dangled to her lips.

Angie screamed. She couldn't help it, even though she could form no words. The pain was searing, then slowly became a deep throb. He smeared some cream on the smooth metal, slid it around, mopped up some of her blood, and flipped her over on her back, releasing her hands as he did so. Angie's agony was made worse because her captor just stood there, watching her cry, with the club in his hand. Angie knew that if she gave in to the pain, he would hit her.

Angie's tears streaked down her face, mixing with blood. She was too fearful of his reaction to allow herself to cry aloud. After a few minutes, she controlled her whimpering, and he moved away, his body language less threatening. She managed to drink from the water bottle again; he made no move to take it from her. With the ring dangling in front of her mouth and the gag in it, she could do little more than pour it in, hoping some would filter back into her throat. Swallowing was agony.

A bit later, he gave her another of the diapers. After that he left — she hoped for the night. Angie looked at the door, longing for escape. Knowing it was futile, she settled in with only her pain and fear for company.

'Twas a rough night. Theatre folk might believe it was bad luck to quote *Macbeth*, but Angie didn't see how hers could get any worse. She was hot at first, and her body was soaked with sweat. During the night, it became cold in the shed. She ran out of water, too. By the time morning light filled the sky, it had been 24 hours since she'd eaten. Angie was still alone in the shed, naked, chained up, and in pain—waiting for whatever her captor would bring in the morning.

*   *   *

Chapman had not slept at all. She used three different private detectives and two off-duty officers from Avery Electronics Security division—each working on one of the three different scenarios she had worked out.

The car had been easy to find. With its front end crushed in brush and trees, it was less than five hundred feet from the end of the drive. The top was down, the keys still in the ignition, and Angie's purse, including her wallet with money and credit cards inside, was on the floor in front of the passenger seat. Billie and Danny had combed the woods close by, finding no trace of her; then they had sought help and planned strategy.

"If she decided to leave, she had help," Chapman declared. "Who has she befriended—someone who would come and take her off like that?"

"Billie, I don't think that happened. We've kept her on a leash, in terms of her social life."

"I agree," Chapman said. "But we have to consider the possibility."

That was the first possible scenario—an accomplice had helped her run.

Number two—she had hit her head and lost her memory. She might still be wandering in the woods. Far fetched, but plausible.

Number three—someone had snatched her.

If Angie had been the privileged daughter she sometimes pretended to be, then the third scenario would've been the most likely. But since she was who she was, a captive, the first possibility seemed to be more apt, so Chapman made that her top priority. She sent a P.I. to Angie's hometown, hoping that if she showed up there, she could be intercepted. Agents from Avery Security were looking at connections on campus and at work. The time frame—Saturday and Sunday—would make their jobs doubly difficult.

The gatekeeper and his son had been enlisted to search the woods near the car. That would address possibility two.

Danny was assigned to review tapes of the estate security monitors, hoping that if Angie had been abducted by someone hostile to Marc or the company, something unusual might have been picked up. That was their initial approach to the third scenario.

*   *   *

Joel Simpson was exhausted. Having to look for the girl, late into the night, after the work of having kidnapped her was taking its toll. Chapman... the "Sergeant" he called her in his mind... wanted him to work again come first light. Of course, he had to join the search; otherwise, suspicion might be cast upon him. In the early morning, he looked through his father's meager food supply and found a package of breakfast pastries and a carton of juice in the kitchen, which he took to her—before he went out to rejoin the search.

Simpson had to take out the gag. He threatened her and hoped that she was too cowed to call out. The girl seemed grateful for the food—grateful and pathetic. Because she made no sound, he decided that his threats were enough to keep her quiet.

He grabbed the ring, twisting it. She squealed in pain, then choked the sound off as he threatened her again, but there were tears in her eyes.

"Remember, Red," he told her. "I work just outside, and if I hear you, I'll come back and beat you until you aren't *able* to make a sound. You hear me?"

The naked girl nodded, tears streaking the dirty, bloody mess that was her face.

*   *   *

Angie ate the package of pastries and tried to concentrate on listening. Her captor had said he would be close by, but she heard nothing—which neither confirmed nor denied the statement. However, it was of little consequence—she couldn't get loose. Angie felt sure that she was still on the estate, but no one would know where. The territory wasn't familiar to her, either. The jogging and riding paths that Chapman used didn't come near the gate. Angelhurst had little traffic, and what there was stopped briefly at the gate and went on. Her chances of being heard by someone other than her captor were quite small.

She was relieved not to have the ceramic blob in her mouth. Angie was loathe to do anything that would result in having it replaced. She listened intently. If she had any inkling that anyone was within earshot, she would call out. But, she decided to wait for some sound that might be a sign that her cries would be heard.

Angie had held on as long as she could. She used the diaper and added it to the collection near the sleeping bag, wondering when he would return. The waiting was awful—not knowing whether his coming was something to look forward to, or something to dread.

Angie was hungry and thirsty enough to need him, but she had no desire to be assaulted again.

*   *   *

Danny had helped Chapman search for the car, as well as performing the initial search for Angie in the woods. Afterward, she wanted his help in developing possible theories for Angie's disappearance. That done, he had helped round up extra people for the search. Weary, he had fallen into bed at 2:00 in the morning. Chapman told Janice not to wake him until 8:00 that same morning

Danny was updated as to their progress, allowing him to run the command post while Chapman slept. She finally turned in at 10:00 A.M. for a few hours of rest. Mr. Avery had been notified, so he sent a few more security men, ones who would keep their mouths shut.

After lunch, Danny was finally able to scan the security tapes. He began with the monitor of the gatehouse. Before long he saw something that didn't look quite right.

The camera only took a frame every two minutes. He saw Angie in her car. In the next frame she was out of it, leaning in the window of the little shelter at the gate. The next one showed a figure in hunting attire standing over her, with what might be a club in his hand. Danny examined the picture closely, but he wasn't sure of the man's identity. Studying the image, Danny decided that the figure looked an awful lot like Joel Simpson, who was out in woods, supposedly looking for Angie.

Danny ran the film again and picked up the intercom phone.

"Billie!" his voice was triumphant. "I think we have something here. It looks like it's a variation on number three."

"On my way." Chapman had been asleep less than three hours, but her voice didn't reflect her weariness. Her years of service had taught her how to push herself in times of crisis. She could deal with this one, too.

*   *   *

Joel raped her again in the early afternoon. Talking filth, he walked around Angie, looking but not touching. Stomping the ground, he called her names and told her what a stinking mess she was.

That much was probably true. She stole a moment to glance down at her unwashed body.

Roughly, he touched her bruised and swollen face, making her flinch.

"We won't need that chain much longer, Red." He tugged on the chain fastened to her neck. "You'll follow me wherever I lead you, with a ring in your nose. Just like the old bull my granddaddy had." He smeared more cream on her nose and moved the ring enough to keep it from sticking. Grabbing her hair to move it out of the way, he returned the gag to her mouth as well. Once again the chain was cutting into the back of her neck.

After a few more insults—some real, some imaginary—he pulled down his pants. The only good thing was that he was quick about it. When he finished, he gave her something to drink. Inside the shed, the temperature was sweltering again, and she was sweating as she lay on the sleeping bag. Joel left her, after threatening to beat her if she made any noise.

*   *   *

Chapman and Danny looked at the film, again and again. The distance and the angle made a complete analysis inconclusive, but it was a sure thing that Angie's disappearance wasn't voluntary. Chapman told Janice to recall the security team working on that possibility. The next frame showed the car, but no person was visible. The next frame showed the Mazda going down the drive—with a driver who wore a hunting cap.

Angie wasn't visible in any other frames. Was she in the car? Was she somewhere else? Was that really Joel Simpson? Chapman needed answers. Should she go get Simpson and question him? If he were holding Angie, he'd have to go back to see about her, thus leading them to her. If she were dead, he would have no motivation to reveal information, except under extreme duress. Worse, if the perpetrator were someone other than Simpson, she would've wasted so much time!

"Danny, I'm going with the Joel Simpson hunch," Chapman stated, after seeing the films again. "I need some equipment."

"Billie, what if you're wrong?"

"Let's check this first."

"Okay. I'll let Janice know where we're going."

*   *   *

Joel gave her a carton of milk, but drinking it was impossible. Every time she turned it up, it hit her nose. Also, the gag was still in, meaning that most of it ran down her chin instead of into her throat. Angie gave up and lay on her side, tears flowing, trying to make no noise. Joel seemed angry that she had not consumed the milk. She found communicating with him nearly impossible, so she ceased any such efforts.

He kicked her in the side, rolling her onto her back. With some haste, he lowered himself onto her body. Angie believed that he smelled as badly as she did, which was saying a great deal. His voice was in her ear, using his customary vulgarities, trying to ready himself. Angie stayed as still as she could. A reaction seemed to be something he needed. Her nose hurt, a constant throbbing. Her captor knew it, because he took the ring and twisted it—making her cry out against the gag. Tears ran down her cheeks and puddled in her ears.

Angie's discomfort seemed to stimulate him, and he used her again. After giving her another diaper, he left. For once she didn't need it. Her fluid consumption had been so low that she no longer needed to urinate. Angie lay in her own sweat and blood—for her nose had begun to bleed again. Tears mixed with the other fluids, and when she touched her face, her hand was covered in bloody slime. Her nose hurt, and the smell of her surroundings was atrocious, but she was beyond caring. Angie thought of Marc, of Chapman, Danny, of Janice. Where were they, and were they trying to find her?

Chapter 13

Chapman stood in the woods outside the gatehouse. She wore a throat mike and earphone, allowing her to communicate with Danny—who had similar gear. The stun gun was clipped on her waist belt, as were a pair of handcuffs and a law enforcement-quality pepper spray. She had night vision goggles ready for nightfall.

This might not take that long. Joel had just left the shed, zipping up his pants.

"Danny," she said in a whisper. "Watch him—I'll check the shed."

Chapman watched Simpson cross to the house, and she made her way to the shed, using what cover she could find. There were no windows in it, but there were wide cracks between the boards. On a side not visible from the house, Chapman peered inside. While it was getting dark and there was only the remaining twilight, she could see the light flesh of Joel's naked victim, lying on her side, motionless.

"Keep your eyes open. I think I've found her."

"I'm on it," Danny acknowledged.

Chapman looked through another crack, trying to get a clear picture of Angie's condition. She lay on her side, her back to Billie.

"Danny—any sign of him?" Chapman's voice was in his ear.

"No, he's still in the house. Want me to go closer?"

"Negative! Do not, I repeat, do not spook him. I need a better look."

"Roger that."

Chapman sidled around the shed, making no noise. Her brown and gray camouflage would be hard to see against the wall in the twilight, but she was sure that someone looking straight at her would notice her, despite the camo. Chapman stared through a crack and was able to see the chains restraining Angie and the gleaming ring dangling from her nose. More significantly, she saw her move.

"Danny—positive I.D.—it's our girl, and she's alive. Looks like I'm gonna need some bolt cutters to free her."

"Okay, Billie. We have some in the garage."

"Go. I'll cover Angie," Chapman ordered. "Danny, this situation doesn't look good. I doubt she can walk far, if at all. Get transport and park at the side of the gate. Coast in. No noise."

"Roger." Danny's voice echoed in her ear as she moved around the shed.

Chapman returned to the area hidden from the view of the house. She watched Angie, but she listened more, having a mental argument with herself. She wasn't sure if she wanted Joel to come back before they could free Angie. Part of her wanted to take him, and part of her knew that Angie might be at risk. Either way, she knew she'd best be ready. Wishing for more firepower, Chapman pulled out the stun gun, knowing that she had to use stealth.

*   *   *

Angie lay on her side, making no sound. She, too, was listening; she thought she heard something. A rescuer? That was possible. She heard another small sound, so she grunted. An ordinary enough sound, like someone who had stubbed a toe. Just enough to let a passerby know that she was there. Unfortunately, *he* was there.

"I told you no noise, you little, redheaded bitch," her captor said as he stomped into the shed, rolling her onto her back. He leaned over, the billy club in his hand, and drew back to hit her. Chapman launched herself as his arm swung down, her well-honed muscles enabling her to hit him hard in the back. He gave a strangled cry and fell flat, beside his victim. Angie drew back in surprise and saw Chapman, dressed in combat gear, returning the stun gun to its holster and pulling handcuffs from her belt. Her captor was quickly restrained, and Chapman rolled him off the sleeping bag and into the dirt—away from Angie.

Chapman gave Angie's shoulder a gentle, encouraging pat. Angie looked up, tears in her eyes once more.

"Danny?" Chapman said into the mic. "I've stunned Simpson. What is your position?"

"Just got back in the truck. Be there in five."

"Roger that. Call the house and tell Janice we'll need a robe for her."

Chapman leaned close to Angie and turned off the mike. "Danny's on his way with some bolt cutters. Does Joel have the keys?" Chapman's voice was still low as she glanced at the flaccid body of Simpson.

Angie couldn't give a verbal response, gagged as she was, and she wasn't sure, so she shrugged.

Chapman went through Joel's pockets and came up with a small ring of keys. After a couple of tries, she managed to free Angie's neck and ankle. The gag took a little longer, but Angie had just spat that out when Danny arrived.

"Angie, can you walk?" Chapman was behind her, helping her up.

"I don't know." Angie's voice was a hoarse croak.

"Okay, we'll handle it," Chapman promised.

Danny noted her naked body and took off his shirt, which Chapman helped Angie put around her. Because Angie was as tall as he was, it gave only scanty coverage.

"Can you get her in a fireman's hoist? I'll open the back door. Put her across the backseat."

With Chapman's help, Danny put Angie's lanky form over his shoulders and carried her the short distance to the Explorer. After they had her settled in the back seat, Chapman and Danny returned for Simpson. Danny dumped him into the cargo area.

"You ride with him, and if he so much as twitches, hit him again." Chapman handed him the stun gun and swung into the driver's seat.

"It won't be too long," Chapman promised her, putting the truck into gear and pulling toward the house at a crawling pace.

*   *   *

Angie would have sworn that the driveway had grown during her absence. Only 32 hours or so had elapsed, but it had been the worst ordeal of her life. Chapman positioned the vehicle as close to the back door as she could, and Janice ran down the steps, a bathrobe in her hands. Together, she and Chapman pulled the girl from the car, wrapped the robe around her, and helped her up the steps.

"What do you want first, Angie?" Chapman's voice was low. "Shower, bed, something to drink?"

"I want it all, but a shower first, please. Then something to drink. Maybe something to eat, too. I've only eaten once—and it wasn't much." Angie grunted as she struggled with the stairs. "I'm sorry, Billie. I don't think I'm gonna make it."

"You'll make it. You're strong. Come on, girl." Chapman moved her hand to Angie's back, giving more support. Angie felt herself being pushed up the steps. They got her into the bathroom; then Chapman helped her out of her improvised outfit and seated her on the bench in the shower.

Chapman turned the water on, then directed Janice. "Get some soup on, and have something for her to drink. With a straw—I don't know what we can do about her nose."

They moved out of Angie's hearing. She began trying to wash some of Joel Simpson off of her body. In a moment, Chapman was back, and she washed her charge, her touch gentle and thorough. After helping her out of the shower, Chapman held her up until they had entered the sitting area, where Chapman seated her on the chaise lounge. Angie was still naked except for the towel around her middle. Shaking her head, Chapman began an inspection of Angie's body. For once, Angie didn't resist Chapman's search. She paused over each of the bruises, concluding by taking Angie's face in her hands and examining it. Without a word, she turned and got a nightgown out of the closet, helping Angie into it.

As Chapman left, Janice entered with a tray. She placed it over Angie and asked if she needed any assistance.

"Not to eat—no. But if you can, stay." Angie's voice was still a hoarse croak. "Janice, I don't really want to be alone right now."

"Okay." Janice sat in one of the armchairs, looking at the floor. "Are you ready to talk about it?"

"Tell me your side first. How did y'all find me?"

Janice related the story, beginning with Sherry's phone call and ending with Danny's call on the cell phone, alerting her to be ready for their return. "If Danny hadn't recognized Joel on the security camera stills, we wouldn't have found you—at least no time soon. It was so weird, finding the car close by, but having no clue regarding where you were."

Angie spooned soup into her mouth with some difficulty. Her nose was sore and the ring dangled too close to her lips. Instead, Angie switched to the cold, sweet tea Janice had brought and sat back on the chaise. "Where is Billie, Janice?"

"She took Joel to the detention cell. I think she intends to interrogate him."

"You mean he's across the hall?" The very idea horrified Angie.

"He's quite secure. You know that," Janice assured her. "Under the circumstances, we can't call the police. Technically, we're guilty of the same crime."

"I'm sure I thought so at the time, but Janice, it was *not* the same. None of you are guilty of what he is. I've never had anything so bad happen to me. I hate him."

"Billie feels the same way. I don't know what she plans, but that guy is going to regret what he did. That's for sure."

"Does Marc know?"

"He knew about your disappearance. I don't think that Billie's had time to tell him we found you. There's a team from Avery Electronics Security being disbanded right now. We needed assistance trying to figure out what might have happened to you. Marc arranged their help, of course. I'm sure that he cares; he's just busy."

"Do you think—" Angie was having trouble phrasing it. "Will Marc still care for me, considering, well, originally, he wanted someone who had known no other man... to use Biblical language. Will it matter?"

"Why should it?" Janice took the tray and placed it beside the door. "Angie, you need to recover, to get your strength back. Try not to worry about Marc. Just concentrate on getting better."

* * *

Chapman checked to be certain that Simpson had recovered from the stun and was secure. She had leg irons and handcuffs on him, and the door was locked. Using some of his gear—especially the gag— had been tempting, but not professional. On the other hand, letting him wait for interrogation would be helpful. He needed to sweat about his future a bit. Any immediate need for questioning had ended when they found Angie. Simpson could wait until later.

Although she was almost dropping with exhaustion, Chapman went back across to see Angie again. The girl looked better, reclining against the white chaise lounge, talking with Janice.

"Angie," Chapman began, sitting in the other armchair, "Do you want to see a doctor tonight? I could take you if you want. Or we can wait until tomorrow."

"Do I have to see one at all?" Angie glanced up at her, with a pleading look in her eyes. She didn't want to stir from her room. At least no time soon.

"Angie, we have two basic needs. We must deal with the ring in your nose. It doesn't seem to come apart. I can cut it and take it out, but a painkiller would help. You'll need an antibiotic. That should be handled soon—tonight, if possible. And, um, I assume he violated you?"

"Yes, ma'am. Three times."

"Then you must see a gynecologist. There are certain diseases that are transmitted by sexual contact. We won't have to worry about pregnancy, of course. But disease is a risk for which we must be prepared. It's important so that we can take proper care of you—and Mr. Avery, too."

With that realization, Angie slumped, and tears returned. Janice moved to sit beside her holding her hand and giving her a supportive hug.

"I think we need to deal with the ring now. It looks infected and is no doubt painful. I've some fairly strong oral painkillers down in my quarters." Chapman gestured to the tray. "Looks like you ate. That will help." She left, and Janice hugged Angie again, trying to assuage Angie's grief at all that had happened to her.

'She's only twenty-two', Janice thought. 'She's been through so much.'

*　　*　　*

Chapman returned with a couple of capsules. Without protest Angie swallowed them. With a slight nod, Chapman dismissed Janice and put a tape recorder on the table. The former Marine stood erect and sober, as she informed the girl that she needed to debrief her, and that she would rather do it now. Angie pulled herself together to answer the questions. Chapman's tone became increasingly gruff as the girl related the details of her ordeal.

As she talked, the painkiller began to make her sleepy. Angie's attention wandered, so she apologized.

"No, that's what I need, " Chapman assured her and stood, turning off the recorder. "Angie, I'm going to use a bolt cutter to cut that ring. That shouldn't hurt too much. Then I have to push it out of the hole, and that will hurt. Sorry." Chapman turned to the tray on the writing desk.

"I'm also going to give you some more capsules—antibiotic. It's gonna take a few days, but you should heal, and any scar you have will be in a place where most folks won't see it."

Janice came back with the bolt cutters, and Chapman did just what she had said she'd do. Janice held Angie's hand again, and Angie squeezed it until Janice almost cried out herself, when Chapman pushed the metal through the flesh between her nostrils. Angie began to cry, so Janice continued to sit with her, holding her. Chapman cleaned up the blood and put some first aid cream on the hole.

"Let's get her another drink. She's dehydrated." Chapman suggested. "Then everyone on this hill needs sleep. Including me."

Janice left for the kitchen. Chapman took Angie by the hand.

"Let's get you up. Can you walk on your own?"

Angie crossed the two or three yards to the bed, wobbling a little.

"If you need company, I can sleep here."

"I'll be okay. Janice told me you didn't get any sleep last night," Angie told her. "You'll be better off in your own bed."

"You sure you can make it to the bathroom, if you need it?"

"Sure." Angie tried to smile. "I'll crawl if I have to."

Janice brought a small picnic cooler with ice and drinks—and straws.

"Keep drinking, anything that you can," Chapman reminded her. "We'll go for a stroll in the morning, and a longer walk on Tuesday. By the end of the week, you'll be running four miles again. It's over, Angie. Remember that."

"Yes, ma'am. Good night, Billie, Janice. Thanks for everything. I mean it."

"Good night, Miss Donalson." They said it in unison, and withdrew, leaving her to her memories.

*　　*　　*

Perhaps it was the painkiller, perhaps it was relief—regardless of the reason, Angie slept all night. Janice awakened her by bringing in a tray, with juice and coffee—and Angie's favorite cream cheese Danish. Janice sat with her while she ate, then suggested that she dress in workout clothes.

"Billie wants your strength built back up. You're going for a walk, then straight to the weight room. Later, I take you to see Dr. Jones. Danny has a few days off, but as you can see, Mrs. Bowen is back."

Angie bit into another Danish. "Hurrah for Mrs. Bowen!"

"Be careful—you can't have lost that much, not in two days," Janice kidded her. "Oh, and I called in sick for you. I told Mr. Adams that you had a car wreck over the weekend, and that you would be back later this week. Billie and I decided that it was the best explanation. After all, your car *is* wrecked, and this will help explain the bruises and damage to your face."

"Marc?"

"Called. We didn't want to wake you. He sends his regards and hopes for a speedy recovery. He's out of the country."

Angie got more coffee and went back to the chaise lounge. Chapman arrived, looking murderous.

"Do I look that bad? I'm scared to look in a mirror," Angie was trying for humor.

"I've been talking to that... that piece of crap who did this to you." Chapman sputtered. "I may put him down yet. Some people need to be dead."

"I have no objection," Janice stated. Angie was shocked, which must have shown on her face.

"What happened to Miss Donalson could have happened to me—to any woman who crossed his path. If you let him go, he'll do it again." Janice continued.

"I know. I can think of nothing else," Chapman's voice was bitter.

"Come on, Billie, you promised me a walk," Angie stood. "I'll get dressed. I feel a lot better! Let's go outside. We'll both feel better."

"You sound like me," Chapman said with a wan smile.

"You taught me everything I know." Angie replied and disappeared into the closet in search of some athletic wear.

By lunch, Angie decided that Chapman did feel better. They had gone for a walk; afterward, Chapman supervised Angie's upper body workout. Angie was feeling almost human again. Getting rehydrated helped quite a lot. Her nose was sore; her mouth still hurt a little, and some of the bruised areas were stiff, but Angie was far from incapacitated. Chapman did a bit more "debriefing" and called Marc on the phone. Angie was not sure what they talked about, but Marc talked to her at the end of the call. She felt cheered by the warm and caring tone in his voice.

The doctor visit was a different matter. Dr. Jones knew something about the assault and was baffled about the lack of regard for proper police procedure. He reminded Angie that she should have gone to a hospital instead of taking a shower, declaring that important evidence had been flushed down the drain. After a while, the doctor did a physical exam, and they took all the samples (blood and otherwise) necessary for testing her for diseases to which she might have been exposed. He also was concerned about her face and gave her a shot of antibiotic and some medication to reduce swelling.

When Angie returned home, Janice told her that she had rest of the afternoon to herself, so she changed back into a T-shirt and shorts and went to see if Mrs. Bowen had something that she could do in the kitchen. Although the staff undoubtedly thought she needed rest, what Angie wanted was to be busy and around other people. Mrs. Bowen's domain was perfect. Mrs. B. decided that the shelf paper on top of the cabinets needed replacing, so when Chapman began searching for Angie, she found her on top of the counter in the kitchen, with a pair of shears in one hand and a roll of shelf paper in the other. Mrs. Bowen was in her usual chair, giving directions.

"Hi, Billie! I'm making myself useful." Angie waved the shelf paper at her and kept on, since she just had one more section.

"Hi, yourself. How was the doctor visit?"

"It happened. What can I say?" Angie kept her tone light, for she was unsure as to what Mrs. B. knew about the situation. "Danny is off for a while, I hear. Do I need to do any yard stuff while he is gone?"

"Maybe tomorrow. You need to get back to work before they issue a pink slip with your name on it."

"I called Mr. Adams. They expect me on Wednesday. Janice has until then to think of a way to make me presentable." After conferring about it, Janice and Angie both hoped that she would look better by then. The bruises could be explained—not the nose. Angie had decided that she looked like a punk rocker with an infection. "What about my car?"

"I had it towed to a body shop today. You'll have to drive something else for a week or two. Mr. Avery's BMW is available. It does have a phone. I would rather you took it."

"All right! I'll impress the hell out of those kids with that!"

"You might as well get something good out of the situation, Miss D."

Angie finished the shelf and jumped down from the counter. Chapman looked at her, really looked, because she always watched her body. Chapman was accustomed to assessing its level of fitness. Although she said nothing, she nodded approvingly at Angie's lithe movements.

"Let's go for a ride before dinner," Chapman suggested, and they went to saddle the horses, while Mrs. Bowen whipped up something. They took a trail through the forest, and Chapman led at a brisk pace. She seemed to be trying to escape something, and Angie found herself wondering what it was.

"Billie," Angie called to her and she slowed. "What is it? Why are you going so fast?"

"I made a decision, Angie," she said. Angie always listened more closely when Chapman used her first name—it was usually important. "Joel's got a reputation for wandering in and out of his Dad's life. This time, he won't be back."

"What do you mean?" Angie reined her horse in. The gelding that Chapman rode circled back to join her.

"I put him down. He was a monster, and I put him down."

"What did you do with him?" Angie couldn't help asking. She cared nothing for him, indeed, he had degraded her and used her and probably would have killed her as soon as he was finished with her. But she wanted to know.

"I won't tell you that. I debated mentioning it at all, but I thought you might get over this better if you didn't have to keep looking behind you." Chapman looked down, embarrassed.

"Thanks, Billie. I mean it. From me, on behalf of the female half of the race—thank you."

Chapter 14

For Angie, going back to work was a blessing and a curse. She needed something to do, and in that it was perfect. But the young are always curious, and she had trouble explaining her injuries. They wanted a blow by blow account of the car crash, which Angie had to make up, of course. Trying to her story keep straight was a tough job. Janice had used a thick foundation to hide most of the scab on Angie's nose, but that meant Angie had to keep her fingers off it, which seemed impossible; it was beginning to heal and itched without ceasing. Fortunately, most of the kids were soon far more interested in what was on the screens before them than in perusing Angie's injuries.

Another week passed, Angie's car was fixed, and her face and bruises were just about back to normal. The doctor's office called with preliminary test results, telling her that everything was clear for the moment. The nurse told her that some of the tests should be repeated in three months, unless the perpetrator was found and tested. "Uh, I don't think he'll be found, " Angie told her.

"Well, the initial report looks good," the nurse told her again, before ending the call.

Chapman heard the news and was relieved, but she still had double guilt feelings—first for hiring Ellis Simpson, and secondly for letting him go with his son missing. She could hardly tell him that he would never hear from his son again. Yet, she couldn't bear to have him on the property, so she gave him two month's severance pay and use of the cottage for another two weeks.

Then there was the matter of Mr. Avery's relationship with the girl. The staff of Angelhurst had been making excuses for him, but he seemed to be losing interest in Angie. He hadn't spoken of it, and his support for the staff was unwavering, but Chapman wondered. Had he found someone else? Avery had never pretended any desire to marry Angie, only to use her. But Chapman and the others had become Angie's advocates. Each of them hoped he would relent and marry the girl. That she loved him was obvious—and the social differences had gradually been reduced by her exposure to his lifestyle.

170

Chapman feared, more than anything, the day when Avery would call her into his study and hand her information on some other girl—another innocent to be torn away from home and trained to be his paramour. At the time, Chapman had easily rationalized that Angie's home situation was bleak, and that removing her from it was for all practical purposes doing her a favor. But Angie's love for the tiny, run-down cottage in rural Georgia, and for the aunt who had appeared so cold and unloving, had demonstrated that Angie had possessed a home life that she considered happy. Because Angie had accepted her new position, it had worked out, but Chapman regretted the way she had treated the girl. So much so that she doubted that she could ever do it again.

*   *   *

Marc had indeed been busy, and he had lost some interest in Angie. But he wasn't seeking a new mistress; it was time for a wife.

If he allowed himself to think it over, he was overdue in dealing with the wife issue. Marc had passed his thirtieth birthday. But he had been so satisfied with Angie that there was little motivation to look for a wife. In recent years, his father had pointed out, over and over, that he needed a grandchild—that Marc needed an heir. The elder Avery also emphasized that it would be good for business if someone with similar interests could be found.

In time, Marc found someone who would make the perfect corporate wife. A woman from a fine old family, a woman with wealth, breeding, and who would inherit a sizable fortune of her own. To court and win her would take time, but Marc seldom changed his mind when he went after something.

*   *   *

Angie realized that she hadn't seen Marc for more than a month. She continued to wonder how much the attack had affected his view of her. Her summer job had ended, and Chapman had told her that she was free to pursue another, as long as it was within driving distance and wouldn't interfere with any of her duties in regards to Mr. Avery.

"What duties? I haven't seen him in so long I forgot what he looks like." Angie's voice was bitter.

"Or you might try graduate school. I'm sure that would be satisfactory, if you could get accepted some place in driving distance." Chapman ignored her complaint.

"Billie, what's going on? Or maybe I should ask what is *not* going on."

"I don't know, Miss Donalson. Mr. Avery hasn't been in contact with me, either. All the bills are being paid, and that's the extent of my contact. Really."

"I figured it had to do with... with what Joel Simpson did to me."

"I can't rule that out, of course, but his absences started before that happened. Mr. Avery has been here less often for at least six months. For the past two or three, we haven't heard much, in addition to not seeing him. He used to call me on a regular basis to check on the estate, and on you, even when he wasn't coming here himself."

"Can you speculate?" Angie asked her, hoping for some new insight.

"Sure, but it would be fiction. I *know* nothing."

As Chapman and Angie were having this conversation over cereal and muffins in the breakfast room, Janice came to the door. "Billie, Mr. Avery is on the main line."

Angie watched her go, wondering what she might find out. At least Chapman had acknowledged that there was a problem. Hopefully, she would be honest with her.

"I guess you can make yourself a list of questions, Angie. Mr. Avery will be here tomorrow evening." Chapman returned to breakfast.

"A detective, I am not. But I hope we can find out what's going on."

"Perhaps so." Chapman looked uncomfortable. "You need to do upper body today, and you might want to go for a ride. Danny also requested your assistance with some landscaping project, but I don't remember exactly what. Do you mind?"

"No, not at all. I'd rather stay busy."

*   *   *

172

Angie had finished the irrigation system by noon and planted some bulbs in another garden. After a hasty lunch, she went into town to shop for some fall shoes, then she had a check-up at her dentist's office. A brief call to Janice was now routine—"I should be home by 4:45," Angie told her, and the Mazda rolled through the gates at 4:40.

Angie was steering the convertible up the drive as the helicopter took off for its return trip to the city. Angie saw it and knew that Marc had come home at last. Over and over, she had wondered what might be on his mind—why she was no longer attractive. Involuntarily, Angie looked at her image in the rearview mirror. She was pleased by what she saw—clear skin, with just a suggestion of the freckles of her younger days, but no lines as yet. Dark green eyes sparkled with warmth and intelligence. Her hair, always her greatest asset, glinted with reddish gold tones in the sunlight.

Angie parked in the garage to save Danny having to put the car away and shouldered her purse and shopping bags as she walked up the path to the back door. Climbing the steps to the patio, she saw Janice cleaning the tables.

"Hello, Miss Donalson," Janice greeted her, "Mr. Avery would like to see you in his study."

"Thanks, Janice."

"I'll put your things in your room," she offered, and Angie handed over her bags.

Janice climbed the stairs as Angie knocked and entered the door of the downstairs study. The room was traditional, with some carved woodwork, wall-to-wall shelves stocked with everything from bestsellers to a multi-volume set of the Oxford English Dictionary, and a large desk. Marc sat behind the desk, so Angie took one of the two chairs opposite.

"Hi, Angie. You're looking good, as always." Marc's voice was chipper; his cap of dark blonde hair was still thick and had just a hint of curl.

"Hi, yourself. It's been a while." Angie wasn't sure what to say.

"Yes, I know. I've missed seeing you. Being with you." Marc pushed the chair back and rose to come closer to her. He sat on the edge of the desk and took her hand in his. As she looked up at him, he bent his head to her face, kissing her full on the lips, an intense but brief gesture.

"I've been really busy. And I have to tell you about it." Marc reached behind him to the desktop and handed her a newspaper, which was folded so that the society pages were up. The first engagement announcement was Marcus Avery, Jr. to Rebecca Wyatt. Angie was startled—too stunned to react. Frozen, she stared at the picture, seeing the familiar features of the man she loved, his arm possessively draped around the dark haired Rebecca. Miss Wyatt looked petite—"pert" was a word that Aunt Claire would have used, no doubt with that hint of disdain that she used so well. Because Angie couldn't bring herself to read the pedigree of her rival, she focused instead on the date. November 22nd, just before Thanksgiving.

"When do you want me to leave?" Angie found her voice, at last. She sounded calm, in spite of her inner humiliation.

"Leave? Why?" Marc's voice reflected genuine disbelief. "I want you as much as ever. This—" he used the newspaper to gesticulate, "is just business. Dad wants me to have a wife who fits in with our company. Becky will be the hostess. She will have the brats; she'll be the wife. You're my lover, and I still love you. But remember, I brought you here as my *mistress.*"

Angie sat back in her chair. Marc still held the newspaper in his hand, but she was no longer looking at it. She peered into Marc's face, into his eyes. Ironically, he looked just the same. She thought that some revolutionary change would have overcome him, but he still had the face she had grown to love. Now a face of treachery.

"Marc, she won't stand for it. I must go, even if we still care for each other. No marriage has a chance in such a situation." Angie's words reflected a wisdom beyond her years.

"I still care for you, and I have no intention of giving you up. At first, it'll be our little secret. Later, she may find out, but you aren't any threat to her, nor is she to you. You'll both be a part of my life, but only a part. What you, or she, want is of no consequence. This is the way it will be. She'll live in Charleston, and she'll be the wife I need for that side of life. You'll stay here, or meet me on the road, and you'll satisfy my needs, as you've done for the past five years."

"You might be able to keep me a secret for a while, but she'll find out. It's best to end it now. Either break off the engagement, or let me leave. I promise that I won't accuse you or anyone here of any crime. Although I would never have chosen this life, I'm grateful for what I've been given during the last few years. I appreciate it enough that I would never betray you."

"No. You stay here."

Angie stood by the chair. "I'd like to have enough money, clothing, and so forth to get myself started. If you won't make it a gift, then make it a loan which I could repay."

"We'll talk later, Angie. Right now, I need to see Billie, too."

Angie turned to go without glancing back at her captor, turned lover, turned traitor. In the hall, Angie saw Chapman coming to the study, but Angie was speechless.

*   *   *

Angie noticed that Janice had placed her purse and shopping bags on the writing desk. She glanced at them, then flung her body across the bed, weeping. She loved Marc, and despite the unusual nature of their relationship, she had never considered that he might marry someone else. She assumed that one day he would marry her. If not that, then a continuation of their current relationship. For the first time, Angie realized that he could have been involved with any number of women over the years. Somehow, she had believed that he was only involved with her.

Naive. That was what she was when Marc first took her. That's what she was to this day. What sort of promise was there in a relationship which began with an abduction? Angie punched the pillows, attempting to release the anger that filled every nook and cranny of her body.

*   *   *

"What sort of reaction did you expect, sir? The girl does love you." Chapman was annoyed with Avery. Angie had ceased to be a victim and had become a protégé years before; therefore, Avery's new plans were as much a threat to Chapman as to Angie.

"I never promised her marriage. I told her up front, day one, that I wanted her as a mistress. I told her she couldn't get pregnant. Producing the Avery heir has never been part of the plan for Angie."

"That's true. But there's an implied promise in any long-term relationship. She's been here for five years. Somewhere in there we all began to think that you were in love with her, as she is with you."

"I care a great deal about Angie. If I didn't, I'd have ordered you to get rid of her long ago. You may sympathize with Angie, but you work for me. You'll help me keep Angie in line, and you'll follow my orders without question. Is that clear?"

Chapman stood, regarding him without backing down. "Understood, sir. But be careful. Your own happiness is also at stake. Maybe you were listening to your dad instead of your own heart."

Avery chose to ignore that. "Billie, it's your job to keep a close watch on Angie. She's very important to me. This will be hard for her."

"Yes, sir."

"Take extra good care of her. Dismissed."

Chapman turned to go, shaking her head as she went out the door.

* * *

Angie got though the weekend only because she'd come to a decision. Due to her summer employment, she had a bank account in her own name, with cash she could access without using the credit cards in her wallet. Monday morning, Angie closed out the account, taking it in bank notes of various denominations. She realized it was very little. At least, it didn't compare with what Marc spent on her. However, if she used it with some care, it would get her far from Angelhurst. Although Angie had been living in the lap of luxury, she'd grown up poor. For once that would be a real advantage. She knew something about living with a mere trickle as cash flow.

Monday night, she went to bed as usual, but set the alarm for 2:00 A.M. When it went off, she went into the closet and packed two small cases with an assortment of practical clothing and toiletries. The places she would have to stay wouldn't have a concierge ready to help her with a forgotten toothbrush. Thankful that Chapman had stopped locking the upstairs doors, she took the cases down to the garage and placed them in the tiny trunk of the Mazda. Using Danny's flashlight, she found the transponder, transferring it to a toolbox under the seat of the flatbed truck. It was 4:15 before she finished, but she doubted that she'd sleep anymore. She was too nervous.

When she had finished the morning run with Chapman, Angie told her that she had an interview with the school system that had employed her during the summer. Chapman looked surprised, but Angie told her that she'd forgotten it during the emotional turmoil of the weekend. Angie ate a hearty breakfast and dressed in a professional looking pair of slacks and blazer. These clothes were comfortable enough for driving, yet the outfit was appropriate for an interview.

"I really don't know how long I'll be," she told Chapman and Janice. "It's a technology consultant position, which probably means multiple interviews. Maybe even a trial run on fixing a computer problem. I'll call as soon as I finish."

"Good luck," Chapman and silently, Angie bid them farewell. When she left the gate at Angelhurst, she took out a map of the southeastern states and pointed the Mazda south. Destination wasn't important—she just wanted to get away from Becky Wyatt. Angie shrugged her shoulders. Adamsville was calling. She would do what she'd once longed so much to do; it was time to go home.

Chapter 15

In five years Adamsville hadn't changed much. The old grocery had become a convenience store, and a new grocery with a pizza place and a dry cleaner had been built in what had been a pasture. Apart from that, it looked much the same. On Angie's home street, a real estate sign with "contract pending" was in Aunt Claire's yard. The house had been painted a fresh white. She remembered a tired pea green with peeling dark trim. New reddish brown shingles replaced the curling black ones—ones that had leaked, Angie recalled. A deck, painted a redwood color similar to the shingles, now ran across one side of the house, making it seem larger. She turned down a parallel street and came back for a second pass. Glancing around, she parked on the street, one house up from her old one. This house had been vacant when she'd been abducted, so she took a chance that whoever had purchased it wouldn't recognize her.

A young woman with a baby in her arms answered Angie's knock.

"Could you tell me if the house next door really has sold?" Angie gestured toward the Donalson place.

"I reckon so. They put up that there thing about the contract on it a couple a weeks ago. The folks buyin' it go to my church."

"Did you know the previous owner?"

"Yeah, a little old lady. She was strange—went sorta dotty in the head after her niece went missin' a few years back. Folks said the girl just never came home. Anyway, Miss Donalson died several months ago, I guess, not quite a year. Don't reckon she had any close relatives, so some distant ones came, cleaned out the house, had it fixed up real nice, and put it up for sale. I told Amber about it, and they have a contract."

"Cute little place. Might need a little more work, but it's nice," Angie remarked.

"Yeah, sorry you missed it. But there's some others over at Hunter's Glen. Off the main highway." The young woman was eyeing Angie's clothing and the red convertible. "You oughta look over there."

178

"Thanks." Angie guessed that the woman didn't think she belonged in the neighborhood. Perhaps not. Angie approached the Mazda, still glancing around. Aunt Claire was dead. The last connection to her past was gone—so she would go on. The lady was right. She no longer belonged here. With a shrug, Angie climbed into the small cockpit and pointed the Mazda toward the east. When she got to the outskirts of Macon, she decided to look for a flea bitten motel that would take cash. The next day she went east on I-16, to Savannah, then down I-95 toward Florida.

*   *   *

Tired from another day of driving, Angie was sitting cross-legged on a motel bed in South Georgia, en route to Jacksonville, drinking a diet soda from a can. She had purchased it, gas for the car, and some fruit, crackers, and peanuts from a little store around the corner. Angie was conserving cash by buying only one restaurant meal a day, and snacking the rest of the time.

She had registered in her own name, but paid in cash. Angie heard a knock at the door and resolved to ignore it. Then she heard her name.

"Miss... uh... Donalson? This is security. We have had a gas leak reported, and we gotta check every room."

Angie looked out the hazy peephole beside the security instructions. All she could see was a dark uniform. Although she was apprehensive, she decided to open the door. The place looked so dilapidated that anything might be leaking.

"Okay," she said, opening the door a crack. A foot was placed in it, keeping her from slamming it shut. Then she recognized Danny, dressed in the security uniform, pushing the door in. Chapman was right behind him, a short black stick in her hand.

"Hands on the wall, above your head," Chapman told her. Angie hesitated, so Chapman roughly pushed her into position. Angie felt the hard bar pressed against her buttocks. Angie heard the door close, then Chapman spoke to Danny. "You pack her up."

"Nice outfit, Danny. Did you rent it from a costume shop?" Angie's tone was confident and taunting—much more confident than she felt.

Danny ignored her. Chapman held her in position, while searching her. Finding nothing, she took Angie's purse, pulled out the car keys, and tossed them to Danny. Chapman kept her spread against the wall until they had cleaned out the room. The process didn't take long, because her unpacking had been limited. Chapman returned to the figure against the wall and spoke to her in a quiet but authoritative voice.

"Did you pay for the room in advance?"

"Yes, ma'am, in cash."

"We are going to leave now. There'll be no trouble. Got it?"

"Yes, ma'am."

Danny put her cases into Chapman's rented Ford. When he returned to the room, he held her arm until she was seated in the front passenger seat. Chapman had one cuff of the leg irons around the bar that adjusted the seat; she locked the other cuff around Angie's ankle. Angie could move a bit, but stretching that leg out was impossible. So was exiting the vehicle.

"If you agree to cooperate, I'll leave your hands free." Chapman regarded her, waiting for a response.

"I won't give you any more trouble," Angie acknowledged. "I know when I'm at a disadvantage." She gestured to the cuff around her left ankle.

"Good. You and I are going to the Glynco Jetport in Brunswick. The plane is standing by. Danny is going the slow way; he has to get your car home."

"Billie, how'd you find me? I took the transponder out of the car."

"I know. But Mr. Avery has a friend on the police force in Atlanta. He put a bulletin on your car and license plate. You were spotted on I-95 and followed here. The information was passed on to us, so Danny and I came in via a hired jet. I figured that you'd avoid using your credit cards, so it was a matter of finding the car," she explained.

"The security guard ruse was pretty good. That place was so old, I found it all too plausible that something was leaking."

"Yes. It seemed that it might work." Chapman's tone was neutral.

Keeping the car was stupid, but how could she have gotten so far without it? Angie chided herself, mentally. She gave the leg chain a rueful glance. What was she in for now?

"Is Marc very mad?" she asked aloud.

"Now he is. At first, we were just worried. After what happened to you before, it was hard not to be worried. I'm not happy that you took off, but I guess I understand it better than Mr. Avery does."

"I just couldn't sit there and do nothing while he married someone else."

"It's my job to retrieve you, Miss Donalson. I've done that. I'm not being paid to sympathize." Chapman's voice was harsh.

"So you want me to just sit and wait until he calls for me."

Chapman sighed. "I'm not thrilled over the engagement. But from the start, he told me he wanted you as a mistress. I've helped him make you into one. It's my job to keep you at Angelhurst—safe and sound. You can cooperate and make it easy, or you can make it more difficult. But if you challenge me, you'll pay the price. Know that."

Angie sat back, relaxing a bit. She knew Chapman well, and this time she wasn't mad, she was just doing her duty. "You wouldn't just sit and wait to be wanted, either. You're on my side, you just can't say it or do anything about it."

"You may be right," Chapman said. "But if you keep running, I'll have to do something to restrain you. And I know that more than anything else, you despise that."

"So what should I do?"

"Talk to Mr. Avery. Make him understand what you feel for him. Work on your relationship," Chapman advised. Then her voice took on its warning tone. "But be aware that any infraction in discipline is my area, and I'll deal with you. I have my duty."

*   *   *

Angie was exhausted when they climbed out of the helicopter in the wee hours of the morning. She gazed at her captor, wondering if she might be even more tired. Chapman escorted her to the detention cell and told her to get some sleep. Angie stripped to her underwear, crawled between the musty sheets and slept.

181

The next morning—actually it was almost noon—Janice brought her some sweat shorts and a heavy tee shirt. Chapman met her as she left the cell, and they jogged their usual route, just later in the morning. Stopping by the breakfast room, they ate a hearty brunch of sausage and egg casserole, biscuits with honey, and delicious coffee. After a couple of days of very poor food, Angie enjoyed Mrs. Bowen's efforts. Conversation was sparse, but Chapman did tell her that she needed her to report to the stable to groom the horses and clean out the stalls, since Danny was still on the road with the car.

Angie worked without protest. The job needed doing, and she needed something to keep her mind off her problems. Chapman was busy with some estate business, so Janice had Angie work in the kitchen when she finished with the horses. Before dinner, Angie went back to her room for a shower and a change of clothing. She had just emerged from the shower when Chapman, dressed in her usual polo shirt and khakis, entered the room.

"Miss Donalson, I've decided to allow you to remain here—no more time in detention. We can use your help on the grounds and in the house. Mr. Avery's out of town, and I haven't heard from him—so it's my call as to the consequences of your actions. I will resume the basic security plan."

Angie looked puzzled. "What does that mean?"

"We're just going back to where we were when you were first brought here. You're searched before bed and upon returning to this room. Both the suite door and the hallway gate will be locked unless you are escorted off the floor."

"For how long?"

"Until further notice." Chapman sounded resolute, so much so that Angie chose to acquiesce.

"Yes, ma'am." Angie toweled her damp hair, went into the closet and changed into a simple tee shirt and jeans. She returned to the room. Chapman, to Angie's surprise, was still there, sitting in one of the chairs near the chaise lounge.

"Something on your mind?" Angie asked her.

"I don't know how to say it. I need to know what you're thinking." Chapman regarded her.

"I'm not sure I understand."

"When we first brought you here, we knew that you would try to escape. And we knew that suicide might be a possibility. That's why we used a restraint at night. Are you thinking along those lines? What do you intend to do?"

"Maybe I ought to have a plan. But right now I'm still in shock." Angie sat in the other armchair. "Ms. Chapman, in less than a week I've learned that the man I love is going to marry someone else, and I found out that the woman who raised me from the time I was three until I was seventeen is dead. I didn't have a chance to see her again. Not to say goodbye, not even to attend her funeral. Now, you come along and drag me back here and lock me up," she said. Her voice was cracking and tears trickled down her cheeks. Impatiently, she swiped at them. "I'm not ready to plan. I need to mourn first."

"Angie, I want you to promise to go along with things for a while. Give Mr. Avery time to see that he needs you more than he needs this society girl."

"And if he really does prefer her to me, what then?"

"Then we'll help you deal with the situation."

"Are you planning to let me go?"

"No. Mr. Avery won't allow me to do that. But the best I can do now, for either of us, is to keep you safe and hope that Mr. Avery realizes just how vital you are to his happiness. I believe that he will, sooner or later."

"How long should we wait?"

"At least until the wedding. He might back out. You're not ready to do anything else. You just said so. So give it some time. And if you aren't a risk to yourself, I won't have to chain you up at night."

"All right. Don't worry, Billie. I have nowhere to go." Bitter tears clogged her throat. Chapman looked as if she wanted to say or do more; instead, she rose from her chair and told Angie that she'd be escorted to dinner in half an hour.

Chapter 16

For the next month, Chapman kept Angie busy. Nothing onerous, just routine work on the estate. Chapman relaxed the security after that month, and Angie volunteered to work at the library in town. Still bored, after discussing the matter with Chapman, she did try to find a job; graduate school just didn't interest her. Angie had no luck in the school systems around Angelhurst, so she continued working at home. She didn't see Marc—not once. Her gynecologist assured her that she had no infections from her encounter with Joel when she went in for a follow up visit. Physically, Angie was ready, but Marc never called for her—not until the wedding.

A week before the nuptials, Marc had Angie report to him in Charleston. Chapman came with her, ostensibly for security. Angie decided that moral support was a factor as well. As they made the long drive across the mountains and down to the coast, both women speculated as to the reason for the summons. Chapman seemed sure that Mr. Avery had finally come to his senses and would call off the wedding. Angie, having weathered his arrogant whims many times before, had packed a dress that Janice deemed appropriate for the wedding and figured she would use it.

*   *   *

Marc had assigned one of the administrative assistants in his office to show Angie and Chapman around town, which Angie found entertaining, and Chapman seemed to enjoy quite a lot. The day had been long, so it wasn't surprising when Chapman excused herself to an early bed.

"Why am I here?" Angie asked as soon as Chapman left for her assigned bedroom. She and Marc stood in the kitchen, the remnants of an evening snack still on the counter.

"I wanted to see your lovely face. And I need your splendid body."

"That's wrong, and you know it. What's your real reason?"

"Do you have any feelings for me?"

184

"How can you ask that? Don't you realize that I could still bring you to ruin? All I have to do is tell my sordid story to the police, or to a tabloid."

"Perhaps. But you haven't. I thought you were enjoying your life."

"You think that's why I left?"

"I viewed it as a temper tantrum. We all have 'em."

"You may've had Billie bring me back, but we haven't made love since you got engaged. And we shouldn't."

"Angie, this is your chance to convince me that I've made a mistake." His arm came around her, pulling her close. His other hand moved to massage a rounded breast, which her ribbed turtleneck did little to disguise. He guided her to the sofa in his small living room. They sat, Angie turning toward him, but not responding.

"You're a gorgeous woman, you know that? And you're my soul mate."

"If that's really true, then propose. If I'm so important to you, marry me."

Her smoldering resentment made her resist his gentle yet insistent foreplay. He kissed her, his mouth exploring hers, and she pulled back. "I've accepted that you won't permit me to leave. But a woman doesn't want sex without love. At least I don't. I've been happy with you, the past few years, because I believed that down deep inside you did love me. However, I don't see how you can marry her if you really love me. I guess I'm like a dusty trophy on your shelf. You still have me, but the game ended a while back."

"Give me another chance, Angie. Our game, as you put it, is only in the first quarter. You still have a shot. Just quit playing at being so damn moralistic."

"I can't be happy with you. Never again. Let me go."

"I think you'll eventually change your mind. But I want you willing. If you're not—then I'll find some other work for you. You'll remain on the staff at Angelhurst."

"For how long?"

"I see no reason to concern ourselves with that. Right now, it looks like I'm going through with the wedding, and you'll be going back to Tennessee with Billie."

*   *   *

After the awkwardness of her evening, Angie was surprised when he insisted that they stay on and attend the wedding. Angie felt out of place going to the high society reception. Chapman looked even less comfortable, but she was attired in a fashionable dress that Janice must have helped her choose. The former Marine took this duty as seriously as any other and stayed close by the side of her charge. As they moved down the receiving line, Chapman introduced her as Marc's ward.

Becky Wyatt was appealing, dressed in elaborate, elegant bridal attire. As she and Marc opened the reception with a dance, Angie realized that her dark beauty was a perfect foil for his tall, blonde figure. Chapman and Angie were seated at a table with some Avery Electronics executives, one or two of whom Angie had seen at parties at Angelhurst. During the reception, Avery danced with Angie only once, whispering to her that she was the most magnificent woman in the room.

Indeed, Angie had been chosen as a partner often, even though she knew few people at the reception. Not long after dancing with the groom, Chapman signaled to her that it was time to leave. They changed to casual attire at Marc's apartment and were on their way back to Angelhurst. Angie was tired, but she also wondered just what her future might hold.

*   *   *

A sliver of moon shone over the ridge of the mountain as Chapman pointed the Explorer toward the cabin. They arrived after midnight. Angie had fallen asleep while reclining in the passenger seat. Chapman put Angie in the loft and used the futon in the living area for her own bed. Although she would've been welcome at her brother's house for Thanksgiving, Chapman had concluded that Angie needed a vacation.

"Let's do some tourist stuff," Chapman suggested as they shared breakfast at a small café near Gatlinburg.

"Why?"

"Why not? I told everyone to take off."

"Who's looking after the horses?"

"Danny's boarding them for a week."

They stayed through Thanksgiving, giving the staff at Angelhurst some time with family. Chapman took her on a trolley tour through Gatlinburg to see the Christmas lights; they also toured some of the museums and shops. As the week passed, Angie seemed to brood a little less, and Chapman decided that was success enough.

When they returned to Angelhurst, Angie half expected to be moved from her suite next to Marc's and occupy one of the rooms downstairs where the staff lived. Chapman shook her head when Angie asked about that, a grin on her face.

"Miss Donalson, we'd have to move so much stuff that it's not worth it. Not to me. Mr. Avery said you could stay where you are. However, you'll have to wear the estate uniform when you're on duty. I'll post your schedule along with everyone else's on the board in my office."

"Do I get paid?"

"Yes, but only minimum wage. You are getting free room and board, remember."

"Okay. I guess that's fair. Marc's paid for everything, but I've never gotten a salary."

On Monday morning, Angie dressed in the khaki pants and navy blue polo shirt that Janice had delivered to her and performed all the tasks posted on the white board.

* * *

Marc's wedding trip lasted for three weeks. When he and his new bride returned to Charleston, they moved into the house that Mr. Wyatt had renovated as his gift to the couple. After a couple of weeks of settling in, Marc sent for Angie.

"He wants you to come with a supply of clothing to last for a couple of months, and your car," Chapman told her. "You're to report to his new house, alone. He faxed us a map." Janice joined her to help with the packing. No one was sure as to why he wanted her, so she took a variety of in season clothing, including a couple of pairs of khaki pants and some navy polo shirts. Because the luggage area of the convertible was small, Janice prepared to ship part of Angie's clothing.

Chapman appeared upset when Angie left. Both Janice and Chapman were wondering what would happen. Angie had been nervous enough when the order came, but Chapman's visible apprehension exacerbated Angie's own anxiety. The drive took all day; she was exhausted by the time she located the house. Angie parked in front and rang the doorbell. A maid in a black uniform answered, telling her to wait in the reception room for Rebecca Avery. After sitting for ten minutes, Angie stood as the new Mrs. Avery swept into the room.

"Miss, ah, Donalson? I'm Becky Avery." She was shorter than Angie by some seven inches and had a demeanor generated by too much wealth, too early in life. Her handshake was limp and insincere. "Marc and I appreciate your coming at such short notice. I know that you're not really a domestic, but having you in the kitchen will be a great help. I've had Martha prepare a room near the kitchen for you."

So Marc wanted her to be his cook. Despite her irritation, she kept her voice impassive. "Thank you, Mrs. Avery."

"I understand you have your own car?"

"Yes, I do."

"I'll have Martha help you get your bags in, then you can park in the garage."

"Thanks."

"You'll want to look over the kitchen, I'm sure. Martha will show you." Mrs. Avery strolled back into her sitting room.

Angie followed Martha to the kitchen, which was large and well equipped, if not the equal of the one at Angelhurst. "Do they expect me to get dinner?" she asked.

"No. She said they were going out tonight. You begin tomorrow morning. But I can make a run to the grocery before I leave, if you need anything."

Angie inspected the pantry, mentally planning a day of meals. Having served as Mrs. Bowen's assistant... and substitute on several occasions... Angie was capable. The scenario was just a bit of a letdown. If she had to do menial work, she'd much rather be doing it at Angelhurst.

"How many do we feed? Any other staff?" she quizzed Martha.

"No, I'm the only full-time employee. There's a grounds maintenance crew and a cleaning crew which come weekly."

Angie and Martha chatted a bit and worked out the details of Angie's tasks for the next day. Armed with her research, Angie jotted down a menu for Mrs. Avery to approve. An hour later, she was settling into the room that Mrs. Avery had assigned to her. After getting herself a snack in the kitchen, she ran into Marc as she made her way back to her room.

"Hi, Angie! I saw the menu. Looks great. I'll see you at 7:00 for breakfast."

"Hi, yourself. At 7:00? Okay, I'll have it ready. I would like to run sometime, though. What time does your... does Mrs. Avery arise?"

"Late. You'll have time between my breakfast and hers to run and get a shower. The neighborhood's a good one, so you'll be quite safe. We have a family membership at a health club. I'll have my secretary call and set you up with them. I know Billie will want you to work out."

"Thanks." Angie hesitated. "Marc, there are any number of folks available who can cook. I can't believe you couldn't hire someone. Or you could've gotten Mrs. Bowen and left me on duty at Angelhurst."

"I want you two to get to know each other."

"I don't think this is wise."

"Just a few months. And you're a great cook. Billie was only paying you minimum wage, so you'll get a raise."

"Glad to hear it," she said dryly. "Do you want me to wear a uniform? I noticed that Martha does. I brought some stuff like we wear at Angelhurst."

"That's fine, or you could wear something a bit sexier. I'd like that," Marc said with a smirk on his face. "Angie, this is temporary. Wear the khakis, or jeans or something. Whatever you find comfortable. If you think you'll be inspired, go get a chef's hat."

"I'll go right out and get one," she replied, then sighed. "I'm tired, Marc. Good night."

"See you in the morning." Marc winked and moved along the corridor with a spring in his stride that she hadn't seen in a long time.

*   *   *

Angie set her alarm for 6:00; she was in the kitchen, with an apron over her navy polo shirt and khakis, before 6:30. Rising early was natural. Chapman had cured of her of wanting to sleep late years before. Marc entered at 6:55, and she had coffee and raspberry chocolate chip pancakes ready for him.

"Let's eat in the kitchen together," Marc suggested, so Angie set two places at the counter near the range, and they ate side by side, just as they'd done at the cabin. Avery smiled as he sampled the stack of pancakes.

"You're going to need a cardiologist if you keep eating stuff like this every day," Angie observed. She'd eaten only a couple of pancakes with a few raspberries on the side.

"Make it lighter tomorrow," he instructed. "But every other day, we'll have something good. Deal?"

"You're the boss. I have to do the marketing today. Any special requests?"

"Lasagna."

"Okay. But I'll never rival Mrs. Bowen. You know that."

"Hey, this girl I married can't boil water for instant tea. Seriously. I can't imagine going to the cabin with her. I'll never be able to go anywhere with her and her alone. We'd starve."

Angie was silent. She could've chided him for marrying her, but the subject was too difficult. Not responding, she picked up her plate and put it into the dishwasher. As she watched him finish, she poured herself another cup of coffee.

Marc finished his breakfast with relish, then paused to kiss her—on the lips. Angie didn't pull away, but she didn't kiss him back, either. He left without so much as a backward glance. After she straightened up the dishes from his breakfast, she donned some sweats for her morning jog.

Angie decided that he'd been right about the neighborhood. The streets were quiet; she saw a few other joggers and one or two security guards, but no one who made her feel uncomfortable. But after jogging in the woods with Chapman at her side, the suburban setting seemed strange. The habit was ingrained, however, and she ran about two miles in her usual twenty minutes, then turned around and ran back toward the Averys' large home.

Martha had arrived and greeted her as she entered the kitchen door.

"Any sign of Mrs. Avery?" Angie asked, hoping for a shower.

"None." Martha grinned.

"I'll be finished in twenty minutes. Come by for a cup of coffee," Angie invited her fellow servant.

"Great. I'd like that." Martha went to the living room and began picking up and dusting.

When Angie came back into the kitchen, Martha informed her that Mrs. Avery would like a grapefruit half and a croissant. Angie complied, pleased that both were available. Martha seemed grateful for both the help and the companionship, which made Angie glad about that aspect of the situation. At least someone was benefiting from this odd turn of events.

*   *   *

A couple of hours after dinner, Marc knocked on Angie's door. She'd been cuddled up in a comfortable club chair, reading, and when he came in, she was surprised. As he sat on her bed, he told her she looked fabulous—even in an apron.

"I'm not wearing an apron," Angie observed, gesturing toward her attire of jeans with a long-sleeved tee tucked into them, and sock feet. She had returned to the chair, one of two flanking a large ottoman and put her sock-clad feet back on the ottoman.

"No, and I've seen you in sexier outfits. But you look mighty good to me."

"Where's your wife?"

"Becky is in the bath. She takes these incredibly long baths," he explained.

For half an hour, Marc teased Angie about joining him in the bed.

"I thought you married the woman. Doesn't she perform her marital duty?"

"About as well as she cooks," he grumbled.

"Give her some time," Angie advised, a wicked grin on her face.

"You aren't here as the cook." He stood and pulled her from the chair to the bed. Although she didn't resist, she didn't show him any affection, either.

"Really? I think it's best I confine myself to kitchen duty."

"Just you wait, Angie. You'll do more than cook."

"I don't think so," She pushed him off the bed. He rolled to his feet and left without satisfying his desire, which surprised her. Angie was grateful for his departure—not only did she find the situation unnerving, but also she had to get up and get breakfast early in the morning.

*   *   *

During the next few days, they established a pattern. Angie cooked breakfast twice, once for Marc and herself, and once for Mrs. Avery. Lunch Angie shared with Martha in the kitchen. Sometimes Mrs. Avery ate what they did, sometimes she wanted something special, and about three times a week, she went out. Dinners were more elaborate, with Martha serving each course. Once, when Becky had a "girl's night out," Angie and Marc spent the entire evening together watching a bit of television, and Marc fondled her just as he had when they'd spent weekends together at Angelhurst. For the most part, however, Angie had evenings alone.

Angie saw little of Mrs. Avery. She doubted that they would "get to know each other" as Marc had suggested would happen. Mrs. Avery sent her orders via Martha, and Angie cooked. The lady of the house wasn't the sort to mix with the help, so Angie only saw her when Martha wasn't around to intercede.

If the Averys ate later than their normal 7:00, Martha went home, leaving Angie to serve. For Angie, that was the hardest part. She knew how, of course. During her years at Angelhurst, Janice had served Angie many, many times. However, those same years at Angelhurst had made Angie far too familiar with Marc to do a credible job playing servant. Sometime during the first year, he'd gone from "Mr. Avery" to "Marc"—friend and lover, and she had trouble with the role of servant.

Avery knew it, too. He often teased her, and it was on one such occasion, that the pair first aroused Mrs. Avery's suspicions.

Angie served what she viewed as an appropriate gourmet meal for a winter evening. The main course was a roast lamb loin, accompanied by parmesan-potato stuffed roasted onions, and sautéed vegetables. Angie gave Mrs. Avery her plate first; afterward, she brought Marc's to him, smiling as she noted his expression. Obviously, he hadn't realized how far along her lessons had gotten.

"Don't you have any fresh pepper?" Marc asked.

In retrospect, Angie knew she should have said, 'Yes, Mr. Avery,' and fetched the pepper. But she knew him too well. "This doesn't need any pepper." She scoffed. "Marc, do you plan to sneeze all over Mrs. Avery's dinner, the way you sneezed on mine in San Francisco?"

Marc chuckled at the recollection. He'd had an absolute sneezing fit.

Brown eyes flickering suspicion, Mrs. Avery focused her gaze on Angie. "You seem to know each other well. When were you in San Francisco together?"

"A long time ago," Marc replied, his eyes sparkling with amusement, and Mrs. Avery couldn't help noticing. She eyed Angie with something between curiosity and suspicion as Angie brought in the dessert of mocha mousse in cranberry sauce. After dinner, while Angie was finishing cleaning up, Mrs. Avery did something totally out of character. She came into the kitchen and sat down on one of the stools at the wide counter, to chat with the help.

"So how long have you known Mr. Avery?"

Her tone was warm. Angie knew that she didn't have it in her, the ability to be sociable to the lower class. The intro was as fake as her nails.

Angie was washing up pots and pans; she paused as she returned a skillet to its hook on a rack above the counter. "I've known him since my junior year in high school," she answered truthfully.

"How did you meet him?"

"His company was sponsoring a college scholarship. I met him during the interview process, as I was being considered for it—the scholarship, I mean."

"How did you wind up being his ward?" More and more suspicion crept into her voice.

Angie wasn't certain what she'd been told. Sticking to her usual cover, the adoption story, made sense. Marc and Angie had told it often; perhaps Mrs. Avery had heard it. "My mother died when I was three years old. My father was a truck driver, so he was away from home a great deal. We lived with his unmarried sister, who helped raise me. Then my dad died when I was thirteen. Aunt Claire and I had a difficult time after that. The Averys learned of my situation during the scholarship process. Eventually, Mr. Avery became my guardian. I lived at one of his houses, and members of his staff looked after me."

When Angie told that story, she always let it sound as if Marc's father had been the guardian. But the papers provided by the law firm listed Marcus Avery, Jr. as her guardian. Angie hoped that Mrs. Avery would accept the story, but her face mirrored distrust, and she was obviously there seeking to know the exact nature of their relationship.

Angie continued with her fiction, which she and Chapman had used when people were curious about Angie's circumstances. "I did finish college, so I guess I got the scholarship and a family." Angie ended her recitation with a small smile. Mrs. Avery didn't return the gesture.

"You lived at one of his houses?"

"Yes. The one in Tennessee. It's called Angelhurst. That's where I learned to cook. Mrs. Bowen, the chef there, taught me. It began as sort of a hobby. I've been on the staff there since I graduated from college."

"How often did you see Marc?" she inquired.

"Mrs. Avery, would you like some coffee, or tea?" Angie asked. She didn't want to appear servile; she just wanted this to be more social and less like an interrogation.

"No. How often?"

"It varied, of course, depending on his schedule and mine. I often saw him on weekends, and we've been on vacation together. I went on some business trips when my breaks from school coincided with a conference or sales event." Angie shook her head. "Really. It just depended. I went to Mr. Avery's home for Christmas and some other holidays. None of my family is left, so he and his family have always tried to make things cheerful for me."

Why she was defending Marc and being deceitful to his wife? Angie wasn't sure. But the best lies have a lot of truth in them, and that was certainly the case with her little life story. Most people were polite enough to accept it, verbatim. If they were dubious as to the true nature of her relationship with Marc, they kept their suspicions to themselves. Not Mrs. Avery.

"So you've lived in the same house with him and traveled with him?"

"I never lived in his primary residence, but we've been under the same roof from time to time. And yes, I have traveled with him." Angie kept her answers honest, for the most part. All that Angie had said could be easily confirmed, anyway. She wasn't admitting anything. "Mrs. Avery, I can see where you're going with this. I came here because Mr. Avery asked me to help out. During the time I've been here, I have done nothing wrong. If you want me to leave, just say so. My degree is in instructional technology. I've designed and maintained computer systems for students. To be honest, I find being your cook a somewhat demeaning position. I've played servant out of respect for Marc. But I've no intention of staying here and being insulted by your insinuations."

The kitchen cleanup was finished. Angie took off the apron, which covered her long sleeved navy polo and khaki pants, and hung it up. Tired and disgusted by the conversation, she dried her hands on a towel and turned to the door. "Good night, Mrs. Avery."

Angie left her in the kitchen, going straight to her room, hoping that she wouldn't be followed. With a sigh, she picked up the book she'd been reading, but it no longer held her interest. Angie's mind was on the future—possible versions of it, and none of them seemed bright or cheery. Christmas was in a week, and she faced the prospect of having it alone for the first time in her life. The long-term picture was even bleaker. Angie knew that she couldn't have Marc, yet she wouldn't be allowed to leave, either. Tears pooled in her eyes when she lay down, praying for sleep.

Chapter 17

The next morning, Marc was surprised when Angie related the details of her interview with his wife. But because Angie had admitted nothing, and Becky hadn't accused him, he thought the matter closed. He kissed Angie with passion and told her to take two weeks for Christmas.

"And do what? Everyone at Angelhurst will go home to their families."

"Um... yes. I suppose so. I'll call Billie and get her to stagger leave times so you won't be by yourself the whole week."

"No, Marc. Let them have their time with their families. It's precious. I know, since mine's all gone. I'll go back there to take care of things. I guess Bessie, Thor, Kirk and I will have Christmas together. A horse can be pretty good company." She smiled, although she didn't much feel like it. He hugged her and suggested that she go ahead, so she'd have a chance to see everyone before they left for the holiday.

"Besides, it will give Becky a chance to cool off. It's possible that she'll miss the food enough to want you back."

"I wouldn't mind it if she found another chef. Marc, I never thought I'd be reduced to being your cook."

"It's only temporary. But I would rather her learn what kind of person you are first-hand. Later, I'll tell her the truth."

"What truth?"

"That we're lovers."

"Yeah, right," Angie groused. "Are you going to tell her how I became your mistress?"

"It's not necessary. I haven't had to force you in years, now have I?"

"Perhaps not. But now that you're married, the physical relationship is over."

"No. You're important to me. I'm still in love with your beautiful body."

"It's lust, Marc. Not love. If you loved me, you would've married me. You wanted her instead."

"I want you, Angie. That hasn't changed. You're my mistress, and that's the way I intend to keep it. With her marriage to me, Becky gets more power and an even better position in society. And I need her connections. Oh, she'll eventually guess what you are, but by that time it shouldn't matter. Business is all about compromise. So is life."

"She was pretty close to guessing our true relationship last night. Maybe I should've just told her, flat out."

"Let me decide when the time is right. I love you more than I need her."

Angie sighed, appalled by his churlishness. Remembering the empty house in Adamsville, she knew that she had no other home, no family other than Avery's staff. "Okay, I'll go to Angelhurst. I'll see you, when?"

"Take until January fourth. We'll be out more than in, so you might as well spend your time there. We won't need you, and Billie will."

*   *   *

Angie packed a small bag and drove to Angelhurst right after breakfast, having no desire to spar with Mrs. Avery again. Arriving after dark, Angie joined Chapman for a chat in the kitchen as they shared a late night snack before bed.

"So Mrs. Avery is questioning the relationship?" Chapman busied herself dishing out leftover apple pie.

"Yep. Big time. I doubt the secret will be a secret much longer."

"Do you think she'll leave him?" Chapman asked.

The gossipy side of Ms. Chapman was a new one, and Angie found herself grinning behind her napkin. "I'm not sure. I think she wants to run me off, not the other way around."

"We can't have that." Chapman's tone was light, but the words reflected her policy—never let the girl go. Never.

"Long drive, Ms. Chapman. I'm tired, and I want to go to bed."

"See you in the morning. When have you been running?"

"After breakfast, about 7:45."

"Okay, we'll do it your way. See you for breakfast at 7:00. And you won't have to cook. Mrs. Bowen is on duty." Chapman smiled and took Angie's used plate to the dishwasher.

"Good night."

"Good night, Miss Donalson."

Angie smiled to herself as she went up the stairs; it was good to be home.

*   *   *

Chapman and Janice made every effort to insure that Angie's holiday was a pleasant one. Chapman didn't leave for her brother's house until Christmas Eve. Janice came back two days after Christmas, and the two of them went forth, armed with credit cards, to the after-Christmas sales. Angie grinned, thinking of how she'd spent plenty of Marc's money, too. Apart from being alone for about 48 hours, she had company. Even on the days when she was alone, she had to perform a number of tasks related to running the estate, so she was too busy to fret about her isolation. On Christmas day, she received phone calls from Chapman, Janice, and Marc.

When she returned to her place in the kitchen, Mrs. Bowen had many questions regarding "the position." Angie smiled at her satisfied disposition. Mrs. B. was obviously proud of her protégé.

In what seemed to be no time, Angie was due to return to Charleston, but she was reluctant. With surprising sensitivity, Chapman joined Angie for the ride down, using her estate manager's position as an excuse.

"I've got to check out some restorations down there. References given by contractors, that sort of thing," Chapman announced as she put a carry-on bag in the trunk of the Mazda. "I can fly back in the helo in a couple of days."

There was ample time to talk on the long drive. At times they lambasted Marc Avery and gossiped about his wife. In general, Angie enjoyed Chapman's company. When they arrived, Chapman, ever the estate manager, was curious about the house and how it was run. Angie went in the back door, greeting Martha, who seemed delighted to see her fellow servant. Angie introduced the pair, simply telling her that Chapman served as the manager of Mr. Avery's country house. Martha assigned Chapman to the room across from Angie's.

As usual, Angie surveyed the pantry and refrigerator, making a menu for the first day, then a shopping list. Chapman wanted to see Mrs. Avery again, so Angie took her upstairs when she put forth the menu for approval.

Becky's manner was imperiously cold. She signed off on the menu and turned back to the television program she was watching, effectively dismissing the pair. Chapman raised her eyebrows as Angie led the way back downstairs. Angie shrugged and went on with her work.

Back in the kitchen, Angie fixed fried egg sandwiches for both of them, glad for a chance to enjoy a down-home favorite. Chapman shook her head as she ate.

"That's a fine piece of work in there. I can't believe that he married *her*. Or that he's subjecting *you* to her. No wonder you didn't want to come back. I think I'll fire Mrs. Bowen, just to get you back home."

"Surely you jest." Angie chuckled.

"I might be closer than you think. This is horrible."

"Well, she was a little nicer at first. Not that she was ever a warm, accommodating sort of person. I think her suspicion is what you saw just now."

"We need to get you out of here. Soon. Can you stand it?"

"For a little while." Angie smiled at her former captor. "I was never so happy as I was the day Marc said I could go home to Angelhurst for a visit. I'd prefer to work there—believe me."

"I believe you," Chapman echoed, and with that she turned in.

*   *   *

Angie's tenure as the Averys' cook lasted just one more week. Marc was in Europe, working on a marketing and distribution network change, when Becky found a new cook, one who'd worked for a country club acquaintance. Now that she had a replacement on board, Becky wasted no time giving Angie the boot. She had just one day to clear out, but that was fine with her. An unhappy Martha helped her pack her clothing into boxes and promised to have them shipped to Tennessee. Angie called Chapman with an ETA after midnight and drove straight through. Pushing herself that hard was stupid, but she was so delighted to be out of Mrs. Avery's employ that she didn't want to stop for anything—not even sleep.

Angie spent the next three months back on the staff at Angelhurst. When she checked the board in Chapman's office each morning, there were always tasks jotted down beside her name. Marc had called her twice. The first call was when he returned to Charleston and found her missing. He seemed upset by her departure. The second was on her birthday. Angie also received a gift, a delicate diamond pendant, which she had no place to wear.   She stayed on at Angelhurst—not out of fear of Chapman or out of love for Marc—but because it was the easiest thing to do. With Aunt Claire's death, Angie seemed to have run out of reasons to leave. Due to the social restrictions placed upon her during her college years, Angie hadn't formed the friendships that often come out of such an environment. She'd made Marc's staff into a surrogate family, and they gave her familial affection. During the months since Marc and Becky's marriage, Angie had come to realize that her "love" for Marc Avery wasn't returned. The more she reviewed the relationship, the more Angie realized that what she'd believed was love might be mere infatuation, inexplicably interwoven with her enjoyment of his material wealth.

*　　*　　*

On a fine April day, Chapman asked her to have lunch in the breakfast room, the smaller inside dining area. Not really small, it could seat ten without becoming a tight squeeze. Although they often used the patio with its glass topped tables and umbrellas for casual meals in warmer weather, or the group ate in the kitchen when Marc was away, today Chapman wanted some privacy. Mrs. Bowen had fixed a Mexican salad, a particular favorite of Chapman's, so the pair shared it while Janice and Danny ate in the kitchen with Mrs. Bowen.

"What's on your mind?" Angie began.

"Mr. Avery called me. He's coming here for two weeks. His wife is coming with him. They're to share his usual room. I've asked Janice to get it ready for them this afternoon."

"What about me?"

"He didn't mention you, but considering the way you parted, I asked. Specifically, I asked if you were to be moved. He was adamant that you were to stay right where you've always been. 'Accessible.' That was the word he used."

"Ms. Chapman, I've given up on having certain things my way. You know that. But I don't see how this will ever work. Ever," Angie stated, anguished. "She can't stand the sight of me."

"I know. It's easy to get ready for the visitors. Clean a bit more and buy a little more food. But how do we prepare for the fireworks?" Chapman sighed and turned to her salad.

"When?"

"Tomorrow evening."

*   *   *

Chapman met the guests, along with Janice and Danny, who helped with the baggage. The Averys carried only light luggage in the helicopter, but two large boxes of belongings had arrived via ground shipping earlier. They were prepared for a long stay.

The guests had dinner in the breakfast room with Chapman and Angie. Chapman's presence surprised Angie, for the estate manager customarily ate with the staff when Mr. Avery visited. The meal was casual, served buffet style on the counter in the breakfast room. Angie wore a stylish pants outfit; Marc wore his usual Sunday sweater and casual pants. Becky wore a cream colored dress which set off her coloring and her figure; Chapman wore her usual working garb, a polo shirt and khakis. Conversation was either forced or sparse. Angie decided that she'd seldom endured such a painful social occasion—especially with people she actually *knew*.

They had drinks and music in the family room afterward, but Chapman and Angie excused themselves as soon as possible. Angie went to her room and did some web surfing—not really working, just looking at some ideas, and went to bed before the usual time.

Her surprise was genuine when Marc slipped into bed and woke her with a kiss.

"What are you doing?" she mumbled, drunk with sleep.

"What do you think, darling? That door is here for a reason." He stroked her bare shoulder, caressing her with a gentle tenderness that she grudgingly admitted she had missed.

"Marc, she's in the next room!" Angie whispered, worried that Becky would hear.

"Sound asleep. Come on, Angie. You're a better bedmate. I came all this way just to be with you. Don't make me use force."

"I know better than that." Angie shook away her sleepiness and sat up. "But this isn't going to be much fun, either. You sure you want to make love to a mannequin?"

Not wanting to take "no" for an answer, he remained on the bed, stroking her, caressing her. After so many years, he knew her most sensitive, sensual spots, but she refused to let his gentle hands sway her resolve. After a while, he gave up and left her lying on her side. She remained awake for quite a while longer, wondering if Becky was that heavy a sleeper.

In the morning, she arose at 7:00, as usual, and was dressing for her four-mile run, when the connecting door swung open again. Becky stood in the doorway, and she was livid.

"You... you. To think I let you spend weeks at my home. I should never have let you stay one night under my roof. So Marc brings me here, to *your* place. A nice set up—just open the connecting door and there you are!"

"Mrs. Avery, I know that you're upset. You have every right to be. But be upset at your husband, not at me. He's the one who brought me here. The one who made me what I am. That happened long before he knew you." Angie stood her ground.

"Blame him? Yes, I blame him. But a woman chooses to say 'yes' or 'no'—so you're not without blame."

"And 'no' is all he's heard since you married."

"You expect me to believe that?"

"Believe what you want. I haven't done anything with him since your marriage."

"And before?"

For a long moment, Angie regarded her, coming to a decision. Now was the time to set a few things straight. She went to the bed and jerked back the bedding at the foot. The chain, still welded there, was in her hand. Angie displayed the cuff, ready to confine the bed's occupant. Becky looked puzzled as Angie waved the chain above the foot of the bed.

"That night—when you interrogated me about my relationship with Marc—much of what I told you was the truth. I was seventeen years old when Marc Avery discovered me. Instead of giving me the scholarship I was after, he had me kidnapped. Abducted. I woke up here, in this room, chained to this bed. I was confined here for months. Every night, I had to sleep with this chain around one ankle. So I couldn't leave. And it didn't do too much good to say 'no' to Marc. Believe me, I tried."

"You were abducted?"

"Yes, ma'am. When I tried to run away, I was punished." Angie dropped the chain and gestured for her to follow. The detention cell was empty, but its purpose was easily discerned.

"I spent the better part of one summer in this cell. I had to work outside, then I returned here at night. And I've been sent here again, many times, over the years. Perhaps I did have choices, but not the way you envisioned."

"You seem free enough now. I didn't see any cell in my house in Charleston."

"Oh, I'm more free than I was. You may not believe this, either, but I left when I learned of Marc's engagement to you. Of course, he sent the staff after me, and I was locked up again."

"Who came after you?"

"Ms. Chapman and Danny."

"The woman with the khakis? She could pass for a prison guard, all right. I thought she was your friend." Once again, she looked puzzled.

"You take your friends where you can find them. I haven't been allowed many social contacts, so I've become close to the people here. Psychologists no doubt have a name for it, but the people who are my captors are also my friends. Remember, I've spent the past six years in their company."

The pair, one tall and auburn haired, one petite and raven haired, were still standing there in the dark cell glaring at each other when Chapman climbed the stairs. She saw the open door and entered. Mrs. Avery was still in her gown; Angie was dressed for exercise.

"What's going on here?"

"I'm setting Mrs. Avery straight on why I've made certain choices in my life." Angie's tone was cold.

"Mrs. Avery, please return to your room. If you'll use the intercom, breakfast will be prepared for you—in the dining room, or on a tray if you prefer. Miss Donalson is late for her run. Don't detain her any longer."

"What will you do, lock her up?"

"If necessary." Chapman's voice was filled with authority. "Let's go, Miss D."

Angie followed her down the stairs and out the door without looking back. Neither of them spoke, they just ran. Chapman set a swift pace. They were back at the house in less than forty minutes. As they climbed the stairs, Chapman paused. "I know it's hard, listening to her mouth. But you can't play in her league. She's been intimidating people with that mouth since birth. Just let it wash over you. Like a duck."

"I didn't start that conversation. She came into my room, yelling at me. I just wanted her to know that I haven't been intimate with Marc since they married. And I didn't volunteer for the job in the first place." Angie's tone was quiet and calm.

"Sure. But there are no doubt things that Mr. Avery must keep from his wife. I think he's taking a huge risk bringing her here."

"He thinks we'll become friends. It ain't gonna happen."

"If she exposes this operation, many of us will suffer. That's my main concern."

"I see," Angie said. Chapman had more to lose than anyone did. She'd been "at point" from the get-go. Chapman marched up the stairs with Angie trailing, hoping her remarks hadn't gone too far.

*   *   *

For the next week, Becky made life hell for almost everyone at Angelhurst. Nothing pleased her. She made demands and complained without ceasing. Marc was disgusted with both his wife *and* his mistress. Avery had hoped that they'd make peace and settle their differences. Every member of the staff of Angelhurst was working overtime, trying to please Becky. All suffered some of her verbal abuse, but Angie heard the most. For the staff, the end result was just extra work. Angie faced constant needling. Becky couldn't understand why Angie hadn't just gotten into her car and headed for anywhere, other than her husband.

Sometimes Angie was able to hold her peace. Sometimes she wasn't, leading to the inevitable verbal altercation. As Angie marched up the steps to the patio after her run one morning, the conflict became physical as well.

Chapman had pushed her to do five miles, and Angie had managed, but she was tired. Angie had just poured a bowl of corn flakes when Becky came out the door. She wore a pair of tights and a sports bra with a tunic over it, looking the picture of physical fitness. The picture, not the reality, of course. Angie was sweaty, her hair frizzy from the humidity, her strength all but gone. But Angie glanced at down at her own body, which was straight and sturdy, if devoid of Becky's sensual curves.

"Hi there, floozy. Had a bad morning? I think I'll take a picture of you, just like that, and pin it up in the bedroom. That ought to get ol' Marc raring to go."

Although Becky had no doubt said worse things, Angie was sick of Becky's insults and strong enough to overpower her. Grabbing her adversary by the arms, Angie pushed Becky to the rail and over it, effectively tossing her off the patio. For good measure she poured her bowl of corn flakes on Becky's head, as she lay sprawled in the shrubbery below.

Chapman didn't move. Not a muscle. Janice had just come out with a platter of bacon and eggs. She set it down and began to giggle. Marc came out, swearing and cursing, helping his wife up the steps. Angie turned on her heel and went to her room for a shower, deciding to forgo breakfast.

At lunch, Becky reopened the fracas, at first verbally, then by splashing her glass of Chardonnay in Angie's face. They were on the patio again, and Angie repeated the maneuver that sent her over the rail once more. At a nod from Marc, Chapman apprehended Angie this time, taking her to the detention cell, still dripping wine. Angie went without protest, figuring that Chapman was going along with Marc for show. She expected little or no punishment. Chapman was on her side, right?

*   *   *

However, Chapman slammed the door of the detention cell, shaking her head. This one was beyond her, and it was time to tell Avery that. Marching back to the patio, she signaled to him that she needed to meet him in his study.

"Mr. Avery, we have to keep them apart. I can't control Angie in this situation. It's intolerable."

"*You* think it's intolerable. What about me? I have to live with the bitch. And as for Angie, I don't just want her—I want her *willing*. They both need an attitude adjustment."

"I can deal with Angie, under most circumstances. Your wife is your business. Right now, I need Mrs. Avery out of here. Or let me take Angie elsewhere. I could use the cabin, if that suits you."

"Billie, what I demand is that they be made to get along with each other. Not necessarily like each other, but get along. No more fighting."

"I'm not a miracle worker!" Chapman protested.

"You've always worked miracles. Give me a plan for creating harmony between warring parties."

"You need a diplomat, not a soldier. They have to work out their differences."

"In training soldiers, you had to have any number of people who didn't like each other. How did you make them into a unit?"

Chapman sighed at his naiveté. "Mr. Avery, it's different. In training recruits, or special forces units, you strip away the differences and build them back up through mutual success and teamwork. I probably could make them work together in that situation. But here, they're two individuals who won't back down. I can't help you. The best thing to do is separate them."

"You want me to divorce her. I know you do. But I'm going to keep both of them, because they both have qualities I desire. And I'm not just talking about sex. Not at all. So let's get back to controlled situations. What would you need to make it work? Think as outlandishly as you want."

Sitting back, Chapman mentally rehashed portions of her military career. Certain situations made people or broke them—quickly. Rebecca Avery had never met a real challenge in her whole life. She wasn't the sort of individual who volunteered for military duty, of course, but such people had occasionally been conscripted. The techniques should work, but the situation would have to be extreme. Rebuilding her character would be possible. But the price would be too high. Billie certainly didn't want to go through something like that.

"Billie, I see the wheels turning. Talk out loud."

"We can talk about it, if you want. But we need to get these two separated. I have Angie locked up, and I want to let her out. Get your wife out of here, or let me take Angie away."

"First, let's hear it. Then we'll move Angie."

"Survival training might work. Take the two of them, with just a big pack each, and drop them in a wilderness area for a considerable length of time—say four to six months. No way to get back to civilization. No food, no shelter except through teamwork. Either they get along or they die."

"Did you do stuff like that?"

"Me, personally?" Chapman grinned and shook her head. "Some aspects of my service are classified. But I could be in charge of such a mission. There would have to be teamwork exercises, such as setting up camp, locating food and water, searching for and locating the other individual in the unit, and so forth. Doing without some resupply might be beyond their abilities. But drop a few MRE's each week, and anything else has to be caught, killed, and cooked. Everything but the most necessary essentials would have to be taken away."

"I think this is a fabulous idea. Plan it out, in detail. I'll want a full report by 0900 tomorrow."

Chapman laughed. "Aren't you getting too far into this?"

"Right now, it's only an idea—but I have a problem, and you have an uncanny ability to solve problems."

"What about my girl? Do I leave her locked up?"

"Yes, but in her room. No clothes, unless you need to have her exercise or work. I want her to consider the infraction serious. It's either that or some sort of chain, and you say she hates any sort of restraint."

"Okay. Confined to quarters without clothing," Chapman pondered the situation, "Mrs. Avery entered her room earlier this week. She must be kept out of there. I'll have Danny replace the lock on the connecting room door with a key-only lock."

"No need. Becky goes in the detention cell."

"You're kidding."

"No, not at all. No restraints. No clothes. Same as Angie."

"You can't do that." Chapman was amazed at the suggestion. "It was difficult with Angie, and she came from nothing. The minute your wife leaves here, she'll ruin you with it. You could face criminal charges, and your marriage will be over in a way that'll make daily headlines."

"By the time you're finished with her, she won't remember the detention cell." Marc Avery's smile was confident.

"Take her home, sir. Please."

"You have your orders. I want Becky to learn to get along with the rest of the world. She can start with you."

Chapman rose to her feet. "You'll accompany me?"

"Sure. A part of me enjoyed seeing Angie toss her over the rail. I'll probably enjoy this, too."

*   *   *

Angie heard about Becky's being placed in the detention cell from Janice, who had drawn the duty of bringing meals. Angie sat down in utter disbelief. "You're kidding, aren't you?"

"No, Miss Donalson, I'm not. You should've seen Billie's face after she and Mr. Avery had stripped her and locked her up." Janice sat down to gossip. "And Billie's been assigned to come up with a plan for straightening her out. I have no idea what she will dream up. Billie's a great boss, but she does suffer from an overdose of the military—at an early age."

"I hope that Marc has a good divorce lawyer. Because the minute Becky gets back to Daddy, this thing is gonna blow up like a hydrogen bomb."

"I would think so," Janice agreed. "Sorry, I have to go. I'm bringing trays to everyone today. Mrs. Avery is next. I plan to just shove it through the slot under the door."

"I don't blame you. I've been on the wrong side of her tongue too many times." Angie turned back to her computer. "See ya. Let me know what's happening."

"Sure." Janice locked the door behind her.

After she ate lunch, Angie went back to work on designing a presentation that Marc had asked her to do earlier. She didn't want to do work for him, especially after the events of the past few days; she just needed to keep her mind active. Otherwise, all the crazy stuff that happened around her might affect her more than it did.

Chapter 18

"I'm uncomfortable with much of this for these women. Please understand that. I want you to view this as just a hypothetical situation." Chapman had her notes in front of her and a bare bones proposal typed up for Avery.

"Go on. What would happen in Stage One?"

"Typical indoctrination for new troops. Stage One requires a uniform appearance and lack of amenities. It's an essential part of the breakdown, and getting to survival basics. We're talking fatigues, learning to sleep on the ground, and carrying a week's worth of gear on their backs. No baths, no toilets." Chapman hesitated before throwing in the last item. "A woman fiddling with her hair is not part of the survival picture. Neither one should have any—at all."

"You intend to shave their heads?" His voice was incredulous.

"As part of the breakdown, yes. It's also a convenience measure. We'll be a long way from a bathroom or a beauty shop." Chapman paused, searching his expression. "Remember, it will grow back. Six months is long enough to grow a good bit of hair."

"Okay. After that?"

"Get them into a situation where teamwork is expected and required. Airlift into a wilderness is ideal. There should be series of activities, most of which are meaningful to their survival on a day to day basis. Keeping them too busy to fight and forcing them to work together—or at least in mutually dependent activities. For an extended period of time. A week or two shows it can be done. A few months makes it a habit. Four to six months is an ideal time frame. I'd prefer to be out of any wilderness area before winter."

"Stage Three?"

"Critical. Extraction from the survival situation, but additional time in uniform, to make the training hold in new situations." Chapman had it all figured out, albeit reluctantly.

"You know, Billie, this sounds like it would work." Avery smiled. He was impressed with the thought Chapman had put into her proposal.

"Maybe. But I don't recommend it." Chapman's voice was firm. "There is considerable risk to the women. Mr. Avery, this would have to be for real. Any number of accidents could befall the unit. It would be a most difficult assignment for the officer in charge. Literally a six-month mission, with no days off. And it would be expensive. Initial equipment and uniforms. Helicopter trips at least twice a month to check on the unit and to drop supplies."

"Humph. Compared to their charge bills, this sounds cheap!"

"Both of them would no doubt resent the person or persons who put them in the situation. I would be the initial object of hatred. But I'd also be the one to get them through it. You, on the other hand, would be just as much at fault, and have no opportunity for redemption. Now they are fighting *over* you. In the future, they might *both* want to kill you."

"I want to do it. The whole thing."

"No, Mr. Avery. No."

"What's your timeline on starting?"

"I'm not sure. Perhaps two or three weeks on equipment. Where would we go? There is no place remote enough in this area. It has to be *miles* and *miles* from civilization. No chance of hiking out."

"I own a ranch in Wyoming. Huge place. We're talking thousands of acres. They measure land in square miles out there. No one would disturb you."

"Then we add transport to that remote location. Mr. Avery, reevaluate this. Let's go back to just keeping them separate."

"I want Becky to stay in the detention cell until we begin Operation Goodwill. She'll need some exercise. Could you let her out, under supervision?"

"We'll take care of it. But please reconsider." Chapman didn't plead. Instead, she looked at him with a sincerity that touched him.

"Begin work on the mission. I want an update in two days, including a projected timeline and a cost estimate. Contact my local staff if you need any assistance. There is an Avery-owned mine near the ranch. You can use them for support when you check out the area."

*   *   *

A week had passed. Chapman or Danny had taken each woman out twice a day for exercise sessions—but always at different times. Angie looked well, for she was accustomed to periods of confinement. Mrs. Avery was a different matter. Chapman was beginning to believe that Mr. Avery was right. Becky needed what was being planned. An attitude adjustment, Mr. Avery had called it. Chapman called him in Charleston with an update.

"Mr. Avery, we are ready for Stage One. That will be done here. A week's worth of conditioning will no doubt help them adjust. Stage Two will begin next week. Transport and equipment should be ready by then. It will last approximately 5 months. Then we return here for Stage Three. In six months, you should have two very different ladies—in appearance, anyway. Hopefully in attitude, too. Right now, I just hope that everyone gets back in one piece."

"You need to work out a couple of days leave time for yourself. I know this has been difficult, and it's only beginning. You'll be compensated, starting with this month's check." Marc sounded appreciative. "I'll come up for the weekend to give you that much time off. Then I'll stay for day one of Stage One. It should be interesting."

"I'd still prefer to back out, sir. I haven't told either woman about our plans, although I think Janice may have given Angie some hints."

"No, Billie. We're going through with it. Has your electronic equipment shown up?"

"Yes, sir. Portable transponders and tracer, and radios. We're ready to begin training with those."

"Uniforms and gear?"

"Yes, sir. I've got fatigues, we call them BDU's in the service, and boots for each of us. I've ordered two tents which are scheduled for delivery any day now. I also have ALICE packs, bedding, cooking equipment, and two cases of MRE's. All here." Chapman sounded resigned.

"Stage One begins on Monday morning. Stage Two begins the following Monday, barring last minute complications. Right?"

"Right, sir." Chapman ended the conversation, then packed her bag for a visit to Matthew's. But she doubted that she'd enjoy it. There was just too darned much to think about.

* * *

Angie knew that something big was going to happen. Janice had told her that Billie was working night and day on some project, something with a military slant; she'd also been gone for two days, working on it. Janice was certain that it involved Angie and Becky. Danny had been reticent for once, so Janice had little information. When Angie asked him about it, he said she'd find out soon enough.

Angie ran each morning as usual, sometimes with Chapman and sometimes with Danny, but she returned to her room for a shower afterward and had to emerge without clothing. The closet was padlocked, the small chest in her room held only workout clothes, and she was to wear those only when instructed. To violate that dictum would result in her having to wear restraints, so she cooperated with the instructions. Angie had one other exercise session each day, usually weights with Chapman or tennis with Danny.

Janice told her that Becky had a similar schedule—a long walk/run in the morning and some recreational activity in the afternoon. The pair never saw each other; no doubt that was planned. Janice told Angie that everyone was getting tired, so something had to happen soon.

Marc came back to Tennessee causing the schedule of activities to virtually cease. He did spend some time with Angie, but Chapman was nowhere in sight. Angie figured that the former Marine had the weekend off. She read the signs, realizing that whatever they had in mind would happen when Chapman returned. After she made several queries to Marc, he became angry, telling her to shut up.

On Sunday night, Marc visited her again, lounging on the big bed in her suite.

"Angie, you sure you don't want to hop in here and have some fun?"

"No, I'll stay over here." Angie sat in the big chair at her computer. Although she'd been naked in his presence often enough, she still found the situation embarrassing.

"You sure? It might be a while before you get another chance."

"Why? What's going on?" Angie's uneasiness was exacerbated by his refusal to answer her questions. Perhaps she was paranoid, but the big secret had been brewing too long.

Angie woke up alone on Monday morning, a little later than usual, surprised that she'd been allowed to sleep. Janice knocked on the door, handing her a folded bundle of clothing. Shaking it out, she noticed that it was different from what she'd worn in the past. There was a pair of camouflage pants with adjustable waist tabs and a string for tightening the legs at the bottom, a brown tee shirt, a sort of shirt/jacket combination which matched the pants, and a nylon web belt. Also, instead of running shoes, she had a pair of mid weight trail boots with padded socks. This clothing was tougher stuff, designed with a cooler climate in mind, than the uniform she had worn before. Topping off the bundle was a peaked camouflage cap, like the one she'd seen Chapman wear from time to time.

"Billie said you have ten minutes. She wants you standing outside the door." Janice's voice was devoid of emotion.

"So it begins—whatever *it* is."

"I suppose so. I'm still in the dark. Honest." Janice shrugged and closed the door.

Donning the uniform and taking a deep breath, she went into the hallway. To her left, Chapman was marching up the stairs in a uniform identical to the one Angie wore, a black bag in her hand. Chapman motioned for Angie to enter the detention cell.

As she complied, Chapman's voice commanded. "About face. At rest."

Even after all the years, her reaction was automatic—Angie turned. As she did, Chapman snapped handcuffs on her wrists, then she gestured for Angie to go to the center of the room. Becky was also dressed in camouflage and handcuffed. In a brief glance around the small, dark room, she noted that the furnishings had been rearranged—there were now two bunks, with footlockers at the end of each one, on either side of the room. A chain had been welded to each, and a cuff was attached, very much like the bed across the hall. The bunks were bolted to the floor, as well.

A straight chair stood in the center of the room, and Chapman guided her to straddle it, her chin even with the back of the chair. Angie sat, uneasy, and watched Chapman. Marc came into the room, standing between Chapman and his wife.

"What's going on?" Angie asked, finding it impossible to keep the nervousness out of her voice. "Tell me something."

"I call it Operation Goodwill—Billie calls it survival training," Marc answered. "I have to have you two get along, so we've determined to put you through a mission, together. I know Billie has trained you before, Angie, but that was nothing compared with what you'll experience in the next six months. Today, we begin Stage One, preliminary training. Stage Two begins next Monday. It involves some interesting and somewhat hazardous training in the field. At the end of Stage Three, each of you will no doubt be a different person, if, as Billie likes to point out, you survive."

A hair clipper appeared in Chapman's hand. "Miss Donalson, you must remain absolutely still. This will hurt if I have to restrain you further." Her other hand came down on Angie's shoulder, pushing her back into the chair even as she tried to stand.

"What are you going to do?" Her voice was frantic. Angie knew damned well what she intended to do, but she couldn't believe it. For years, Chapman had endeavored to keep her appearance perfect. Now she intended to destroy Angie's best asset. Marc joined Chapman's effort, grabbing Angie's arms and pushing her down, holding her in the chair.

"Be still. You won't be needing all this hair for a while, so we're getting rid of it." Billie's voice was a low growl in her ear.

She was quick and efficient. With one hand at the back of Angie's neck and the clipper in the other, she began. In strokes from the forehead to the back of her neck, she took off all Angie's hair. Still in shock, Angie had a vague awareness that her head felt naked. A downward glance showed her that the floor was covered in reddish brown locks. Chapman inspected the girl's head, seemed satisfied, and ordered her to stand by the left bunk. Avery stepped back, releasing her. Appalled by the damage, she approached the cot that

Chapman had indicated. Then Chapman turned her attention to Marc's wife.

"Mrs. Avery, sit down." Chapman commanded her. Becky didn't move. No verbal tirade, but she did not move. Marc and Chapman took a side each and moved her beside the chair, pushing her onto it. Marc held her, as he had held Angie, while her black hair joined Angie's on the floor. Angie saw her hands pull hard against the cuffs, other than that she didn't move. There was about an eighth of an inch of hair left; just enough to show that she'd once had black hair. Chapman told her to go stand beside her bunk, and when she failed to move, they picked her up and placed her near the one on the right. Chapman retrieved Angie's cap, adjusting it to fit her now nearly naked skull. She did the same for Becky. Marc stood near the door, staring, as if he couldn't take his eyes off the pair.

"You will wear these everywhere you go for the next six months," Chapman said before slipping a metal chain attached to a curious gadget around Angie's neck. "This is a big step up from dog tags. Each one has a transponder, similar to the one in your car, Angie, which emits a microwave signal. Listen up! This is most important. It will allow members of the unit to find you, and if extraction becomes necessary, it will allow a helicopter to zero in on your location. It could mean the difference between life and death. I'm not kidding." Chapman unlocked Angie's handcuffs and put them in one of her many pockets.

Angie still stood, rubbing raw wrists. She watched Chapman remove the cuffs from Becky, and she, too, rubbed her chafed wrists.

"Where are we going?" Becky had found her voice.

"Stage One will be here. You will get used to the uniforms and other gear. Your exercise level will increase; you need to be in better shape for this mission. Stage Two, next week, involves the unit being taken to a remote wilderness—somewhere in the western U.S. I won't be specific, but it's plenty rugged. We are dropping for a five-month survival course. When you return, Stage Three, you will have other training and debriefing. Then it's over." Chapman recited this as she inspected their uniforms and checked the contents of the lockers.

Marc said nothing, but he watched intently.

"My father will have your hide. He'll nail you to the wall and—" Becky hadn't forgotten how to curse, even in the detention cell, in a uniform which looked ridiculous on her, with her hair lying in a pile on the floor. Angie waited for Chapman to intercede, but the former Marine let Becky go on with her graphic threats until she grew tired.

"The three of us are going out that door, downstairs to the back door," Chapman said, when Becky slowed her tirade, "and the minute your feet hit the grass, you run. We are doing five miles today and every day until we leave. Move out."

The pace Chapman set was slower than usual, but that was no doubt to help with the extra distance. At the end, Angie was exhausted, but she'd matched the pace Chapman set, losing sight of Becky after the first mile. Sitting on the bench outside the pool fence, Angie and Chapman waited. Angie didn't know what had happened in between, but Becky was running, Danny right behind her.

Becky collapsed on the bench beside Angie, chest heaving and gasping for breath. Chapman let her recover, then told her charges to get to their feet. They entered the pool house, a rather primitive facility with a shower, a toilet, and benches for dressing. Chapman introduced them to an MRE—"meals, ready to eat." Immediately, Angie decided that this was a horrible concoction for someone trained as a gourmet chef.

They ate them cold from foil pouches, then Chapman gestured toward the facilities and left. A few minutes later, at Chapman's command, they went outside. Each of them was assigned a work detail. Angie felt fortunate; she got a gardening assignment, something she would've done for recreation. Becky got grass cutting, and it was obvious that she'd never been near a lawn mower. Danny had to show her everything.

After a late lunch of crackers with little packets of peanut butter, Chapman marched them to the weight room for a full body workout, with the weights at Angie's maximum levels, insuring that she was tired when it was over. Although she did fairly low weights compared to Angie, Becky looked as if she were dropping. Chapman scrutinized the pair, shook her head, and escorted them back to the detention cell, ordering them to strip to underwear and chain themselves to the bunks.

Dinner was, Angie thankfully realized, something Mrs. Bowen had prepared. Janice brought it on trays; although they weren't allowed off the bunks, the food was good. At dusk, Chapman returned with a light pack for each girl. They dressed again, packed a flashlight, a canteen, a foam mattress, and a blanket. After a two-mile hike in the ever-growing darkness, Chapman demonstrated how to lay out their beds for a night under the stars.

Angie huddled in her blanket, realizing that she couldn't remember ever sleeping outside—not in her whole life. Angie didn't sleep much, but it was obvious that Becky was terrified. She seemed afraid to lie down, and Angie understood how she felt. At dawn, they were told to anoint the nearest tree, pack up their meager belongings and at a slow jog, return to the pool house. Breakfast was another MRE, then they performed another work assignment, followed by a five mile run, more crackers and peanut butter, and back to the woods. Chapman led them on a hike deep into the woods between the paths, which were used for riding and jogging.

Angie and Becky had hardly spoken to each other, and Angie hadn't spoken to Chapman since she'd performed the GI haircut. They reached a clearing, and Chapman decided it was time for another lecture. Drawing a line in the dirt with the toe of her boot, Chapman commanded the pair to form up at the line and paced in front of them as she talked.

"I've told you that wearing the transponder is critical. But being able to locate the other members of the unit is of paramount importance. Each of you must be able to use the mobile tracer to find the others. In theory, I would be the one to rescue you, but you might have to rescue me. The reality is that this will be a dangerous situation; each of us will be dependent on one another in this mission." Chapman paused in her pacing. "Donalson, you are more familiar with this terrain. I want you to go out into the woods—no more than a half-mile or so—and hide. It will be our job to find you. Take off, go ahead, find a spot, and stay put."

Angie didn't respond, but she was certain that Chapman still trusted her, despite the lack of conversation between them.

"Move out. You'll have fifteen minutes to secure your position."

Without hurrying, Angie went into the woods. Getting out of sight was easy, because the woods hadn't been landscaped here, and there was plenty of brush to make moving and locating difficult. Because she saw no alternatives, Angie obeyed the order. If they really were going into some wilderness area, Angie just might want Chapman to be able to locate her. Finding a fallen log in a thick patch of brush, Angie climbed in and sat down. She took off the camouflage cap and ran a hand over her prickly head. She scratched to alleviate some of the itching, then replaced the cap so that the brim hid her face. Looking around, Angie decided that she was well hidden, especially in the camouflage clothing. Making no sound, she took the canteen from her belt and drank some of the tepid water. This was going to be a long six months.

*　　　*　　　*

Becky had not yet recovered from her shock. Being locked up had been horrible—just like being in jail, she had told herself, or a dungeon, with the chain around her ankle at night. Then being made to wear these army clothes and having her head shaved, just like a victim of a concentration camp. Now she'd had no sleep and bad food, and her legs ached from all the running and hiking. She didn't know how much more she could bear.

Becky glanced at the compact woman before her, dressed in these same army clothes, and tried to understand some complex device for tracking in the wilderness.

"Do you see the signal?" Chapman was asking, again.

"Where?" Becky finally seemed to look at the tiny LCD screen.

"There. You see it?"

"There are three things blinking."

"I have the unit set for all three frequencies. The two at center are me and you. The third is Donalson. See it?" Chapman's voice was patient.

"Yes. So what do we do?"

"We move, trying to bring her signal closer to the center. When Donalson's signal is centered, along with ours, we've found the target. Just like a bull's eye."

"Okay."

"You take the point." Chapman gestured for her to move out.

"Huh?" Becky had no military frame of reference.

"You go first." Chapman was being more patient than she'd ever been in her whole life. She was sure of it.

"Oh," Becky said and moved toward the brush. "I'll have to go through those briars and stuff," she complained, hesitating.

"That's why you're wearing a uniform made to take some punishment, Avery. And it's why you don't need to be worrying about what's getting into your hair."

"Well, you solved that problem," Becky observed, her tone dry.

"Precisely. Move out, Avery."

*   *   *

They found her in about fifteen minutes. Angie had heard them approaching, then Becky appeared right in front of her. The search had taken not much longer than she spent finding her little hiding place. Then Chapman turned the exercise around, giving Becky the hiding job and giving Angie the point. She found Becky with little effort. Angie shook her head in wonder; it was a handy device.

"Each day, we'll check the transponders with the tracer. We need both parts functional, every day. If your transponder does not show up, then someone needs to keep a visual check on you. With only three in the unit, it's gonna be impossible to always stay together. The transponders will give us the ability to find each other." Chapman lectured the pair as they returned to the house.

Both of them were both happy to see their bunks. Neither protested Chapman's order to strip to skivvies and chain themselves up. Becky examined a blister that she'd made, burst, then chafed into a bloody mess. Angie's heel and one toe were also raw and bleeding. Angie sighed, noting that they both looked awful, and no doubt felt worse. This ordeal was going to be a long haul at best—worse if the lines of communication didn't open up. Operation Goodwill, indeed

"We look pretty bad, huh? And we haven't gone anywhere yet." Angie decided to break the conversational ice.

"I just feel tired—beaten." Becky sighed and stretched out.

"Running in new boots isn't such a good idea. My right foot is a mess."

"My feet are sore, too," Becky admitted.

"Do we have a first aid kit?"

"No," she replied. "I watched 'Army Woman' stock the lockers. We'll have to ask, if we ever get the chance."

"I'll leave that to you."

"So you and 'Army Woman' aren't friends anymore?" Becky taunted her.

"I guess not. I respect Billie. She knows her job. If anyone can take us to the wilderness for months and get us through, she's the one. But I don't deserve this. No way."

"Meaning, of course, that I do? No way, bitch. This is Marc Avery's fault, 'Army Woman's' fault, and your fault. Not mine." Becky's tone invited retort, but Angie held her tongue.

They couldn't fight, physically, for the chains on the bunks separated them. But Angie realized that verbal sparing would just make this intolerable situation even worse. So she shut up. Because they'd gotten so little sleep the night before, it wasn't long until they both crashed. Janice woke them with trays from the kitchen.

"Miss Donalson," she said in a somber tone, touching Angie's shoulder.

"Oh, hi, Janice. Sorry, I must have dozed off. We had a bad night."

"I brought some chicken salad and some fruit. Billie said you hadn't had much fresh food." Janice kept her eyes on the floor to avoid staring at either woman.

"No, we haven't. Thanks, Janice."

Angie smiled to herself as Janice assisted her with the tray, like she was a hospital patient. Angie certainly felt like one, her body sore and tired. Janice returned in a moment and helped Becky.

"Janice, we need some first aid stuff—band aids and antibiotic cream. I'm used to running, but not in boots. Just something for busted blisters and stuff like that. Could you get us something?"

"Sure. I'll be right back."

The pair ate, and when she came back, Janice helped each woman with her injuries. She took the trays and wished them the best of luck.

Seeing a familiar face had been comforting, Angie mused. She guessed that Becky didn't even have that consolation. Janice was just another member of the crew torturing her. Of that, Angie was certain, because she'd once felt that way about everyone here herself.

"Janice is a really nice person," Angie assured Becky.

"Yes. For a kidnapper, she has a great personality." The sarcasm was strong in her voice. "Miss Donalson, spare me."

"Okay," Angie replied and lay back on the bunk. Silence enveloped the dark room.

*   *   *

Chapman returned to give them an instructional booklet on their packs. Angie shook her head in amazement. Yes, instructions for packs. Really. There was also a military survival manual.

"You will familiarize yourselves with these manuals. You'll be using the All-Purpose Lightweight Individual Carrying Equipment described in them. The rest of your gear will be here tomorrow evening. While it's important to read both manuals, be sure to concentrate on the shelter and food sections of the survival manual. We're leaving the kitchen and the bedrooms behind, you know."

"What, are you giving us a test or something?" Becky asked in her most derisive tone. "Maybe if we flunk, we just won't go." This last comment she directed at Angie.

"No, you'll just have to try to carry 30 pounds of gear in your pockets. Or maybe we'll leave your stuff behind. But Angie will not carry your gear, nor will I. If you insist on going in just what you're wearing, you won't survive. If you insist on going with no information, you reduce all our chances."

"What if I refuse to carry all that stuff?"

"Avery, if you fail to survive, you will solve Angie's biggest problem. And mine." Chapman's voice was curt. "As you were." Chapman executed a perfect right face and left the room.

"'Yes, ma'am,' 'No, ma'am,' and 'No excuse, ma'am'." Angie said almost under her breath.

"What?" Becky sounded irritated.

"You won't listen. It's not in your nature to do so. But when I was still a teenager, Ms. Chapman taught me the three responses to give a woman suffering from an overdose of the military. 'Yes, ma'am,' 'No, ma'am,' and 'No excuse, ma'am.' If you can keep your mouth limited to those, you'll save yourself loads of humiliation."

Reluctantly, Angie picked up the survival manual and began reading. Becky sat staring at the ALICE manual. For the first time, Angie realized that this woman just might not make it, and she wondered what that might mean for her—and for Marc.

Chapter 19

In one way, the week known as Stage One went by far too slowly, but was grueling and onerous, because the lifestyle to which they were accustomed was literally just across the hall. In another way, it was too fast, because on Monday the threesome would fly out, and all this would cease to be training and become surviving. Although they were not friends, Becky and Angie knew that somehow they'd have to get through this together, so they kept the verbal barbs to a minimum.

A week had past, and Angie still not spoken to Chapman, other than to answer a direct question. Chapman had ignored this and continued to work with both women, teaching them what they had to know. They spent one afternoon, learning how to assemble the huge packs that would be used after the drop. Another day they learned to set up the tents and to build an emergency shelter with only a camp ax. On the highest hill on the estate, they practiced rock climbing in tandem and learned the safety procedures. They dug a latrine—a hole in the ground between two trees with a pole lashed to the trees as a support for their fannies. There were additional sessions with the transponder locations, even in the dark. On several occasions, Chapman put them through the search and locate exercise again, testing the radios to see how much range they had, and under what conditions. And, in addition to all that, they did a couple of work details to help Janice and Danny, who had been on duty for quite a while.

On Sunday night, Chapman had them assemble the tents and sleep in a clearing in the woods. At dawn, Chapman woke the women and ordered them to take down the tents and stow them in the large compartments of their packs. After jogging back to the house, they had breakfast, and as Chapman kept her watchful eyes on them, they loaded the rest of the stuff from the lockers into the various compartments or small duffel bags which were attached to the bottoms of the packs. When they had crammed everything from ponchos to folding shovels into their olive drab bundles, Chapman double-checked everything and, without a change of clothing or a shower, had them lug all their gear to the helipad. Both of the women seemed apprehensive, but neither vocalized her fears.

When the helicopter arrived, Danny helped them into it. Bearing the Avery logo, it was a Bell LongRanger with seating for seven, thus being able to carry both the passengers and their equipment easily. The copilot handed back three pairs of hearing protectors, which they donned without removing their caps. Such helicopters, Chapman knew, had a range of a bit more than 300 miles, meaning that there would be three stops. From her seat in the helicopter, Chapman watched the landscape change from the trees and farms of Tennessee to the flatter plains, marked by large fields and occasional streams of varying size. As the day progressed, they flew over areas which were more semi-arid than anything else.

*   *   *

By varying degrees, the altitude increased, and they approached the most magnificent mountains Angie had ever seen. The pilot consulted his map while Chapman looked for their destination. With Chapman in the front, scanning the terrain, the helo pilot maneuvered a bit and lowered them to an area of sparse grass. Without streams, trees and large bushes didn't seem to grow very well.

All three had dozed some in the helicopter, thus gaining some rest to go along with the extra daylight gained as they traversed two time zones. After the helo left, Chapman ordered them to set up a basic shelter, hang the food packs in a spindly tree a good march away from the camp... to discourage bears from visiting, Chapman informed them... and gave each woman an assignment to scour an area for firewood. The weather was cooler and dryer than that in Tennessee, and Chapman reminded them that they'd welcome the fire come nightfall.

Chapman began to parcel out jobs for the pair; it was no surprise that Angie was in charge of food, while Becky was designated to be in charge of shelter. When the camp moved, Angie would carry the food and cooking equipment and Becky would carry the tents. Bedding and clothing, each would carry for herself. Chapman carried "command gear," including the mobile tracer for the transponders, the radios, and the communications equipment. She also lugged a first aid kit and some tools, including a rope for climbing.

After the fire began to burn well, Angie brought out the MRE's. Counting the packages, Becky pointed out that they had only a three-day supply.

Chapman laughed. "We are in survival mode now. One MRE per person, every other day. The rest of our food we procure in the field. We'll get a helo drop in two weeks. That gives us a couple each in reserve, just in case the weather prevents the helo run."

Last week the MRE's had seemed insufferable. Now, with the prospect of only one every other day, and nothing else, suddenly they had become important. Angie got out the cooking pot and a folding grate, placing them over the fire. Becky sat down, using her pack as a pillow, ready to be waited on. Angie had sacrificed part of her water supply to heat the MRE's. Chapman noted it and turned to Becky.

"Avery, we need a supply of fresh water. Climb up on that hill and see if you can see a stream. Look for ribbons of vegetation. This is a dry climate."

"Now?" Her voice was plaintive.

"Now. It'll get dark soon. We'll need water tomorrow, or certainly the next day. And we won't be able to refill canteens, much less wash anything until we locate a water source. I assume that you wish to bathe, or do you plan to wait five months for a shower?" Chapman dug in her pack, then she handed Becky a compact pair of binoculars.

Becky got off her behind and climbed the hill, her pace leisurely.

Chapman got out the tracer using the opportunity to calibrate it as Becky climbed out of sight.

"Ms. Chapman, I just hope we get through this," Angie stated, starting the first real conversation they'd had in a week. "I can't believe you brought us here, wherever here is."

"I'm sure. I'm not unaware of the potential for problems." Chapman's voice was level. "This is gonna be tough for the untrained. That week you had wasn't sufficient instruction. I have a few advantages that a military commander wouldn't have, such as these transponders. But in a military operation, I also would have a larger compliment, and more than one experienced officer. If anything happens to me, you two will be up that proverbial creek."

"Why'd you send her out alone like that?"

"She needs to build up her confidence. So do you. You'll work together, plenty. But you'll also have to work alone, too. And we do need that water source."

"Didn't you spot one from the air?"

Chapman nodded. "I did look. I believe there's one on the other side of that hill where I sent Avery. But distances can look a whole lot different on the ground. Besides, reconnaissance is one task that we'll all have to take on from time to time."

"I heard you say that we were going to a place with the fewest people per square mile in the U.S. —that means we're in Wyoming, I guess."

"You must have had a good geography teacher," Chapman said with a grin.

"Why are you being so circumspect?"

"Miss Donalson, one requirement for this mission's site was that it must be impossible for either of you to hike out. And I don't want you or Avery getting killed trying it."

"Don't worry, I have no intention of taking off on my own." Angie looked about the wilderness and shook her head. "I've never seen such a big rock pile. You're looking at one Georgia girl who realizes she ain't ready to tackle this on her own."

"Good. How's that supper coming along?"

"Got one warm enough," Angie told her. "I'll wait for Becky. If you want, go ahead and eat."

Chapman looked at the tracer again. "She's returning. You eat this one, and I'll get the next one warmed up for her." Chapman squatted beside the little grate and plopped in another foil pouch.

*   *   *

After the first two or three days, their situation got a little better. A little. Becky had indeed found water, so they moved their campsite near it. With some arduous labor, they managed to catch some fish in the rapid waters of the stream, and Angie found some nuts that still had some good meats within. They had to crack a great many to find anything, but it was still food.

After washing out their three day old uniforms, they bathed as best they could in the frigid water and donned the crumpled, but clean ones from their packs. With a rueful shrug, Angie began to see some benefit in her 1/4-inch long haircut. They swiped the soap over their heads just like the rest of their bodies and got out of the creek on the double. During the first week, Chapman established the pattern of the evening meal being based on whatever they had gathered during the day, since it often required a lot of prep time. The coveted MRE was eaten in the middle of the day, on the days they had one, and if they had enough luck to save any food, that became breakfast. Often, the threesome went without breakfast, but starting with nothing was a great incentive to go out and find something.

Shelter was imperative. Fire was more imperative. But food was most imperative. In a short time, Angie realized that they spent more time and energy on finding food than on any other aspect of existence. She guarded the food with her life. Really. If Becky had decided to satisfy her hunger, then it might mean starvation for the other two. So Angie viewed her food responsibility as her most urgent task.

Angie was surprised when she realized that her physical appearance was now of no importance. She forgot about her hair... or the lack of it... and nails and other aspects which had formerly been so important to her. Now staying warm and reasonably dry and having food were the most imperative goals in life. Each woman's weight dropped with the combination of scant food and hard work.

Chapman made them move each week, generally tracking along a stream to a new campsite. Moving to the resources was necessary, she informed them. As far as firewood was concerned, she was right; it was hard to come by. Game was also quickly exhausted. So the moves made sense, but each one meant a day or two of breaking down camp, hiking to a new location, and setting up again. On those days, they didn't spend much time finding food. So, in spite of some improved procurement techniques, they were still subject to lean days.

On this particular day, Angie was looking for ferns. Chapman had shown her some small examples struggling to survive on a creek bank, and Angie's job was to gather enough to boil for supper.

Walking quite a distance beyond the range of her small radio, Angie debated as to whether or not she had enough for a scant cooking. While Angie sought veggies, Chapman had taken Becky to check the snares they'd set two days ago. If the snares yielded some prey, they'd have something with the greens. At least, Angie tried to think of them as that. She sighed, remembering Aunt Claire's cornbread. Angie and her aunt had made many a late summer meal off turnip greens and cornbread. No matter how much she wished, there would be no cornbread this evening.

Since she was running out of streambed as the creek got smaller and out of radio range, she turned to follow the creek back toward camp. In an hour or so, she was back in touch with Chapman by radio, and she soon saw the two low slung, camouflaged tents. Angie's pack liner was only partially filled with the tender heads of the ferns, but she could see that her companions had already started a fire in the pit. On the first day at this site, Becky and Angie had dug a shallow pit, lined it with rocks, and rigged a stick that would hold a pot over the coals. The arrangement was straight out of the survival manual, but it worked well enough. Angie filled the pot with water from her canteen and started the greens, but they would need more water, so she went toward the creek to refill it. There she saw Becky kneeling, washing off an animal skin. Becky glanced up, nodding in recognition. Although she saw her numerous times each day, Angie was still amazed by her companion's appearance. Her BUD pants hung on her now lean frame, and her hat covered most of her short, black hair. Angie couldn't imagine a sharper contrast to the snob that she'd known in Charleston. Not that she looked any different, she reminded herself, running a hand over her own stubby hair.

*   *   *

During the entire experience, the women never saw the helicopter land. Every sixteen days, they would journey to a location Chapman indicated and find the packages which had been dropped from the helo. The usual shipment contained a case of 24 MRE's, along with batteries for the communications equipment, and once there were fresh tee shirts and some camp soap. Angie knew that Chapman had some sort of device for communicating with Avery headquarters via satellite, because she sent in a weekly report, but neither woman was allowed to know the arrangements.

Unit communications were handled via the transponders and short range radios. Each morning, Chapman checked to see that the transponders were working, and they were given a radio for use that day. The radios had a range of a mile or so, depending on terrain, which allowed them to work alone yet stay in touch.

As far as the unit idea went, the women worked better together than Angie would have thought possible. After the first few days, Becky Avery lost most of her rich girl "wait on me" attitude. As she got leaner and stronger, she was able to take her place on the team. Each woman was in exactly the same situation—a subordinate to Chapman, an ugly waif in dirty clothes with a closely cropped head.

In actuality, both women were quite dependent on each other. Angie's dry shelter rode on Becky's back, and Becky's next meal rode on Angie's. Neither of them could afford to undercut the other; indeed, the situation required cooperation and teamwork. Chapman fostered their togetherness by having two tents, one for herself and the gear, and another one which Becky and Angie shared. Chapman parceled out the day-to-day duties, and if teamwork was called for, usually Angie and Becky got the job—whatever it might be.

*   *   *

The plan was working, Chapman thought to herself, as she watched the pair setting up their tent. The fifth week was just beginning, and they had just moved to a hillside overlooking a beautiful valley. They were a bit farther from water this time, but it was close enough. More trees were here, so wood would be less of a problem. Week by week, Chapman was working her way higher into the mountains, where there was more rainfall, therefore more vegetation, and hopefully more game.

The day was warm, and both women had removed their BDU jackets to work in their tee shirts. Their caps were off, and Chapman could see the sunlight glinting off the hair that was beginning to grow back on their heads. Each one had enough so that she could easily tell them apart, even at a distance, by color—Becky had a dark black cap of hair, while Angie's was reddish brown. Neither would need a comb for another month or so, but they seemed to be finished with the itchy stage.

A measure of their progress had to be their emotional balance. Angie was becoming less fearful, both of their surroundings and of starving to death. Her natural self-confidence had begun to reemerge. To say that she was happy would be an overstatement, but she looked less miserable than she had when they first arrived. Even more encouraging was the occasional laughter that Chapman had begun to hear at night from the tent that the young women shared.

Becky was also adjusting, albeit more slowly. She'd lost more weight than Angie or Chapman and had built more muscle. She was also less fearful than she'd been at the beginning, but she still started at the smallest noise. Chapman doubted that she ever got a full night's sleep. Certainly, she was still reluctant to venture forth, whether it be an assignment or simply recreation.

During the past couple of weeks, Chapman had begun to plan hikes for recreation. At first, every foray had been to find food or wood. Those tasks still took much of their time, of course. But as they became more skillful, they had additional time, and Chapman wanted them to see the gorgeous country and respect its wildlife. For the operation to be successful, the initial breakdown of will had to be followed by a positive restructuring. Appreciating nature, as well as living off its bounty, was part of that. Succeeding at the tasks at hand would finish the re-creation of their self-esteem.

For her communications with the outside, Chapman had been given an experimental PDA with a satellite uplink to Avery Electronics Security, who in turn relayed messages to Marc. He had seen digital images of the women as they worked around the camp, taken with the digital camera contained in Chapman's "command gear." She also used it to send text only updates, which told him that there'd been no physical fighting and little verbal debate. He'd also been assured that they were healthy and had no critical needs to be addressed.

As she composed her weekly message, Chapman decided to venture that the experiment seemed successful. The women were becoming closer, and their tendency to bait each other had waned. Despite their lack of equipment, they were indeed surviving. Angie and Becky had eaten things that they'd never touch in civilization, but the sacrifices were helping mold them into a unit, a team.

In an area with moose and coyotes and bears, Chapman felt almost naked without a rifle. At first, she had decided to forgo having one in camp, primarily because she didn't trust her charges. However, the situation with the two women had improved enough that she decided to request a weapon and take the chance that they wouldn't use it in on each other—or her.

As a precaution against something happening to her, Chapman had begun teaching them to use the compass and read the maps that she used to pick campsites and find the helo drop areas. Angie picked it up fairly well, but Becky seemed to have little math talent. However, Becky had learned quite of bit of woodcraft, and she was now able to go on food gathering expeditions alone. Chapman was becoming quite proud of the way the women had developed during their ordeal.

*   *   *

Angie and Becky had found a pool in the stream where the water was still, the closest thing to a mirror that either of them had seen in three months. They squatted on the bank, peering closely at the strange images before them. Angie mused that she'd have known what she looked like—she looked just like Becky. The only differences were minor changes in the details—her red hair instead of Becky's glistening black.

Their hair was now more than an inch long all over, giving good coverage, but it didn't get in the way. The BDU's had been used hard; they were ragged. Washing them in cold water by beating them on the rocks with a little soap from the small containers of camp soap that they used for washing everything had not kept them looking too spiffy. Both young women tried to keep clean, but they had to wear one uniform while the other dried out, so it wasn't unusual to be in the same one for three days. And often, it was so cool at night that they slept in them, too.

Angie's boots were getting worn on the toes, and the threads were beginning to unravel. Both of her tee shirts were stained and had small holes at the seams, and one pair of pants was ripped from a fall on a rugged rock climb. But considering, the gear was holding up well. Better than they were.

Chapman had instituted sick call, and neither woman liked her idea of nursing. They had an assortment of problems that required her ministrations. Angie had a sore on one foot that refused to heal. Although Chapman kept dressing it, it always broke open and bled through the dressing. Becky had cut her hand badly enough that Chapman decided to sew it up—without Novocain, which they didn't have. Angie figured that she would lament about the scar. Although Becky flinched during the sewing, she never mentioned the white scar tissue. Angie speculated that she would probably choose to have plastic surgery later; however, no one discussed it. Each of them had gotten burned using the primitive cooking equipment, but Angie naturally had the worst time of it, because cooking was her responsibility.

The former Marine kept up with their general physical condition as well. She knew when they had menstrual periods... actually Angie didn't, a typical side effect of the depo provera. Angie was surprised that Chapman gave her an injection, right on schedule. Becky's periods were erratic, no doubt due to the rapid shift in her fat/muscle balance. Also important was fluid intake and output. Chapman even knew if their bowels were functioning correctly. If they came down with diarrhea... and both did, more than once... she dispensed pills and restricted diets. There were no secrets, of any sort, during the operation.

Angie, having lived all her life in the south, found the weather interesting. There was little humidity, and the bugs, which had been ubiquitous at home, seemed to be non-existent. They were high enough that it was warm only in the afternoons—sometimes so warm that the threesome shed their jackets. Once or twice, the women pulled off their pants and tee shirts as well. But the evenings were cool, and the nights downright chilly, even in the middle of summer. Their gear included blankets, and they used them, along with a fire, every night.

After Chapman got the rifle, the food situation improved. She was a skillful hunter, and she took each of them along, teaching them how to hunt game. Mrs. Bowen had not taught Angie anything regarding the processing of a beast... be it fowl or mammal... into something ready for the frying pan, so Chapman taught her that. As they began eating more meat, Chapman issued each woman a wicked looking skinning knife and taught them how to get the kill into the skillet.

Eating a lot of meat, along with an occasional MRE, didn't constitute a varied diet. Angie figured the cholesterol count was terrible, but they were young, except for Chapman, who wasn't *too* old, and the situation was supposed to be temporary, she reminded herself. Mrs. Bowen had stressed eating balanced meals while teaching Angie about fine dining, and Angie found that she missed the kitchen more than anything else.

Becky proved surprisingly good at dressing meat. She was still scared of live beasts, but once they'd been killed, she was adept at cleaning them up. Angie couldn't believe it when she saw her, knife in hand, digging out the guts of a rabbit that Chapman had brought in.

"I'll bet you were a whiz at dissecting in biology," Angie observed, watching this phenomenon.

"Actually, I was. It was my favorite subject," she acknowledged.

When they finished, it looked almost as good as the meat that came from the local butcher. Angie longed for a real kitchen, instead of the folding pan and homemade grate over the fire pit that was all she had for cooking.

*   *   *

Marc looked at the report for Stage Two, week sixteen, which included six pictures: two landscapes with the women in each shot for perspective, two shots of them in camp doing chores together, and a close up of each girl. They looked better. Still a bit dirty, with close cropped hair, but he could see that it had grown out. They looked less haggard, and Becky looked as if she might have gained some of her weight back. Despite the hard living, they were still beautiful examples of their physical types.

The text message in Chapman's plain, almost terse style summarized the week's activities, informing him that both women had suffered only minor injuries and were healthy considering the circumstances. She noted that teamwork continued to be good and that she wasn't having any discipline problems at all. The pictures told him more than Chapman's narrative, at least in some ways. In the landscapes, the women looked as if they were enjoying the scenery, rather than being victims of it. The chore scenes showed them working together with no apparent hostility. Once again, Marc was amazed at Chapman's ability to bring out the best in her personnel.

*   *   *

The three women had been in Wyoming for five months; it was late September, and the weather was cooling off quite a bit. At this campsite, they had built a windbreak and fire reflection wall to help heat the campsite. The bi-weekly helo drop had included some long sleeve thermal knit shirts, which they wore under the BDU jackets for warmth. Each of them had an extra blanket now, as well. The extra equipment meant more to carry when they relocated, but Angie was hoping that they'd made the last move. Tonight's main dish consisted of a couple of quail that Chapman had managed to snare, and Angie sat doing mental arithmetic, trying to calculate the number of weeks that they'd been in Wyoming, just to be sure. Before Angie could speak her thoughts aloud, Chapman brought up the subject herself.

"Stage Two of this operation will be complete in two days. The helicopter will meet us at a pickup point a couple of miles north of here. We'll return to the Tennessee estate, by helo, then you'll have three weeks of training and adjustment—Stage Three. At the close of that, if Mr. Avery has no objections, you can go back to doing whatever you were doing before we began."

"We really made it!" Becky's voice was filled with amazement.

"Oh, you more than made it," Chapman said with genuine appreciation in her voice. "Mrs. Avery, you may not believe it, but I told Mr. Avery that I didn't think we had better than a 30% chance of getting through the five months without having an extraction. To be honest, I figured you would be the one who wouldn't make it. So I'm doubly proud of you."

"It only took you a week to get us ready to come. Why do we need three weeks on the other end? Why not just go home?" Angie asked, not sure that she'd get an answer. During the entire trip, Chapman had been more reticent than usual regarding her motives.

"You needed a chance to get used to the diet and gear, before we began. And you probably needed more time than you got, but I wanted to take advantage of the weather. I'd prefer not to remain here much longer. It's going to get really cold." Chapman finished her portion of quail and tucked the bones away for Angie to bury when she stored the food for the night. "You need to adjust to civilization again. If I know you, you'll want to go jump into the Jacuzzi, first thing. We're gonna go a little more slowly. We'll sleep in the pool house, using our gear, for the first week. You'll move to the detention cell for the second week. For the third week, you'll return to your rooms. We'll eat fewer MRE's and more real food. I plan to let you out of uniform in the evenings. Of course, we'll reintroduce recreational and work activities. Miss Donalson, I'll have Janice set up appointments with your hairdresser, your dentist, and your gynecologist. Mrs. Avery, you can use the locals in Tennessee or you can wait for Charleston. But you'll need to take care of those items. Life will return to normal, but we'll do it my way."

"We could handle a gradual return to normal activities on our own," Becky observed. "I don't see the need for three weeks."

"I do." Chapman's face turned hard. "Unless you want me to order up some cold weather gear and stay until Christmas. There is a contingency plan in place—all I have to do is transmit one instruction, and within a week we'll have gear to make it in the winter. What'll it be, Avery?" There was a challenge in Chapman's voice.

"I want to go home," she said in a quiet voice.

Angie thought that Becky had not known how to back down, not until they spent five months in the wilderness.

"All right. See to your evening details, troops."

With flashlight in hand, Angie took the refuse out and buried it away from camp. Then she suspended the rest of their food from a tree with a rope and pulley system—designed to make it easy for the women to retrieve, but hard for a bear or other scavenger. Becky busied herself getting the fire punched up and the tent ready. When Angie returned, she called to Chapman to let her know that she was back in camp. Stooping over, she crawled into the tent she shared with Becky and slid into her bedding, ready for sleep.

But they were so excited that they lay in the tent and talked later than usual. After the first few weeks, when their anger had worn itself out, the women had talked a great deal. Angie had never had a companion that she knew as well as she now knew Becky. They'd been side by side for five months, with no other associate than the taciturn Chapman, so they were now good friends.

Over the months, their conversations covered many topics. Now Becky knew her story, including details about her life with her folks in Adamsville, about the abduction, all the way up to the day Angie had gotten orders to go to the Avery home in Charleston. Angie knew the details of Becky's education in exclusive private schools, as well as her informal education in how to live as rich people do.

This night, they talked about what they missed the most—Angie was fondly reminiscing about cream cheese Danish, and Becky was extolling the virtues of hot showers. Both of them avoided discussing any real plans, because Marc Avery refused to let either of them go, and if they went back to fighting over him, all they had gained would be lost. Angie realized that she could never fight with Becky again. She giggled at the thought.

"What? What's so funny, Angie?"

"I was just thinking about how we got here. You do remember when I tossed you off the patio and poured corn flakes on your head."

Becky chuckled. "Yes, I remember. Then you did it again at lunch."

"Without the corn flakes, though," Angie said, laughter in her voice.

"Yes. I kept calling you names—'a floozy' was the one that got me pushed over the rail, as I recall."

"What happens now? Becky, I don't think I could get that mad at you again. But the basic problem still exists. Marc married you, yet he refuses to let me go. If he had any intention of letting me leave, I wouldn't be here now."

"I know. And I'm not sure that I want to stay married to him. Not after this. Can you imagine a man doing *this* to his wife?" Her voice was incredulous.

"I was in total shock when it happened. I knew something was going to happen, but I couldn't believe it when Billie cut my hair off."

"I know. I watched you go first, remember? I knew that she would do it to me, but I just sat there and let her. It's hard to think about how awful that was. And now I have to decide if I tell the world what a bastard my husband is, or if I just pretend I went on a six month camping trip voluntarily."

"I don't know what I'd do if I were you. But I have no real choice. If I run, Ms. Chapman comes after me. And as you now know, she's loyal to a fault. If she's ordered to punish me, then I'll be punished. I could very well wind up here again—in the winter. Gosh, it's cold." Angie shivered.

"Yes. I can imagine." Becky was filled with remorse. "I couldn't understand before. Not even when you showed me the detention cell. It never seemed real until I was there, with a cuff around my ankle. Then it became tangible, and I knew why you had stayed, even before Billie cut off my hair and dragged me out here."

"But that's a big part of why you are here," Angie assured her. "I'm sure that she and Marc decided that you and I had to experience this together. The goal was to end our feud. And to give the devil his due, it did work. I won't be fighting with you."

"Nor I with you. I'm sorry for the things I said about you. To you." Becky's tone was sincere.

"Me, too. I was pretty awful. Especially the patio thing." Angie was still tickled, just thinking about Becky Avery under the corn flakes.

"I wonder—" Becky mused.

"Wonder what?"

"If my clothes will still fit. Or do I get to buy new ones?"

They both laughed at that one.

"Settle down over there," Chapman called out.

"That's what Stage Three is for. To fatten us back up," Angie commented. "I haven't had any breasts to speak of for months."

"Ah, the truth comes out—"

Chapter 20

The Bell LongRanger was descending, and Chapman smiled as she watched Avery and Donalson. Her charges, their packs overloaded, were anxiously awaiting the trip. The whole mission had been difficult, but keeping them in line these last three weeks might be the hardest part. She was tired, and the women would be pulling on the reins hard, ready to be finished with Operation Goodwill. Despite the success she had enjoyed thus far, Chapman knew that it was critical to phase them back into their old lives, without the conflict that had existed before the mission.

Chapman had sent Mr. Avery a detailed report, part of which was to be forwarded to Janice, so that they would be ready at Angelhurst. The young women would need to be kept busy enough to pass the time quickly. Fall wasn't the best time for finding tasks for them, but she was sure that Danny and Janice had come up with something.

The women ran to the helicopter and were given a hand in. The crew showed them where to stow their packs, and they took their seats and strapped in. Chapman followed them, glad for a successful end to this phase of the operation. They faced a long trip, which would seem longer as they crossed two time zones, arriving after dark. No doubt she would find it difficult to make them set up in the pool house, but compared to tents, a facility with a roof, running water, and toilets ought to seem magnificent.

*　　*　　*

Both tired and excited, the young women jumped out of the helicopter, accepting their huge packs once more and helping each other get situated in a proper fashion. Chapman led them the short distance to the pool house, informing them that it was home for the next six days. Angie set up her sleeping bag against one wall; Becky moved to the opposite wall. Angie realized with a start that they not been so far apart in months. She was aware that Chapman was allowing them a chance to regain some space, to become individuals again. Although they'd eaten a hamburger in a small airport during the trip home, they were hungry enough to wolf down a cold pouch of mystery meat as Chapman broke out a new case of MRE's. After a brief conversation, the pair drifted off to sleep.

Dawn seemed to come early—then Angie remembered the time change. With only a short segment of time devoted to the facilities and dressing, Chapman led them on a five mile run. They ran—not hiked, *ran*—the entire five miles. Angie found it exhausting, especially in boots rather than running shoes. Once more they had had breakfast from the box. As they emerged from the pool house in mid-morning, they saw Danny for the first time. He was low key in his greeting, but Angie noted the way he stared at their worn clothing and odd hair cuts. Angie swiped her hair back from her face. After five months, each woman's locks were about three inches long, all over their heads, which was acceptable in back, but prone to get into their eyes—almost impossible to manage without using the caps to hold it in place.

Danny spelled out the chores of the day. Becky had to rake up some leaves and prune some shrubs; Angie got the job of planting bulbs for a spring tulip garden. After working at surviving for so long, the tasks seemed trivial. After lunch, they straightened what Chapman termed their "barracks" and painted the stable fence. Later on, they enjoyed their first shower and climbed into freshly laundered BDU's. In the evening, the young women climbed the steps for dinner in the breakfast room. Mrs. Bowen prepared a mini-feast, featuring some of Angie's favorites, so the threesome "pigged out," to use Angie's turn of phrase. Danny and Janice joined them for dinner, which was served buffet style, so the group could all enjoy it equally. After dinner, Janice asked Angie and Becky to help clear it. Mrs. Rebecca Wyatt Avery didn't blink—she just cleaned up with the rest of the crew.

The remainder of the week was organized along the same lines as the first day—running and work in the morning, work in the afternoon, and a social dinner in the evening. Those evenings were really a chance to debrief. Janice and Danny served as the audience, and the girls found some interest in filling in the details of their adventures. Of course, the debrief worked better for Angie than for Becky, for she was more comfortable with the staff. However, by the end of the week, even Becky had warmed up somewhat. For the weekend, Chapman transferred her charges to the detention cell. In Angie's mind, the foremost improvement was that all of the meals now came from the kitchen. Both girls laughed about Chapman trying to fatten them up, just as Angie had speculated. During week two, they began the days in BDU's; first they ran, then they had breakfast in the breakfast room. This was followed by doing chores around the estate. After lunch, they changed into workout clothes and did either upper or lower body weight lifting sessions, followed by tennis or horseback riding. Angie assisted Mrs. Bowen in the kitchen a couple of evenings, then Becky and Angie shared kitchen duty the following weekend, so Mrs. Bowen could be off. In reality, Angie cooked and Becky helped, but she really did help.

Sunday evening found them back in the detention cell, stripped to their black sports bras and cotton underpants, ready for sleep. Chapman entered, dressed in her usual working garb of khakis instead of the camouflage BDU's. Angie thought she looked tired. Each woman stood by her bunk, at attention.

"Avery, Donalson, this operation is coming to a close. We have until the end of this week. I'm transferring each of you to your rooms across the hall tomorrow. And I want to be certain that this mission remains a success. We accomplished several objectives, but the main one is on going. The two of you have to get along with each other." Chapman stood between the bunks, looking from one to the other.

"Does it look like we've been fighting?" Angie queried.

Her half smile was a trifle wan, Angie thought, as Chapman shook her head.

"Actually, I'm here to congratulate you on your success, but also to warn you that if your behavior becomes a problem, the operation could be repeated. We have proved that you can cooperate with each other. The survival training did work. Continue to demonstrate that you have learned cooperation, and you'll have only some interesting memories of what happened to you this past summer."

Angie made no reply, and Becky followed her example.

"As you were." Chapman glanced at them again and left.

Just as she promised, on Monday morning, Chapman supervised the women as they stowed gear, filled laundry bags, and moved across the hall. Angie was allowed to go back to her room, and Becky occupied Marc's. They were still under supervision, including an early run in the mornings, as well as scheduled recreational activities each day. For the first time in a long time, however, they had some unscheduled time. Time for just themselves. Angie kept the appointments that Janice had set up for her, beginning with the hairdresser. Angie was ready for the visit, for she would need Sherry's help before she was really presentable.

Angie drove herself, with Becky in the passenger seat, into town to see what Sherry could do for her hair. Becky just went for moral support, but after she saw Angie's haircut, she demanded a chance to sit in the chair, too. Sherry was the closest thing to a hair magician in Tennessee, and she made those three inches of hair into something stylish! Smiling as they returned to the Mazda, the girls realized that short haircuts did work well with the convertible. The weather was warm, especially compared to Wyoming, and the top was down. With no real destination and for once, no deadlines to meet, they cruised around for a while, enjoying simply wasting time. After touring the mall and picking up a few things for Becky, who was now a size smaller than when they left, they had an ice cream at a local shop. As she pointed the small car home, Angie realized that she hadn't had so much fun in a long time.

Janice seemed surprised when they bustled through the kitchen door with shopping bags in hand, laughing together. But Chapman had succeeded when no one thought she could. They were spending time together voluntarily. Well, almost—Chapman had told them that Becky couldn't leave her custody until Friday evening, so Becky wasn't free to go back to Charleston just yet.

Marc returned for the weekend. Neither of the women had seen him for six months. Chapman had told Angie that he'd seen pictures from the trip and that she'd made reports while they were gone. Angie knew she would find it difficult to just say "Hi, how are you?" to the guy who had ordered them into the wilderness, where they might make it or they might starve. Neither of the women had spoken of it, but their mutual jealousy was bound to come into play again as well.

Chapman made a bit of a production of Avery's arrival; she ordered them to dress formally for dinner. After such a long time of just surviving, Angie found it difficult to spend the time and energy that was expected on grooming. But after Janice checked and rechecked, Angie thought she looked as good as she ever had. At Chapman's request, Angie waited outside Becky's door, so that they would descend the stairs together.

Becky's black hair gleamed. Angie speculated that this might be the first time since childhood that her hair was free of chemical treatments. Glancing at her former rival, Angie noted that her skin glowed with health. She wore a white gown with gold lamé trim that set off her dark hair and golden skin. Angie wore emerald green, her best color, a subtle but elegant sheath of shining material, and shoes that were made of similar material, dyed to match the dress perfectly. Her mouth quirked in faint amusement as Angie noted the marked contrast which Marc would see. His last sight of the pair had been in the detention cell as they stood with shaven heads, wearing camouflage BDU's and trail boots. In mutual silence, the pair descended the stairs. Angie wasn't sure what Becky was thinking, but she found herself apprehensive. Despite Chapman's efforts to usher them back into their old lives, Angie was aware that she had changed. No doubt Becky had changed even more.

Chapman stood at the foot of the stairs in her usual khakis and polo shirt; she glanced up and nodded her approval. Angie grinned at that. With a grand gesture, Chapman ushered them down onto the shining wood floor of the foyer. Marc stood in the hall in a tuxedo jacket and striped pants. Angie had forgotten just how handsome this man was. A smile split his face as he turned his gaze toward the stairs.

"Mr. Avery, may I present Mrs. Rebecca Avery and Miss Angela Donalson. Lean and trim, safe and sound. And with your permission, sir, I am off duty."

"Aye, aye, Sergeant. One more mission accomplished with your usual aplomb. Thanks again."

Angie turned to her, towering over her in high heels.

"Off on vacation? I thought you just got back from a camping trip." Angie's tone was dry.

Chapman snorted. "Good bye, Miss Donalson."

"Bye, Billie. Have a good time."

Maybe it was her imagination, Angie thought, but Becky seemed to look fondly at the rigid back marching down the hallway.

*　　*　　*

Mrs. Bowen cooked Italian, Marc's favorite. Janice served a blush wine with it, neither dry nor overly sweet, and Angie enjoyed the meal, but not the company. Conversation was awkward, which was strange—she'd been having "girl talk" with Becky for months, yet with Marc sitting there, the banter stopped. Angie was self-conscious, and it seemed that Becky felt a similar constraint. They talked of trivialities—the fall-like weather, the dresses they'd seen in the mall, their hairstyles. What they didn't talk about was the trip west, or what the future might hold.

As they left the dining room for the family room, Marc broached the subject of their immediate future. He asked them to come up with a cover story, primarily for Becky, of course. The people at Angelhurst knew where Angie had been and what she'd been doing. Marc chuckled, speculating that he could create one, but that they would no doubt be better at making up something that Becky could stick to as she reestablished her social life.

"What did *you* tell everyone? I can't believe that I was gone for six months and no one even noticed." Becky's voice held a hint of her old sarcasm. "I imagine that my story has already been told—by you."

"Well, I had to be rather inventive. You went on a retreat, you know, one of those combinations of spiritual and physical R & R. I had my computer folks take some of our honeymoon pictures and digitally edit me out, then insert a forest background. I thought that would be in keeping with whatever you wished to relate regarding your experiences. The pictures, along with some faxes, went to your dad. There are copies of everything here, and I want you to read them over before you leave."

"I told you he had it all figured out." Becky turned to Angie, who just shrugged.

That was their affair, not hers, Angie thought.

"I won't hurry you, Becky," Marc was saying. "Stay here as long as you like. If you want to go to Charleston, you can go with me Sunday. Or I can arrange something later. But you must promise me, and really mean it, that the exact nature of your great escape will remain our little secret."

"That's what you want, isn't it? You want to treat me like... like—" Becky became incoherent.

"Like a soldier? Billie did that. But be honest with yourself. Aren't you better off for it?" Marc regarded his wife. "You look great. And you learned so much about yourself, didn't you?"

"The end does not justify the means. Oh, hell, that's a cliché, I know, but true. What you did to us, both of us, was effective. We quit fighting. But the risks were too great. I'm damned sure that Chapman told you that. We could've starved. Or been dinner for one of those bears." Becky had not lost her temper, not this time. Her argument was reasonable, her voice steady.

"Mr. and Mrs. Avery," Angie spoke in a formal tone. "You need to discuss this, but I don't need to be a party to it. Please excuse me." She got to her feet, ready to go.

"Angie, sorry. I know that you aren't interested in this. But I thought you might want to tell me a bit about your Wyoming trip."

"It was interesting. I didn't want to go, and I sure didn't like having to go the way we did. As you say, I did learn quite a bit. But you know all about it. You helped plan it, you read the reports and saw the pictures that Ms. Chapman sent. We survived, and that was what you both called it—survival training."

"Yes, but the details. Women always have all these interesting details to share. Maybe I should put the two of you in a room and just listen to you reminisce." Marc was standing at the door, smiling at them.

"And you have just the place, upstairs, with the chains at the ready," Becky observed.

"I'll pass. Good night." Angie's voice was firm as she swept out of the room and up the stairs.

*   *   *

Angie was alone when she ran the next morning. Chapman was gone; Danny and Janice had the weekend off, so she did the five miles on her own. With only Mrs. Bowen on duty, Angie helped in

247

the kitchen at mealtime and with the clean up. Marc agreed that they could eat buffet style in the breakfast room, so Angie carted the food in from the kitchen and back again. Becky offered to help, and she accepted. Marc almost gloated at the change in his wife.

Angie was uneasy as she went through the motions of living at Angelhurst. On Saturday, Angie asked to speak to Marc alone, and they retired to the study after lunch. He sat behind the desk and gestured for her to take her usual chair. His smile had a Cheshire Cat quality; Angie wondered what it was about her that made him grin.

"What is it?" she asked. "Why are you looking like that?"

"Billie told me that you would be different when you came back. And there is something," he explained. "It's not just the weight or the hair. There's something new in the way you carry yourself. I can't quite put my finger on it." He shook his head. "What's on your mind, Angie?"

"I want you to look into your crystal ball and show me your vision of the future. What are your expectations for me? And for Mrs. Avery? You spent a lot of time and resources on making us more compatible. You could have stopped the fighting by just going back to Charleston and taking her with you. So you had something in mind. I need to know just what you want of me. I may never get a chance to do more than clean out the stables here, but that doesn't mean that I have no interest in my future."

"Okay. That's logical. I want to have the option of having you both under one roof; that may not reflect our usual circumstances, but I want to be able to have you visit the house in Charleston, and we may visit here. There is to be no hostility. Billie told you both that we might repeat Operation Goodwill. I'd gladly do it again to achieve that goal."

"What am I to do on a day to day basis? I like living here, but I don't want to be Danny's little helper the rest of my life. Or Mrs. Bowen's, for that matter. It's enjoyable, working with them, but not real. I've tried to get a job, but this area is too isolated—I can't live here and work in my field."

"That's a problem. I have no objection to your working, but I won't allow you to relocate away from me. If you want to try the Charleston area, you can stay at my home there for a while," he offered. "By the way, you don't have to cook. Of course, if you want the chef job, you can have it back. The guy Becky hired isn't nearly as good as you are—doesn't look as good either."

"I would prefer to avoid that situation. It wasn't a good fit before."

"Things are different now," Marc assured her.

"Maybe, maybe not." Angie sat back in her chair. "Once your wife returns to her old friends, she'll behave the way they do," she reminded him. "One thing that keeps me centered is spending more time with your employees than with you. I don't act rich, not only because I didn't grow up that way, but because the people I hang around with aren't rich."

"Angie, that's what I like about you. You are wise beyond your years. You always were."

"I learned what I learned the hard way. Not many people twenty-three years old have been through what I have." Angie's smile was wan. "Including your Operation Goodwill."

"What do you want to do? Shall we air out a guest room?" Marc asked.

"Give me a couple more weeks to get settled back in. You'll need to get reacquainted with your wife. I guess she's staying with you?"

"Yes, she really doesn't want a divorce. Part of me was surprised when she agreed to stay, but that's what she said."

"I wondered. Back in Wyoming, she was wrestling with the decision. Guess I'll come visit you both in Charleston, but this time I'll look for a job. Will you be a reference?"

Marc laughed. "Sure. Use Becky, too. She has connections. That's why I married her."

"Don't push it too far, Marc. We've made our peace, but you could ruin it."

"Okay. Just a little joke. Get your résumé together. If you can locate something in Charleston to your liking, go ahead. But I'd gladly pay your bills to have you available full time."

"I'd rather work, even if I have to stay on the staff here." Marc raised his eyebrows at that. Angie continued, "I don't like being bored. But I'd appreciate your help in getting something better."

*   *   *

Becky agreed that the easiest explanation was to go along with the retreat story. The Averys returned to Charleston on Sunday, and Becky lost no time making the rounds to show off her new look. She found it almost comical. Her friends saw her lean, muscular body and wanted to know the secret. Some said they'd pay twice what their personal trainers were getting to look and move as she did. Becky found it difficult to keep a straight face, just thinking of her pampered friends with a GI haircut and a uniform in the Wyoming wilderness.

But, it was either go along with it or go through with a divorce. The day her father found out what really happened to her would be the day the lawyers drew up the papers. Of that there was no doubt. Daddy Wyatt was already miffed at her leaving without so much as a goodbye.

Becky had paid him a visit the next day after she returned to Charleston. Others praised her lean appearance, but her father looked beyond the slender figure and the sparkling hairdo, right into her soul and saw that something else had happened. His darling wasn't Daddy's little girl anymore. Her brash bravado had been replaced with something a bit deeper, stronger—a quiet confidence.

Bill Wyatt was pleased by the change. But he couldn't understand it any more than he could understand her leaving for some retreat and just sending him an occasional fax. Whatever else she was, Becky had always been a devoted daughter. Something about her demeanor was different, however. Maybe it was marriage. The responsibilities of a home and a husband might have made her mature a bit.

"What was it like, this retreat?" Wyatt asked. Becky wished she'd taken Marc's suggestion to work on her cover story a bit more seriously.

"Different. Like a really long camping trip. No amenities—no phone, no television, no direct access to computers! We wrote down stuff and it was sent down the mountain for the office people to fax it wherever. At first, I wasn't sure I could deal with it. We were out in the wilderness—primitive facilities, moose and elk around the camp. Dad, we lived in tents! No showers, no toilets. They told us to watch out for bears, too. No food in your tent, that sort of thing. I was terrified! But we got used to it. And everything we did depended on teamwork. I think having so much wasn't always the best thing, Daddy. I've expected everything in the world to just come to me. But it doesn't work that way, does it? It sure didn't out there in Wyoming."

"You've learned a valuable lesson, if you learned that, Rebecca," Wyatt told her in a serious voice. "It's true that you grew up without having to worry about anything. Perhaps this retreat helped you get over being so spoiled. But why would I deny you things? I have so much; it's only natural to share. When you have children of your own, you'll understand."

"I guess so, Dad. I kinda hope that it will be a while before we get into the baby business." Becky tried to draw the conversation to a close.

"Don't ever go off like that again without telling me, honey. I'm glad it went well, but I was worried."

"Okay, Dad. I should have talked it over with you, but I just thought you'd try to talk me out of it."

Wyatt still had some unanswered questions, but Becky did look as if her adventure had done her some good. Her short hair was shiny and healthy looking, as was her lean body. So he smiled at his only daughter, then invited her and her husband to dinner at the club Thursday.

Chapter 21

Angie slipped back into her life with no further adjustment. During Stage Three, she had managed that. Her days began with a five-mile jog through the woods, then she joined the staff for an informal breakfast in the kitchen. Her workout schedule had been reestablished, and she got Danny to ride with her a few afternoons a week. Mrs. Bowen was easily persuaded to let Angie be responsible for a few meals. Angie also worked on her résumé and her contacts at the college, trying to drum up some job interviews in the Charleston area. Also, she made arrangements to take some courses to get a South Carolina teaching certificate, knowing that she'd no doubt need one to make her eligible to get a job there.

Chapman came back to Angelhurst the weekend before Angie was to leave for Charleston. When Chapman came in, Danny and Janice took off, so Angie began her day's work by caring for the horses. On Saturday, Angie had jogged her five miles, breakfasted with Mrs. Bowen, and gone to the stable to see after the handsome threesome. Chapman found her there, clad in khaki pants and her "Angelhurst" polo shirt, cleaning out the stalls.

"Miss Donalson, looks like you have a job on your hands," Chapman observed.

"Yes, I don't see how Danny gets so much done." Angie piled the used straw into the wheelbarrow and took it behind the barn to the compost heap.

When Angie returned, Chapman had the fresh straw out and was spreading it in the stalls. Angie went outside with a currycomb in one hand and a brush in the other to groom the horses, one by one. Chapman stood watching, but their conversation was sporadic.

"Angie, are you over—? Do you think you'll ever—Oh, I'm not saying this very well." Chapman was uncharacteristically inarticulate.

Angie smiled as she finished Thor and moved to Bessie. "What are you asking, Ms. Chapman? If I hold a grudge?"

"I guess that's one way of putting it. I've been concerned. We had a good relationship before Wyoming. I have to wonder if we'll ever have the same sort of rapport again."

"Sure. If I can forgive you for abducting me, beating me with a whip, and putting me into a bed with a chain on one ankle so I would have to have sex with a guy I had met just once, then I guess I can forgive you for cutting off all my hair and taking me to the wilderness, with Becky Avery for a roommate. Just give me some time, okay?"

"You have a way of putting things. You know that, don't you?" Chapman's sigh was so filled with regret that Angie almost felt sorry for her.

"I call 'em like I see 'em. You and Marc had your reasons. And it worked. Becky and I came back friends. I doubt that can hold, given the circumstances, but we both have plenty of motivation to be civil to each other." Angie moved to the other side of the horse she was grooming. "And Marc will no doubt be satisfied with civility. For now, anyway."

Chapman took Thor and Kirk, and Angie led Bessie to the pasture below the stable, where they turned the horses loose for the day.

"You're right about that," Chapman said. "I heard that you're going to Charleston on Monday."

"Yes, I asked Marc for permission to seek a job elsewhere, and that was the only option he offered. He said I had to remain close to him. And I doubt I'll get a position here. I've tried, and there isn't anything. I want to *do* something."

"I understand. We'll miss you. This is a bit like a family, for me and for the others. We wish you well, but it's hard to see you go."

"I may not have any luck in Charleston. It's the wrong time of the year. Jobs in education usually open up in spring and summer. And I wasn't around."

"I know. Sorry about that." Chapman seemed remorseful.

"Who was really behind Operation Goodwill? Was it you or Marc?" Angie kept her voice level.

Chapman sighed again. "I guess we both get the blame. I cooked up the proposal, but I told him at the outset that I was reluctant to go through with it. Mr. Avery insisted. I was concerned that one or both of you would be damaged or killed. It was a real possibility. We were very lucky."

"I suppose so," Angie muttered. "I'm going to stay at Marc and Becky's house, but as a guest this time. I'd prefer an apartment, but until I have a reason to be a more permanent citizen of Charleston, I guess the Avery residence will have to do."

"Are you concerned about Mrs. Avery? You don't think she'll treat you the way she did before, surely?"

"That's not it. But I went there before to cook. Now I'm supposed to be one of the family? Not!"

"How long will you stay?" Chapman asked as they climbed the hill back to the house.

"I guess until I run out of places to look for a job."

"A month?" Chapman guessed.

"Who knows? I have nothing else to do," Angie replied. "I'll play it by ear. It depends on my luck in the job market, and my reception at the Avery household."

*   *   *

Angie drove the Mazda right up to the back door, after using her car phone to alert Martha to her arrival. Climbing out of the small car, Angie handed her a couple of small bags and lugged the larger garment bag up the steps herself. Martha put her on the same floor with Marc and Becky, explaining that Clark, who had taken her place in the kitchen, occupied her old room.

"This is a nicer room, Miss Donalson," she began and Angie interrupted her.

"Call me Angie, for heaven's sake. We know each other too well for any such formalities. Can Clark cook?"

"Well, I wouldn't say he's as good as you were, and he certainly isn't good company, but no one is going to starve."

"What is Mrs. Avery up to today?"

"Tennis at the club, and a swim in the indoor pool afterward. I think she sees some friends there, because she's always gone a while."

"You think Clark would mind if we invaded his domain for some coffee or cappuccino? We need to catch up."

"I doubt it. He's gone this afternoon. Mrs. Avery is meeting her Dad for dinner. I'm to serve cold chicken salad for dinner to Mr. Avery—and you, of course."

"Come on down then," Angie said, washing travel dirt off her hands and heading for her former spot in the kitchen.

Martha and Angie gossiped. Martha was dying to hear about the "retreat" because she had heard that Mrs. Avery and she had both gone. That was tough for Angie, because she wasn't too sure how much Becky had told her household. Angie did her usual subterfuge—lie by telling as much truth as she could. After a bit of waffling, Angie told her that they'd been in Wyoming, in a very rugged landscape, and that during the time there they had set aside their differences.

"We never heard too much about it, but when she came back, she was so different. She looked wonderful... thinner and stronger, and not nearly as demanding. Why, before, she wouldn't lift a finger. When she came back from—Wyoming, was it?—she came into the kitchen to fix herself a snack one afternoon. Clark was beside himself. Thought she didn't trust him to do his job."

Angie laughed aloud and drank more cappuccino.

"You know, Becky's okay if you get her away from her rich friends. But if she's back at her club and dining with Daddy, that retreat stuff ain't gonna last long."

"For sure. The changes are already happening. I just hope some of it carries over. She was a lot nicer to work for when she first got back."

"I'll bet."

"Angie, why are you here? I mean, I'm glad to see you, but why did you come if they're going to keep Clark on as chef?"

"I came to look for a job. Believe it or not, I learned to cook more or less as a hobby. I have a degree in instructional technology—using computers in the classroom, being a media specialist, that sort of thing. I'd like to get a job in my field. I mean, there's nothing wrong with being a cook, but I would like to do what I studied all those years."

"Well, sure you would. I hope you find what you are looking for!" Martha seemed surprised by Angie's new status.

They were still chatting when Becky came into the kitchen. She looked different, Angie thought. Already the brittle layer of sophistication was rebuilding itself. Her hair had been subtly restyled, and she'd probably gained five pounds. But she hadn't lost everything they had gained, for she greeted Angie with a warm smile.

"Hi, Angie. Marc told me you were coming. It's good to see you again." Becky approached her, and Angie stood. After a brief embrace, Becky moved back to look at her.

"Hello. Martha and I were just catching up. It's been quite a while. Close to a year since I was here."

"Yes, Mrs. Avery," Martha stood, disconcerted. "May I assist you with changing your dress? I understand you're to dine with Mr. Wyatt at his club."

"Oh, that's why I'm here. Daddy decided to come over to us, because Marc said he's too tired to do anything but come home. And Clark has the evening off, so what can we do? Any ideas?"

"Clark left some chicken salad, but I don't think it was meant to stretch that far. Just enough for Mr. Avery." Martha shrugged. "I can pick up something at that big deli near the interstate."

Becky turned to the lanky, auburn haired figure. "I know you just drove across the state, but could you look around and see if you could pull something together? We'll do deli if we have to, but I'd like something more elegant. You're the best chef I know."

Rueful in spite of the flattery, Angie went to the refrigerator. She glanced at her watch; it was already after 5:00. There was indeed a small bowl of chicken salad, not enough for three, unless they were anorexic. There were some salmon fillets, no doubt set out to thaw, and a good selection of fresh veggies in the crisper. In the pantry, Angie noted a plentiful supply of staples and bread. Nodding, she declared herself ready.

"But Clark will want to kill me, because I am no doubt ruining his menu for tomorrow," Angie told them as she searched for an apron.

"We'll worry about that tomorrow." Becky declared, like Scarlett. "Do you need some help?"

"Check the wine. Do you have something appropriate in the box?"

Becky bent down to the wine cooler and looked. "How about this?" She held up a bottle of pinot grigio and Angie nodded.

"When do I need to be ready?"

"Probably 7:15 will do."

"I can do that," Angie replied. "Martha, are you off tonight?"

"I was supposed to leave at 6:00."

"Go ahead. I can serve. Would you check the dining room before you go?"

"Sure, I'll be glad to."

"How about me?" Becky asked again.

"Let's sketch out the menu, then you go get dressed up. I can handle this."

"Thanks, Angie. You don't know how much I appreciate it."

*   *   *

Angie remembered Mr. Wyatt from the wedding and reception, of course, but she hadn't seen him up close and personal. As she served their dinner, course by course, beginning with a salad made of cucumbers, carrots, and red onions, Angie began to notice similarities between Becky and her dad. They had some of the same mannerisms, and they were both inclined to speak their minds, even if they disagreed with each other.

As she removed the plates from the main course—grilled salmon with lemon-dill sauce and new potatoes—Angie saw Becky mouth "Thanks," but it seemed that she didn't want to say it aloud with her father there. Marc also noticed, but he spoke up.

"Great job, Angie. I thought the salmon was fabulous."

"Thanks, Marc. I'll have dessert here in a couple of minutes."

Angie grinned to herself at the look that passed between Becky and her dad. Mr. Wyatt was never going to understand why the cook had been allowed to call Avery by his first name. The grin remained as she carted the dishes back to the kitchen. On a small tray, Angie set three dishes of caramel sorbet, returning to the dining room with as much speed as she could muster.

"Here we are," she said unnecessarily. "You all need anything else?"

"No, thanks," Becky said, looking down at her lap.

"Angie, could you bring us a pot of decaf coffee?" Marc asked in an affable tone.

"No problem," Angie replied and retreated to the kitchen. Digging through the cabinets, she located an insulated carafe. In fewer than fifteen minutes, she had a tray with the coffee, cups, and cream and sugar back on the end of the dining room table.

"I understand you're not the regular cook, Angie?" Mr. Wyatt asked, as Angie poured.

"No, sir. I'm Mr. Avery's ward. At least I was when I was growing up. I'm here to look for a job. Since the chef had the night off, Becky asked me to fill in."

"Nice dinner." Wyatt's voice was gruff. "Good luck with your job search."

"Thanks," Angie replied; then she grinned her urchin grin and made her exit. In the kitchen, Angie dined on chicken salad. Afterward, she cleaned up. She was still in the kitchen, writing a note for Clark, explaining to him what she had used, when Becky entered.

"Thanks again for doing dinner," she said, "I know you must be tired."

"Somewhat. I was just leaving a note for your regular guy. I want to go to bed pretty soon. You know, I still run early, so I need my sleep. Do you want to get up and jog around the neighborhood?"

"I ought to. I haven't done much exercise other than tennis since we left Angelhurst."

"I won't twist your arm, but I've done it so long, it's habit. Becky, I think you could manage, if you go ahead and start back. It's only been about three weeks since we were running five miles a day."

"What time?" Becky sounded apprehensive.

"How about 7:30? Then we can have breakfast afterward. When do you usually eat? You averaged 9:00 when I worked here."

"I can manage 7:30," she agreed. "I'll ask Marc to get me up."

"Poor little rich girl. Don't you own an alarm clock?"

"Ah, be nice, Angie!"

"I am, I am. I usually run earlier."

"We won't have Billie to urge us on." Becky chuckled.

"I'll do my Billie imitation." Angie's voice dropped half an octave. "Move out, Avery."

Becky laughed aloud and waved as she departed.

*   *   *

Although the sun had risen, it was still cool as they ran. Despite the brisk temperature Becky began to lag a bit as they made the last leg of the route. Angie urged her on, praising her for making it as they climbed up the steps into the hall next to the kitchen. Becky asked Clark to give them breakfast at the bar in the kitchen, and they chatted over coffee. Angie expressed her concerns regarding her slim job prospects and her intention to work in the area. Becky described her return to her social life; then they fell silent.

"It's funny," Angie observed. "We talked all the time in Wyoming. What's the difference?"

"Something in common. We have very different lives and interests." Becky's tone was logical. "Just surviving was fuel for many of those conversations. Then there was the mutual longing for home. We're back. We made it!"

"So we did. Speaking of civilization, I'm going upstairs for a shower. I have to drop off some résumés and make a few calls. I have an interview tomorrow. Just preliminary, to seek information. But still, it's a start."

"Good luck, Angie."

"Run tomorrow?"

Becky looked down at her body. "Okay. I need the exercise." She laughed ruefully. "Pretty soon my new clothes won't fit if I don't do something."

*   *   *

Angie conducted several "informational interviews," a fancy name for fishing expeditions, but she didn't get so much as a real nibble. Most were with personnel directors or principals of schools within driving distance of Charleston. As she had pointed out to Chapman, autumn was the worst time to seek a position, since school systems tried to have a complete staff under contract when they opened. In fact, she couldn't even start taking courses for certification in South

Carolina until the beginning of the semester in January, but Angie got all her applications filed and was awaiting letters of acceptance from two colleges.

Discouraged, she packed her bags and headed back to Angelhurst. Marc had seemed frustrated by her continued refusal to let him hop into her bed while she was in Charleston, but Becky remained civil to Angie, although Marc's sexual innuendoes did place a strain on both women at times. Becky found it difficult to refrain from a swift retort when Marc made one of his increasingly frequent comments regarding Angie's desirable form, but she did manage to keep quiet. The specter of Billie Chapman was enough to motivate her to keep her temper under control.

When Angie decided to leave, Marc proposed creating a position for her at the local corporate office. She shook her head, knowing that his attitude toward her would give them away in short order.

"Marc, I'll return in January to begin school. It's too boring here with nothing to do. Ms. Chapman will find something to keep me busy."

Surprisingly, Marc nodded his assent.

Chapter 22

Angie was once again welcomed home at Angelhurst. Ms. Chapman wasted no time in putting her on the work schedule, and Mrs. Bowen adjusted her menus to include some of Angie's favorite dishes. Before long, it seemed that she'd never left.

Marc and Becky visited Angelhurst once or twice a month. Bit by bit, the fall weather became winter weather, so Angie moved her run to later in the day and used the treadmill if rain or extreme cold prevented use of the trails around the house. Angie spent more time on inside tasks and less on outside ones. In a move that seemed out of character, Chapman asked Janice and Angie to decorate for the holidays. Marc and Becky took advantage of their efforts by hosting a family party—for both Mr. Avery and Mr. Wyatt, as well as a few more distant relatives. Angie split herself between being on the fringes of "family" and being Mrs. Bowen's assistant. Becky helped with the preparations, even though she only served as hostess during the party itself.

They had six guestrooms filled, and Mrs. Bowen and Janice needed Angie, so she did as much as she could. Angie was bringing in platters of bacon and eggs to the breakfast room when she saw Becky enter, turn a bit green, and flee into the hall bath. Angie set down her burden and followed her. Knocking on the closed door, Angie called to her.

"Becky, are you all right?"

"Not exactly," came the muffled reply. Then there were sounds of retching. Angie glanced up and down the hall to make sure no one saw her, then opened the door. Becky was on her knees, hands on the rim, heaving over the toilet. Angie wet a washcloth and began bathing the face of her one-time rival. Eventually, the retching stopped, and Becky sat back on her haunches.

"I hope it wasn't something I cooked," Angie teased, rinsing out the cloth again. She handed it to Becky and regarded her.

"No, I guess it was the smell of the food. It's begun to bother me."

"The smell? Why?"

"Angie, you idiot. I'm pregnant." Becky's voice held no heat.

"Oh. I never had any experience with that. You aren't using birth control?"

"No. It's my job to produce the Avery heir. Remember?"

"I guess I knew that. I just have always been required to—"

"I know. Billie gave you a shot in Wyoming. It keeps you from having periods, too. Lucky you."

"And it makes me gain weight. Which is one reason Ms. Chapman is adamant that I do so much exercise. Of course, you won't be having periods for about nine months." Angie reached out a hand and pulled Becky to her feet.

"I'll gain a good bit of weight. My doctor says twenty to thirty pounds is an average. So much for my Wyoming sculpted figure."

"Let's get you to your room upstairs. If I don't return to the kitchen, Mrs. Bowen will think I got lost. Do you want a tray later?"

"Maybe. Much later. I'll use the intercom."

"Good."

Angie helped her down the hall and into the foyer, afraid she would collapse again, but Becky traveled up the steps without mishap, and Angie rushed back to the kitchen, announcing that Mrs. Avery must have a virus or something. Becky needed to decide when to share the news.

About 10:30, as she finished cleaning up after breakfast, Angie used the intercom to check on Becky.

"Think you can eat a cracker?" Angie quizzed her.

"Maybe. I can come down to the kitchen."

"No. I'll bring you something. Something without a smell."

Seated in her customary rocking chair, Mrs. Bowen looked puzzled at the interchange. Angie set a small plate of crackers and another of fruit on a tray and headed up the stairs to Marc's room. She found Becky seated on the bench beside the windows, a pallid smile on her face.

"Let me know if I can do anything to help," Angie told her before returning to the kitchen to assist Mrs. Bowen with lunch.

*　　*　　*

The following day, Marc and Becky held a formal luncheon for their guests to share their news with the family. Together they stood at the head of the table and informed the gathering about the impending birth. The delighted grandparents responded with congratulations, handshakes and hugs. Angie took her place in the line of well wishers, despite an inner jealousy. No Avery heir would have her auburn hair and long, strong limbs. For many years now, Marc had taken good care of her, but all he'd ever allow her to be was the mistress—eternally marriageless and childless.

At a distance, Chapman watched both young ladies, being no doubt the only person in the room aware that Angie was jealous of Becky's impending motherhood. Such envy was an emotion that Chapman herself had never had, but she knew that Angie liked children and that before his marriage, she would gladly have borne Marc's heirs. As Chapman looked on, she noted that Angie was behaving herself with perfect decorum, though, and that was a relief.

*   *   *

This made two Christmases spent alone at Angelhurst, Angie thought. In a flash of generosity, Marc and Becky had invited her to be with them, then Chapman had offered to stay, but Angie assured them that she'd have Christmas with the horses, "just like last year."

As was her custom, Chapman again visited her brother, Matthew. This was the first Christmas for Matt's granddaughter, the offspring of his oldest daughter, who was the same age as Angie. Observing the festivities, Chapman couldn't help comparing the young women in her mind. Angie needed the same things—a husband and a child. Not for the first time, Chapman felt guilty for her role in molding Angie into Avery's idea of the perfect mistress. If Angie had been allowed to remain in Adamsville, she might not have enjoyed the wealth that she did now, but in all probability she would've been chosen as a mate by one of the local boys. Now, Avery would never allow her to fulfill that role.

While she drove the twisting road back to Angelhurst, Chapman thought of leaving her job with Avery. She'd devoted almost seven years to his pet project. During those years, she had invested most of her salary. That, with her military retirement, should make her comfortable. No doubt, she could afford to leave. Chapman considered taking Angie with her. But Mr. Avery commanded great resources, and there was no way to escape him, if he chose to bring Angie back. She would only make the situation worse by trying to evade him.

If she left, Mr. Avery might decide to hire another keeper for Angie, and the girl's circumstances would no doubt worsen. All too often, such a setting would attract an abusive, power hungry individual. Chapman found herself envisioning Angie being tortured with restraints, or worse, with no advocate to aid her. As she drove, a new mission began to form in Chapman's mind. Her new objective would be to persuade Mr. Avery to release the girl. Getting him to acquiesce would take some time, but perhaps, as he got busy with his own offspring, Mr. Avery would decide to allow her to leave.

*   *   *

Wasting no time, Chapman called Marc's secretary and got an appointment to meet with him in his Charleston office, for the express purpose of asking him to release Angie into her keeping, and to tender her resignation. Assuredly, this would be a bold request, and she doubted that she would be successful, but it was a way to sow some seeds that might be harvested later.

Leaning back in his high-backed executive chair, a loosened tie about his neck, Marc was shocked by Chapman's request. Throughout the years, Marc had been certain of her total loyalty, and equally sure that she would never question his orders. He found it hard to picture the estate without her, and harder still to even consider letting Angie go.

"Why? Why would you want to take Angie away?" Marc struggled for a reason for her unusual request. "Are you… attracted to her?"

With some measure of disgust, Chapman sighed. She supposed a woman with her background and no relationships with men would be suspected of having lesbian tendencies. Once or twice, Chapman had wondered if she might do better on that side of the street. However, her own sexuality was not relevant to the discussion.

"No, sir. I'm not gay, and even if I was, Angie is obviously straight. You surely have no doubts regarding that." Chapman's mouth smirked at the very thought. "No, sir. My motives lie somewhere between guilt and altruism. I was wrong to help you abduct the girl in the first place. At the time, I bought the argument that she'd be better off, eventually. We all—Danny, Janice, and I— agreed that her situation was appalling. You know, when she first came to us, she was amazed that we had plenty of food! One of my main motives was that you seemed to have plans for her, plans that would ultimately lead to her being more than she could have achieved any other way. So I helped. But now, I look at your wife, who will have children to love, and I look at my niece, who is Angie's age and has a husband and a baby of her own. Angie will grow old waiting for you, then she'll be cast aside, and we'll have stolen her youth. I have a guilty conscience. I've been feeling remorse for quite a while. Even before Wyoming, and what she went through there. Now she works in the kitchen or helps with grounds maintenance. What a waste."

Marc sat back and listened. From their first meeting, Chapman had been a loyal employee, so she deserved his attention. A small part of him agreed with her. However, he had a huge monetary and emotional investment in Angie, now at her peak, and although he couldn't spend a great deal of time with her, he was loath to let her go, to become a wife to some other man.

"Billie, I appreciate your position. I agree that Angie would make someone a fine wife. But she's mine. I made her. You made her. *We created her.* She wouldn't be as beautiful, as educated, as cultured if we hadn't removed her from that hovel down in Georgia. No doubt you're imagining her life without our intervention. But interject some realism. What sort of fellow would she have married in her desperation to leave her aunt's little house? When that imagination goes into overdrive, picture her in a trailer, surrounded by dirty brats and a guy with a beer gut who hasn't bathed in a week—who beats her when she opens her mouth to protest. That's an accurate snapshot. Remember, she is not Rebecca Wyatt. She isn't your niece, either. Angie's an orphan, who came from nothing."

"Sure, that's one possible scenario. I've worked and lived with this girl for seven years. Not many people have as much intelligence and ambition as she has. I think she would've made more of herself than that. She still has time, if we let her go." Chapman stuck to her plan of action. "If you'll allow it, I'm offering to ride herd on her, to make sure that no recriminations come back your way. In a way, I taught her to please you. Now I want to help her learn to stand on her own two feet."

"I can't make you stay. But I don't really think you're ready to resign, you just want to do right by Angie. I believe that you have— you've just lost sight of that. Yes, you helped me procure her, but since then she's had the best and strongest advocate possible. You're friends, perhaps better friends than you realize." Marc leaned back in his chair. "I used to be jealous of the relationship between you two. She held me at arm's length for quite a while. But not you, Billie. Angie took to you at once. Now you want to do your best for her, and I appreciate that. But reconsider. What Angie has learned, what she has become, is due to my money and your efforts. Angie has a college degree, magna cum laude; she's an accomplished cook—if she wanted, she could no doubt get a chef's job in a gourmet restaurant. We've allowed her freedom of choice in her studies, and I'm still supportive of her efforts, financially and otherwise. While she may be required to perform certain duties, Angie has the best of everything— clothes, car—and she always lives in one of my homes, enjoying the lifestyle of a member of my family."

"Mr. Avery, I'm not saying she's being mistreated. I'm saying that she's like a dog on a leash. Pampered, yes, but never free."

"A dog on a leash is at least a safe dog. She'll be kept safe. No, I won't release Angie. If your position becomes vacant, I'll have to hire another estate manager. Someone else will have to become responsible for Angie. For her behavior, for her physical condition. I doubt that I can find anyone as good as you, but I will find someone. No one is irreplaceable."

"I know. But couldn't you let Angie go and use, you know, hired help?"

"I rejected that idea years ago. AIDS is no closer to being really cured, and other sexually transmitted diseases are so prevalent, hookers are no more attractive than when I decided to procure her. Angie may need more time to get over my marriage, but she will. You may wish to think over your own plans. If you must go, then I'll seek a replacement, but I don't really think retirement is the answer just yet. Angie is planning to return to Charleston to do a semester's work in graduate school. Why don't we wait until that's over?"

Chapman hesitated for a moment. Success on the first try had been, of course, unlikely.

"Okay. We'll discuss it again when she's finished her studies." Chapman got to her feet.

"She may not be as unhappy as you think, Billie. If she could get a job, I'll bet she'd be more fulfilled. It has always seemed to be enough for you." Marc stood to escort her to the door.

"Thank you for seeing me." She turned to go. "Mr. Avery, I would appreciate it if this conversation stayed between us. Angie must have a certain respect for me, otherwise I'd have no control."

"Understood. This remains between us."

Marc noticed that she was a bit slower and her posture was less rigid than it used to be. He pondered as she marched down the hall. Maybe she really was getting old. That's no doubt why she was having second thoughts after all this time.

*   *   *

The day after New Year's, Angie left for Charleston once again. For the car, they packed a few everyday clothes and sweats, and Janice shipped a box of clothes to Marc's Charleston address. For once, Angie actually looked forward to the trip. Beginning graduate school might not be great, but she had felt stagnant for too long. Also, she was eagerly anticipating spending some time with Becky, who had called a couple of times, just to talk.

The drive was as long and tiring as she remembered, so she was thankful when Martha came out to help her get her bags into the house. Martha put her in the same room she had used on her last visit, but Angie noticed that it had been redecorated, and the room next to it had been fitted out as a study and office for her. A new computer and desk with a scanner and printer filled one wall. Another wall held bookcases and a writing desk. There was also a small sitting area in the room, making it almost as comfortable as her suite at Angelhurst.

"Wow," Angie said as Martha showed off the improvements. "I'm impressed. Who did all this?"

"Mr. Avery suggested it—Mrs. Avery chose the furniture and drapes, that sort of thing. They wanted to surprise you."

"Consider it done. I'm surprised. It's a good one, though!"

"Wonderful. I'll tell Mrs. Avery. She has one of her doctor appointments today, and she's late." Martha glanced at her wristwatch. "I hope everything's all right."

"Me, too. Has she been doing well?"

"I suppose. She still has a good bit of nausea. Clark is rather frustrated right now. Most of his favorite herbs seem to send her straight to the bathroom."

"She looked sort of green when she was at Angelhurst. That's how I found out about the pregnancy."

"Mr. Avery is so tired of her being sick. If you ask me, he ought to be more supportive."

"Yes. It's his fault, isn't it?" Angie observed with good humor.

"I would think so. Do you need anything, Angie?"

"Not at the moment. I'll want something to eat after a while. Are the Averys dining in?"

"Yes. You're expected to join them. I'm staying late to serve."

"I'm honored. Sure you want to stay?"

"It's not really an option. I still *work* here." There was an edge to Martha's voice.

"Oops." Angie looked contrite. "Well, maybe while I'm here I can take care of that some of the time. I'll only have three classes."

"I'd enjoy a few evenings off, if Mrs. Avery doesn't mind, of course." Martha smiled.

"Let's remember to ask." Angie returned the gesture. She knew that Martha had an elderly father, and she made dinner for him when she could.

Becky came into the room. There was a ghost of a smile on her face, but Angie thought that her heart wasn't in it. Indeed, looking at her, Angie wondered if it was a good idea to even be there.

"Hi, Angie. Good trip?"

"Long. I wish there was a way to attach my car to the bottom of the helicopter."

"Yes, I guess so. But I hate the noise and vibration of the chopper almost as bad."

"I know what you mean. I love the room—rooms. This is great!"

"Good. I know that Marc will be glad. I think you'll have to pay him back, though."

Angie almost choked before she responded. With a furtive glance at Martha, Angie opened her mouth, but Becky seemed to read her mind.

"He said he needed you to do some sort of proposal and a presentation for the board of directors. I think you'll be using that computer for a lot more than your term papers."

"Oh," Angie said and nodded. "Well, I can handle it. But he has a whole department devoted to doing stuff like that."

"I gather that's the problem. When he wants his ideas confidential, you may be the best answer. You have done these things before, I understand."

Angie nodded again. "Sure. From time to time, Marc has asked me to do presentations. It's not exactly what I trained for, but I've taught myself quite a bit about it. You know, trying to keep from being bored in the country."

"Is there anything you can't do?" Becky shook her head in wonder. "Dinner's at 7:00. Need anything?"

"Nope. Martha has taken good care of me." Angie grinned at the pair, who then left her to unpack.

*   *   *

Despite her hunger, Angie hated dinner. Not the food—the ice between Marc and Becky made it an agonizing affair. She wasn't sure what the problem was, but Angie was pretty darn sure there was a problem. Both of them were polite, of course, but it just seemed that speaking to the other one was almost more than either of them could bear. Martha had hinted that Marc wasn't supportive of the pregnancy, or of Becky. Angie had the feeling that it might be something more. And for once, she felt she wasn't the problem.

They parted company shortly after eating, Angie using the valid excuse that she was tired after driving across the state. She returned to her room to finish straightening out the things she'd brought, laying out all the materials for class, then checking e-mail. Having that squared away, she showered and dressed for bed, intending to read herself to sleep. At one point, she heard Marc and Becky in the hall, and once again, it sounded as if they weren't getting along. Angie had read that pregnancy and having small children put a strain on a marriage, but she decided that it was too soon for such problems to be developing. Becky wasn't even showing yet.

In the morning, she jogged an abbreviated route that took her only a couple of miles, thus allowing her to finish quickly. Afterward, she got Clark to fix a light breakfast. Angie noticed Martha passing by, so she asked her to join her for coffee. As they chatted, Angie asked the questions that had plagued her at every waking.

"Martha, what's going on with the Averys? I felt like I was having dinner with the chief combatants of World War III."

"That bad, was it?" Martha sighed and swirled her coffee in its cup. "Angie, almost from day one, Mr. Avery has viewed the pregnancy as a problem. Like it's his wife's *personal* problem. He doesn't want to know what's going on with her, and he doesn't like the fact that she's sick. Believe you me, she is sick a lot. Sleeping a great deal, too. He never liked her sleeping late, and now she sleeps early and late. I would guess she's not—I mean, you wouldn't feel like—"

"I get the picture," Angie said dryly. "You think he isn't getting any."

"Yes, ma'am. That would be my guess," Martha said in a sage voice.

"That could be it. Poor Becky. I can't relate. It's never happened to me. But it would have to be awful to feel like that, and be on the receiving end of his animosity, too."

"Yes. They need to get straightened out before the baby comes."

"I sure hope so. When is she due?"

"July 4—Independence Day."

Angie glanced at her watch. "Good luck with the Averys. Let me get to school."

*   *   *

School never changed. After waiting in lines and meeting her advisor, she finally got her registration done, bought her books, and picked up the syllabus for each class. When she got back to Marc's house, Becky was in her sitting room, reading a book—well, she was looking at it, anyway.

"Hi." Angie knocked on the frame of the open door.

"Angie, come in. How was school?" Becky leaned back and ran a hand through her hair, which was growing out, almost as long as it had been before Chapman got a hold of it.

"Just a paperwork day. Class starts tomorrow. How are you feeling?"

She made a face. "Pregnant."

"I have no frame of reference. What do you feel?" Angie took an armchair across from her.

Becky sighed and pulled her legs up. "I feel nauseated. Almost constantly. I don't throw up all the time, I just feel as if it's imminent. There's a bad taste in my mouth. Nothing tastes right, and some things are instant trips to the bathroom. Onions. Coffee. Bacon. I ate a blueberry muffin yesterday, and I had a blueberry explosion. In the bathtub. Marc was grossed out. He just left me with floating vomit."

"Yuck. Will you be like this the whole time?" Angie inquired.

"I should be about over it, according to my doctor, but I can't tell that it's any better. I sleep all the time. I can't concentrate. I feel nervous. Is this depression?" Becky looked miserable. "It was easier back in Billie's camp. I thought she was the worst thing that had ever happened to me, but I was wrong. This is the worst."

"I take it Marc has no sympathy."

"Not anymore. He was excited about it for a week or two. But I haven't been interested in sex or anything else. That's the root of the problem. I mean, he always wanted children. Or so he said."

"Yes. Just not mine." Angie couldn't help herself. Those feelings came barging out, even though she should've kept her peace, especially in front of Becky.

"Angie, right now, I wish I had the mistress job, and you could be the wife. Believe me." Becky seemed totally honest, and Angie was surprised by her revelation. "If Billie had only given me one of those shots."

"I don't know what to say. But Becky, we're not going to be changing places. Is there anything I can do?"

"Go to bed with him."

"Say again?" Angie had trouble believing her ears.

"I mean it. Go to bed with him. I sure don't feel like it. He's horny—so you can help him out. Seduce him."

"Believe it or not, Becky, I've never done that. He comes to me, not the other way around. And I haven't done anything with him since you two became engaged."

"I can't imagine that."

"It's true. Oh, he's asked. But he told Ms. Chapman that he only wants me if I'm willing, and I haven't been. Willing, that is."

"Angie, I'll sleep downstairs. Are you, as you say, willing?"

"I don't know." Angie paused, considering. "Are you sure about this?"

"Never more serious in my life. Put on your sexiest gown and go across the hall. He'll welcome you. And if he's in a better mood, maybe I will at least be an object of his pity rather than his hatred."

"I had in mind fetching you some crackers or something."

"Crackers I can get for myself," Becky stated, her tone dry.

Chapter 23

When Angie left Angelhurst, Janice had sent quite a number of clothes, and Martha had unpacked those for her. The spacious closet was filled, but what it held wasn't as extensive as the wardrobe in her suite at Angelhurst. Angie stood at the door searching for some nightwear that would help her fulfill Becky's request. Whether or not Becky knew it, Angie had been truthful when she informed her that seducing Marc would be a new task. Yes, she had a supply of seductive garments, some gifts from Marc himself and others that Chapman had purchased or instructed her to buy. Part of Chapman's job, as she saw it, was to make Angie attractive to him, and packaging was part of the deal.

She found a deep midnight blue teddy with matching underpants. Although it wasn't sheer, it was short enough and lacy enough to create a certain atmosphere. With a shrug, Angie put it out, ready for use later. Marc was dining with some visiting executives, so she and Becky ate in. Clark served dinner himself—a simple meal of salad, spaghetti in meat sauce and garlic bread—which Angie enjoyed, but once again, Becky turned green at the smell of the first course.

Afterward, they watched a movie on cable, or rather Angie did; Becky fell asleep half an hour into the movie. When Marc came in, they awakened her, and she went to the guestroom, pointedly staring at Angie as she left the room. For a few moments after Becky made her exit, Angie chatted with Marc, her tone light and flirtatious. Yawning, she went to her room to dress for bed.

Angie didn't have to go across the hall. As if it had been choreographed, she slipped the garment over her head and the door opened. Marc Avery entered with a look of longing on his face that Angie recognized. As a man in a desert will drink deeply from a well, Marc savored the activities of the evening. Afterward, he went to sleep in her arms, his face peaceful and satisfied.

*   *   *

273

Marc slipped out of Angie's room early in the morning, grateful for her presence. Chapman had been right in one respect; loving Angie was much easier than loving Becky. His mistress was the best sex partner, the best friend he'd ever had. For the first time in a long time, he was reminded that having Angie was an indispensable part of happiness.

Marc dressed and went down to breakfast, whistling and happy. Later on, he poked his head in Angie's room. She was dressing in heavy workout wear, ready for her morning jog. With some vigorous steps, he crossed the distance and cuddled her in his arms.

"You keep that up and we'll both be late," she purred at him, like a cat content after a meal.

"It would take very little for me to cancel my meetings. Angie, you look so good…like a goddess."

"Good?" Angie scoffed. "I'm ready to run. I probably don't look good, and I'll look worse when I get back. If I'm a goddess, I'm the goddess of running shoes. But I need the exercise. Billie says I spend too much time sitting on my rear end as is."

"Smart lady, Billie. Listen to her, girl." Marc smiled and released her so she could don her running shoes. "See you at dinner. Now I have a reason to come home."

"That's not quite fair—Becky didn't get pregnant all by herself."

"Angie, she hasn't just gotten pregnant. She's morphed into a sleepy barf monster."

"Marc, she'll get over it. At most, it will last nine months."

"A long nine months. But you'll make it much more enjoyable. Why did it take you so damn long?"

"I've missed you, Marc. When Billie would chain me to my bed, I was certain that I hated you. Later, I thought I loved you. I felt betrayed when you told me about Becky. Attending the wedding made me realize that you couldn't possibly love me. So I couldn't just pretend it didn't happen. In a way, I suppose Wyoming was good for both of us. I can deal with it, as long as she doesn't mind."

"What do you mean?"

"Why do you think she slept in the guest room?"

"I'll be damned."

Angie had her running shoes on and her keys dangled from a lanyard around her neck. Her auburn hair shimmered as she moved toward the door.

"No doubt. See you later." She smiled devastatingly and slipped out of the room.

Marc watched her slim but well shaped behind as she let herself out, a whistle of admiration slipping through his lips.

*   *   *

Becky was up, after a fashion, when Angie got home from school. They chatted for a few moments, then Angie retired to her room to begin the extensive reading that always seemed to come with any new college course work. She'd been reading for about an hour when the intercom buzzed.

"Angie, you have a call on line one." Martha's voice was hollow and tinny.

"Okay, thanks," Angie replied, surprised to hear Billie's voice.

They talked of Angie's courses and her exercise program... or, according to Chapman, the lack of one... and of Becky's continued problems with pregnancy sickness. When she hung up, Angie realized how much she liked Chapman, despite the strange relationship which they shared.

At dinner, Marc was attentive to Angie, only Angie. Becky had to notice, but she said nothing. Apparently, relief at not being on the receiving end of Marc's sarcasm was enough for her. Angie felt awkward and tried to involve Becky in the conversation, but Becky gave her a rueful look, then a slight shaking motion of her head. Intuitively, Angie realized that Becky wanted her to keep Marc happy.

Once again, Marc joined Angie, this time before bedtime. He brought in the fact sheet for her to design a slide presentation and report for his next board of director's meeting.

"I cannot have this leaked, Angie. If you do this presentation, it'll be confidential. I don't trust the graphic arts department with this one." Marc placed the materials on her computer desk beside the huge stack of texts. "What's the time line? Looks like they've already loaded you down with stuff to do."

Angie sighed. "Yes, they always do. And I need to start weight training; I called the club and they still have me on the membership roster. Good news is I have only one class tomorrow. How about Thursday night? Can you manage if I have it done by then?"

"Sure. I'll schedule the meeting for Friday. Thanks, Angie."

"Thanks for paying all my bills. This month will be pricey." She grinned. "One day, you're going to realize that this is a losing proposition."

"Nope, you're worth every penny. You always have been." Marc sat beside her on the love seat, and began to nuzzle her. A playful swat caused him to duck.

"You're going to have to get over being so horny if you want me to get all this work done."

"Oh, I'll be quick about it," he said, his hand moving over her breasts.

* * *

Between looking after Marc's needs, keeping up with her schoolwork and trying to maintain her fitness, Angie stayed busy. Every month, Chapman had her come back to Angelhurst, and while she was there, Chapman checked her weight and measurements and charted her strength as well.

As Becky gained weight with the pregnancy, the disparate physical differences became even more striking. Angie's willowy figure became a foil for the ever-widening Becky. Marc viewed his wife with disgust as she expanded. Due to her petite stature, it seemed that the baby had nowhere to go but straight out, and once she began showing, Becky needed full-cut maternity clothing in a hurry. In a gesture of moral support, Angie went with her to help her choose clothes. The lack of a mother was one thing that they still shared—a lack that brought them together, in a mutual understanding of something they had lost.

Once again they were a team. Just as Chapman had forced them to work together to survive in the wilderness, they now worked together to keep Marc happy and Becky on track for a healthy pregnancy. Angie performed her bedtime duties with enthusiasm; in the daytime she used her spare time helping Becky. Although Becky was reluctant, Angie encouraged her to exercise, to eat even when she didn't feel hungry, and even accompanied her on some of her doctor visits. Ironically, the Averys' marriage, which had been hanging by a mere thread, was now held together by Angie, who helped each of them maintain some sanity and some continued satisfaction with their lives.

*   *   *

Marc watched the pair of women coming up from the garage. Angie gave Becky a hand as they came to the steps. The short hair that Angie had retained gave her a boyish look from a distance. Becky, on the other hand, had allowed hers to grow, and with the growth hormones in her system, it was thick and luxuriant. As the nausea had finally abated, Marc's feelings for her had settled down to a mixture of tolerance and annoyance. He looked forward to the birth of his heir, but he sometimes wished that Angie, not Becky, was the woman with the distended belly and swollen ankles.

"Hi, girls. How'd it go at the doctor's?"

"We've got another week to go—at least. I'm not dilated as yet." Becky frowned.

Marc knew that she just as anxious as he was to be finished. His secretary had told him that the ninth month was the worst. "It's designed to make you ready to deal with labor and delivery," Mrs. Conner had confided.

Angie carried a shopping bag in one hand and released Becky's hand, as her awkward, pregnant body seemed to regain its balance.

"She's getting tired, Marc. We need to take good care of her."

Marc put his arm around Becky and steered her toward her sunroom, turning to address Angie. "Of course. We're close to having an heir for the Avery fortunes, whatever they may be in twenty years."

"I'll check with Clark and make sure that he has a snack ready for her," Angie said. "Perhaps something with calcium. We want that baby to have strong bones, you know."

"Thanks, Angie."

As Angie withdrew into the kitchen, Marc smiled to himself. Having Chapman put them through Operation Goodwill had been a brilliant success. When they faced stress, they still pulled together—just as Chapman had taught them. Despite their differences, they had come to appreciate each other, becoming friends.

As they entered the room, Marc helped his wife settle onto a loveseat in the small room and took his place beside her. "Any problems?"

"Not really. I had a non-stress test. No big deal. My weight was up again. Guess I'll have to go on a super diet when this is over."

"Want me to put Billie in charge?"

Becky looked at him. Sometimes she couldn't figure out if his comments were a joke or not. After last summer, she couldn't be sure.

"Only if you agree to take care of the baby. I don't think I could manage Wyoming with an infant riding in my pack."

Marc chuckled.

With a flourish, Angie entered, bearing a tray. She had dishes of ice cream for each of them.

"It's cold, it's delicious, and it's loaded with calcium. Hey, it even reminds you of family reunions."

"I never went to any of those," Becky said.

"No family? Or do rich people do it differently?" Angie inquired, her voice light.

"Rich people do it differently," Becky acknowledged. "If we ever saw our relations, we'd meet at a beach resort with some of Dad's family. We had a shrimp boil on the beach—catered by the hotel, of course."

"So you never made homemade ice cream on the back porch?"

"No. Was it fun?"

"The Donalsons didn't have much family, so we didn't have reunions," Angie mused. "But, when I was in grade school, my best friend, Amber, took me to her family reunion. Her Aunt Ruth made peach ice cream, and her Uncle Bob turned the crank. While it was making, they let each of the children take a turn." Angie smiled at the memory. "Yeah, I guess it was fun. Odd, I hadn't thought of that in a long time."

"Maybe it's my being in the family way," Becky's smile glowed with hope.

"That must be it." Angie smiled with her and sampled the ice cream.

"I'll tell Billie about your acquiring these poor eating habits," Marc teased her.

"She'll find out when I climb on the scales," Angie scowled.

"You mean she weighs you?" Becky asked, incredulous.

"Ever since I first came to Angelhurst. She keeps records, too. I'd be willing to bet that she can tell you what I weighed in July two years ago without looking at the chart. Not only that, she can tell you what I bench-pressed. It's truly amazing."

"When are you going back?" Becky inquired.

"To Angelhurst? This weekend. I go once a month, so Ms. Chapman can keep up with me. She's been upset, of late, because I've been slipping."

"I still can't believe it." Becky shook her head.

"Oh, yes, you can. You know how she is."

"She's different, that's for sure."

Marc watched as his women finished the snack and Angie piled the dishes on the tray to take it back to the kitchen. Becky seemed really tired, so he suggested a nap and helped her to their room.

*   *   *

Angie leaped from the helicopter late Friday evening and joined Chapman, who'd come to meet her. She had only an overnight bag, which she probably didn't need, what with having duplicates of almost everything in her room at Angelhurst. Glancing around, Angie realized how much she missed the remote estate, which had been home for so many years.

"Good trip?" Chapman queried, her voice raised so that Angie could hear it, despite the helo receding over the treetops.

"For a chopper, yes. Its only real advantage is speed." Angie had seldom flown in the craft, and it was never her first choice.

"Mrs. Bowen has dinner ready for you. I think she believes you're her granddaughter or something."

Angie grinned and picked up the pace toward the house. Chapman, Angie, Mrs. Bowen, and Janice dined in the kitchen, and once again they caught up on Angie's schoolwork. Angie listened as the staff spoke of their traditional duties. Chapman grumbled that since no one was spending any time at Angelhurst, she was thinking of opening a bed and breakfast.

"I think they'll come once the baby gets here," Angie explained. "Becky can't travel this far from her doctors. Of course, Mr. Wyatt will no doubt want his grandchild close, so I don't expect long vacations."

"How about you?" Chapman asked.

"The first session of summer school is half over," she mused. "I might skip the second part and come home for a while. But if I want a job in Charleston, I need to be in Charleston. So I don't know. Becky may need some help with the baby; Marc just might give me the nanny job."

"What do you know about babies?" Janice challenged.

"She can learn," Mrs. Bowen put in. "Angie's a smart girl. She can cook, she can fix computers, what's so hard about keeping a baby?"

"Thanks, Mrs. B. I don't know much. But I did go with Becky to the 'Caring for Newborns' class. I do think I could help. I just don't know how she'll feel about it."

"You aren't having trouble again?" Chapman asked in a guarded tone.

"No, not like that." Angie read her inflection. "It's just—people are funny about their kids. Especially the first one. Becky might prefer a professional. She may even, believe it or not, want to do it herself. It should be up to her. I just hope Marc realizes that. Things are a bit better between them right now. Maybe it'll last."

"I'd wondered about that," Chapman said.

"It's been rough from time to time," Angie replied. "But he has been reasonable lately. It will be important that they have a spirit of teamwork, going into the labor room."

"Well, that's an area wherein I know nothing," Chapman declared. "So Mr. Avery can't order me to take care of that."

The foursome chuckled at the thought of Chapman in charge of labor and delivery.

*   *   *

When Angie ran with Chapman on Saturday morning, her light workouts told on her. With some surprise, Angie had to push hard to finish the five-mile run at even a slow jog. The session with the weights that followed wasn't much better. Chapman muttered under her breath as she recorded the results. When Angie climbed on the scale, she'd added three more pounds. Chapman could contain herself no longer.

"Miss Donalson, this is atrocious. Terrible. Your running was anemic; your strength is fifteen percent below normal. Not *below* your *maximums, below normal.* You weigh more than you ever have in your whole life. I can't fix this. You have to do it. As long as you live elsewhere, it's a matter of self-discipline to keep yourself in shape. All I can say is that I'm disappointed in you. You've been taught how to care for your body, and you're ignoring it. You'll look like Becky Avery in no time, and you won't have pregnancy as an excuse."

Chapman glared at her. Angie stood still, wearing only lightweight workout wear and cross-training shoes. Earlier in her life, she would have trembled at the verbal onslaught. Or been annoyed. But she had mellowed. Chapman was mad because she cared. Keeping her in shape was her way of caring for her.

"You're right, Billie. I do need to get back into shape. I guess I'll forego the second session; I'll come back here and get myself back on track. If an interview comes up, I can always fly down."

"See that you do. But in the meantime, you need to get back to running every day. Work out as often as you can. If you give me six weeks, I can help you regain your norms." Chapman's voice was firm, but she seemed somewhat happier.

*   *   *

The helo returned for Angie on Sunday afternoon. With some reluctance, she took the passenger's seat, placed the headset over her shining auburn hair and gave Chapman a spiritless thumb's up. Three and one half hours later, she climbed out of the cramped cockpit and made her way to the little Mazda which she'd left at the community airport near Marc and Becky's suburban home. Tired and hungry, she stopped in the kitchen and made herself a snack, then reviewed her texts before bed, knowing that her hardest classes were on Monday.

Marc was aware that Angie had come in; the sounds from her room indicated her return. Fondly, but without passion, he looked at his sleeping wife. Becky had been a trooper, especially of late. He saw that she had propped her expanded abdomen onto an extra pillow, and he was relieved that *he* would never face pregnancy or childbirth. Looking at her, sleeping in silence, made something stir within him. In haste, he slid out of their suite and across to the rooms that Angie occupied.

The next morning, mindful of Chapman's lecture, Angie dressed in shorts and a tank top and ran the five-mile route around the neighborhood. By the end, sweat poured from her head and upper torso, for it was hot and humid, even at 7:00 in the morning. After breakfast, a shower and a change of clothing, she was ready to head to class. Becky was making her way, her pace slow as molasses, down the hall. Although she was late, Angie paused. "Good morning."

"Off to the doctor today, Angie," Becky told her. "Wish me luck."

"Certainly. Good luck. See you this afternoon."

The Monday classes were challenging—not only the subject matter, but Angie was tired after her weekend journey. As she was driving home, the cell phone rang. Surprised, Angie picked it up and heard Martha's voice, sounding nervous.

"Angie, Mrs. Avery is in the hospital. Could you go over there?"

"Sure, no problem. Something wrong?"

"Not exactly. Mr. Avery's in a meeting, and she's alone."

"On my way. Don't worry, Martha. I'll stay until Marc can get there."

*   *   *

Having been to some of the childbirth classes, Angie knew right where to go. After spending a few minutes convincing the nursing staff that she was close to Becky, Angie was allowed into the labor room. Becky seemed to be in a lot of pain, which came in spurts, usually every three or four minutes.

"Is Marc coming?" Becky panted, the contractions keeping her winded.

"I'm not sure. Martha got me on my cell phone on the way home from school. I can make some calls, if that's what you want."

"He should be coming. I spoke with Mrs. Conner."

"How long you have been here?"

"Since this morning. They sent me over from the doctor's. I was already dilated and having mild contractions."

Just then, a member of her OB-GYN group came by, so Angie stepped outside and found a pay phone. Marc's secretary told her that he was in a meeting, but that it should end any minute.

"Tell him that she seems okay, but she could use his support."

"Yes, Miss Donalson. I'll tell him to come right along," Mrs. Conner sounded concerned. "I've canceled the rest of today's appointments and I'm working on tomorrow."

"Good deal. Thanks."

Angie made her way back to the labor room, but a nurse's aide stopped her.

"Are you with Mrs. Avery?"

"Yes." Angie turned.

"You need to stay in the waiting room. Dr. Patton is checking on some things. We'll let you know when you can come back."

Angie returned to the waiting room and sat for a few minutes. Bored, she decided to call Martha.

"Hi, Martha. Looks like we've got a baby on the way. Is the nursery ready?"

There was a chuckle on the other end of the line.

"Sure. We've only had about eight months to prepare. How is she?"

"Lady, I'm telling you, she looks awful. I never realized it was so damn painful. The contractions are about three minutes apart. They have this machine which charts the contractions—big humps on the paper mean lots of pain. Her doctor came, and they ran me out, so I called you." Angie paused. "Another thing. Marc isn't here. She needs him. I rang his office and his secretary told me she'd try to get him here."

"He's still not there?" Martha's voice rose with emotion. "I called him long before I called you. He should've been there a while back."

"I know. She asked for him." Angie's voice was close to breaking. "I hope he'll hurry up."

Just then, Angie saw him briskly entering the labor and delivery floor.

"He's here. I'll call when I know something. Bye." Angie dropped the phone and started toward him. Avery, still dressed in a lightweight suit and tie, stopped the first nurse in the corridor.

"I'm Marc Avery. My wife, Rebecca, is here."

"Yes, sir. She's in labor room five. I'll show you the way."

Angie stopped, unsure. She wanted to be there, for Becky, for Marc. But she was an outsider, and this was a family situation. Still hesitant, she paused and decided to quiz the nurse about Becky when she returned to the station.

Standing in the corridor, trying to become part of the woodwork, she noticed that there was quite a bit of traffic into Becky's room— fast traffic. Serious faces, hurried movements. Then Marc emerged, his face pale, looking very much like a child who had lost his mother.

"Angie."

She hurried down the corridor. "What is it? What's going on?"

"Angie, she's gone. I can't believe it."

Marc sagged without prelude, and Angie staggered for a moment under his weight. Instinctively, she put her arm around him and swung him so they were propped against the handrail that lined the corridor.

"Marc? What do you mean? I was in there, not thirty minutes ago. She was in pain, but nothing seemed amiss."

"When the doctor first came in, she lost consciousness. They tried to revive her. They're taking her down to the O.R. for an emergency C-section. To save the baby. They aren't sure if it was a heart attack or a stroke or something else. But she wasn't breathing and her heart wasn't pumping. She's on life support, for the baby."

A nurse came by and saw them.

"We have a room down near the O.R. We'll take you there, and the doctor will come talk to you after the baby's born." She slipped her arm around Marc's waist and together she and Angie walked him down to a small room that was a combination waiting room and chapel. Angie noticed a Bible on the table and inspirational art on the walls. Gently, Angie and the nurse seated him.

"Are you family?" the nurse whispered to Angie. She shook her head.

"No, friend of the family. Both of them."

"Is there anyone we need to contact? A minister?"

"Becky's father must know. I'll get someone in Marc's office to call him." Angie was whispering, moving far enough away so that Marc wouldn't hear. "I don't know that Becky was particularly religious. Marc's isn't. His father lives here in town. I'll need to get him, too. Is there a phone, not here, but close?" Angie had noticed the signs forbidding use of her cell phone.

"Sure. Just down this hall. I'll stay with him for a few minutes."

"Thanks."

Angie called Marc's secretary and Martha, just telling them that something had happened to Becky and that the two fathers were needed. As soon as she could, she returned to Marc's side.

There was another half hour's wait. The young obstetrician came in, still in his scrubs, and sat down to talk to Marc. Angie stood to leave.

"No, Angie, stay." Marc's voice was soft.

"Are you family?" the doctor asked.

"No, a friend."

"Please, Angie. I need a clearer head to hear this, too. It's like I'm in a daze."

Angie sat. The doctor cleared his throat.

"Mr. Avery, you have a son. He's doing well. We'll watch him closely because we lost some data during the other crisis, but indications are good that he's just fine." The doctor paused, obviously struggling with the news that he had to convey. "We tried to revive your wife. We ran every test. I would like to do an autopsy to be certain, but all evidence points to an aneurysm in the brain. Everything was going well; then she reported an acute pain in her head, followed by immediate collapse. It was quick. She was with us, everything was fine; then she wasn't with us."

Marc hung his head, saying nothing. The doctor looked at Angie, wanting a cue.

"I was in there just before you came. The nurses seemed to think everything was okay. Why didn't we know something was wrong?"

"If it was an aneurysm, there was no way to know. People walk around with this time bomb in their heads. Perhaps the strain of labor was the trigger. But if she had it, sooner or later she would have hemorrhaged. It just happened here, today. I'm sorry. I know this is difficult. It's rare to lose a woman in childbirth, but even today, it does happen."

"When can we see the baby?" Angie's voice was low and furry with emotion, but she just had to change the subject.

"It won't be long. The pediatric nurses are with him, and when he's transferred to the nursery, Mr. Avery can see him."

"Thank you, Doctor."

"We need to handle disconnecting the life-support and set up the arrangements for Mrs. Avery. Do you have a clergyman? Has the staff handled that?"

"No." Marc's voice was husky, but he was following the conversation.

"I'll have someone in Social Services come and help you. Do you have other family on the way?"

"Yes, Mrs. Avery's father and Mr. Avery's, as well. I left word for them to come," Angie answered.

"I'll have them directed to you here. If you need anything from the medical staff, please have someone contact us. And again, I'm sorry about the way this turned out."

Angie grasped Marc's hand as soon as they were alone.

"Angie, I just can't believe it. I can't believe she's gone."

"Me, neither. I was in there, talking to her. They asked me to leave when the doctor came in, and I never saw her again."

"Apparently they had just finished trying to revive her when I came in. There were tubes and things, and a sense of defeat in the room. Then they got me out of there—I guess so they could take the baby." Marc dropped his head to his hands. "Angie, what am I going to do with a baby?"

"Marc, I'm so sorry that Becky—that she didn't make it. But we'll help with the baby. I took the class on newborn parenting. Martha can help. And you can hire a nanny or something. But you have to look after that baby. Remember, he's all you have left of the relationship."

"Yeah. You're right. We have to look after it." Avery sat, his head in his hands.

"Not 'it,' Marc. Him. He's a person. And every child needs parents. God knows I'm an expert on that," Angie declared in a voice strong with emotion.

"I suppose you are. But I'm not ready for this. Not for any of it." Marc's voice broke then, and the tears that had glistened in his eyes rolled down his cheeks. Angie began to cry also, and they embraced, but this time for comfort, not passion.

A nurse interrupted them after a while, with a status report on the baby.

"I'm Julie Parsons from the pediatric nursery, I'm here to tell you about your son. He's doing well. Eight pounds, four ounces, twenty-one inches long, APGAR of 7. He's going to be under observation in the nursery, but if you want to come down there in a while, you can look through the glass. Both of you. Mr. Avery can go in after the pediatrician gives us the okay. But he's a beautiful baby."

"Thank you for coming to tell us." Angie found her voice first. "I'll get Marc to come down there. It's been so traumatic. We appreciate having some good news." Angie paused. "I know it doesn't seem like it, but I know Marc will love his son. It's just—"

"Yes, I'm sure. Well, he's in good hands. We'll take extra special care of him, since his mamma can't." Nurse Parsons smiled through her own tears and was gone.

"We ought to go down there when someone else gets here. We wouldn't want anyone to get the idea that the child isn't wanted."

"I've never held an infant. I was depending on Becky to do all that stuff."

"We're gonna learn, Marc. We have to. Period."

"I can't do this without you, Angie. You know that don't you?"

"Becky would want the best for her baby. I'll do everything I can. Don't worry."

"I've never appreciated you as much as you deserved. You're the best thing that ever happened to me. I'll make it up to you—"

The Social Services representative came to the tiny room and began to coach Marc through the details of his wife's untimely departure. They selected a funeral director and made arrangements. At different times during the process, Mr. Wyatt and Mr. Avery arrived. Bill Wyatt was a man who was self-assured and composed in almost any circumstance, but hearing the news about his only child shattered that composure. He ranted, raved, questioned, and cried. Angie didn't know him well, but she thought the reaction was only natural for a man who had suffered such a loss. Mr. Avery was calmer and put an arm around his son in an attempt to comfort him. Angie stayed through the shock and question stages, helping Marc articulate answers for the elder family members, but she soon began to feel awkward.

"I want to go see the baby. I can't go in, because I'm not family, but I want to look," Angie explained.

"Sure, go ahead." Marc turned toward his dad.

The Social Services rep also took her leave, guiding Angie to the nursery on the maternity floor.

Chapter 24

Marcus Avery III was swaddled in white, like the other babies in the nursery. He had a small blue and white sock cap on his head, and his eyes were closed as if the hoopla accompanying his entry into the world had tired him out. Little cards taped in the clear bassinets told the child's last name and vital statistics. "Baby Boy Avery" looked like all the infants—head too large, mouth a rosebud, and skin pale. Angie thought he was beautiful, because he was the product of the man she loved.

A nursery worker noticed her interest in the Avery baby and came to the glass to hold up the sleeping child, her touch gentle but confident as she supported his head and body. Angie couldn't see a resemblance to Marc or Becky, specifically, and the fine wisps of hair that escaped the little blue and white striped cap weren't Marc's golden blonde or Becky's coal black, but a rich, dark brown.

The nurse returned the young Mr. Avery to his bassinet and went to attend to another baby who had awakened, crying. Angie stood almost in a trance, amazed at the twists of fate, and wondering for the first time how this strange turn of events would affect her. Although she had not wanted to be friends with Becky, the Wyoming wilderness trip had made them comrades. Angie knew that she'd miss Becky, but she also realized that once again Marc was free—and now he needed someone to be a mom to that little man over there. As she stood, still in awe, she made up her mind to be the best second-string mom on the planet.

*   *   *

"Oh, my word, no!" Martha's voice reflected disbelief. Angie stood beside the hospital entrance, her cell phone at her ear, pacing the sidewalk. With Marc and the grandparents making arrangements, it seemed like the best time for Angie to do the necessary, but unpleasant, task of beginning to notify members of the Avery staff of Becky's tragic demise.

"Yes, they are here," Angie said, answering the obvious questions. "I'm not sure where they'll end up, but it may very well be at the house. Both Mr. Avery and Mr. Wyatt have apartments, so the house seems like a better place. I don't know yet."

After putting together preliminary plans for keeping the bereaved comfortable, Angie ended her conversation, only to start over as she punched the main number at Angelhurst.

Chapman was in her office, so Angie wound up going over the same details with her that she had just given Martha.

"We'll make hotel reservations and be there by tomorrow evening," Chapman said, matter-of-fact, even in the wake of Angie's shocking news.

"Thanks, Billie. I know Marc will appreciate the gesture. And I could use a shoulder to cry on myself. I'm not sure if I'm strong enough to do this."

"It won't be easy. Such times never are, but you'll do fine. Remember to take care of Mr. Avery. All three of them."

Angie was nodding, recognizing the wisdom of Chapman's words. "Yeah. I can't lose sight of that, can I?"

"No. Help them all you can."

"Yes, ma'am."

Angie concluded her conversation with Chapman, then rang Mrs. Connor at Marc's office. That was, perhaps, the hardest call to make, because Angie didn't know Mrs. Connor well, but she knew that Marc and Becky had relied on her steady support and compassion.

"I'll be waiting to hear, as soon as they decide where they'll be." Mrs. Connor gave Angie her home number, as well as her cell number. "I want to be there as soon as I can be of some help."

"Thanks, Mrs. Connor. I know that Marc will appreciate it. Everyone will."

Having made the essential contacts, Angie paced the sidewalk one more time, thinking. She had believed Becky Avery to be the worst sort of mate for Marc, but now that she was gone, Angie found it hard to comprehend. What would Marc do? Would he go out and find another society girl, or was this really a second chance?

Did it really matter? With Claire's death, Angie had no other family. And she didn't want to face the future alone. Marc's family had become her family. Chapman's advice reverberated through her mind. *Help them all you can.*

Mindful of the responsibilities associated with having a family, Angie forced herself to walk briskly back into the emotional storm on the third floor.

*   *   *

"We're going to the house," Marc told her as she knocked on the doorframe. Just a courtesy, since the door was open. The Social Services rep had a clipboard in hand and peered hopefully at Angie. The gentlemen needed a guide, and she had other patients' families who needed assistance.

"Where's your car?" Angie asked Marc. The practical side was taking over, and Angie knew she couldn't fit Becky's relatives into her two-seat convertible.

"I used valet parking. Here's the stub."

"I'll have the car brought to the front," Angie said, pausing at the information desk at the waiting area. The volunteer manning that station was most helpful, and in a few moments, she was at the wheel of Marc's Lexus, piloting it with skill toward the Avery home. As discretely as she could manage, Angie phoned Martha and Mrs. Connor. The atmosphere in the car was glum, as each of the men seemed to withdraw into himself, trying to deal with the unthinkable.

*   *   *

At the funeral, Angie stayed with Marc's employees, leaving the rows reserved for family to Becky's kin. The service was as brief as her life had been, and Angie was soon standing in a cemetery with Chapman on one side and Janice on the other. Marc was dressed in a somber charcoal gray suit and stood at the graveside talking quietly with his father and father-in-law.

"What happens now?" Janice spoke aloud, but kept her voice low.

"Marc has asked me to take care of the baby. Martha has been on the phone, trying to round up a nanny. But the hospital says he's ready to come home. I think we are going later this afternoon to get him." Angie's voice was pitched low as well.

"What about your classes?" Chapman inquired.

"I plan to withdraw. I'm sure Martha would be willing to pitch in, but school's not all that important right now. Helping Marc and the baby get straightened out is my first priority. I was only taking those classes so I could get a teaching certificate, and I don't think I'm going to be needing it anytime soon."

Chapman nodded. "Do you need Janice?"

"I don't know. I think Martha and I can handle him, especially if we can find a part-time nanny. We would both like to have an 'expert' we can consult. There's a dearth of grandmothers in this clan."

Janice grinned. "Maybe we should send Mrs. Bowen instead."

The conversation ended as Marc approached. The crowd had dwindled, and Mr. Avery and Mr. Wyatt were being escorted to the black limousine that had carried them from the funeral home to the gravesite.

"Hi. Thanks for coming," Marc began with the conventional phrasing. "Are you coming back to the house?"

"I'm not sure that's appropriate, Mr. Avery," Chapman began, but he waved her to a stop.

"It's my house. I'll say what's appropriate. Angie and I will be going to get the baby after lunch, and I want you there."

"Yes, sir. If you're sure."

"She'll need some help, and Martha and Clark will have their hands full. You're needed."

"Okay. Jan and I will have lunch on our own, then we'll change into working clothes," Chapman told him. With an unusual gesture, she hugged Angie, then Marc.

"Get him back home, Angie. We'll see you later."

"Yes, ma'am."

Chapman and Janice left in the Explorer.

"I want to ride with you," Marc said, and motioned Angie toward his Lexus, which Mrs. Connor had driven to the cemetery.

"Okay." Angie wondered at the arrangement, but she saw Mrs. Connor joining Mr. Avery and Mr. Wyatt in the limo. Marc's hand touched her elbow, and he steered her toward the car.

"Want me to drive?" Angie offered.

"No. I'm okay."

In silence, they watched the rest of the mourners leave, then Marc started the car.

"You're going to see this as piss poor timing, I know," Marc began, as they pulled onto the highway, "but I want you to understand something."

He paused as he changed lanes, then resumed. "Angie, I learned to keep my strategies to myself, even in high school. Watching Dad as he executed his plans and ran an often cutthroat business taught me that. It's better to take action than talk about it. That's the way I've dealt with you, right from the start. But that isn't always the best way."

"I'm not following you." Angie turned to him. His face was intent on the road; the conversation seemed almost secondary. He braked for a stoplight, and while they were still, he returned her gaze.

"We'll be picking up Marc the third in a couple of hours. And I want you to know that I'm looking to you to raise him. I want that, and if she could have chosen, I think Becky would've picked you as well."

"I kinda figured that I would be the nanny. For a while, at least. I'll do my best. For you, for Becky, and for him." Angie swiped at a tear.

"Angie, you won't be his nanny. You'll be his mother."

"What?"

"I'm not good at asking, am I? I give orders, I don't take 'em." The light changed and he accelerated.

"Are you proposing?"

"That's one way of putting it. Oh, we'll have to wait a while. A year or two. And we'll have to be careful before then. I don't think Martha knows about our relationship, and I'm damned sure Becky's dad doesn't know. I want to keep it that way."

"How?"

"I imagine that we'll spend a lot of time in Tennessee. I don't have to play any games there. Billie will make it work out. She always does."

"I see. What about Mr. Wyatt?"

"We'll work out a schedule or invite him to Angelhurst. That falls into the category of minor details. But the game plan must be in place. What do you say?"

"I used to dream about this moment. Now I don't know what to say."

"It's simple, really. Say 'yes', and in a year or two, you'll be the next Mrs. Avery. Say 'no', and I'll keep you on staff. It's more or less the same task—the biggest difference is in job title."

Angie looked at him in wonder. To Marc, everything was a business deal.

"In that case, I'll be Becky's successor."

"Good. You know me well enough to realize being my wife won't be all that easy."

"Perhaps. But I'd rather be a wife than a mistress."

"I hope you feel that way in five years." He reached over to take her hand.

"I'm adaptable. It's my worst weakness."

"Or your greatest strength. I love you for it." His hand squeezed hers and released it.

"Thanks. I guess." Angie's face reddened as she heard the compliment—backhanded or not. "When do we get the baby?"

"This afternoon at 4:30. That's when you begin your new career."

"I look forward to it."